In Darkness

In Darkness

- A Poetry Collection -

Atticus James

In Darkness

Published through Ingram Spark

This is a work of fiction. Names, characters, places, and incidents are the product of the author's imagination or are used fictitiously. Any resemblance to actual persons, living or dead, events, or locales is entirely coincidental.

All rights reserved
Copyright © 2025 by Atticus James
Book Cover Designed by RevCreation

ISBN: 979-8-218-54300-6 (Paperback Edition)
ISBN: 979-8-218-54299-3 (Ebook Edition)

No part of this publication may be reproduced, stored in a retrieval system, or transmitted in any form or by any means electronic, mechanical, photocopying, recording, or otherwise, without the written permission of the author or publisher.

Dedicated to you.

"Only when we are brave enough to explore the darkness will we discover the infinite power of our light."

– Brené Brown

Table of Contents

A Note from Atticus ix
The Beginnings 1
Chapter 1 Rabbit Hole 7
Chapter 2 Downward Spiral 18
Chapter 3 Tightrope 34
Chapter 4 Suicide Pact 40
Chapter 5 Jealously 47
Chapter 6 Cross Your Mind 54
Chapter 7 Hold Her Hand 60
Chapter 8 The Cracked Mirror 66
Chapter 9 Obscurity 73
Chapter 10 A Dazed Poets Mind 79
Chapter 11 Who Am I? 88
Chapter 12 Sincerely, me 93
Chapter 13 What I Gave You 99
Chapter 14 Rock Bottom 107
Chapter 15 Shattered Heart 117
Chapter 16 You For Me 126
Chapter 17 The Gloomy Meadow 134
Chapter 18 Midnight Thoughts 142
Chapter 19 In Darkness 147
Chapter 20 Demons 153

Chapter 21 Nightmare	159
Chapter 22 Major Depression	167
Chapter 23 Chaos	181
Chapter 24 Amnesia	188
Chapter 25 Intoxication Blues	199
Chapter 26 It's You	207
Chapter 27 Second Love	215
Chapter 28 Falling	224
Chapter 29 Full Moon	230
Chapter 30 The Weeping Willow	234
Chapter 31 Gravity	240
Chapter 32 The Darkest Hour	246
Chapter 33 Sadness	251
Chapter 34 Dandelion	257
Chapter 35 The Quill	262
Chapter 36 Lost Love	269
Chapter 37 Distance	276
Chapter 38 In Some Life	283
Chapter 39 Moving On	288
Chapter 40 Let Go	294
Chapter 41 Healing of the Broken Heart	300
Chapter 42 The Light	307
Chapter 43 Saving Grace	314
Chapter 44 Out of the Darkness	320
Chapter 45 Happiness	325

A Note from Atticus

For as long as I can remember, I have harbored a dream – a dream of publishing a book that allows me to share my stories with the world in the way I've always envisioned them being told. I've longed for my words to breathe life into experiences, thoughts, and emotions, just as they did when they first emerged from the deepest parts of my soul. Growing up, I found solace in writing. It became my way of processing life's many mysteries. I wrote, and I wrote, and I wrote some more – each stroke of the pen an attempt to capture the emotions of a world that often felt too vast to contain. It felt as though every day I was filling pages with poems, stories, speeches, and quotes that reflected the fleeting moments, the subtle shifts in my surroundings, and the intangible feelings within me.

But, as many stories often go, life's twists and turns pulled me into currents I couldn't control. Circumstances beyond my grasp caused me to make decisions that slowly eroded my confidence in the power of my own voice. That once endless flow of creativity became a trickle, then a drought, leaving me questioning whether my words would ever find their place in the world again.

Before we embark on this journey together, I want to share a piece of myself with you, so you may better understand who I am and what you will encounter in these pages. You will know me as Atticus James, a name I chose for its sense of privacy and protection. The identity, however, is real in every sense that matters, for in this name lives my heart and my mind – the essence of the stories I am about to share.

When I was young, I received a diagnosis that would shape the trajectory of my life: Major Bipolar Depressive Disorder. The weight of that label fell upon me like a heavy cloak, obscuring the light I once knew. From that moment, my life was no longer just a journey of discovery, but one of learning to navigate a tumultuous landscape of mental illness. There were days where joy was a fleeting visitor, and others where darkness was an unwelcome companion, whispering insidious thoughts that sought to bury me beneath the ground.

In one of those darker moments, I made a decision that haunts me still – I set fire to every piece of literature I had ever written. Every poem, every song, every story that had once held my dreams was reduced to ash. In that moment, I silenced my voice. I cannot fully explain what compelled me to destroy the very thing that had once brought me so much peace, but I know that in the aftermath, I lost not only my words but also the desire to write them. For nine long years, I could not pick up my quill. The creative fire that once burned so brightly inside me had been snuffed out, replaced by a void that I did not know how to fill.

During those years, I worked hard to manage my mental health, to find stability in a world that often felt unstable. Yet, despite that progress, I remained in denial. I stopped my treatments, isolated myself from those who mattered, and immersed myself in work as a means of escape. I lived in a state of survival, not truly embracing the life I had once yearned to create.

Then, on November 3rd, 2022, my world shifted. In what felt like the blink of an eye, everything changed. I went from being the ruler of my own destiny to a servant to forces I couldn't recognize. It was my darkest hour, a moment where the ground beneath me seemed to crumble. And in that moment, when I could see no way forward, I did the only thing I knew how to do – I wrote. I wrote, and I wrote, and I wrote some more, pouring out every emotion, every thought, and every piece of myself that had been locked away for so long.

This collection is born from that outpouring. It is a journey – a journey through darkness, but more importantly, it is a journey toward the light that always awaits on the other side. As you, my dearest reader, walk with me through these pages, I hope you feel the rawness, the passion, and the resilience in every word. My aim is not only to share my story but to offer solace and hope for those who may be facing their own battles. I want to remind you that, no matter how deep the darkness may seem, there is always the promise of tomorrow, always a way to rise again.

This book is not just a collection of words, but a testament to the resilience of the human spirit. It is a reminder that even in our darkest hours, we possess the power to create, to heal, and to rise from the ashes of our struggles. Each word on these pages reflects not only my journey, but the journeys of all who have faced the abyss and found their way back.

You may find that these pages reflect your own emotions, your own battles. You may see pieces of yourself in the stories, the poems, the moments where darkness clings too tightly. But know this – you are not alone in your struggle. The very act of picking up this book and reading these words are proof that you are already moving forward, already seeking the light. There is a strength in you that cannot be silenced, a flame that cannot be extinguished, no matter how fierce the storm may seem.

Before I send you on your way, allow me to leave you with one final thought. When the darkness grabs ahold too tight, just close your eyes and breathe. Feel the pulse of life within you, the quiet strength that has carried you this far. You are stronger than you know, and the possibilities that lie ahead are endless. Even in the most profound darkness, there is always a flicker of light, waiting to guide you.

So as you navigate the twists and turns of this journey, as you face the shadows that may arise, remember this: the light within you is eternal. No matter how lost you may feel, no matter how heavy the burden becomes, you have the power to rise, to write your own story, and to shape your destiny. And when you feel that you cannot go on, know that I, too, have stood at that edge, and I am here with you.

I will see you on the other side – where light meets shadow, and where hope is always waiting to greet us.

With love,
Atticus

In Darkness

The Beginnings

The evening air turns cold and damp, and in the distance, I think I can hear a hummingbird. As I sit on the bench inside our family greenhouse, I wonder what it would be like to be a butterfly.

"Curious," I ponder, "how curious it is that such a beautiful creature could start so small, unbothered by the walk of life around it. Then, almost without connection, metamorphose into a winged creature that soars through gardens and landscapes and flowers."

As I stare at the natural life around me, the smell of lavender takes over the artificial air created by the variety of herbs, flowers, and trees that are contained within the building. To the naked eye, one would think that this was an ordinary greenhouse that was simple and small, but to us Atkinsons, it is much more than that.

My mum's name is Rachael, and we live in a coveted part of Ireland, a small village in the southern part of Dublin. For as long as I can remember, my family has been the center of gravity for the people of our town.

Our village sat just a mile from the farm, nestled among fields and dotted with old stone cottages, a small church with a bell tower, and the corner pub where neighbors shared their stories over a pint. As a child, I'd walk there with my Dad on Saturday mornings, our steps slow and easy along the cobblestone path. The smell of freshly baked soda bread from the bakery would meet us at the edge of the village, mingling with the faintest whiff of sea air carried in from the coast.

ATTICUS JAMES

It all started long ago, when my great-great-grandfather founded a small congregation in our town of Ranelagh. He was a farmer, and a damn good one at that. His fields yielded the highest quality produce and foliage that the town had ever seen. His most successful plant? As ironic as it may seem… potatoes. It was before the industrialization of the area in the seventies when times were still tough on the people of the community. It was still an impoverished town with little life – with an economic collapse riding on the horizon. We had just witnessed what something like The Great Depression brings onto community… onto culture. But we came out of it. How? How did we survive a collapse? How could we have prevented it?

With little to his name, he took a leap of faith: coupled himself with a lawyer, a doctor, and a preacher and formed a roundtable. For months they met on a varying cadence to avoid being seen. They did not know what they were planning, nor did they know where it may lead… but they did know that whatever was coming next, it needed to be kept a secret.

"Gentlemen," my great-great-grandfather spoke softly, "a collapse is coming, and we need to stop it. I do not know what our approach should be, but we must think of something before it is too late. I have asked you all here because I have not that much education – that much exposure to what we can do as a society of people. For my whole life, I have served my community through the harvesting of my farm. But now? Now, I must ask for help. My son and my daughter need their future secured. I plead to you to share your insight and help me put together a plan to stop this."

The mere utterance of these words sent shockwaves through the room. The lawyer's face was drained of blood, leaving behind a shade as white as snow. The doctor struggled to find words to comprehend what was just told to him. But the preacher, the preacher broke the silence that seemed to last an hour.

"Shameus, I do not know what you see or how you have come to see it… but this proclamation is not merely one that we can take lightly. So, let me ask you…" he pauses for a moment, allowing his thoughts to fully calibrate. "… are you sure this is something you wish to exclaim?"

"It is not as simple as a yes or no," Shameus tames, "for weeks my crops have been yielding less and less. My well-off customers are sharing how their wealth is thinning. My middle-class customers are sharing how their wealth is no longer allowing them to save for things like their children's education. My low-class customers, my community, are asking for installment billing.

"What even is installment billing? And why has such a capitalistic idealism infiltrated our community? I do not need to explain to you, Father, and to these two scholars what weight this may bear on our future."

In my early life, I was surrounded by family. I had a father who worked tirelessly to provide for his wife, his son, and me. He was a farmer, just like his great-grandfather was, with a minute difference: he built a vast empire that contributed to more than half of the overall produce supply for all of Ireland. He was the definition of success and had plans for continued growth in the future. My mum was a schoolteacher. She loved working with her students, teaching them the importance of reading and writing and the impact literacy will have on their future. My twin, Logan, who was minutes older than me, was one of the most genuine and pure souls you may have ever met. He was full of energy and full of life.

When he was eight, Logan began working alongside our father on the farm. He had been showing high-level competency that left those around him feeling inspired. One morning, he and our father went to take the tractor out to do routine maintenance on the far field that is on the horizon line of our mere 100-acre farm, that spanned far beyond our own town and even the town beside us.

The farm had been in our family for generations, each field and stone wall a testament to the Atkinson name. Our farmhouse, with its weathered stone walls and deep-set windows, seemed as much a part of the landscape as the rolling hills stretching out to the Dublin Mountains in the distance. Inside, the scent of peat lingering from the hearth reminded me of winter evenings with my father, sharing stories while he tended to the fire.

The sun was shining bright in the sky and the clouds were painting a picture that was so captivating that my mum and I spent hours pointing out different animals, symbols and even at one point, figures, arguing what they could mean. The air was crisp, and there was a light scent of rosemary that laced the atmosphere. It was intoxicating.

At the drop of a dime, the weather shifted. Dark, ominous clouds blocked the shining sun. The thick smell of dew clouded the radiant smell of rosemary that once filled the air with a soft, bold scent that would leave the average person yearning for a cocktail and prime-cut steak.

My mum sat, in silence, outside on our patio for hours. Refilling her whiskey glass as she swaddled down the bottle. When the tractor failed to return, she knew something had happened. She did not know what, she did not know where and she did not know how. For the first time in her marriage, she was infuriated by the luxurious life her husband provided. If something had happened, there would be no way to know where to even begin to start. There would be no way to know… anything.

She rings her parents, who live a short drive away and calls for me, who is wearing a sundress, laced with pink and blue roses, that flows through the air like a ballerina gliding across the stage. My hair has a tight braid that wraps around my head with a white lily placed perfectly proportional to my ear.

"I have called your grandparents; they are on their way to pick you up. Go and grab some clothes for this evening and tomorrow, I will come and grab you as soon as I am able. And Lily?" She pauses, "I love you, and I will see you soon."

There is such a tone to my mum's voice that I can tell that something is off. I scan the field for my brother but fail to notice anything that could remotely resemble him.

Within minutes, my grandparents are pulling into view, and I am instructed to wait in the car. I can tell that there is something that is not being told to me, and I am starting to get a sick feeling. One I had never experienced before. My gut was telling me that something had happened to my brother. At that moment, I began to cry… silently. I did not want my mum, or grandparents, to see or hear. As I opened the car door to get inside, I listened closely to my mum's voice. I was not able to gather much from the muffled conversation, but I was able to hear one line… a line that changed my life:

"… there has been an accident."

Chapter 1
Rabbit Hole

My alarm clock shattered the stillness, pulling me from another night of restless dreams haunted by memories I wished I could forget. I longed for my brother, especially on days like today – the day we should have celebrated together. In fleeting moments, I felt him with me, as if he were standing right by my side. I saw him in the clouds and stars, heard his whispers of encouragement when I needed them most, his familiar presence wrapping around me like a comforting blanket.

The morning light was soft, filtered through a veil of mist that clung to the fields like a whisper of something forgotten. In Ireland, the rain had a way of painting the world in muted greens and grays, a color palette I had come to find both comforting and melancholy. The damp earth smelled rich, like the soil held centuries of stories that only the rain could coax out.

"Are you awake, honey?" My mum's soft voice floated through my door, the sound both comforting and painful. "Today is a big day for you. Your senior ball."

I felt paralyzed, trapped between the weight of reality and the fog of my dreams. No words came as she moved closer, a familiar warmth against my chilly despair. I wished I could muster the energy to respond, but the heaviness in my chest was too great.

"Lily..." she paused, waiting for any sign of acknowledgment.

But I remained lost in thought, drifting back to the months that followed that fateful night.

The greenhouse my mum had built in memory of my father and brother transformed our backyard into a lush haven, a sanctuary that felt both sacred and suffocating. It was a place where beauty flourished, but it also served as a constant reminder of loss. At its entrance, a world of endless possibility lay hidden beneath layers of vibrant life. Standing at the threshold, I often lost myself in the silence that enveloped the space, where even the smallest echo felt monumental.

The greenhouse was filled with my father's pride and joy: rows of shamrocks, delicate heather, and resilient Irish ferns, each plant carefully nurtured in memory of his parents. I could still hear his voice, teaching me how to tend to each one. "These aren't just plants, Lil," he'd say, his voice low and reverent. "They're family, too."

Inside, terraces spiraled deep into the earth, a labyrinth of green where I could breathe and think. The air was thick with the sweet scent of blossoms and damp earth. I had planted lavender around the bench on the fourth terrace – the spot where I did most of my contemplating. The calming aroma wrapped around me like a warm hug, and in those moments, I felt my brother's spirit watching over me, protecting me with every whisper of the breeze.

But as the weeks turned into months, the shadows deepened. I watched my mum search for solace in the bottom of a bottle, each sip a desperate attempt to escape the pain that lingered in our home. Hennessey became her new love, and I often found her sitting on the living room floor, lost in a fog of her own making. I had lost my father, my brother, and now, the mum I once knew. I wished for a flicker of hope, but the path ahead remained shrouded in darkness.

As I stood in the greenhouse, surrounded by the vibrant greens and fragrant blooms, the weight of my losses pressed down on me like a heavy cloak. The memories of happier times seemed so distant, as if they belonged to someone else's life. I would often sit on that lavender-scented bench, thinking of all the moments we should have shared – school dances, family gatherings, laughter echoing through the house. Instead, silence filled the void, and grief wrapped around me like an unshakeable shadow.

"Lilith, it's time to get up!" my mum called, her voice sharp against the quiet of my room. "You cannot lay in bed all day, it is nearly time for you to leave for your ball."

"Mum–" I pleaded, "I know what day it is. Just give me a minute, please."

"Oh, okay…" she sighed, her disappointment palpable. "I'm sorry."

As the door clicked shut, I sank back into my pillow, overwhelmed by the weight of reality. She was right; it was an important day, and I should find a way to embrace it. I struggled to maintain control over my emotions, but days like this often felt like an uphill battle. Logan would have understood – he would have supported me. I had to put my best foot forward, for him.

Finally, I dragged myself from the bed, catching a glimpse of my reflection in the mirror. The moment I looked up, a wave of emotions crashed over me. I saw the girl who once radiated joy now shrouded in shadows. My hair hung limp around my shoulders, lifeless and dull, a stark contrast to the vibrant girl I used to be. My eyes were puffy and red, remnants of sleepless nights filled with tears that felt like they would never stop falling.

As I stared deeper into my reflection, I felt an ache in my chest. This girl in the mirror felt like a stranger. Her face was marked by sorrow, the corners of her mouth turned down as if gravity itself was pulling her into despair. I wanted to reach out and shake her, to tell her that life could still hold beauty despite the overwhelming darkness that surrounded us. But instead, I felt paralyzed, locked in a battle between the girl I was and the pain that had become my constant companion.

Memories flashed before my eyes – moments of laughter with Logan, the warmth of our shared secrets, the way he could light up a room with just a smile. Now, those memories felt like echoes in an empty hall, reverberating painfully in the silence. I thought of how he would have laughed at my outfit, how he would have insisted I twirl around so he could see the full effect of the dress. I could almost hear his voice, mischievous yet gentle, reminding me of the joy hidden beneath my sorrow.

Dad was a natural storyteller. On quiet nights, he'd sit by the peat fire and tell me tales of the Good People – fairies who'd appear in the misty mornings if you looked hard enough – or the haunting wail of the banshee, heard only when someone's time had come. Those stories had a way of sticking, echoing in my mind on the foggiest days. Even now, I couldn't look out across the fields without half-expecting to catch a glimpse of something hidden, something magical.

But the harsh reality of loss clung to me like a shadow, reminding me that he was gone. My heart ached for the moments we would never share, the dances we would never have. I wanted to scream, to let the world know how deeply I was hurting, but instead, I stood there, tears spilling down my cheeks, the reflection staring back at me with a mixture of longing and despair.

In that moment, I felt a fierce wave of determination rising within me. Yes, I was hurting, but I was still here. I was still breathing. I would not let the darkness consume me completely. I could honor Logan's memory by living, by embracing the life I had left.

My hands were shaking, but still, I reached out to wipe away the tears, taking a deep breath to steady myself. I looked into my own eyes, searching for a flicker of strength amid the sorrow. It was there, buried but undeniable – a small flame of hope. I had to believe that even in the depths of despair, there was a chance for renewal.

As I began to prepare for the evening, a heaviness settled in my chest. The thought of stepping into that ballroom felt daunting, like staring down the dark tunnel of the rabbit hole I often found myself trapped in. I could almost feel the shadows creeping in, whispering doubts that twisted and turned through my mind. But in that moment, I remembered Logan's laughter, his ability to light up the darkest corners of my heart.

I took a deep breath, resolving to face the night ahead. I wouldn't let the weight of my grief pull me down. Instead, I would carry his spirit with me, transforming my pain into a source of strength. I wanted to believe that even amid the chaos, there could be beauty – a flicker of hope shining through the cracks.

With trembling hands, I reached for my journal, the pages blank and waiting for the weight of my thoughts. I flipped to a fresh page, gripping the pen tightly as I began to pour out my feelings, allowing the darkness to spill onto the paper:

April 14, 2018

There's a long, dark and narrow way,
A passage called the rabbit hole;
It twists and turns and tears to pieces,
Forcing the mind to go astray.

As if the lights that fades dim,
Could hideaway all the pain;
It's an endless battle lost,
Long behold the dragon's reign.

For years and years the flame flickered,
Until that brisk evening it had stopped;
If only the light could maintain control,
No one would fall down that rabbit hole.

It's a long, dark and narrow journey,
One that is full of misery and pain;
One wishes to have headed that warning,
Before they had go —

I closed my journal, a bittersweet smile breaking through the haze of tears. Writing had become my sanctuary, a way to keep Logan's spirit alive amid the darkness. Each word was a thread, weaving him back into my life, reminding me of the love that could not be extinguished, even in the deepest sorrow.

Wiping my eyes, I took a deep breath, grounding myself in the present. The weight of the rabbit hole still tugged at me, that familiar pull of grief and despair. It was always there, lurking at the edges of my mind, tempting me to fall back into its depths. But I refused to let it pull me under tonight. Tonight was supposed to be different. It had to be.

I stood up from my desk and moved toward the mirror, facing the reflection I had avoided earlier. The girl staring back was not the same one from months ago. She was quieter now, her joy tempered by loss. But there was also a new kind of strength in her eyes, a strength born from pain, from surviving in the shadow of grief.

I ran my fingers through my hair, trying to smooth out the wild strands. The dress hanging on the back of my door was still waiting, a reminder of the night ahead. I could hear my mum downstairs, pacing, the soft clink of glass against glass punctuating the silence. She was struggling too, perhaps in ways I couldn't fully understand, and the weight of her grief pressed down on our home like a fog. But as much as I wanted to help her, tonight had to be about reclaiming something for myself.

With trembling hands, I reached for the dress. Logan would have laughed if he could see me now – nervous, fidgeting, overthinking every little detail. He always knew how to ease my anxieties, with a joke, a nudge, or just that reassuring smile. I could almost hear him ribbing me, telling me not to take things so seriously.

"C'mon, Lil, you've got this," I whispered to myself, imagining his voice beside me. I wasn't sure if I believed it yet, but I wanted to.

I slipped into the dress, the cool fabric skimming over my skin like a promise of something new. The turquoise shimmered in the soft glow of my room, the lace delicate yet structured enough to hold me together, even as I felt a bit like I might unravel. As the zipper clicked shut, I stood still for a moment, letting the sensation of wearing something so beautiful sink in.

I turned back to the mirror and caught my own gaze. It was hard to believe this was me – standing there in a dress meant for a night like this, a night of moving forward. For so long, I had felt stuck in place, like my life had been frozen in that moment when we lost Logan. Everything since then had been a blur of gray, but now… now there was color.

The dress felt almost like armor, wrapping me in its vibrant hue. I took a breath, trying to adjust to this version of myself. Not the broken sister, not the girl trying to hide her pain beneath layers of denial, but someone who was daring to step into the light again, even if it scared her.

I traced my fingertips along the intricate lace, noting how delicate it was, how easily it could tear. But it didn't. The dress was beautiful, yes, but there was a strength in its construction. A quiet resilience. I hadn't expected to feel that way about a piece of clothing. I hadn't expected to feel anything, really.

My hands, which had been trembling moments ago, steadied as I smoothed the fabric along my sides. Maybe this was what it felt like to step into something new. Not to forget the pain, but to allow myself to grow around it.

With the dress now in place, I wandered over to the small vanity where my hairbrush lay waiting. A half-empty bottle of perfume sat beside it; the scent still strong enough to remind me of simpler days when getting ready for a night out was something I looked forward to. I hadn't worn it in months.

I picked it up, hesitating for a moment, before spritzing a small amount into the air. The familiar fragrance filled the room, swirling around me. It was the same one Logan had teased me about once, saying it smelled like a garden – something earthy and alive, just like I used to be. I smiled faintly at the thought, letting that memory comfort me rather than weigh me down.

With slow, deliberate movements, I took the brush to my hair, gently untangling the knots that had formed throughout the day. The repetitive motion was calming, a small ritual that grounded me. My wavy strands cascaded down my back, wild and untamed like they always had been, but tonight, they would be different – just like me.

I ran my fingers through the soft waves, thinking about how Logan used to playfully mess up my hair whenever I got too serious about fixing it. He would have had something to say about tonight, some sarcastic remark that would have made me laugh. And just like that, the heaviness threatened to creep in again, the familiar ache of his absence tugging at the edges of my resolve.

But I refused to let the rabbit hole pull me in. Not tonight. This was a night for standing tall, for finding myself again.

Setting the brush down, I grabbed the small pins that had been laid out next to the vanity. Carefully, I separated two sections of hair, one on each side, and began weaving them into simple braids. My fingers worked methodically, the movement almost second nature after years of practicing. The braids felt like tiny threads of control in a world that had spun wildly out of mine.

Once the braids were done, I fastened them at the back, letting the rest of my wavy hair fall loose. There was one final touch left – the lily. I picked it up from my vanity, holding it delicately between my fingers. It was vibrant and alive, its white petals glowing softly in the dim light of my room. The flower had always been a symbol of Logan, of the life we had shared, and now it would be a part of me as I stepped out into the world again.

Gently, I placed the lily on the left side of my hair, securing it in place. It stood out against my dark waves, a small but powerful reminder of the beauty that could still exist, even in the wake of loss. The flower was fragile, like the lace of my dress, yet here it was – alive, enduring, just like I hoped I could be.

As I finished, a knock echoed from the hallway. Ava's voice broke through the soft silence of my room. "Lily? Are you ready yet?"

I blinked at my reflection, taking one last look before stepping away from the mirror. Ava was always the more practical one between us. Calm, composed, and forever patient in her quiet way. When I opened the door, there she stood, leaning against the banister at the top of the stairs, her soft brown eyes studying me.

A small smile tugged at her lips as she took me in, her gaze approving yet filled with something deeper, something intense. "You look stunning," she said softly, her voice barely more than a whisper. "Logan would've been proud."

Before I could respond, the space between us disappeared. Her hands slid up my arms, pulling me closer until our bodies were pressed together, and without hesitation, her lips met mine. The kiss was deep, charged with an urgency that took my breath away. I felt the world around us dissolve, leaving nothing but the fire between us. My heart pounded in my chest, and every nerve in my body ignited with the electricity of the moment.

Her words, simple yet filled with a knowing weight, nearly undid me. Ava had seen me through it all – the long nights, the moments when I felt like falling apart. She never asked for anything in return, just sat with me when I needed silence or held me when the sobs were too much.

She hadn't always been my closest friend, but grief had changed us, bonded us in a way that felt unshakable. Ava had become an anchor when the ground beneath me gave way, offering stability without asking for anything in return.

"Thanks," I murmured, my voice catching slightly as I stepped toward her. "And you're always on time. Of course."

She shrugged, teasing the corner of her lips upward in a smirk. "Someone has to make sure you don't spend the entire night second-guessing yourself." Her hand reached out, gently squeezing mine as we both descended the stairs.

The night air greeted us as we stepped outside, cool against my skin. The headlights of the car illuminated the path ahead, and the driver waited, holding the door open.

Ava nudged me gently toward the car, her eyes catching mine one last time before we stepped inside. "Let's get this over with," she said, her voice carrying the right blend of humor and understanding.

I smiled as I slid into the seat beside her, my heart pounding with a mixture of nerves and determination. "Let's do this," I whispered, more to myself than to her.

As the car pulled away, I leaned back, watching the house disappear behind us, the weight of the night ahead settling in but no longer feeling so impossible. With Ava beside me and Logan in my heart, I felt ready – or at least, ready enough to try.

Chapter 2
Downward Spiral

The car rolled to a gentle stop, the hum of the engine cutting off abruptly, leaving only the distant sound of laughter and music drifting through the night air. I stared out the window, momentarily frozen, my fingers gripping the cool fabric of my dress. The soft crunch of gravel beneath the tires, the distant gleam of the ballroom lights – everything felt too much, like I was watching someone else's life unfold through a screen.

"Lily?" Ava's voice reached me, soft but grounding. She had that way of cutting through the fog, pulling me back to the present. "Ready?"

I turned to look at her, her eyes warm and reassuring, and nodded, though my heart hadn't quite caught up with the idea. With a deep breath, I slid out of the car, the driver opening the door just as my feet touched the ground. The cool evening air wrapped around me like a reminder of reality, but the grand estate before me felt anything but real.

The ballroom stood towering in front of us, its massive arched doors gleaming under the golden glow of lanterns strung above. The manor itself was a sprawling, Gatsby-esque masterpiece, with towering columns and grand windows framed by ivy that seemed to grow like veins, clinging to the centuries-old stone. Fairy lights were strung across the entire courtyard, twinkling like a thousand tiny stars, casting a soft, magical glow over everything they touched. It was the kind of place that belonged in another era, a world where time moved slower, and everything felt larger than life.

"Wow…" I whispered, my voice barely audible.

Ava grinned, looping her arm through mine as we made our way toward the entrance. "Yeah, it's pretty incredible, right?"

Incredible didn't even begin to describe it. It was stunning, overwhelming even. The kind of grandeur you only saw in movies or read about in novels. The air smelled of freshly cut grass and roses, the night punctuated by the distant sound of a bubbling fountain somewhere in the expansive gardens. There was something surreal about it all – the elegance, the beauty – like I'd walked into a dream that wasn't mine.

I could already feel my heart pounding in my chest, the weight of everything pressing down on me. The ballroom loomed ahead, filled with glittering chandeliers and the sound of clinking glasses. It was so alive, so vibrant – everything I wasn't.

The entrance was flanked by intricately carved marble statues, their blank, serene faces gazing down at the guests as if judging who was worthy to pass through these gilded doors. People were gathered in small groups near the steps, their laughter light and effortless, their dresses and tuxedos tailored perfectly to match the elegance of the evening. They seemed like they belonged here, like they'd always belonged here.

I couldn't have felt more out of place.

I glanced down at my dress, the turquoise lace shimmering under the soft lights, and felt like a child playing dress-up. It was beautiful, yes, but it was hard to shake the feeling that I was an outsider in a world that was never meant for me. I swallowed hard, the growing lump in my throat threatening to make itself known.

"You look stunning, you know," Ava said quietly, her hand squeezing mine as we climbed the steps together.

I forced a smile, though my insides churned with nerves. "Thanks."

As we approached the entrance, the music inside grew louder – a soft, jazzy tune, the kind that was meant to set the mood for an elegant evening of mingling and sophistication. The doors were opened for us, and suddenly, we were inside. And if the exterior had been impressive, the ballroom itself was like stepping into another world entirely.

The ceiling stretched impossibly high above, adorned with massive crystal chandeliers that sparkled like stars suspended in midair. The walls were draped in deep emerald green fabric, the color so rich it seemed to absorb the light and reflect it back in shades of gold and silver. The floor was polished marble, its surface gleaming under the glow of the chandeliers, reflecting the swirling gowns and elegant shoes that moved across it like a flowing river of color.

Long, sweeping curtains framed the enormous windows that lined one side of the room, offering a view of the expansive gardens outside – hedges trimmed to perfection, fountains bubbling softly, and rose bushes blooming in full, vibrant reds and whites. Every detail was deliberate, every inch of the space designed to make you feel like you had stepped into something grander than yourself.

"Lily, this is amazing," Ava whispered beside me, her excitement palpable.

But all I could feel was a growing weight in my chest, a sense of being too small for a place this grand. The people here weren't just dressed to impress – they belonged. Their laughter rang out like music, their movements graceful and effortless, while I felt clumsy, like a shadow on the edge of something too bright.

We moved further into the room, Ava pulling me gently forward, her presence a lifeline in the sea of unfamiliar faces. Her confidence was magnetic, her smile easy and warm as she greeted people with a nod or a wave. She was in her element here, and part of me envied that. She belonged, but I wasn't sure if I ever would.

I could feel the air around me, thick with the scent of roses and expensive perfume. The clink of champagne glasses echoed softly, mixing with the murmurs of conversation and the low hum of music playing in the background. The whole scene was elegant, perfect even, but it felt miles away from where I was emotionally.

Ava's voice pulled me back again, her arm looping through mine. "Are you okay?"

I nodded, though the tightness in my chest remained. "I just... need a second."

Her eyes softened with understanding, and she gave my arm a reassuring squeeze. "Take your time. I'll be right here."

I offered her a small smile before stepping toward the far side of the ballroom, where the windows stretched from floor to ceiling, offering a glimpse of the night outside. The gardens were bathed in soft light, and beyond that, only darkness. I pressed my fingertips to the cool glass, staring out at the quiet world beyond this loud, beautiful space, and tried to find my breath. The air in the room felt heavy, like it was pressing down on me, reminding me of everything I had lost. Everything I was still struggling to hold onto.

The ballroom was a swirling mass of people now, the music lifting them into graceful movements, their laughter mingling with the soft rhythm of the jazz band playing on the stage at the far end of the room. Ava stayed close, her presence like an anchor amid the chaos of color and light, but I could still feel the unease growing, like I was slowly sinking beneath the surface.

We moved through the crowd, Ava's hand occasionally slipping into mine, guiding me, making sure I wasn't swept away by the night. She was a natural at this – her charm effortless, her smile disarming. People gravitated toward her, drawn by the warmth in her eyes and the way she spoke, always making the person she was talking to feel important. I could see it in the way they responded to her, the easy laughter that flowed, the looks of admiration they couldn't hide.

But for me, it was like walking through a dream. I smiled when I needed to, nodded at introductions, but none of it really felt real. The whole evening had this strange, distant quality – like it was happening to someone else and I was just a witness.

And then, the music shifted – a slower song, one that pulled the couples together on the dance floor. The soft notes of the piano filled the room, echoing off the high ceilings, wrapping around us like a lullaby. It was beautiful, but it only made the space between me and everything else feel wider.

"Wanna dance?" Ava's voice cut through my thoughts, her smile playful as she turned toward me, her hand extended.

I blinked, my mind scrambling to process her words. "What?"

"Dance with me." She gave a small, encouraging nudge, the light in her eyes sparking with mischief.

"Ava, I don't –"

"C'mon, Lily," she said, her tone gentle but insistent, "it's just a dance."

There was no getting out of it. I could see the determination in her gaze, the way she was willing me to say yes, to let go of whatever it was that was holding me back. And maybe, just for a moment, I wanted to let go too.

I sighed but couldn't help the small smile tugging at my lips. "Fine."

Ava grinned triumphantly and pulled me toward the center of the dance floor, where couples were already swaying to the slow, melodic rhythm. She held out her hand, and for a moment, I hesitated. But then, with a small nod to myself, I placed my hand in hers.

We began to move – slow, tentative steps at first, but Ava guided us smoothly, her movements confident and graceful. Her hand rested gently on the small of my back, her other hand holding mine in a way that was firm but reassuring. It was a simple dance, nothing elaborate, but it was more than just the movement. It was the way Ava made me feel safe, like she was holding me together in a way I hadn't realized I needed.

The music carried us, the soft, lilting melody filling the space between us, but it was Ava's presence that truly grounded me. The sound of her laughter, the feel of her hand in mine – it brought me back from the edge, back from the swirling mess of emotions that had been threatening to pull me under.

"You okay?" she asked, her voice low, as we moved together.

I nodded, but the lump in my throat returned, and I wasn't sure I could trust my voice. Ava's gaze softened, her thumb brushing gently over the back of my hand as she held me, steady and sure. It was such a simple thing – this dance, this moment – but it felt like something was shifting. Like for the first time in months, I could breathe again.

"You know, you're stronger than you think," Ava said quietly, her voice cutting through the music like a lifeline. "You've been through so much, but you're still standing."

I looked down, blinking back the sudden sting of tears. It was too much – her kindness, her understanding. I didn't know how to respond, didn't know how to let her see the cracks I had been trying so hard to hide.

Ava stopped moving for a second, her grip tightening just enough to keep me steady. "It's okay to let go, Lily," she said softly. "Even if it's just for tonight."

Her words hit me in a way I hadn't expected, and for a moment, I wanted to. I wanted to let the walls down, to let her see how broken I felt. But as much as I craved that release, there was still a part of me that was afraid – afraid of what might happen if I did. So instead, I just nodded, letting her hold me a little tighter as we swayed to the music.

And for those few minutes, it felt like the world had slowed down. Like it was just the two of us, moving together in this quiet, intimate moment, far away from the noise and the expectations and the weight of everything I'd been carrying.

But all too soon, the song came to an end, and with it, the brief sense of calm that had settled over me. Ava pulled back slightly, giving me a searching look as if she was trying to read something in my expression. I smiled weakly, hoping it was enough to reassure her, though I wasn't sure I believed it myself.

"Thanks," I whispered, my voice barely audible above the murmur of the crowd as the next song began to play.

Ava smiled, her eyes warm and understanding. "Anytime."

Before I could respond, a familiar voice called out from across the room, breaking the spell between us. I turned to see a small group of our friends approaching, led by Sophia Anderson. Her red, luscious hair flowed around her shoulders like a fiery halo, drawing the eyes of everyone nearby. The boldness of her auburn dress accentuated her curves and shimmered under the soft lights, exuding confidence and charisma that made her the center of attention.

Sophia had an effortless way of lighting up a room, her laughter ringing out like music, inviting others to join in. She had this magnetic energy that seemed to pull people in, and I couldn't help but feel a pang of envy as she flashed her dazzling smile. It was easy to forget the insecurity that sometimes lingered beneath her vibrant exterior; she wore her charm like armor, concealing the softer parts of herself from the world.

As she approached, I noticed her eyes flicker toward Ava with an intensity that felt charged. It made my stomach twist with uncertainty, but I pushed the thought aside, forcing a smile as she drew closer.

"Aye, you two!" Sophia grinned, her eyes lingering a little too long on Ava before turning to me. "We've been looking for you. You ready for the after-party?"

I blinked, caught off guard by the sudden change in energy. "After-party?"

"Yeah, at my place," Sophia said with a sly smile, her gaze flicking back to Ava for a moment before returning to me. "It's gonna be amazing. You're coming, right?"

I hesitated, my mind still spinning from the dance. The idea of going to a loud, crowded party after this felt overwhelming, but before I could say anything, Ava chimed in.

I watched Ava shift her stance, her earlier nervous energy replaced by a bright spark of excitement. When Sophia's question floated in the air, asking about the plans for the after-party, Ava didn't hesitate for long.

"We are in," she said, her voice firm and light all at once.

The words settled uncomfortably in my chest, pressing down on me like a sudden weight. I hadn't expected her to speak for both of us, and it rattled me. My gaze snapped to her, catching her eye, but Ava only smiled and shrugged as if it was the most natural thing in the world.

The group's chatter resumed, but my mind buzzed with unease. I needed a moment away from the others, from the excitement of plans I wasn't sure I wanted any part of. Without saying anything, I gently tugged at Ava's arm, leading her toward a quiet corner of the ballroom, where the low murmur of conversation couldn't reach us.

"Ava, why did you say we're going?" I asked, keeping my voice steady, though irritation simmered just beneath the surface.

Ava blinked, clearly confused. "I just thought it'd be fun. What's the big deal? You can always say no later if you're not feeling it."

"That's not the point," I replied, my voice sharper than I intended. "You didn't even ask me. You just decided for both of us."

Ava sighed, running a hand through her loose curls, frustration etched on her face. "Lily, we've barely done anything like this in months. I thought you could use a little fun, a break from... well, everything."

I swallowed, feeling the weight of her words. She was trying to help, but I couldn't shake the discomfort of being dragged into plans I wasn't ready for. "I don't need you making decisions for me," I said, crossing my arms defensively. "Especially not tonight. You know I've been overwhelmed with all of this." I gestured around at the grand ballroom, the noise, the clinking glasses, and laughter that felt so distant from my current reality.

Ava softened, her eyes darting between my face and the floor, guilt creeping in. "I wasn't trying to push you, okay? I just... I want you to feel like yourself again, like you used to."

I took a breath, the frustration mingling with guilt. "I know," I finally said, my voice quieter now. "But I don't think I'm ready for that. Not tonight."

We stood there in silence for a moment, the tension slowly dissipating between us. I could see the understanding settling in her gaze, a shared acknowledgment of the journey we both faced.

"Okay, let's just take it one step at a time," Ava finally said, a tentative smile breaking through. "Tonight is about enjoying ourselves, remember?"

I nodded, forcing a smile of my own. "Yeah, okay."

As the music swelled around us, I felt a flicker of hope, like a candle fighting against the darkness. Maybe I could find a way to enjoy this night, to reconnect with the pieces of myself I had buried under grief.

Ava reached for my hand, guiding me back into the fray. As we rejoined the crowd, the warmth of our love enveloped me, and for a moment, I let the weight of my sadness lift just a little. We swayed to the music, losing ourselves in the rhythm, and I could almost believe that everything would be okay.

The night stretched ahead of us, filled with laughter and dancing, but somewhere in the back of my mind, the reality of my struggle lingered. I couldn't ignore it forever.

After several songs, I felt the need to take a break. The noise and brightness had started to close in on me again. Ava caught my eye, a knowing look passing between us as if she sensed my unease.

"Want to step outside for a bit?" she asked.

"Yeah, I'd like that," I replied, grateful for her understanding.

As we stepped out onto the balcony, the cool night air washed over me, refreshing and grounding. I closed my eyes for a moment, taking in the sounds of laughter and music echoing behind us, blending with the gentle rustling of leaves from nearby trees.

The stars twinkled above us; a sea of tiny lights that made the sky feel endless. I leaned against the railing, inhaling the fresh air, and for a moment, I was just Lily again, separate from the pain that often consumed me.

"Aye," Ava said, joining me, her voice softening the air around us, "you okay?"

I nodded, opening my eyes to look at her. "Yeah, just needed a moment."

"Want to talk about it?" she asked, concern etching her features.

I shook my head. "Not right now. Let's just enjoy the night."

We stood side by side, gazing out at the world around us. I felt a flicker of hope igniting within me again, a small reminder that I was not alone in this.

As the night wore on, we danced and laughed with our friends, the earlier tension forgotten. But deep down, I still felt that nagging unease about the after-party. I wasn't sure I was ready to dive head-first into the chaos, especially after seeing the way Ava and Sophia interacted. Their chemistry was palpable, an energy that thrummed just beneath the surface.

Eventually, as the clock ticked closer to midnight, I knew I needed to make a choice. The noise of the ball had begun to feel like too much, the energy overwhelming. I turned to Ava, who was chatting with Sophia, her laughter ringing clear and bright.

"Ava, I think I'm going to head home," I said, the words slipping out before I could stop them.

She turned to me, surprise flashing in her eyes. "What? Why?"

"It's just been a lot," I admitted, the guilt creeping back in. "I think I need some time to myself."

"But we just got here," she argued gently, concern lacing her tone. "What about the after-party? I thought we were having fun."

"I know, but…" I hesitated, feeling my heart race. "I just don't think I can handle it tonight."

Ava's brow furrowed, her eyes searching mine. "Come on, Lily. It'll be fun. You can't keep hiding away from everything. You need to let loose!"

"I'm not hiding," I protested, though I could hear the tremor in my voice. "I just –"

"Lily, you can't keep doing this. I'm trying to help you!" she said, her voice rising slightly, attracting a few curious glances from nearby friends.

"We're supposed to be in this together," I replied, frustration flaring. "But I can't do what you want me to do tonight."

She stared at me, her expression shifting from frustration to something softer, as if she were finally understanding.

"Okay," she said finally, her voice low. "I get it. You need to take care of yourself. But… please, just think about it."

I nodded, wishing I could explain how hard it was for me to step back into that world. I wanted to be the carefree girl she remembered, but the shadows were still too close.

After a moment of hesitation, I watched as Ava's expression shifted. She turned back to our friends, her earlier enthusiasm replaced with a contemplative silence.

"I'll see you later then," she said, a hint of disappointment in her tone.

"Yeah, have fun," I replied, forcing a smile even as my heart sank.

As Ava walked back to join Sophia and the others, I felt a wave of sadness wash over me. I wanted to tell her that I didn't want this rift between us, that I valued my relationship with her more than anything, but the words were stuck in my throat.

With a heavy heart, I turned and headed toward the car, the laughter and music fading into the distance. As I walked, I stole one last glance back at the party, my heart aching at the sight of my friends lost in their own world.

Then I caught sight of Ava and Sophia standing close together, their heads bent toward one another, laughter spilling from their lips like a secret. Sophia's red hair shimmered under the lights, framing her face in a way that made her look almost ethereal.

Ava leaned in, a playful smile dancing across her lips as she whispered something that made Sophia laugh again, the sound light and musical. There was an electricity between them, a magnetic pull that drew my eyes, tightening my chest as I tried to shake the feelings it stirred.

Sophia reached out, brushing a loose strand of hair from Ava's face, her fingers lingering for just a moment longer than necessary. Ava blushed, a soft pink blooming on her cheeks, and the sight pierced through me like an arrow. It was a fleeting moment, but it felt significant, like a spark igniting beneath the surface.

I turned away, my heart heavy with an emotion I couldn't quite place – was it jealousy? Insecurity? Or was it simply the fear of losing the one person I felt connected to in this chaotic world?

As I reached the car, I slid into the passenger seat and leaned my head against the cool glass, closing my eyes. I took a deep breath, feeling the weight of the night press down on me. The image of Ava and Sophia lingered in my mind, blurring the lines between friendship and something more.

Maybe I was reading too much into it. Maybe I was just projecting my own fears onto their interaction.

But as the car drove away, the echoes of laughter and music fading behind me, I couldn't shake the feeling that something had shifted between us – a distance forming where once there had been a closeness I desperately wanted to hold onto.

The drive home felt longer than it should have, each moment stretching out like the shadows that danced across the road. The vibrant lights of the ball faded into the night, leaving behind a dull ache in my chest that I couldn't quite shake. The laughter and chatter of the evening replayed in my mind, intermingling with the sting of uncertainty.

As the car pulled into the driveway, I glanced at the darkened house, the windows dark like empty eyes staring back at me. I could feel the silence creeping in, filling the spaces left by laughter and joy.

The car parked and I sat in silence for a moment, my hands gripping my knees tightly, the sound of my heartbeat echoing in my ears.

Why had I let my feelings for Ava get so complicated? I wanted her to be happy, of course, but the sight of her leaning into Sophia – so effortlessly close – had left me reeling. I was happy for her, I thought. I really was. But the jealousy simmering beneath the surface whispered insidiously, urging me to question everything.

Was I losing her? Could I bear it if our friendship slipped through my fingers, especially when she seemed so at ease with someone else? I felt like a fool, caught between wanting to support her and the selfish urge to keep her close, to guard our bond like a fragile treasure.

With a heavy sigh, I climbed out of the car, the cool night air wrapping around me like a shroud. I walked to the door slowly, each step heavier than the last, the reality of the evening weighing on me like an anchor. As I entered the house, the familiar creak of the door echoed through the stillness, a sound that had once brought comfort now felt foreboding. Shadows stretched across the walls, creating dark corners that felt almost alive, whispering remnants of laughter and joy that now seemed out of reach.

Moving through the darkened halls, I was overwhelmed by memories that clung to the walls like ghosts. Each frame held a moment frozen in time – family dinners where laughter echoed, holiday gatherings filled with warmth, and the casual chaos that came with simply existing together. Logan's absence was palpable in the air, an ache that twisted deep within my chest. It gnawed at me, reminding me that happiness had a way of unraveling when grief pulled at its threads.

As I reached my room, I flicked on the lamp, its warm light spilling across the space, casting a soft glow on the walls that felt like a hug. This room, once my sanctuary, now felt like a battleground where I constantly fought to reconcile the girl I was with the one I had become. I sank onto my bed, the weight of the night pressing down on me. I took a moment, my breath hitching as I gazed around, absorbing the familiarity that felt both comforting and stifling.

I moved to my desk, the journal waiting patiently for me, its pages blank but filled with the promise of release. It felt like an old friend, ready to hear the truth of my turmoil. I grabbed my pen, hovering over the page, my heart racing as I battled with the surge of emotions clamoring for attention.

The dance with Ava kept replaying in my mind, vivid and exhilarating, yet tinged with an unsettling edge. I had felt so alive in those moments, a fleeting escape from the heaviness that constantly weighed me down. But then came the sharp reminder of Sophia's gaze, filled with a warmth that seemed to wrap around Ava, leaving me on the periphery. Was I being possessive or just longing for something that felt so fragile? The thought made my heart ache. I yearned to embrace this new chapter with Ava, yet the flicker of jealousy sparked within me, igniting questions I was terrified to face.

In that moment, sitting at my desk, I felt an urgency to confront the chaos swirling in my mind. The thoughts were relentless, like a torrent rushing through me, threatening to drown out any sense of clarity. I needed to make sense of it all – to capture the whirlwind of emotions and release the weight of my insecurities.

Taking a deep breath, I finally pressed the pen to paper, allowing the words to flow freely. It was time to unravel the tangled knot of feelings, to honor both the joy of the night and the shadows that lingered within me. I was ready to explore the depths of my heart, to acknowledge the complexities of friendship and desire, and to embrace the vulnerability that came with it all.

But as I began to write, the words poured out effortlessly, unfiltered, like a stream of consciousness spilling onto the page. I let my thoughts flow, each sentence capturing the rawness of my feelings, the tension between the joy of the night and the heaviness in my heart.

In the corner of my room, my puppy, Ophelia, lay curled up in her bed, blissfully unaware of the emotional storm brewing within me. Her soft, black fur glinted in the lamplight, and I could hear the gentle sound of her breathing, a reminder of the innocence and joy that still existed in the world. I paused for a moment to watch her, a smile breaking through the turmoil. Her presence had a way of grounding me, reminding me that there was still beauty to be found, even amidst the chaos.

As I resumed my entry, I allowed the pen to dance across the page, capturing the highs and lows of the night, the overwhelming feelings of being out of place, and the delicate vulnerability I felt in my relationship with Ava. Each word flowed through the pen effortlessly, as if they had been waiting for this moment, reflecting my fears and uncertainties about where we stood amidst the shifting dynamics of our relationship.

With my heart laid bare before me, I continued to write:

April 14, 2018

On top of the world you comfortably sat,
Waiting for your future to make itself known;
Watch your footing and try not to slip,
For you do not want to venture far off on your own.

On top of the world you comfortably sat,
Scanning and searching the paths down below;
All of the sudden your reality shifts as you fall,
Through that downward spiral you had to go.

Twisting and turning as your reality falls,
You look all around to see where you went wrong;
All you can see are the sights of reflection,
For it so happens to have been you all along.

You look up above to the world you once ruled,
As memories flood through the lens of perspective;
Take a moment and reflect on where you are,
And align yourself with your life's new objective.

You look up above to the world you once ruled,
As your journey restarts on this path anew;
Breathe long and breathe deeply today and tomorrow,
For where you once sat is not what you once knew.

Chapter 3
Tightrope

The morning light streamed through my curtains, illuminating the chaotic aftermath of the ball. My mobile buzzed incessantly on the nightstand, and I hesitated before reaching for it, my heart racing with a mixture of dread and curiosity. As I scrolled through the messages from my friends, my stomach dropped with each notification.

Messages poured in, collectively sharing stories of the night's events, snippets of laughter tinged with disbelief. But one thread caught my attention – a message from Leo. My best friend's words hit me like a punch to the gut:

"Ava and Sophia were getting really close last night. I swear I saw them sharing passionate kisses before slipping away behind closed doors."

I blinked, rereading the message as confusion washed over me. It couldn't be true. Ava would never do that to me, would she? My heart raced, memories of last night flooding back – the way Ava laughed, the way she danced, her eyes sparkling under the dim lights of the ballroom. I had felt so connected to her in that moment, so safe. But now, the realization of what had transpired sent me spiraling.

Images of Ava and Sophia wrapped in each other's arms filled my mind, their bodies pressed together, laughter mixing with whispered secrets. The thought was like a fire igniting within me – rage and sadness battling for control. I could feel the tightrope of my emotions stretching taut, each step forward sending me deeper into uncertainty.

I envisioned them together; lost in a world I had been excluded from. My mind painted a scene, intimate and raw, as if I were a voyeur in my own heartbreak. The way they would touch each other, fingers tracing skin, breathless gasps punctuating the silence – each moment burned in my mind, churning like a storm inside me.

The thought of Ava, the girl who had promised me the world, entangled with someone else twisted the knife deeper. What had I done to deserve this? I had opened my heart to her, allowed her to see my vulnerabilities, and in return, I was met with betrayal. The familiar rabbit hole of grief and despair beckoned me closer, threatening to pull me under once again.

I stumbled out of bed, the weight of my reality pressing down like a lead blanket. I paced my room, my mind racing. I could feel the anger boiling beneath the surface, a raging fire that demanded release. I needed to confront her. I needed answers.

The thought of facing Ava filled me with a mixture of fear and determination. I grabbed my mobile and typed a quick message, demanding she come over. I couldn't let this sit any longer. I needed to know the truth, no matter how painful it might be.

When she arrived, the air between us crackled with tension. I could see it in her eyes – the hesitation, the guilt. My heart raced as I confronted her, emotions bubbling over like a pot about to boil.

"Ava, what happened last night?" I demanded, my voice shaking slightly.

She hesitated, her gaze shifting away from mine. "I... I don't know how to explain."

"Try," I pressed, the words spilling out like a dam breaking. "Did you kiss Sophia? Did you leave with her?"

Her silence spoke volumes, and the realization hit me like a slap across the face. "You did, didn't you?"

"I didn't mean for it to happen," she said, her voice barely above a whisper. "It just... happened. I'm sorry, Lily."

Sorry. That one word echoed in my mind, twisting like a dagger. I felt my heart shatter, the pieces scattering like autumn leaves in the wind.

"You're sorry? You were supposed to be there for me, to support me! And instead, you're off with her?"

"I never meant to hurt you," she pleaded, her eyes glistening with tears. "But I can't pretend I don't have feelings for Sophia."

Her confession sliced through me, leaving me breathless. I felt as if the ground had fallen away beneath my feet, leaving me teetering on that tightrope of emotion once again. "How could you do this to me? After everything we've been through?"

"I... I didn't plan for this. I thought we were happy," she said, but her words felt hollow, echoing against the walls of my broken heart.

My vision blurred, tears spilling down my cheeks. "You know what? I can't do this anymore. If you have feelings for her, then maybe you should be with her. I deserve more than to be a second choice."

"Ava," I whispered, my voice cracking. "I can't believe you would do this."

As I turned away, I felt a profound sense of loss, not just for her but for what we once had. The very foundation of my world felt like it was crumbling beneath me, leaving nothing but confusion and rage in its wake.

After she left, I collapsed onto my bed, the silence of my room pressing down on me. I felt broken, alone, and defeated, as if this betrayal had marked the end of everything I had cherished. My heart ached; each beat a reminder of the pain I felt.

Unable to find relief in the silence, I reached for my journal. It had always been a haven, a place where I could pour my soul out without judgment. Tonight, I needed that more than ever. I opened to a fresh page, the blank space staring back at me, waiting patiently for the flood of emotions I had no words for.

The pen hovered for a moment, my mind racing with fragmented thoughts. And then, as if guided by an unseen force, the words began to flow effortlessly:

April 15, 2018

Off in the distance you see the rope,
Connecting the two islands of false hope.
You stop and you ponder your future decision,
As your walk between islands will require precision.

You approach the rope of ambiguity,
And you study the odds of continuity.
As you place your foot forward carefully,
You are overwhelmed with thoughts left wearily.

The rope can snap at any moment in time,
And your life could change at the drop of a dime.
To overcome this unparalleled mission that's here,
You must allow your mind to remain quite clear.

One deep breath and a courageous sigh,
Sets the tone for the walk through the sky.
With each step you feel another part of you heal,
Even though it does not quite seem real.

As you clear that rope and escape insanity,
You trip into another type of fantasy.
When off in the distance to no surprise,
Another tightrope appears before your eyes.

I set the pen down, the entry staring back at me like a mirror reflecting my inner turmoil. It felt like I had captured a piece of myself in those lines, yet there was no peace to be found. Just another tightrope to cross.

Feeling no more relief than before, I grabbed my mobile, desperate for comfort, and sent Leo a message. His quick response left me feeling a shimmer of comfort.

"Lily, what happened?"

I sat there, my body heavy with exhaustion and the weight of the crumbling world. In moments like this, my mind drifted to Leo. He had always been there, for as long as I can remember. A constant in the whirlwind of my life, he had this quiet strength that never faltered, no matter how chaotic things became. Leo wasn't just a best friend; he was one of my anchors, and above that, the one person I could always count on. Through every storm – Logan's death, my father's absence, and now Ava – Leo was the rock that kept me grounded.

When the grief became unbearable, when the walls started closing in, Leo would be there. He knew me better than anyone else, knew when to listen, when to speak, and when to just hold my hand in silence. They had shared countless memories, and it seemed like every defining moment of my life had him by my side. The way he would crack a joke at just the right moment to pull me out of my own head, or the way his eyes could speak volumes without a word… he was my sanctuary.

As the memories of our friendship played out in my mind, I realized just how much I needed him now, more than ever. This was a kind of pain even I couldn't bear alone. I reached for my mobile, my hands shaking slightly as I scrolled through my contacts. When Leo's name appeared on the screen, I stared at it for a moment, feeling the flood of emotion rise in my chest.

I hit call. The ringing on the other end felt eternal. When his voice answered, warm and familiar, a single sentence slipped out, fragile and full of everything that I didn't have the words to say:

"I need you."

Chapter 4

Suicide Pact

I sat there, numb, my mobile still in my hand long after I'd hung up with Leo. The room felt too quiet, too still – like the air itself was thick with everything that had just happened. The space where Ava used to fit in my life felt like a void, and the realization left me hollow. I didn't know how long I'd been sitting, staring at nothing, until I heard the familiar crunch of tires on the gravel outside.

Leo.

He always showed up. It was like he could sense when I was breaking, even when I hadn't fully said the words.

The front door creaked open, and soon enough, there he was, leaning against the frame of my room. His eyes scanned me for a moment, and then he stepped inside without a word, just him – Leo, the person who knew me better than anyone else ever could.

"Lily," he said softly, his voice grounding me in a way I didn't think was possible tonight.

Ophelia stirred from her spot on the floor, wagging her tail slightly as she nudged his hand. It was like she knew too. I glanced at her, and then back at Leo, my chest tightening. He crossed the room, sitting next to me on the bed without hesitation. No questions, no judgment – just his presence, solid and steady.

I leaned into him before I even realized I was doing it, the weight of the night crashing down all at once. "It's over," I whispered, my voice shaking. "Ava... everything's over."

His arm wrapped around my shoulders, pulling me closer, like he could physically hold me together. "I'm so sorry, Lily," he said, his voice full of quiet understanding. "You don't have to go through this alone. I'm here."

And for a while, we just sat there in silence. The pain of it all felt like too much, but Leo – he made it bearable. He always did.

I don't know what it was, but something about the way he held me, so sure and constant, made me think back to when we were younger. Back when everything seemed simpler but so much harder at the same time. I pulled away slightly, wiping at my eyes, and gave him a tired smile.

"Remember that stupid pact we made when we were kids?" he asked, his voice half a whisper, half a laugh. "The one about... the suicide pact?" I didn't know why it came to mind, but it did. Maybe because it was one of those memories that felt dark but comforting at the same time – knowing he was always there, even in the most painful moments.

I chuckled softly, his arm still around me. "Yeah, I remember. We thought the world would never get better, so we swore we'd leave it together." I paused for a moment, my voice losing all of its emotion. "But we didn't... we didn't leave, and here we are."

He nodded, his eyes stuck on me as if he was trying to analyze my response. "You're right. We're still here."

For some reason, that memory, that pact, it felt like a reflection of tonight – how fragile everything was. How it could all snap in a moment, like a tightrope stretched too thin. I stood up from the bed, walking over to my desk where my journal lay waiting. The words I needed to write had already started to form in my mind, and I knew I wouldn't feel any sort of peace until they were out on paper.

I glanced back at Leo, his eyes soft and reassuring as they met mine. Without saying a word, he understood.

Sitting down at the desk, I opened the journal and let the pen glide across the page, the weight of the night spilling out onto the paper:

April 15, 2018

Remember when you and I had said,
No matter how our life had gone;
We would be standing side by side in death,
As the ground beneath us turned red?

At this time we knew what one would only know,
That this life was wasted time for you and I;
Only to see that in the end it would seem,
The world seems peaceful while we stare below.

In this time and in this final act,
We as friends for life appear to be;
Following through on that final dream,
For when we were young and full of hurt —
We made what would be that suicide pact.

I closed the journal, the weight of my thoughts still heavy in the air and looked up at Leo. He was leaning against the wall beside my desk, his arms crossed with a mixture of concern and determination in his eyes.

"Do you remember the promise we made after that?" he murmured, breaking the silence. His voice was soft, almost hesitant, as if he were treading carefully on a fragile path.

I nodded, the memory flooding back. We were just kids then, naive and full of dreams, believing we could conquer the world together. "Of course. We promised we'd always be there for each other, no matter what."

"Yeah," he said, a small smile tugging at the corners of his lips. "You were always the brave one, talking about our grand plans to escape this place. I was just trying to keep up."

"Brave? I think I was just stubborn," I laughed, the sound foreign to my ears. "But you were always there, right next to me. I don't think I could have made it without you."

His expression shifted slightly, the lightness giving way to something deeper. "You know that pact was more than just a childhood fantasy for me. It meant I'd always look out for you, no matter how tough things got. And I still mean it."

I felt my heart flutter slightly at his sincerity, but I pushed the feeling aside, focusing instead on the memories. "Remember the time we snuck out to the old treehouse? You insisted we could see the stars better from up there, but all we ended up seeing was the neighbors arguing," I said, trying to lighten the mood.

"Right! And you thought we'd get caught, but I swore I'd protect you," Leo chuckled. "That was a disaster. But it felt like an adventure."

"It did. We were so convinced we were on some mission, saving the world," I mused, my voice trailing off as the reality of my current situation crashed back over me. "Now it feels like we're just surviving."

"Aye," Leo said, his voice dropping an octave, grounding me. "You're not alone in this. I'm still here. We're still here. You mean a lot to me, Lily."

There was a sincerity in his words that sent a jolt of awareness through me. The moment felt electric, charged with unspoken feelings that hovered just beneath the surface. "I know," I whispered, a lump forming in my throat.

We shared a moment of silence, the air thick with everything we didn't say. It was like we were both aware of the unsteady tightrope we were walking, each step requiring precision, and one misstep could plunge us into unknown territory.

Finally, Leo broke the silence, his tone shifting back to a lighter one. "Well, if you ever need a reminder of why life is worth living, just remember our old plan. We're still on that mission, whether it's silly childhood dreams or dealing with the mess of now."

I managed a smile, feeling the warmth of his presence wash over me. "You're right. It's just hard to remember that sometimes."

"Then let's make new memories," he said, his eyes brightening. "Let's find reasons to laugh again."

"Deal," I replied, feeling a flicker of hope igniting within me.

As the conversation continued, I felt my spirits lifting, if only slightly. Leo's support wrapped around me like a safety net, and I knew that no matter how rocky the path ahead felt, I wouldn't have to face it alone.

But as the laughter faded and silence enveloped us once more, the weight of my earlier emotions settled back in. The reality of what I had just faced – the betrayal, the heartbreak – loomed over me like a dark cloud. My thoughts spiraled, and the knot in my stomach tightened.

"Leo…" I started, my voice barely a whisper, "what if I can't get past this? What if I'm just stuck in this pain forever?"

He stepped closer, his expression earnest. "You're stronger than you think, Lily. You've faced so much already. You'll get through this, too. I promise."

His words were meant to comfort, but I could feel the raw edges of my vulnerability showing. I looked away, blinking back tears. It was hard to accept that, while he was trying to lift my spirits, I was still grappling with the ghosts of my past and the weight of my present.

"I need you," I finally admitted, my voice breaking slightly. The confession hung between us, heavy yet freeing, like a lifeline thrown into turbulent waters.

Leo's gaze softened, and he nodded slowly, understanding the depth of what I meant. "I'm here. Always."

In that moment, I felt a flicker of hope, mixed with the undeniable truth that everything was still uncertain. But maybe, just maybe, I could lean on Leo a little more, let him be the light guiding me through the darkness.

As the minutes passed, our conversation ebbed and flowed, memories of our shared childhood surfacing amidst the weight of my current turmoil. Each laugh, each shared moment, built a fragile bridge toward healing. But I knew that beneath the surface of our easy banter, there was an unspoken tension, a longing that neither of us dared to address just yet.

The world outside began to dim as evening set in, and I realized that, for now, I was grateful for the presence of someone who cared enough to help me navigate the choppy waters of my heart. With Leo beside me, I felt a sense of comfort, a whisper of possibility – perhaps this was the first step toward reclaiming my happiness.

And as the night deepened, I understood that, while the road ahead might still be fraught with challenges, I wouldn't have to walk it alone.

Chapter 5
Jealously

The moment I stepped through the school doors, I could feel it. The stares. The whispers. It was as if everyone knew what had happened between Ava and me. My feet dragged against the tile floor, the sound echoing through the hallways louder than it should have been. Each glance in my direction felt like an accusation, as if I wore my heartbreak like a scarlet letter for all to see.

Classes blurred together. Early American Literature came and went in a haze of unread words. Calculus, usually a welcome distraction, only added to the suffocating feeling gnawing at my chest. Time slowed, refusing to move forward at any reasonable pace, as if mocking me.

And then, between periods, I saw them.

Ava and Sophia.

They walked down the hall, hand in hand, their fingers intertwined like a lifeline meant to strangle me. My stomach twisted in knots, a sour heat rising in my throat. Ava didn't even glance in my direction, but I couldn't tear my eyes away. My heart shattered all over again, pieces too jagged to ever be whole.

The sight of them, so casual, so intimate, hit me like a punch to the gut. My legs felt weak, my heart pounding in my chest, and my head swam with questions. How could she? After everything, after all the promises... How could she just move on? With Sophia, of all people.

I turned on my heel, desperate to escape. My breath came in shallow gasps, my eyes burning as I blinked back the tears that threatened to spill. I ducked into the nearest restroom, locking myself in one of the stalls as I tried to pull myself together. But it was no use. My hands shook violently, my pulse racing as jealousy wrapped itself around my throat like a vice.

The image of Ava's fingers interlocked with Sophia's refused to leave my mind. I felt sick. I couldn't breathe.

I stayed in that stall for what felt like hours, the bell signaling the start of lunch barely registering in my fog of emotions. When I finally stumbled out, the hallway was empty, giving me a momentary reprieve from the invisible eyes I imagined tracking my every move. But no amount of solitude could stop the storm raging inside me.

By the time I sat down for lunch, I was numb. My food remained untouched; my stomach too knotted to even consider eating. I pulled out my journal, hoping that pouring my thoughts onto the page would offer some sort of release. But even the words felt heavy, like they weren't enough to express the venomous mix of anger and betrayal that burned inside of me.

I stared down at the page, my hand hovering over it as I tried to find the right words. The feelings were there, like a knot in my chest, but putting them into sentences felt almost impossible. My hand trembled as I finally set the pen down, letting the ink bleed into the paper.

I wrote:

April 16, 2018

You will find yourself staring in the mirror staring into your soul,
Listen close to your minds true story and you will never forget your worth.
If you lose your sense of self-worth and love as you look that mirror,
Jealousy will overwhelmingly take control.

It comes in forms of bitter action,
And can often lead to fatal attraction.
It comes in forms of irrational envy,
And can send your soul into a frenzy.

Do yourself a favor and look deep within your surroundings,
Where you have been and where you will go is no accident.
You are living a life that was hand crafted for you,
So allow yourself to take in the journey and enjoy the view.

Let the jealousy go and the purity rise,
And save yourself from that pitiful demise.
Let the jealousy go and your life fully blossom,
And save yourself from hitting rock bottom.

There will come a time when you feel so disgusted at the person you have
                                                                      become —
Your purpose in this lifetime is to be who you are and not who someone else
                                                                      wants you to be;
You will find a person that accepts you for you and loves your imperfect
                                                                      perfections —
Let go of that envy and jealousy and feel what it's like to be set free.
Jealousy craves when you look down on your soul,
Do not let it win and you will be realigned with your goal —
You will find your self-worth again
                              And then.

The moment I finished, I felt drained, but not lighter. The words were there, scrawled across the page, but they hadn't helped. They just sat there, staring back at me like a reflection of everything I was trying to hide.

The bell rang, pulling me back to the present, though the ache in my chest refused to leave. I closed my journal, tucking it away before heading to my next class. But by the time I reached the door, I knew I couldn't do it. I couldn't face another hour of pretending to be okay.

Instead, I slipped back into the restroom, the stall becoming my refuge once more. This time, the tears flowed freely. Silent sobs shook my body as I buried my face in my hands, wishing I could just disappear.

The stall felt like the only place where I could fall apart, where no one could see the pieces of me crumbling. The sobs came harder, echoing in the small, cold space. I hated myself for this – letting Ava get to me like this, letting her and Sophia's hands, intertwined and mocking, haunt my every thought. How could she throw away everything we had so easily? How could I be so easily replaced?

Time became a blur. I don't know how long I stayed in that stall, but the passing periods came and went, the noises outside dull and distant. People moved on with their lives while mine stood still, breaking apart in a school loo. The reality of it all – the lies, the betrayal, the public humiliation – was too much to carry. My heart twisted as the anger swelled, bleeding into my sadness.

By the time I emerged, the school day was nearly over, though I hadn't attended a single class since spotting Ava and Sophia together. I wiped my swollen eyes, but the redness wouldn't fade. It was written all over me, how broken I was, how deeply I'd fallen into the jealousy I'd been trying so hard to push away.

I didn't speak to anyone as I gathered my things and headed straight home. Mum wasn't home yet, but even when she arrived later that night, I couldn't bring myself to face her. Her knock on my door was soft and caring, the sound of someone trying to understand what was wrong without prying. I didn't answer. I didn't want to explain. What would I even say?

I tossed my backpack into the corner of my room, the weight of it nothing compared to the heaviness I carried inside. My chest felt tight, each breath catching like it had to push through layers of ache. My mind raced between the sight of Ava and Sophia together and the growing feeling that I was losing everything. It was like a punch to the gut, seeing them together, and now the image played on repeat, gnawing at the edges of my sanity.

I collapsed onto my bed, face buried in the pillow, as if I could somehow smother the pain along with the sounds of my own spiraling thoughts. But the softness of the pillow did nothing to soothe me – it only pressed harder on the ache in my heart. The tension in my body felt like a coiled spring, ready to snap, and no matter how tightly I clenched my fists, I couldn't loosen it.

The room felt too quiet. The silence didn't bring peace; it only made the chaos inside my head louder. I lay there, staring into the darkness of my pillow, my mind a whirlwind of confusion and anger. How could everything change so fast? How could Ava, who was everything to me, slip through my fingers like this? I replayed every moment, every word exchanged, trying to pinpoint where I had gone wrong.

Tears burned in my eyes, but I refused to let them fall. Crying would make it too real, and I wasn't ready to face it yet. Instead, I gripped the edges of the pillow, my knuckles turning white as I fought to hold back the sobs that threatened to escape.

I should call Leo. I needed to hear his voice, to feel that steady calm he always gave me when the world was falling apart. He'd been my rock for as long as I could remember. But something held me back, like admitting how much this hurt would unravel me completely. What could I even say? I didn't have the words to explain the emptiness swallowing me whole.

I rolled onto my back, staring up at the ceiling. The room was dim, only the faintest traces of light filtering in through the curtains, casting long shadows on the walls. The stillness of the space contrasted sharply with the noise in my head. My heart raced, my breathing shallow. My hands trembled slightly, and I tucked them under my arms, trying to still the shaking.

I wanted to scream. I wanted to break something, anything, to release the tension twisting inside me. My body was on edge, like I was barely holding myself together, and I wasn't sure how much longer I could keep it up. Each second felt like an hour, the weight of the day pressing down on me until it became unbearable.

And Ava... God, how could she? How could she hold Sophia's hand like that? The laughter, the smiles – it was like she'd forgotten about me, like I was just some shadow in the background of her life. The thought hit me like a punch in the chest, knocking the air from my lungs. I gasped, the pain so real it felt physical, my hands pressing hard against my chest like I could stop the hurt from spreading.

The tears that I had held back so fiercely finally broke free, rolling down my cheeks in hot, angry streams. My body shook with silent sobs, each one more painful than the last. I was losing her. I was losing everything. And there was nothing I could do to stop it.

I wanted to call Leo. I needed him, more than ever. But admitting it felt like admitting defeat. And I wasn't ready for that. I wasn't ready to say the words out loud – to confess how completely broken I felt.

The tightness in my chest grew, squeezing my lungs until each breath felt like a battle. I curled into myself, hugging my knees to my chest, trying to hold on to something solid. But nothing felt solid anymore. Everything was slipping away, and no matter how hard I tried, I couldn't stop it.

Ophelia, my sweet black lab, padded into the room quietly, sensing my distress. She nudged her cold, wet nose against my arm, trying to comfort me the only way she knew how. I reached down and buried my fingers into her fur, the soft warmth of her presence grounding me for a moment. But even that comfort felt distant, like I was too far gone to feel anything properly.

I pressed my face into Ophelia's soft fur, letting her warmth seep into me as the tears continued to fall. My sobs turned into shallow breaths, each one pulling me deeper into exhaustion. I was empty – completely drained – and yet the pain still lingered, gnawing at my insides.

Ophelia stayed close, her presence a small anchor in the storm, but it wasn't enough. Nothing was enough. I couldn't push the image of Ava and Sophia out of my mind. It replayed over and over, haunting me, until the room itself felt suffocating.

I should call Leo. I needed to hear his voice, to feel that steady calm he always gave me when the world was falling apart. But something held me back, like admitting how much this hurt would unravel me completely. What could I even say? I didn't have the words to explain the emptiness swallowing me whole.

The tightness in my chest squeezed harder, and I closed my eyes, hoping that sleep would take me, though I knew it wouldn't come easy tonight. My fingers curled into the sheets as if holding onto something solid might keep me from spiraling further.

"I need you," I whispered, the words barely making it past my lips, not sure if I was talking to Leo or just the silence around me.

Chapter 6
Cross Your Mind

As I sat beneath the sprawling branches of the weeping willow in the local park, its drooping leaves formed a curtain, shielding me from the outside world. This place had always held memories of laughter and warmth, but today it felt heavy, as if the tree itself shared in my sorrow. The gentle rustle of the leaves whispered secrets of the past, and I couldn't help but reflect on the time Ava and I had spent here, playing hide and seek, our laughter echoing against the tree's gnarled trunk.

But now, as I stared at the ground, I could only think about how far we had drifted apart. I was overwhelmed with memories, each one more vivid than the last, yet tinged with the sharp pang of longing. Was there something more we could have done? The question loomed large in my mind as I traced the patterns in the dirt with my finger, wishing I could rewrite our history.

The sun dipped low, casting long shadows that seemed to mirror my own thoughts – dark and confusing. I felt like I was walking a tightrope, suspended between the desire to reach out to Ava and the fear of further rejection. Would she even want to see me again?

As I lost myself in this turmoil, I spotted Ava walking towards the park, hand in hand with Sophia. My heart raced, and I felt a mixture of anger and sadness surge within me. How could she be so fine, so happy? Did I even cross her mind? The thought struck me like a bolt of lightning, and I instinctively pulled my legs closer to my chest, feeling the weight of jealousy pressing down on me.

I watched as they laughed together, a moment of pure joy that felt like a knife twisting in my chest. The willow stood as a silent witness, its branches swaying gently, almost as if it were trying to comfort me. In that moment, I realized how much I missed Ava – not just her presence, but the connection we had, a bond that felt both irreplaceable and lost.

With a deep breath, I closed my eyes and let the memories wash over me. The moments we had shared here, under this very tree, felt like shards of glass scattered in my heart. I could feel the heat of tears prickling at my eyes, but I refused to let them fall.

What would it take for me to move on? I thought as I recalled our last conversation, the lingering words between us that left so much unsaid. The pain of separation was a heavy weight on my chest, yet I knew I couldn't hold on to the past forever.

As the sun began to set, casting an orange hue across the park, I picked up a small pebble and tossed it into the nearby pond. The ripples spread outward, each one a reminder of how our actions, our choices, could alter the course of our lives.

The weekend slipped away, filled with moments of introspection and heartache. I found myself wandering the streets, retracing the steps I'd taken with Ava, searching for pieces of a past that felt like a dream now. Every shadow cast by the setting sun reminded me of the laughter we once shared, and every gust of wind whispered secrets that felt painfully familiar.

By Monday morning, the air was thick with the remnants of my sorrow, even as the school bell rang, signaling the start of another week. As I walked through the familiar halls, I felt the chill of winter in my bones, a stark contrast to the warmth of the willow's shade. Did time stand still beneath that tree, or did I merely lose myself in its branches? Now, I was back in a world where laughter echoed yet felt so far from reach.

As I walked through the familiar halls of Riverview High, a sense of dread washed over me. The laughter and chatter of my classmates felt like a distant echo, a world I no longer belonged to. I had barely slept since that day beneath the weeping willow, the image of Ava and Sophia hand in hand haunting my thoughts. I couldn't shake the feeling of being on the outside looking in, as if everyone else had moved on while I remained trapped in a moment of despair.

In Early American Literature, the words of Shakespeare filled the classroom, discussing love, loss, and the tragic consequences of miscommunication. Each line struck a chord deep within me, amplifying the ache in my heart. I couldn't focus on the teacher's words; my mind was clouded with memories of Ava. Did she think of me while she was lost in her newfound relationship? Did I cross her mind, even once, as she strolled through the halls with Sophia?

The bell rang, snapping me out of my reverie. As I moved to my next class, I felt the weight of my emotions pressing down on me. My thoughts drifted back to the willow tree, its branches swaying gently in the breeze as if it were beckoning me back to that moment of clarity. Beneath its shade, I had found solace, but now, I felt lost in a world that felt increasingly hostile.

During lunch, I slipped away to a quieter corner of the cafeteria, my heart heavy with longing. I pulled out my journal, hoping to capture the whirlwind of emotions that had taken root in my mind. The pen danced across the page, mirroring my internal chaos:

April 23, 2018

I cannot think of a time whether it be day or night,
When you are not at the forefront of my mind;
But I am left wondering how you could be so fine,
And if I cross your mind like you cross mine.

I take a moment and pause beneath the winter sky,
And ponder thoughts inside my mind and heart;
We parted ways and gave each other space,
But I often times wonder if that was smartest way to part.

Was there something more that we could have done,
To reignite the love we held inside our minds?
We could have realigned and worked through all that pain inside,
Instead we parted ways and began to run.

The days moved slower and the nights seemed longer,
And everything in life seemed out of place;
All control was lost and all hope was in decline,
As I wonder if I cross your mind like you cross mine.

Perhaps in a different life our journey never ends,
Or perhaps in this life we manage to make amends.
The truth is I am lost without you by my side,
And there are no stars aligned to guide.
So I will sit and stare and say I am fine,
As I know that I no longer cross your mind like you cross mine.

Closing my journal, I felt a wave of emotions wash over me. The writing hadn't lifted the weight I carried; if anything, it deepened it. Just then, Leo approached, sliding into the seat across from me, a bright smile on his face.

"Aye! You've been hiding out here," he said, his tone light but genuine. "I brought you something."

I looked up, curiosity piqued. He reached into his bag and pulled out a small container of biscuits. "I figured you might need a pick-me-up. My mum made them, and you know how she gets when she bakes."

I chuckled softly, the warmth of his gesture momentarily easing the heaviness in my chest. "You're right. She does bake like it's an Olympic sport."

Leo grinned, leaning back in his chair. "Exactly! So, what's the deal with Shakespeare? You know, it's all about love and tragedy. Maybe you'll find some inspiration there."

"Yeah, well, the tragedy part seems pretty fitting," I replied, forcing a smile.

He studied me for a moment, his expression softening. "You know I'm here if you need to talk, right? Or if you just want to get out of here for a while. We could hit the park. I could use some fresh air."

I nodded, appreciating the offer. "Maybe later. I just need to get through today."

"Okay," he said, a hint of understanding in his eyes. "But remember, I'm not going anywhere."

As the day wore on, the hours felt like an eternity. I moved through my classes like a ghost, unseen and unheard, my mind wandering back to the willow. The tree had become a refuge, a place where I could shed my burdens, if only for a moment. I longed for that sense of peace again, away from the prying eyes of my classmates and the ache in my heart.

Finally, the last bell rang, and I rushed home, desperate to escape the walls of the school that felt so constricting. The weight of the day pressed down on me, and I barely registered the world outside as I walked home. Dinner was an afterthought, the thought of food making me feel ill. I trudged to my room, collapsing onto my bed, tears streaming down my face.

How could I move on when the memory of Ava lingered in every corner of my mind? As I cried myself to sleep, I realized I needed to confront my feelings. I had to find a way to reconnect with myself before I could even think about moving forward.

Chapter 7
Hold Her Hand

The days have grown darker, and all I want to do is reach out and grab the hand that comforted me. But that hand is not here; it's miles away, leaving me to feel the weight of solitude press down like a heavy blanket. Today, I suppose I will continue to feel blue.

The school bell rang, pulling me from my thoughts as I gathered my books for Chemistry. The lab was filled with the familiar scent of chemicals and the faint chatter from my classmates, a symphony of voices that felt both comforting and suffocating. Today's experiment required precision: we were mixing acids and bases, creating reactions that could either bubble over with excitement or explode into chaos if not handled delicately.

As I set up my station, I felt the pressure of my peers' gazes, their eyes like weighted stones pressing down on me. I tried to focus on the task at hand, but thoughts of Ava crept in like a persistent shadow. Each step of the experiment was designed to be executed with exactness: measuring out precise amounts of hydrochloric acid, carefully adding sodium bicarbonate to avoid an overflow. I knew what I was supposed to do, but the bubbling solutions and clinking glassware faded into the background, drowning in a sea of memories I couldn't shake.

I poured the acid, my hand shaking ever so slightly, and watched as it splashed into the beaker. It fizzed and bubbled, but instead of excitement, all I felt was dread. The teacher's voice faded, replaced by the echo of Ava's laughter, memories of us joking about our chemistry class, making puns about reactions that felt so alive. Now, the lab felt like a prison, and I couldn't escape the feeling of everyone judging me.

"Lily are you okay?" my lab partner asked, snapping me back to reality. I shot her a tight-lipped smile, not trusting myself to speak. I tried to stir my mixture, but the motions felt robotic and heavy, my mind a whirlwind of memories and emotions. The acid started to fizz over the edges of the beaker, and I hurriedly grabbed a paper towel, my cheeks burning with embarrassment as I fought to contain the mess.

I glanced around the room, noticing the whispers and furtive glances directed my way. Were they talking about me? Did they know how lost I felt? Each minute stretched like an eternity, the clock ticking louder than the teacher's instructions. I found myself lost in daydreams of when Ava and I were together, our laughter filling the empty spaces of my heart. I couldn't help but wonder if she missed me too.

With a deep breath, I focused on the next step: adding the indicator. My hands trembled as I measured the solution, but before I could add it to the mixture, my thoughts spiraled back to Ava's smile, the way it lit up her face. The indicator slipped from my fingers, clattering to the counter, the loud noise drawing more attention to me.

"Lily, concentrate," the teacher said, and the words felt like a sharp jab. I nodded, forcing myself to refocus. It was just chemistry. Just an experiment. But in that moment, it felt like everything was on the line. I took a deep breath, swallowed hard, and steadied my hands, pouring the indicator into the beaker with all the care I could muster. The solution changed color, a vibrant blue against the stark white of the lab table, but my heart felt heavy.

As the class finally came to an end, I walked through the bustling halls, my heart racing with every glance. It felt as though everyone knew about my heartbreak, judging me with their looks. Leo caught my eye as I turned the corner, and he quickly approached, concern etched across his face.

"Aye," he said softly, his voice cutting through my fog. "How are you holding up?"

I shrugged, trying to play it cool. "I'm fine."

He didn't buy it. "You don't look fine."

I opened my mouth to respond but quickly swallowed the words. Instead, I nodded toward the door leading outside. "Let's go to the park."

With a reluctant agreement, we headed to the nearby park, where the weeping willow stood like a sentinel, its long branches swaying gently in the breeze. It was a spot I had often visited with Ava, a place where we would sit and talk for hours.

Once we settled beneath the willow, I could feel my walls beginning to crack. The memories poured in, and I leaned back against the rough bark, letting out a shaky breath.

Leo watched me, his eyes reflecting a mixture of concern and empathy. "Do you want to talk about it?"

I shook my head, overwhelmed by emotions I couldn't articulate. Instead, I pulled out my journal, the pages filled with my tangled thoughts. I flipped to a blank page, searching for the right words to express the pain and longing that consumed me. As the willow branches swayed above me, casting dancing shadows on the ground, I began to write:

April 26, 2018

The days get darker and all I want to do,
Is reach out and grab the hand that comforted me;
But that hand is not there as it is miles away,
Today I suppose I will continue to feel blue.

Tomorrow will bring the same regret as today,
As I think back to a time when I had all that remained;
Now silence resides where love once lived,
And the world all around me just seems so grey.

One day I believe deep down in my heart,
Our paths will cross and allow us to restart —
And on that day by the worlds demand,
I will reach out and hold her hand.

As the last bell rang, signaling the end of the school day, I felt a mix of relief and dread. I gathered my things and made my way to the weeping willow, where Leo often waited for me. The familiar sight of its drooping branches provided a sense of comfort amidst the chaos of my emotions.

When I arrived, I found Leo sitting against the trunk, flipping through a chemistry textbook, though his eyes were clearly far away from the pages. As I sat down beside him, he closed the book and turned to me, his expression softening.

"How was class?" he asked, his voice gentle, as if he could sense the weight on my shoulders.

"Just another day," I replied, forcing a smile. "You know how it is."

"Yeah, I do. But it seems like something's bothering you more than usual. Want to talk about it?"

I hesitated, the familiar knot tightening in my stomach. Part of me wanted to open up, to share the turmoil that had been swirling inside me since the breakup. But I wasn't sure where to start. Instead, I opted for a lighthearted deflection.

"I just couldn't focus in chemistry," I admitted. "It's like everyone's watching me, judging every little mistake I make."

Leo chuckled softly. "I get it. Those experiments can be tricky, especially when you must measure everything perfectly. But you've always been good at that stuff."

"Not today," I said, shaking my head. "I nearly knocked over a beaker and almost set the entire lab on fire." I laughed, but the sound felt hollow.

"You'll get it next time," he reassured me, nudging my shoulder playfully. "Besides, who cares what they think? You're way too smart to let anyone else's opinions get to you."

His words hung in the air, and for a moment, I allowed myself to breathe, to let go of the weight I'd been carrying. Maybe I was overthinking it. Maybe I just needed to get out of my own head.

"I know you're right, but I still miss –" I stopped myself, feeling the heat of my words rising in my throat. Missed what? Ava? Leo? The way things used to be? I swallowed hard, shifting my gaze to the ground.

Leo seemed to read the turmoil in my eyes. "Do you want to talk about Ava?" he asked gently.

I shook my head, the lump in my throat growing larger. "Not really. I just… I don't know."

"I'm here for you, Lily. Whatever you need."

I felt a warmth spread through me at his words. They were comforting, grounding me in a way that I hadn't realized I needed. As we sat there in silence, I could feel a connection growing between us – an unspoken understanding, a potential for something more.

Before I could say anything else, my mobile buzzed in my pocket, breaking the moment. I pulled it out, my heart sinking as I saw the name flashing on the screen.

Ava.

For a brief second, I hesitated, feeling the weight of that name pressing down on my chest. Leo's eyes flickered to my mobile, and I could see a flicker of concern cross his face.

"Are you going to answer it?" he asked quietly.

I stared at the screen, a million thoughts racing through my mind. This was the moment I had both dreaded and anticipated.

Just as I opened the message, the world around me faded away. I felt Leo's gaze on me, but all I could focus on was the screen, the words that might change everything.

"Can we talk? I need to explain."

As I read the message, my heart pounded in my chest. I looked up at Leo, whose expression was a mix of hope and concern, and in that moment, I knew I had a choice to make.

Chapter 8
The Cracked Mirror

Ava had asked me to meet. I shouldn't have agreed, but I did. I stood outside the café, my breath clouding in the cool evening air, trying to convince myself that I was ready for this conversation. The message still echoed in my mind: *"Can we talk? I need to explain."* It had been days since I'd seen her, and now I was here, waiting, my heart a mess of anger, confusion, and a dangerous hint of hope.

When she finally appeared, walking toward me with that familiar grace, I wished I could feel nothing. But I couldn't. The sight of her – her face, her eyes – made the weight in my chest grow heavier. I wanted to demand answers, to ask her how she could betray me like that. Instead, I just stood there, feeling small and brittle.

"Thanks for coming," Ava said, her voice soft, almost hesitant. There was something guarded in her eyes, something that only made me feel more distant.

I crossed my arms, not trusting myself to respond right away. I didn't even know why I'd come here. Maybe to hear her out, maybe to rip the bandage off once and for all. But now that she was standing in front of me, I wasn't sure I wanted to hear any of it.

"What do you want, Ava?" I asked, finally forcing the words out, my voice sharper than I intended.

Ava flinched, just barely, but I noticed. She sighed, taking a step closer. "I didn't mean for things to end the way they did. I didn't want to hurt you."

That was it? That was what she had to say?

I shook my head, the frustration bubbling to the surface. "You didn't want to hurt me, but you did. You did, Ava."

She looked down at the ground, and for a moment, I thought she might say something that would change things, something that would make it all make sense. But instead, she just stood there, her silence speaking louder than any apology ever could.

"I…" she started, but the words seemed to die in her throat.

That was enough for me. I couldn't do this. Not now, not ever.

"Don't," I said, stepping back. "Just don't."

Without waiting for her to respond, I turned and walked away, the heaviness in my chest sinking even deeper. I could feel her watching me as I left, but I didn't look back. I couldn't.

The walk home felt endless.

Each step was heavier than the last, my boots hitting the pavement in a dull rhythm that matched the pounding in my head. The cool evening air nipped at my skin, but I hardly noticed. My thoughts were too loud, circling around Ava's face, her voice, her silence.

The sun was beginning to set, casting long shadows across the street, draping everything in hues of orange and purple. The sky above was a canvas of fading light, with streaks of pink melting into darker shades of blue as the last bit of daylight slipped beneath the horizon. Streetlights flickered to life one by one, their glow dim at first, as though hesitant to take over from the fading sun.

I pulled my jacket tighter around me as the wind picked up, carrying the crisp scent of autumn leaves. It should've been comforting, in a way – the quiet evening, the soft hum of life winding down for the night – but instead, it felt suffocating. The world was slowing down, but my thoughts refused to do the same.

Each passing house was bathed in the warm glow of indoor lights, shadows moving behind curtains, families coming together at the end of the day. I envied their normalcy – their ability to just exist, to go inside and be with the people they loved. It felt like another lifetime ago when I could have had that with Ava.

I quickened my pace as the darkness deepened, the last slivers of light fading, leaving the streets bathed in the cold, distant glow of the streetlamps. The chill of the night settled deeper into my bones, and the silence of the evening grew more oppressive with each passing minute.

How could she still do this to me? How could a few words – *soft* words, as if they could undo the damage – tear me apart all over again?

I shoved my hands into my pockets, my fingers curling into tight fists, nails biting into my palms. I wanted to scream. I wanted to cry. I wanted to stop thinking about her, but no matter how hard I tried, her voice kept echoing in my mind: *"I didn't want to hurt you."*

Of course, she didn't want to hurt me. That would make her the bad guy, and Ava couldn't be the bad guy. Not in her version of the story. In her version, things just… happened. But I wasn't a character in *her* story. I was *me*. And in *my* story, things didn't just happen. People made choices. Choices that tore everything apart.

I turned down my street, my feet moving even faster now, as if I could outrun the thoughts swirling in my head. The houses on either side were quiet, warm lights spilling from windows, families sitting down to dinner, people laughing, talking, living their lives. I wondered what it must be like, to just… exist. To go home and not feel like everything was falling apart.

The pavement blurred beneath my feet, and I blinked hard, trying to focus. My hands were trembling now, the adrenaline from the confrontation with Ava still coursing through me, leaving me raw and exposed. I couldn't shake it – her face, the way she looked at me, like she still had a right to be sad about what had happened. Like I wasn't the one who'd been left standing in the wreckage.

By the time I reached my door, my chest was tight, and I had to fight to keep the tears at bay. Not here. Not now.

I fumbled with my keys, my fingers shaking as I unlocked the door and slipped inside. The silence in my house felt louder than the city streets. I dropped my bag by the door and leaned against the wall, trying to catch my breath.

I shouldn't have gone. I shouldn't have agreed to meet her.

But I had. And now I was left with all the same questions, all the same hurt, but no answers. Nothing but her empty apology ringing in my ears.

I dropped my bag by the door and leaned against the wall, trying to catch my breath. The quiet in the house pressed down on me like a weight, heavier than I'd remembered it being. I felt Ava's words circling in my head, pulling at every loose thread until I could hardly think straight.

I needed… something. Anything to pull me out of this spiral.

Without thinking, I moved up the stairs, into my room and to the mirror, standing in front of it as if seeing my reflection might ground me somehow. But the moment my eyes landed on the girl staring back at me, I felt a sharp pang in my chest.

I looked at myself – really looked – and I barely recognized the person I saw.

My eyes traced the lines of my own face, taking in every detail as though I was a stranger. My hair hung limply around my shoulders, dull and lifeless. My skin, usually warm and full of color, seemed pale and drawn, like the energy had been sucked out of me. Dark circles had carved themselves beneath my eyes, evidence of too many sleepless nights, too many tears shed in the quiet hours when no one was there to see.

My gaze drifted lower, over the curve of my neck, my collarbone – thin, like I hadn't been eating enough. My hands reached up to smooth down my hair, but the action felt mechanical, meaningless. I felt hollow, like I was just going through the motions, pretending to be someone who had it all together.

But I didn't. I didn't have anything together.

My eyes moved down to my arms, the way they crossed tightly over my chest, like I was trying to hold myself together, like if I let go, I might fall apart. My fingers curled into the fabric of my sleeves, and I noticed how they trembled slightly, a telltale sign of everything I was trying so hard to hide.

I was unraveling.

I stared at the girl in the mirror – at her tired eyes, her tense shoulders, her clenched fists – and I couldn't help but wonder... When had I become this person? When had I started to disappear?

I blinked, and that's when I noticed it. The crack.

It started in the top corner of the mirror, barely visible at first. But now, as I studied it, the thin line seemed to stretch farther, running jaggedly across the glass. How long had it been there? Had it always been this big?

I took a step closer, my breath fogging the glass as I leaned in. My fingers reached up to trace the crack's path, as if touching it might somehow make it real. The cool surface of the mirror felt rough beneath my fingertips, and for a moment, I imagined that I could feel the crack spreading, just like the fractures inside me.

It was small, yes – but it carried so much weight. The more I looked at it, the more I saw the way it grew, how it twisted and split apart. Just like me.

. As I drew back, my reflection stared back at me, tired and broken. I tried to smooth my hair, to make myself look like I had it together, but it was useless. No matter how hard I tried, I couldn't fix what was broken.

I felt the tears building before I could stop them. My hands started to tremble, and I clenched my fists at my sides, trying to hold it together. But it was too much. All of it. The crack, Ava, everything.

I couldn't fix this. I couldn't fix any of it.

With shaky hands, I grabbed my journal from the desk, sinking down onto the floor. The pen felt heavy in my hand, but the words poured out, raw and painful:

April 26, 2018

Look in that mirror at that slight little crack,
It starts in the corner that carry's all the weight;
At first glance it seemed small but the more that you looked,
The more that you see the pain that is staring you back.

Days and hours and nights carrying the weight,
The burden became more than it could hold;
The crack begins to grow as life cripples in its grip,
Its pain becomes something that cannot be told.

A tear falls from the pockets of your eyes,
As you stare back at yourself wondering why;
Asking why it was so hard to consider,
That this life and the next will be just like that cracked mirror.

I sat on the edge of my bed, staring at the cracked mirror across the room, watching as the light from my mobile flickered and faded. The soft glow of the screen had been my only source of light, casting a pale reflection on the walls before the darkness swallowed it whole.

The silence pressed down on me, thick and suffocating. It wrapped itself around me like a blanket I couldn't shake off, each second heavier than the last. For a moment, I just sat there, the room around me still and quiet, but my thoughts still loud, echoing off the walls of my mind.

I sighed and stood up slowly, flicking the light switch off. The room plunged into complete darkness, only the faint glow of the streetlights filtering through the curtains. I pulled them closed, shutting out the world outside, but it did little to chase away the weight that had settled in my chest.

With a slow, deliberate movement, I peeled back the blankets on my bed and crawled underneath them, the cool sheets brushing against my skin. I curled up on my side, pulling the covers up to my chin, trying to find some comfort in their warmth. But it didn't help. Not really.

I buried my face into the pillow, wrapping my arms around it as if holding it tightly might fill the emptiness inside me. The silence, now thicker than ever, settled in like a presence, and all I could hear was the slow thudding of my own heartbeat.

I closed my eyes, but even then, I couldn't escape. The images of the day – of Ava, of that crack in the mirror – kept replaying in my mind. My chest tightened, and I squeezed my eyes shut tighter, willing sleep to take me. But it wouldn't come.

I let out a long, slow breath, trying to settle myself into the bed. The darkness in the room was mirrored by the darkness in my thoughts, and I sank deeper into the blankets, trying to block out everything. But the weight of it all lingered, heavy, suffocating.

As I lay there, cocooned in my blankets, the only sound that remained was the rhythmic beating of my heart, steady and hollow, echoing in the stillness of the night.

Chapter 9

Obscurity

The blaring sound of my alarm jolted me awake, cutting through the silence like a knife. I fumbled for my mobile, groggy and disoriented, the light of the screen harsh against my eyes in the dimness of the room. The numbers blinked back at me – 6:30 a.m., time to get up for school.

But I couldn't.

The thought of dragging myself out of bed, putting on a brave face, and walking through those halls like everything was fine – it was too much. I stared at the glowing screen for a long moment, my thumb hovering over the snooze button before finally pressing it, letting the sound fade into silence again.

Five more minutes. Maybe I could convince myself to move in five minutes.

But when the alarm went off again, that same wave of exhaustion hit me, heavier this time. My entire body felt like it was made of lead, and no matter how hard I tried, I couldn't summon the energy to lift myself out of bed. I just couldn't face – not today.

I reached for my mobile again, swiping quickly to open the message app. My fingers moved automatically, typing out a quick, simple text to my mum: *I'm not feeling well. I can't go to school today.*

I stared at the message for a second before hitting send. It wasn't a lie, not really. I didn't feel well, but it wasn't something a day of rest could fix.

After a few moments, I dropped the mobile back onto the bed and rolled over, pulling the covers tighter around me. The weight of it all pressed down on me – school, Ava, the broken pieces of myself that I didn't know how to put back together. Everything just felt… too much.

It was easier to stay here, hidden away from the world. Where the chaos in my head could spill out unchecked, unnoticed.

I stayed curled up in bed long after the sun had risen, watching the light seep through the curtains and slowly inch its way across the floor. I knew I should get up, do something, anything to break free from the suffocating weight of my thoughts. But I couldn't. I just couldn't move.

The hours slipped by unnoticed, time stretching and distorting until I couldn't tell if it was morning or afternoon anymore. My mobile buzzed a few times, distant and disconnected, but I ignored it. I didn't want to see the messages from my friends, didn't want to deal with the concerned questions or the polite invitations to hang out. They didn't get it. They couldn't.

Eventually, I forced myself out of bed, my legs heavy and reluctant as I shuffled toward the window. The day outside was bright, painfully so, the world moving on without me. People going about their lives, smiling, laughing, living, while I stood here, stuck in this haze of nothingness.

I turned away from the window, unable to bear the sight of it. The emptiness inside me stretched out, vast and all-consuming. It was like I was standing on the edge of a void, staring into the distance, and all I could see was the faint, dimmed light of something just beyond my reach. Something I couldn't name, couldn't touch.

What was the point of any of this?

That thought lingered, heavy and oppressive, settling into my bones. I wandered around the room, restless but directionless, my mind spinning in circles. Everything felt so pointless. Every movement, every breath – it was like going through the motions of a life I didn't even want to live anymore.

I found myself sitting at my desk, staring down at the journal in front of me, the pen still resting where I had left it the night before. The words I'd written stared back at me, mocking me. A cracked mirror, just like me. Broken. Irreparable.

I picked up the pen and flipped to a blank page, letting it hover over the paper for a moment. The emptiness inside me felt heavier than ever, pressing down on me like a weight I couldn't shake off. I wanted to write, to let it all out, but the words felt stuck in my throat, trapped somewhere between my heart and my mind.

Finally, I let the pen move, the words spilling out slowly at first, then faster, tumbling onto the page:

April 27, 2018

Looking off in the distance at the faint dimmed light,
Searching for answers within the bird that took flight;
Unaware of what is coming or going or staying,
Remaining somewhat aware of the emotions that you are displaying.

The images of life in this moment are left with a stream of a blur,
As some events begin that you had hoped would never occur;
But beyond the blurry chaos of these distant stars,
Lies the moments of the journey that we get to call ours.

It may be hard to notice the light in a life left uncertain,
Breathe deeply and slowly and know not to carry that burden;
For in simplistic form your life and mind are full of purity,
As you look off in the distance at the sight of obscurity.

I stared at the words for a long time after they had left my pen. They didn't feel like they belonged to me, like they had come from someone else entirely. Someone who still had hope, who still believed there was something beyond this emptiness. But I wasn't that person anymore. I hadn't been for a while.

The journal lay open on the desk, the ink drying slowly on the page. My hand hovered over the words, almost as if I didn't want to let them go, as if they held some kind of power that I wasn't ready to release. But the silence in the room was creeping in, filling the space between me and the page, growing louder, heavier, until it was all I could hear.

I leaned back in my chair, my body sinking into the worn cushions as I stared up at the ceiling. The quiet pressed down on me like a weight, and for a moment, just a brief, fleeting moment, I thought maybe I could find my way out of this. That maybe there was a way forward, something – anything – beyond the darkness I'd been stuck in.

But that moment was like a puff of smoke, vanishing as quickly as it came. The weight settled back over me, crushing, suffocating. The air felt thick, harder to breathe. I could feel it pressing down on my chest, the familiar heaviness that never seemed to go away.

I pushed the journal away, shoving it off to the side as if getting rid of the words would somehow get rid of the feelings. But it didn't. The tightness in my chest only grew stronger, and my mind started spiraling again. Thoughts circled like vultures, picking apart every piece of hope I had left. My pulse quickened, each beat pounding in my ears, growing louder, faster.

The walls felt like they were closing in on me, the air too thick to breathe. I needed to move, to do something, anything, to escape the thoughts clawing at my mind.

I stood up abruptly, knocking my chair back, the sudden movement jarring in the quiet room. My feet carried me out of the room, but I wasn't thinking – I was just moving, desperate to outrun the storm brewing inside me.

I found myself in the loo, my hands gripping the edges of the sink as I stared into the mirror again. But this time, I didn't see the crack. I didn't see the tired, broken girl from yesterday. I didn't see anything. My reflection was just a blur, a hazy version of myself, distorted by the fog of my own mind.

It was like I wasn't even there anymore. Like I was already starting to disappear.

The thought of disappearing didn't scare me. It felt… comforting.

What if I just let it happen?

The question hung in the air, heavy and dark. It wasn't the first time I'd asked myself that, and it probably wouldn't be the last. The idea of letting go, of slipping away into the blur, seemed almost peaceful. No more weight on my chest, no more racing thoughts, no more pain.

Just nothing.

I closed my eyes and let the thought sink in, my body sagging under the weight of it all. The world around me felt distant, like I was watching it through a thick pane of glass. I could hear my own breathing, slow and shallow, but it sounded muffled, like it didn't really belong to me.

What if I just let go?

Let the obscurity take me. Slip away into the haze until I didn't have to feel any of this anymore. Until I could be free.

Chapter 10
A Dazed Poets Mind

The school week had blurred together, each day bleeding into the next with an exhausting monotony. By the time Wednesday rolled around, it felt like time had lost all meaning. I went through the motions, dragging myself from one class to the next, but I wasn't really *there*. My mind was elsewhere – stuck in a haze of questions and "what ifs" that I couldn't seem to shake.

I slumped into my seat in Literature class, the familiar weight of the textbook on my desk, but my fingers barely touched the pages. We were supposed to be studying something important today, some classic poem or sonnet, but the words swam in front of my eyes, the letters blurring together into an indistinguishable mess.

The classroom felt suffocating, too warm, the dull hum of students' voices drifting around me like white noise. The teacher droned on at the front of the room, reading from the textbook, dissecting verses that I couldn't seem to make sense of. I caught snippets of the discussion – a metaphor here, a simile there – but none of it felt real.

"The poet's mind is often dazed," the teacher said, her voice barely breaking through the fog in my head. *"Lost in thought, wandering through the labyrinth of language and emotion."*

The words felt like they were directed at me, like she was peering into my mind and seeing the tangled mess of thoughts that refused to quiet down. My head felt heavy, weighed down by the questions I couldn't answer, the feelings I couldn't explain.

I pressed my fingers against my temples, trying to will myself back into focus, but it was no use. My mind drifted, floating away from the classroom, away from the sound of my teacher's voice, into that familiar space of "what ifs."

What if things had been different? What if I hadn't lost Ava? What if I'd said something else, done something else? Would it have mattered? Would I still be here, lost and confused, unable to find my way out of this mess?

I squeezed my eyes shut, fighting against the ache in my chest. The noise in my head was too loud, drowning out everything else. The discussion continued around me, the class oblivious to my silence. I was just a body in a seat, my mind somewhere far away.

I opened my eyes again and glanced around the room, feeling like an outsider. My classmates were engaged, raising their hands, answering questions, their voices confident and steady. How were they all so... *present*? How could they focus on the beauty of poetry when my whole world felt like it was falling apart?

I picked up my pen, tapping it absentmindedly against the side of my notebook. My thoughts wandered back to Ava, back to the things left unsaid, the cracks in our relationship that I hadn't been able to fix. I wondered if she was thinking about me too, if I ever crossed her mind the way she still crossed mine.

Probably not, I thought bitterly. She had Sophia now. She had moved on, while I was stuck here, drowning in the past.

The bell rang, snapping me back to reality. I blinked, startled, realizing that the class was over. I hadn't written a single note, hadn't heard a single word of the discussion. I shoved my textbook into my bag and stood up quickly, hoping no one noticed how absent I'd been the entire hour.

As I walked out into the hallway, the noise of students rushing between classes filled the air, their voices loud and carefree, but it only made the fog in my head worse. I felt detached, like I was watching everything from a distance, unable to connect with the world around me.

Lunch came and went in a blur, like everything else today. I found myself sitting at the usual table with the usual people, but everything felt off. Their voices swirled around me, conversations bouncing back and forth, laughter bubbling up every now and then. But I was barely there. It was like I was watching from behind a glass wall, distanced from the group even though I was right in the middle of it.

My tray sat untouched in front of me – a half-eaten sandwich, a few limp chips, and an apple I hadn't even bothered to pick up. I poked at the food absentmindedly with my fork, moving things around just to look busy, but the sight of it made my stomach turn. The cafeteria was loud, the hum of a hundred conversations filling the air, but I felt like I was stuck in a vacuum, every sound muffled, every word distant.

Across the table, Leo and Maddie were talking about something, their voices blending in a way that I couldn't focus on. I heard snippets – something about plans for the weekend, someone's birthday party – but I didn't engage. I just nodded every now and then when it seemed like they were looking for a response.

Leo glanced at me from time to time, concern flickering in his eyes. I could feel him watching me, but I didn't meet his gaze. I didn't want to see the worry there. I didn't want him to ask if I was okay, because I wasn't, and I didn't have the energy to pretend that I was. He had been my rock for so long, but lately, it felt like even he couldn't reach me. No one could.

Maddie's voice cut through my thoughts suddenly. "Lily, are you going to the party this weekend?"

I blinked, the question hanging in the air as I tried to process it. *A party?* The last thing I wanted was to be surrounded by people, pretending everything was fine while the world crumbled around me. I forced a small smile, shrugging slightly. "I'm not sure," I muttered, my voice barely audible over the noise of the cafeteria.

Maddie frowned, her brow furrowing as she exchanged a glance with Leo. I could feel their concern, the unspoken question in their eyes: *What's going on with you?* But I couldn't answer. I didn't even know what was going on with me.

Leo leaned in a little closer, his voice soft but full of meaning. "You don't have to go if you don't want to. We can hang out somewhere else."

I appreciated the offer, but the thought of being anywhere at all – whether at a party or just with Leo – made my chest tighten. It didn't matter where I was. I couldn't escape this feeling, this emptiness that followed me everywhere.

I nodded again, not trusting myself to say anything. Leo seemed to understand, or at least he didn't push any further. He went back to his conversation with Maddie, but I knew he was still watching me, waiting for some sign that I was okay.

But I wasn't.

I picked up the apple, turning it over in my hands, the smooth skin cold against my fingertips. I should have been hungry. I hadn't eaten much today, but my appetite was gone. Everything inside me felt twisted, knotted up in a way that I couldn't unravel. I placed the apple back on the tray, untouched.

The cafeteria felt like it was closing in on me – the noise, the movement, the sheer number of people. It was all too much. I needed air. I needed quiet. I needed to get out of here.

"I'm going to the loo," I said quietly, pushing back my chair and standing up before anyone could respond. I didn't want them to ask if I was okay, didn't want them to follow me. I just needed a few minutes to myself, away from the noise, away from everything.

As I walked toward the loo, the sounds of the cafeteria faded into the background, replaced by the soft echo of my footsteps on the linoleum floor. I felt like I was moving through a fog, my mind numb, my body on autopilot. I wasn't sure if I was going to the loo to escape or to fall apart.

By the time History class rolled around at the end of the day, I was barely holding it together. The familiar hum of students shuffling into their seats felt distant, like background noise to the storm in my head. I slid into my usual spot near the back, my notebook lying unopened in front of me, the blank page staring up at me as if daring me to write something down.

The teacher, Mr. O'Donnell, was already at the front of the room, flipping through a stack of papers. He launched into the day's lesson, his voice monotone, devoid of enthusiasm. Something about revolutions, or maybe the Industrial Revolution – either way, I wasn't listening. I could see him writing dates and key events on the board, but the words didn't register. They might as well have been written in a foreign language.

"Can anyone tell me what the key factor was that ignited unrest during the Industrial Revolution?" Mr. O'Donnell's question floated into the room, met with the usual silence as everyone tried to avoid eye contact.

I should've known the answer. Normally, I'd be the first to raise my hand, eager to show that I was paying attention. But today, my hand stayed glued to the desk, my fingers tracing the edge of my notebook absentmindedly. My mind drifted, and the buzzing in my head grew louder.

Mr. O'Donnell looked around, waiting for someone to speak. When no one did, he sighed and moved on, writing a few more bullet points on the board.

I glanced at the notes my classmates were hurriedly scribbling down, but I couldn't bring myself to care. Their pencils scratched across paper, but it felt distant, like I was watching them through a fog. I leaned back in my chair, staring out the window, watching the clouds drift lazily across the sky. The world outside felt so far away, so removed from everything happening in this room, in my life.

The teacher's voice continued to drone on, but it was drowned out by my own thoughts. *I should be listening.* I knew I should be, but all I could think about was how detached I felt from everything.

The day had been a blur – just like the ones before it – and now, sitting here, I couldn't remember a single thing I'd learned.

I turned my gaze back to the classroom. The other students were leaning over their desks, engaged, writing notes, raising their hands when prompted. They were *present*. And then there was me, sitting in the back, barely holding myself together. It felt like I was an outsider, watching the world from behind a thick glass window, separated from everything and everyone.

A flash of movement caught my eye. A few desks away, one of my classmates passed a note to another, both of them giggling quietly. I watched them for a moment, feeling that familiar pang of isolation in my chest. They seemed so... normal. Like they weren't weighed down by this heaviness that had settled into my bones.

Mr. O'Donnell's voice broke through again, his words echoing faintly in my mind. *"The unrest among the working class was driven by inequality – people feeling trapped, powerless, pushed to the edge."*

The words hung in the air, and for a moment, they resonated with me. Trapped. Powerless. Pushed to the edge. Maybe I wasn't so far removed from the lesson after all.

I picked up my pen and began to tap it lightly against the notebook, my mind still wandering, still disconnected. The tapping became a rhythm, a beat that matched the pulse in my head, steady and insistent. The noise around me faded as my thoughts turned inward, spiraling through all the things I couldn't control.

That's when I flipped to the last page of my notebook, my fingers trembling slightly as I uncapped the pen. Maybe if I wrote it down – maybe if I let it out – it would make more sense. Maybe the words would help me make sense of this mess inside my head.

May 2, 2018

Dazed and confused like a mind made to wander,
Unaware of the world that is revolving around you;
Sit down and write like you are almost out of time,
Give your followers something that they could ponder.

Ponder the world that your poet designs —
Follow the word of his passionate lines,
Envision the world through the lens of his eyes —
Remove the world from the masks of disguise.

Inside the depths of a dazed poet's mind lies the secrets that once were let out
                                                                                       with a cry;
These secrets are composed of the memories and the truths —
These moments that come and go as they please,
Leaving behind pictures of a life that they may try to deny.

I stared at the words for a long time after I had written them, my mind still buzzing with all the things I couldn't say out loud. The words didn't give me answers, but they gave me something to hold onto. Something that felt real, even if just for a moment. I carefully closed my notebook, almost as if sealing away the thoughts and emotions I had allowed to spill onto the page. It was strange – how writing something down could take even a little bit of the weight off my chest.

The classroom around me continued to hum with the quiet sound of students flipping through their textbooks and scribbling notes, but I was still floating in my own world. The bell rang sharply, jolting me from my thoughts, and I quickly gathered my things. My hands felt steadier now, more sure than they had all day. I wasn't entirely certain where this sudden calmness had come from, but I wasn't going to question it.

As I walked out of the classroom, the cool air from the hallway hit my skin, and for the first time in a while, I breathed deeply, as if my lungs had forgotten how much air they could actually hold. The chaos of the day – Ava, the constant noise in my head, the feeling of drowning in my own thoughts – it hadn't disappeared, but it felt quieter now. Less all-consuming.

The corridors were full of students heading to their next class, but for once, I wasn't caught up in the rush. I slowed my pace, letting the crowd move around me. It felt like I was still moving through a haze, but this one was different. This one didn't weigh me down.

For the first time in a long while, I felt a flicker of resolve deep inside me. I wasn't sure where it had come from, but there it was – a small, fragile flame. Maybe I wasn't as helpless as I had thought. Maybe, if I let myself believe it, I could begin to rebuild the pieces of who I used to be.

I need to try, I thought to myself, gripping my bag a little tighter. *I owe it to myself to try.*

The thoughts were simple, but they carried a new weight. They weren't just fleeting notions like they had been in the past – they felt like something more concrete. Something I could hold onto when the darkness started to creep back in.

As I walked toward the exit doors, I made a quiet promise to myself: I would work on me. I would focus on my own healing, no matter how difficult it was or how long it took. No more avoiding it, no more getting lost in the noise of what had happened. I had to move forward.

With each step down the hallway, the determination grew, layer by layer. I knew it wouldn't be easy. I knew there would be days where it felt impossible, where I would want to give up. But right now, in this small moment of clarity, I made that vow. I wouldn't let anything – or anyone – disrupt my path forward.

The world around me hadn't changed, but maybe – just maybe – I could start to.

Chapter 11
Who Am I?

The weekend had come and gone, slipping away like sand through my fingers. It wasn't like I had expected anything to change – nothing had, really. The same weight that had been pressing down on me before was still there, just as heavy, just as suffocating. I had spent most of the weekend locked in my room, ignoring the world outside, burying myself in old books and scribbling nonsense into my journal in a half-hearted attempt to feel something other than the gnawing emptiness.

But it hadn't worked. No matter how much I tried to distract myself, the thoughts always crept back in – Ava, Sophia, the feeling of being left behind, discarded. It was like a loop that played endlessly in my mind, and I couldn't hit pause.

Now it was Monday, and the start of a new week hadn't brought any relief. If anything, the dread that had been simmering beneath the surface all weekend had only grown. I had made it through the past couple of days by keeping busy, forcing myself to focus on little tasks – laundry, homework, cleaning up my room. Anything to keep my mind from wandering too far down that dark path.

But the moment I walked into school, I could feel it creeping in again. The halls, the classrooms, the people – they all felt the same, like nothing had changed since last week. But *I* had changed. Or at least, it felt like I had. I wasn't the same person who had walked these halls before.

I had been doing better – or so I thought. I kept telling myself that every morning when I forced myself out of bed. I kept repeating it like a mantra, like if I said it enough times, it would become true. I had spent the past few days trying to move forward, trying to stay focused on anything other than the gaping hole that Ava had left behind.

But deep down, I knew I was only one small push away from falling apart again.

It happened between classes.

I had just left Chemistry, my notebook still clutched under my arm as I navigated through the crowded hallway, my mind drifting somewhere far away. The steady buzz of conversation and laughter was background noise, blending into the chaotic symphony of high school life. I wasn't paying much attention, too lost in my own thoughts, too focused on making it to my next class without tripping over my own feet.

And then I saw them.

Ava and Sophia.

They were walking together, side by side, but it wasn't just that. It was the way they were holding hands – Sophia's fingers laced through Ava's, their heads tilted toward each other as they shared a quiet laugh. The sound was soft, almost intimate, and it hit me like a punch to the gut.

I stopped in my tracks, the hallway spinning around me as I stared at them. My stomach twisted, bile rising in my throat as the scene played out in front of me, but I couldn't look away. My heart pounded in my chest, the sound of it loud in my ears, drowning out the chatter of students around me.

How could she? After everything, after the promises she had made, how could Ava be here with her? Smiling, laughing, holding hands – like none of it mattered, like I didn't matter.

Before I knew what was happening, my body moved on its own. My feet turned, carrying me away from the scene, away from the sickening sight of them together. I stumbled into the nearest restroom; the door slamming shut behind me as I collapsed against the wall.

My breath came in ragged gasps, my chest heaving as I struggled to keep it together. The room was spinning, my vision blurry as I sank to the cold tile floor, my hands shaking uncontrollably.

It's happening again. It's all happening again.

My thoughts were spiraling, crashing over me like waves, one after the other, until I was drowning in them. I pressed my hands to my temples, squeezing my eyes shut, willing the pain to stop. But it didn't.

The image of Ava and Sophia kept replaying in my mind, over and over again, like some twisted movie that I couldn't turn off. The way Ava looked at her, the way she smiled, the way she held her hand – it was all too much. Too much to bear.

I had been doing better. I had been moving forward, hadn't I? But now, it felt like everything had come crashing down, like all the progress I had made had been ripped away in an instant.

Who am I?

The question echoed in my mind, relentless and unforgiving. *Who am I without Ava?* I had lost so much of myself when she left, and now I didn't even know who I was anymore. Was I just the broken girl left behind? The girl who wasn't enough?

I buried my face in my hands, the tears spilling out before I could stop them. I had tried so hard to hold it together, to be strong, but this – this was too much. I felt like I was falling, spiraling deeper and deeper into the pit of despair, and there was no one there to catch me.

Who am I? Who am I now that she's gone?

I don't know how long I stayed there, huddled in the loo stall, my knees drawn up to my chest as I cried silently. The minutes blurred together, the world outside fading away until all that was left was the hollow ache in my chest.

When the tears finally stopped, I wiped my face with the sleeve of my jumper, my hands still trembling. The weight of everything hung heavy over me, suffocating, but I knew I couldn't stay here. I had to move. I had to do something – anything to release the crushing thoughts spiraling through my mind.

With a shaky breath, I reached into my bag and pulled out the new journal I had started only a few days ago. My last one had been filled to the brim with all the pain, confusion, and fragments of hope I had poured into its pages. Now, this fresh journal felt heavier in my hands, its blank pages waiting to absorb the chaos in my mind.

I flipped it open, my fingers trembling slightly as I turned to a blank page. My hands hovered over the paper, the pen poised, ready to capture everything I couldn't say out loud.

May 7, 2018

Who am I without you here by my side,
Without you holding my hand through the night?
Who am I now that you have moved on,
Now that you have decided to run off and hide?
Who am I?

Who am I to be now that I am all alone,
Now that I am left to walk through the woods?
Who am I to be when I have already lost the fight,
When I have already lost my throne?
Who am I?

Who am I to you now that I am but a memory,
Now that I must see you move on with someone new?
Who am I to you tonight while the sky is looking grey,
Tonight when I am down and feeling so blue?
Who am I?

Who am I supposed to call when things go good today,
When things seem out of place?
Who am I supposed to call if I need to let out a cry,
If I feel like I am just a disgrace?
Who am I?

Who am I?
Who am I?
Who am I today if tomorrow isn't guaranteed?
Who am I to be if I am to succeed?
Who am I?
Who am I?

Chapter 12

Sincerely, me

The house was quiet. Too quiet.

It had been that way for days – this eerie silence hanging in the air, like the world itself was holding its breath, waiting for something to happen. Waiting for *me* to make a move. I stayed in my room most of the time, trying to avoid the weight of everything outside these four walls. My mum was working late shifts again, so it was just me. Just me and my thoughts.

That was dangerous.

The rest of the week had been a blur. Monday had started like any other, with me putting on the mask I had perfected – getting out of bed, going to school, pretending that everything was fine. But the days that followed were harder. Each day felt heavier than the last, like something was pulling me deeper into a place I couldn't crawl out of.

By Tuesday, the effort of keeping up appearances had worn me down. I found myself staring off into space during classes, unable to focus on anything the teachers were saying. I went through the motions, nodding when I needed to, answering questions half-heartedly, but inside, I was somewhere else. Each time I looked at my mobile, I half expected to see a message from Ava, some sign that maybe things could go back to how they were. But the screen stayed dark, as empty as I felt.

Wednesday wasn't much different. I skipped lunch that day, choosing instead to sit by myself in one of the quiet hallways. I told myself I needed the break, but deep down, I knew I was avoiding everyone. The thought of facing my friends, pretending to be okay when I was anything but, felt impossible. Leo had noticed. He always did. But even when he asked if I was alright, I didn't have the energy to explain what was going on inside my head.

By Thursday, the cracks in my facade were showing. I could see it in the way people looked at me – the concerned glances from Maddie, the cautious tone in Leo's voice. I knew they wanted to help, but I didn't know how to let them. I was too far gone, too lost in my own thoughts. It was like I was walking through a fog, disconnected from everything and everyone around me. The weight on my chest was growing heavier with each passing day, and I didn't know how much longer I could carry it.

By Friday, I was completely numb. The pain was still there, of course, but it had buried itself so deep that all I could feel was this dull, empty ache. I had stopped trying to fight it, stopped pretending that things were going to get better. I knew now that they wouldn't. I was spiraling, and there was no point in holding on anymore.

And now, here I was. Saturday. The end of the line.

I lay on my bed, staring up at the ceiling, feeling that familiar heaviness settle over me again. The weight of everything. The weight of *nothing*. I hadn't eaten much today. I hadn't done much of anything. It was easier that way – just letting myself drift, untethered to the world around me.

Somewhere in the back of my mind, I knew what was happening. I was slipping, falling deeper into the darkness, but I didn't have the strength to stop it. Part of me didn't want to stop it. I'd spent so long fighting this feeling, pushing it down, trying to convince myself that things could get better. But now, it felt like all that effort had been for nothing.

What if this is it? The thought gnawed at me. *What if this is all I have left?*

I rolled onto my side, my eyes falling on the small journal resting on my nightstand – the one I had started only a week ago, the one that already felt so heavy with the weight of my words. My fingers brushed against the cover, but I didn't pick it up. Not yet.

I had been planning, hadn't I? That thought slipped in like a whisper, cold and dark. I had been thinking about what it would look like – *rock bottom*. What would it feel like to finally give in? To let go? It was no longer just a passing thought, something that crossed my mind during the worst moments. Now, it was real. Tangible. Like a shadow creeping closer, waiting for me to make a move.

I had been making plans, quietly, in the back of my mind. How it would happen. What I would do. And now... it felt like those plans were ready to be set into motion.

I sat up slowly, feeling the weight of those thoughts pressing down on me like a vice. My head felt cloudy, heavy, but there was a clarity in my decision. I didn't want to feel this way anymore. I didn't want to carry this weight any longer.

I reached for my journal, flipping it open to the first blank page. My hand shook as I picked up the pen, but the words came easily this time. They had been waiting for this moment.

May 12, 2018

I hope this letter finds you in a better spot,
In a place that you thought you once forgot.

Finding peace and harmony in your days,
Beneath the clouds and suns warmest blaze.

Remember when you were too weak,
Feeling like life was far too bleak.

You made it there then and here now,
And I know at times you must have wondered how.

Your strength and pride pushed you through that time,
And gave you the courage to make the climb.

The mountains were endless or so they seemed,
For the tip of that mountain was all that was dreamed.

When you forget your purpose or your way of life,
Remember to let go of all that strife.

For when you do and you see the way,
Well the light will guide you as clear as day.

One more final thing for me to share,
Before you continue flying through this air —
You are right where you are meant to be,
For you are here and there,

Sincerely me.

The pen slipped from my fingers as I finished the last line, the weight of the journal now more than I could bear. I closed it slowly, pressing it to my chest as I leaned back against the headboard. The room around me was silent, the air still and heavy. I could feel the calm creeping in, like the end of a long journey.

I had written the letter to myself, but it felt like a goodbye. Maybe that's what it was. A goodbye to this weight, to the pain, to everything that had been pulling me under.

For a moment, I closed my eyes, listening to the stillness that surrounded me. It was unsettling, this quiet. It made the thoughts in my head echo louder, bouncing off the walls of my mind, filling the room with things I couldn't say aloud.

What if this is it? I thought again, the words wrapping themselves around me like a familiar cloak. Part of me wanted to fight it, to push the darkness away like I had so many times before. But another part of me – maybe the part that had grown tired of the fight – welcomed the quiet. The calm. The sense that, for the first time in a long while, I didn't have to pretend anymore. I didn't have to be okay.

I had been pretending for so long.

I opened my eyes, staring up at the ceiling, my chest tightening with the weight of it all. I wasn't sure if I was ready to let go, to give in to the finality of it. But at the same time, I wasn't sure if I had the strength to keep holding on. I was stuck in between, caught in this strange limbo between wanting to fight and wanting to surrender.

A soft sigh escaped my lips as I pulled the blankets around me, cocooning myself in their warmth. I wished I could fall asleep and wake up in a different life – one where things weren't so complicated, where the weight on my chest didn't feel so crushing. But I knew that wasn't going to happen. This was my life, and no matter how much I wanted to escape it, I was still here.

My eyes drifted to the window, where the last bit of daylight was slipping away, casting the room in deep shadows. The night was settling in, quiet and still, just like me. The journal sat beside me, its pages full of words I hadn't wanted to write but needed to. Words that felt like they had taken a piece of me with them.

I hugged my knees to my chest, staring blankly at the wall, the numbness settling in once more. There was no more energy left to fight it. No more strength to keep pushing against the tide. I felt like a leaf drifting on the wind, carried by forces beyond my control, not knowing where I would land.

Maybe it's better this way, I thought, my mind quiet for the first time all day.

The calm that followed was eerie, but I embraced it. After weeks of chaos, of spiraling thoughts and uncontrollable emotions, the silence felt almost comforting. Like everything had finally come to rest.

And maybe I had too.

Chapter 13
What I Gave You

The day stretched out endlessly, each minute dragging longer than the last. I hadn't spoken much since waking up, and I could tell my mum noticed. She hovered in that familiar way, like she wanted to say something but didn't know how to approach it. Her usual check-ins were softer today, more hesitant than normal, as if she was waiting for me to break the silence first. She asked how I was doing, how I slept, whether I wanted anything for breakfast, but it was clear she wasn't just asking about food. I gave her short, clipped answers, avoiding her gaze as I stirred cereal in a bowl I didn't really want to eat.

The tension between us was palpable. She was giving me space, but I could sense the worry in every glance, every quiet sigh that escaped her. I could almost feel the weight of her thoughts pressing down on me, as though she was trying to understand something she couldn't reach. I knew what she wanted – some sign that I was okay, that I was holding on – but I didn't have the energy to offer her anything. Not today.

Everything felt like it was building toward something, some invisible line I was inching closer to crossing. The sense of inevitability sat heavy on my chest, tightening with each passing hour. I tried to shake it off, to find some sense of normalcy in the routine things – the shower, breakfast, mindlessly scrolling through my mobile – but it wasn't working. No matter how hard I tried to distract myself, the weight of that unknown edge, that moment waiting to tip over, stayed with me.

It was like standing at the edge of a cliff, knowing the fall was coming, but not knowing how long it would take before I lost my balance. Every breath I took felt like it might be the last before everything crumbled. But I couldn't stop myself from standing there, waiting for the inevitable. There was this strange comfort in the certainty of it, even though I wasn't ready to admit it to myself.

I wandered through the house, my steps dragging as I moved from room to room. I sat in the living room for a while, staring blankly at the TV, the volume turned down so low that the voices barely registered. I don't even remember what was on – some mindless show that I wasn't really watching. It didn't matter. Nothing really held my attention for long. I was too caught up in the noise inside my head, that constant hum of thoughts spinning out of control, one after the other, until they all blurred together in a tangle of worry and fear.

I felt disconnected from everything around me, like I was watching my life play out from a distance. I could see myself moving, hear myself answering my mum when she asked if I needed anything, but it all felt mechanical. Hollow. My thoughts were loud, but they didn't make any sense. They were like static in my mind, a jumble of unfinished ideas and emotions that refused to quiet down, no matter how much I tried to push them away.

There was a part of me that wanted to scream, to cry, to do something – anything – that would break through the haze. But I couldn't. I couldn't even muster the energy to feel the things I knew I was supposed to be feeling. It was like I had been emptied out, like there was nothing left inside me except this weight pressing down on my chest, reminding me that something was wrong, even though I couldn't pinpoint exactly what.

All day, I went through the motions. I showered, ate breakfast, sat in the living room, but it was as if my body was moving on autopilot, while my mind drifted elsewhere – caught between wanting to escape and knowing there was no way out. I was trapped in this limbo, waiting for something to break, waiting for the moment when everything would tip over the edge and send me falling.

The worst part was that I knew it was coming. I could feel it. That moment was getting closer, and there was nothing I could do to stop it.

By the time the afternoon rolled around, I couldn't handle the silence in the house anymore. I grabbed my jacket and slipped out the front door, letting the cool spring air wash over me. I didn't have a destination in mind, but I knew I needed to keep moving. Walking had always been a way to clear my head, to get some distance from the chaos inside, but today the steps felt different. Each one felt final, like they were leading me somewhere I wasn't ready to go.

I found myself wandering toward the park, the same one Ava and I had spent so many afternoons together. The familiar sight of the trees, the swing set, the path winding around the small pond – it all felt so distant now, like a memory from another life. I sat down on one of the benches, staring out at the water, letting my mind drift.

The conversations I had been having with people over the past few days had been… strange. Cryptic. I didn't know if they had noticed, but I felt it. The way I spoke felt like I was saying goodbye without actually saying the words. I couldn't bring myself to tell them what I was really thinking, what I was planning. It felt too raw, too final.

Leo had asked me earlier if I wanted to hang out, but I had brushed him off with a vague excuse about needing to study. He didn't push, but I could hear the concern in his voice. He always knew when something was off.

Maddie had texted, asking about plans for the week, and I hadn't responded yet. The message sat there on my mobile, unread but taunting me with the normalcy it represented. I should have wanted to make plans, should have cared about what came next. But I didn't.

The hours ticked by as I sat there, feeling the weight of the day sink deeper into my bones. Above me, the sky slowly shifted, changing from the soft blue of afternoon to the deep orange and pink hues of sunset. It was like watching time melt, slipping through my fingers, one quiet moment blending into the next. Each color that bled into the horizon seemed to carry a piece of the day with it, marking the slow, inevitable descent into night.

The sun, which had once been high in the sky, began its slow fall toward the horizon, casting long shadows over the park. I watched as the light shifted, the golden warmth of the afternoon giving way to a cooler, dimmer glow. The trees stood tall and silent, their leaves rustling softly in the evening breeze, whispering secrets I couldn't understand. The world around me was moving forward – people passing by, cars humming in the distance, the faint laughter of children echoing from the playground – but I felt frozen, stuck in this in-between place, caught between the light of day and the darkness of night.

It felt like the world was telling me something, like the changing sky reflected the battle happening inside of me. The day was slipping away, and with it, the last bits of hope I had been clinging to. I couldn't stop it. I couldn't slow it down. Just like the sun was destined to set, I was destined to fall. It was only a matter of time before the last light disappeared, leaving me in the dark.

A group of teenagers passed by, laughing as they made their way down the path. I watched them from the corner of my eye, their carefree energy brushing past me, a stark contrast to the heaviness I carried. They didn't notice me, didn't see the girl sitting alone on the bench, staring blankly at the sky. To them, I was invisible, just another part of the scenery, like the trees or the pond. Their world kept spinning, while mine felt like it had come to a halt.

I envied them. Envied their laughter, their ease, their ability to keep moving forward, unaware of the weight I was carrying. It was strange how the world could feel so alive around me, yet I felt like I was trapped in this bubble of silence, disconnected from everything and everyone. The sun was setting, the day was ending, and yet, I remained – frozen in place, unable to move, unable to let go.

My mind wandered to the journal sitting in my bag, its pages filled with the words I had been too afraid to speak out loud. I had written so much in the past week, pouring my thoughts, my fears, my confusion into the pages, trying to make sense of the storm inside of me. It had been my lifeline, the only place where I could let it all out, where I didn't have to pretend I was okay. But now, even the journal felt heavy, like it couldn't hold any more of the weight I was carrying. It was as if the pages were saturated with my pain, the ink bleeding through, unable to contain it all.

I stared at the sky again, now a deep shade of purple, with streaks of pink and orange clinging to the edges like the last remnants of the day. It felt symbolic somehow – the colors fading, just like I was fading. The light was still there, but it was disappearing, slipping beneath the horizon, just out of reach.

The journal called to me, the weight of it pressing against my thoughts, urging me to let the words out. I pulled it from my bag, flipping to the next blank page, the paper smooth and untouched, waiting for whatever I was ready to give it. My hand hovered over the page for a moment, unsure of where to start, unsure if I even had anything left to say. But the words came anyway – soft, quiet, like a whisper in the dark. Words full of the vulnerability I had been carrying, the vulnerability I hadn't been able to share with anyone else.

May 13, 2018

I gave you the world but you wanted more,
More than what I would ever be able to give;
You left me alone with nothing but a tear shedding from my eye,
Learning how to live without you by my side.

The journal sat open on my lap, the words staring back at me like they held the answers I couldn't find. I had written so much in the past week, but this entry felt different. It felt heavier, more final. Like it wasn't just about Ava, or the pain of losing her. It was about something deeper, something I had been carrying for longer than I could remember.

I stared at the page, my chest tight with the weight of everything I hadn't said out loud. The park around me was quiet now, the laughter and footsteps of passersby fading into the distance as the evening settled in. The sun had disappeared completely, leaving behind the last traces of its light, a deep purple and blue painting the sky. The air was cooler now, the breeze picking up as the night took over.

For a moment, I closed my eyes and let the silence fill me. It was strange how peaceful it felt, even though my thoughts were anything but. The chaos inside my head was still there, swirling, pulling me in every direction, but the world outside had stilled. It was just me and the night now, and there was something comforting about that. Like I didn't have to fight anymore. Like I could finally let go.

I opened my eyes, staring out at the darkened park, the shadows of the trees stretching long across the ground. The world felt so big in that moment, so wide and empty, and I felt so small. So insignificant. I wondered if this was what it felt like to disappear – to become part of the background, to fade into the quiet, unnoticed and unseen.

I leaned back on the bench, my eyes drifting upward to the sky, where the first few stars were starting to peek through the dark. They were so distant, so far away, like tiny pinpricks of light in an otherwise endless expanse of nothing. It reminded me of how I felt – distant, far from everything and everyone, lost in the space between.

I hugged my knees to my chest, pulling my jacket tighter around me as the chill of the evening settled into my bones. I felt tired. Not just physically, but in a way that went deeper, a kind of exhaustion that sleep couldn't fix. It was the kind of tired that came from fighting for too long, from carrying too much weight for too many days, too many years.

The journal entry stared up at me, a silent reminder of the things I couldn't bring myself to say aloud. The vulnerability was there, on the page, laid bare in front of me. But it wasn't enough. Writing it down hadn't lifted the weight from my chest, hadn't made the pain go away. It was still there, lingering just beneath the surface, waiting for the right moment to drag me back under.

I closed the journal slowly, pressing it to my chest as I stared out at the park, the last traces of daylight fading into darkness. The night had fully arrived, wrapping the world in its cool embrace, and with it came the sense of finality I had been dreading all day.

There was something calming about the darkness. Something that made everything feel quieter, softer, even though the thoughts in my head were anything but. It was as if the world had finally settled, even though I hadn't. I didn't know what tomorrow would bring, but the weight of it was already pressing down on me, like it was waiting to swallow me whole.

For the first time in a long time, I wasn't afraid of that.

I stood up from the bench, slipping the journal back into my bag as I began the slow walk home. The streets were quiet, the hum of the day long gone, leaving behind only the sound of my footsteps on the pavement. The weight was still there, pressing down on me, but there was also a strange kind of calm that had settled over me.

I didn't know how tomorrow would play out in every detail, but I knew one thing for certain – it would be the day my plan came to fruition. The day I stopped fighting. The day I let go.

As I walked through the darkened streets, the sky full of distant stars above me, I allowed myself to believe, just for a moment, that maybe – just maybe – this was how it was always meant to be.

Chapter 14

Rock Bottom

I woke up with a strange sense of calm. It was almost unsettling, this quiet that had settled inside me, as if the storm that had been raging for months had finally run out of strength. There was no rush of panic, no overwhelming wave of fear that usually greeted me in the mornings. Just stillness. It was almost too quiet, like the silence after a long battle – when the dust has settled, and all that's left is the wreckage.

I could still feel the weight, still feel the darkness pressing down on me, but it no longer felt like I was fighting it. I had given in. Today wasn't a day for fighting. Today was the day I had been planning for. The day I would finally let go. There was a sense of finality in the air, a heaviness that wrapped around me like a thick blanket, suffocating yet strangely comforting. This was the end. I knew it, and somehow, that knowledge brought with it a kind of peace.

The morning passed in a blur, the hours ticking by faster than I expected. Everything seemed distant, muted, like I was watching my life from behind a glass wall. The world moved on around me, but I wasn't really part of it anymore. I was just a ghost, floating through the motions, waiting for the moment when everything would finally stop.

My mum had already left for work by the time I dragged myself out of bed. The house was eerily quiet, the kind of silence that feels too thick, too unnatural. I wandered into the kitchen, where a small note sat waiting for me on the counter, the same note she always left on mornings when she had to leave early. *Have a good day, sweetheart. Don't forget to eat something.*

It was so ordinary. So painfully normal.

But today wasn't normal. Today was anything but.

I stared at the note for a long time, the familiar handwriting pulling at something deep inside me that I didn't want to acknowledge. There was a time when this simple gesture would have brought me comfort, when her care and concern would have meant everything. But now... now it just felt like a reminder of how far I had fallen.

I wondered if she would find this later, if she would remember leaving it for me – this simple note, filled with love and concern for a future she didn't know was slipping away. Would it haunt her when she realized what it truly was? When she looked back and understood that these were the last words she ever said to me?

I could almost see it playing out in my mind: her coming home, finding the note still sitting on the counter, untouched. The slow realization sinking in. The pain that would follow. The questions she would ask herself. *Did I miss the signs? Could I have done something?* But I didn't linger on the thought for long. I couldn't. Not today.

I walked over to the sink and filled a glass with water, the cool liquid sliding down my throat, refreshing but hollow. I was going through the motions – brushing my teeth, washing my face – but it all felt empty, like a shell of a routine I no longer belonged to. I didn't feel hunger or thirst, didn't feel the normal pull of daily tasks. Everything was focused on one thing:

Today.

The hours seemed to slip away faster than usual, as if time itself knew what was coming and was rushing toward it. I moved through the house slowly, deliberately, touching the things that used to mean something to me. The framed photos on the mantle, the old books I had stacked in the living room, the throw blanket my mum had knit last winter. These were the pieces of a life I had once cherished, but they no longer held any weight. They felt like relics from a time I could barely remember.

The sunlight streamed in through the windows, casting soft beams across the floor. It was beautiful, in a way, the way the light filtered through the curtains, dancing in the quiet. But even that beauty felt out of place today, like the world was mocking me with its brightness, with its insistence on moving forward.

The school day moved in slow motion, every interaction feeling distant, every conversation echoing as though it were happening in another room. People around me laughed, joked, complained about homework – living their lives, blissfully unaware of the weight I carried. They talked about plans for the weekend, for graduation, for the future, as if tomorrow was guaranteed. I moved through it all like a ghost, my body present but my mind somewhere far away, already rehearsing what would come later.

By the time second period rolled around, the plan was already set in my head. It had been for days. Each step was carefully laid out, rehearsed over and over again in the quiet moments when the darkness pressed in too tightly. I had pictured it in my mind, imagined how it would feel to finally follow through with it. I knew where the pills were – hidden in the back of the medicine cabinet, out of sight, but always there, waiting for me. They had been there for months, a prescription that had once been for something else, something my mum had stopped using but never thrown away.

I had thought about it so many times. What it would be like to take them. All of them. To swallow them one by one, letting the weight of each pill settle inside me like a promise of peace. I imagined the relief that would follow – the slow, quiet fading as the world slipped away, as my thoughts finally stilled, and the pain disappeared. It wouldn't be loud. It wouldn't be violent. It would be quiet, like falling asleep. Peaceful.

I had already imagined the bottle in my hand, the sound of the pills rattling softly as I tipped them into my palm. I had imagined the feel of the cold water washing them down, one after the other, until the bottle was empty and there was nothing left to do but wait. It would be easy. I had rehearsed it in my mind so many times that it didn't even scare me anymore. It was just a matter of time.

With every passing minute, I could feel the certainty of it growing. No more second-guessing. No more wondering if things would ever get better, or if I could somehow claw my way back to the surface. I knew now that I couldn't. That was the lie I had been telling myself all along – that there was still a chance, still something left to hold on to. But today, I saw the truth. I had nothing left. The fight was over, and this – this was how it would end.

I glanced around the classroom, my eyes falling on the faces of my classmates, each of them lost in their own lives, their own worries, completely unaware of the battle that had been raging inside me. They had no idea that today was different. That today was the last day I would sit in this room, the last day I would be a part of this world. And that was fine. I didn't need them to know. It wasn't their burden to carry.

But I could feel eyes on me, here and there – Leo's concerned glances from across the room, Maddie's hesitant questions between classes. They could sense something was wrong. They always could. But they didn't know how to reach me, didn't know how far I had already fallen. I could see the worry in their eyes, the way they lingered just a little too long when I gave them the same hollow responses I had been giving for weeks. But I didn't let them in. I couldn't.

I smiled when they asked if I was okay, but the smile didn't reach my eyes. It hadn't for a long time. I nodded, told them I was fine, that I was just tired, that everything was under control. And they believed me. Or maybe they didn't, but they didn't push. They never did. They never asked the questions that I couldn't answer. They never forced me to explain the darkness that had taken root inside me.

It was after lunch when I decided it was time to go. I couldn't stay at school any longer. I couldn't pretend anymore. The walls felt like they were closing in on me, the noise of the crowded halls pressing against my chest, making it harder and harder to breathe. I slipped out the side entrance, unnoticed, my footsteps silent as I made my way toward home.

The walk felt longer than usual, each step heavier, more deliberate. The sun hung high in the sky, bright and unforgiving, casting long shadows across the ground as I walked. The world around me was moving, cars passing by, birds chirping in the distance, but it all felt disconnected from me, like I was walking through a dream. A dream I wouldn't wake up from.

By the time I reached my front door, my hands were shaking. But I wasn't afraid. Not really. I had made my decision. I had accepted it. The relief of knowing it would all be over soon was stronger than the fear.

I threw my bag beside the door as I walked inside and moved through the house in a daze, barely aware of my surroundings. Everything felt muted, distant, like I was watching someone else go through the motions. I didn't bother turning on the lights. The dim afternoon light streaming through the windows was enough. I didn't need much. Not anymore.

I made my way to my room, closing the door softly behind me, the quiet settling around me like a blanket. I could feel the finality of it now. This was it. The moment I had been waiting for, the moment I had planned for.

I sat down on the edge of my bed, my heart pounding in my chest, my hands trembling in my lap. For a moment, I stared at the journal sitting on my desk, its pages filled with the weight of everything I had already poured out. The idea of writing one last entry flickered in my mind, but I didn't have the energy. Not in the way I used to. This time, the words didn't need to be carefully placed in a journal. This time, it was simpler than that.

I reached for the small, forgotten bottle of pills hidden in my nightstand drawer, where they had been waiting all along. My fingers shook as I opened the cap, the sound of the pills rattling against the plastic filling the silence around me. I tipped the bottle into my hand, feeling the weight of the small, white capsules pile up in my palm. The decision felt so far away now, like I had already made it days ago, and now I was just carrying out the final act.

One by one, I swallowed the pills, each one sliding down with a gulp of water until the bottle was empty. The room was quiet again, the tension in my chest easing as I set the empty bottle down on the nightstand. I sat there for a long moment, staring at nothing, feeling the slow crawl of calm settling into my limbs.

It wouldn't be long now.

I glanced around the room and saw a crumpled piece of paper lying on my desk. My thoughts were clearer than I had expected, a strange sort of clarity settling over me as the weight lifted. I didn't need the journal anymore, but the need to write one last time – just to say goodbye – was still there.

I picked up the piece of scrap paper, smoothing it out on my lap as I reached for a pen. The words came quickly, without hesitation. A final note, a last message, but this one was just for me.

At one point in life you will hit the bottom,
And not know which way to turn;
It will be dark and ominous and at times quite eerie,
As you begin to plan a return.

The journey back upward will not be that easy,
The journey back upward will cost someone greatly;
But that journey back upward has a reward that will leave you,
Feeling much different than what has been being felt lately.

This fall is inevitable so do not try to avoid it,
Allow your life to take root and blossom;
For this moment in your life will help you remember,
Just how much you do not want to be back at rock bottom.

I stared at the words for a moment, my vision starting to blur around the edges. The paper felt heavy in my hands, the ink smudging slightly where my fingers had pressed against it. I let the pen fall from my grip, the faint sound of it hitting the floor barely registering.

The room was getting quieter now, softer. The tension in my chest was gone, replaced by something lighter, something almost peaceful. I folded the piece of paper carefully, setting it on the nightstand next to the empty pill bottle.

The finality of it all settled over me like a blanket, wrapping me in its weight. This was it. There was no more fighting, no more pretending. This was the end, and for the first time in a long while, I wasn't afraid.

I lay back on the bed, closing my eyes, feeling the quiet settle in.

And then… the sound of the front door opening. My mum's footsteps, fast and panicked, moving through the house. Her voice calling my name, growing louder, more frantic.

But it was too late.

I lay back on the bed, closing my eyes, feeling the quiet settle in. My breathing slowed, the edges of my thoughts blurring as the effects of the pills began to take hold. There was a strange comfort in the stillness, as if the weight that had been crushing me for so long was finally starting to lift.

For a moment, everything was peaceful.

And then… the faint sound of the front door opening. My mum's footsteps echoed through the hall, at first calm, but then pausing – hesitating, as if she had noticed something out of place. I could picture it clearly in my mind: her eyes falling on my school bag, sitting by the door where I had left it. Unused. Unmoved. She knew I should have been at school.

It was that small detail – the sight of my bag, out of place – that must have triggered something in her. The stillness of the house, the absence of noise. The sudden realization that something was wrong.

Her footsteps picked up again, faster now, more urgent. I could faintly hear her moving through the house, searching, her voice cracking as she called out my name, each syllable laced with rising panic.

"Lily?"

She was closer now, her footsteps louder as she moved from room to room, the fear growing in her voice.

"Lily!"

But it was too late.

I couldn't hear her now, the fog thickened around me, pulling me further away from the sounds of the house, from her frantic calls. I was weightless, drifting in a quiet sea of numbness. There was nothing left to fight, nothing left to hold on to.

And then, the door to my room flew open with a crash, the sound reverberating through the quiet.

"Lily!" Her voice broke as she rushed toward me, her footsteps heavy, unsteady. Her breath caught in her throat, a strangled sound of fear as her eyes scanned the room – taking in the sight of the empty pill bottle on the nightstand tilted over and the piece of paper crinkled beside it.

Her presence was close, but I couldn't feel it. Her hands trembling as she reached for me, shaking me, calling my name again and again, as if the force of her voice alone could pull me back.

"Lily! No, no, no... Lily, please!"

Her hands moved to my face, her fingers brushing against my cheek, searching for any sign of life, any sign that I was still there. But I was slipping away, the edges of the world growing darker, quieter, as her voice faded into the background.

She grabbed the note from the nightstand, unfolding it with shaking hands, her sobs filling the room as she scanned the words. And then, the realization hit her like a blow, her body collapsing beside me, her breath coming in short, desperate gasps as she fumbled for a mobile... any mobile... my mobile.

Her voice cracked as she spoke into the receiver, her words jumbled, frantic. "Please! I need an ambulance! My daughter – she's taken something – please, hurry!"

If could feel the warmth of her arms as she pulled me into her lap, cradling me against her chest, her tears falling onto my skin, it would have felt like a heating pad pressed against my body. She rocked back and forth, whispering my name between sobs, begging me to hold on, to stay with her.

"Don't leave me, Lily… please don't leave me…"

The room was black, the distant wail of sirens barely reached my mum through the haze. Her heartbeat was fast and uneven, as she held me tighter, rocking me like she had when I was a child. Her sobs filled the quiet, and for a moment, as if she was wishing that I could reach out to her that it was okay, to tell her that I wasn't afraid.

But that was not possible. I was too far gone.

The door burst open again, this time with a rush of voices – strangers' voices – urgent, calm, but filled with purpose. The EMTs moved quickly, their hands on me, checking for signs of life, speaking to my mum in hushed tones. Intense pressure of their hands on my chest, the cool metal of their equipment pressing against my skin.

"Ma'am, we need to move her now," one of them said, his voice steady, but urgent. "She's still breathing, but we're losing time."

My mum wouldn't let go. Her arms were tightening around me as they tried to pull me from her grasp, her voice breaking as she pleaded with them.

"Please, save her – save my baby…"

Chapter 15
Shattered Heart

I blinked slowly, my eyelids heavy as if the weight of the world pressed them down. The room around me was a blur of sterile whites and muted beeps, my mind swimming in a fog so thick I couldn't grasp where I was – or why.

What happened? The question echoed in my mind, but I had no answer.

My throat felt dry, aching as I tried to swallow, my muscles weak, like I hadn't moved in days. I could barely lift my hand, which rested limply at my side. Confusion clawed at me, and a rising panic stirred deep within. The air felt too still, too cold, and the pale light filtering through the window did little to bring me comfort. I tried to sit up, but my body protested, a deep soreness seeping into my bones. My eyes wandered the unfamiliar room, taking in the machines and IVs surrounding me. Where am I?

I was alone. At first glance, the chair in the corner seemed empty, but then I noticed the jacket draped over it, a familiar scarf hanging loosely on the armrest – my mum's. She had been here. She must have been waiting for me. I shifted, the faint crinkle of paper drawing my attention to a worn notebook on the side table. My journal. Why was it here?

As the fog in my mind began to clear, I strained to remember… to piece together the last thing I could recall. But nothing came.

It was as if someone had wiped the slate clean, leaving me with fragments of memories that refused to connect. Panic surged in my chest, and I fought against the rising tide of confusion.

Where was everyone? What had happened?

Just as I began to feel the edges of a sob building in my throat, the door opened quietly, and my mum stepped inside. The sight of her made the knot in my chest tighten. She looked more fragile than I'd ever seen her – her skin pale, her eyes swollen and red, and there was an unsteadiness to her movements that made my heart clench. Her face was etched with exhaustion, not just physical, but something far deeper. A brokenness.

"Lily…" Her voice cracked as she hurried toward me, barely able to hold herself together. She wrapped her arms around me gently, like I was something fragile, like I might shatter with the slightest pressure. I could feel her body trembling, her breath hitching in her throat, and when I felt the warmth of her tears on my shoulder, the weight of the moment crashed down on me.

"Thank God… Thank God you're okay…" Her voice was a whisper, choked with emotion. She pulled back just enough to look at me, her hands cupping my face as if she needed to see me, to really make sure I was here. Tears streamed down her cheeks, her gaze filled with a mixture of relief, pain, and something else – something deeper that I couldn't quite place.

"I thought I'd lost you, Lily…" Her voice wavered, and I could see her fighting to keep herself together, her lips trembling as she struggled to speak. "My heart… I felt it break when they put you in that ambulance. I couldn't breathe. I couldn't think. It shattered…" She pressed a hand to her chest, as if she could still feel the pieces of herself breaking apart. "I didn't know if I'd ever see you again. I thought I'd lost you, just like your brother…"

The pain in her voice was unbearable, a raw, jagged thing that cut deep. I had never seen her like this. She had always been so strong, so put-together, but now… now it was like I was seeing the pieces of her heart – her shattered heart – scattered around us, each one a reminder of what I had almost taken from her.

I wanted to say something, to reassure her, but the words were stuck in my throat, choking me. All I could do was let her hold me, feeling the weight of her love and her fear pressing down on me like a vice. My heart ached, not just for myself, but for her – for the pain I had caused, the devastation I had almost brought down on her.

"Mum…" I whispered, my voice so faint it barely broke through the silence of the room. "I'm so sorry…"

She shook her head quickly, wiping at her eyes with trembling hands. "No… no, Lily, you don't need to apologize. I just… I couldn't bear the thought of losing you. I couldn't–" Her voice broke again, and she covered her face with her hands, her body shaking with quiet sobs.

I felt like the air had been knocked out of me. Guilt and shame flooded my chest, mingling with the confusion and fear that had been swirling in my mind since I woke up. I didn't remember what had happened. I didn't remember trying to leave… but I knew, in that moment, that I had hurt her in a way that I couldn't take back.

I swallowed hard, trying to keep my own tears at bay, but they came anyway, hot and fast, spilling down my cheeks as I reached out to touch her hand. "Mum… please…"

She looked up at me, her eyes full of so much pain, so much love, and for the first time in a long time, I felt like a child again – small, helpless, and desperate for her comfort.

"You left a note, Lily," she whispered, her voice barely holding steady. "A goodbye note. I found it on your desk, right next to your journal. I… I almost didn't make it in time."

Her words hung in the air like a weight I couldn't carry, pressing down on my chest, making it hard to breathe. I had left a note. I had said goodbye. But I didn't remember. How could I not remember?

I stared at her, my mind struggling to process the enormity of what she was saying. I had come so close to leaving her. I had come so close to destroying everything. And now... now I had to face the aftermath.

My gaze flickered to my journal, sitting on the side table like a silent witness to everything I couldn't say out loud. I needed it. I needed to make sense of what had happened, of what I had done. "Can I... can I have my journal?" I asked softly, my voice shaky.

She nodded quickly, wiping her eyes again as she reached for the journal. "Of course," she said, her voice thick with emotion. "Whatever you need, sweetheart."

As she handed it to me, her hand lingered on mine for a moment, her touch warm and grounding. I took the journal from her, feeling its familiar weight in my hands, but it felt heavier now – like it carried all the pieces of me that had shattered, just like her heart had.

With the journal open in front of me, the weight of the blank page felt overwhelming, like it was daring me to confront everything I had been running from. My hand shook as I gripped the pen, my mind racing with thoughts I couldn't quite hold on to. But the words – they came, pouring out of me in a rush, like they had been waiting for this moment.

I wrote about the pain, the confusion, the desperation. I wrote about how I felt like I was falling apart, piece by piece, just like the shattered heart my mum had described. I wrote about how hard it was to face her, knowing how much I had hurt her, knowing that she had come so close to losing me.

The more I wrote, the more I realized that this entry wasn't just about me. It was about her, too. It was about the way her heart had broken right along with mine, how she had been left to pick up the pieces while I lay here in a fog, unaware of the wreckage I had caused.

I let the pen glide across the page, the words flowing effortlessly as I tried to make sense of everything. And as the lines formed, I felt something shift inside me – a small spark of clarity, of understanding, that hadn't been there before.

I finished the entry, my hand aching from the tight grip on the pen and set it down. My chest felt tight, but there was a strange sense of release, too – like I had finally let out a breath I had been holding for far too long.

The page before me was filled with my thoughts, my fears, my regrets. And at the bottom, the last few words sat heavy on the page, as if they carried the weight of everything that had come before:

June 6, 2018

As quick and as swift as it became yours,
It split and it tore as we drifted apart.
And now I am left to pick up the pieces,
As I look inward at my shattered heart.

They say it won't be easy or kind,
The journey that I have been assigned.
This journey seems so dark and twisted,
And quite frankly I'm frightened to have been enlisted.

I used to believe in love and laughter,
But lately I've been losing faith and hope.
Every morning and night hereafter,
I'll continue searching for the rope.

They say with time comes all the healing,
But yet this time has become unappealing.
I seem to struggle to put words to this feeling,
And am searching for the signs that are revealing.

I meant it when I pleaded for a future,
For I have loved you since we had our start.
But now you are gone and I am alone,
Mending and fixing this shattered heart.

I stared at the words on the page for a long moment, feeling the weight of them settle over me like a heavy blanket. The emotions I had poured onto the paper were raw, exposed, leaving me vulnerable in a way I hadn't been prepared for. It felt like I had laid my soul bare, stripping away every layer until all that remained was the pain. I blinked back the sting of fresh tears, trying to steady the tremor in my hands.

Beside me, my mum sat quietly, her presence steady and warm. I could feel her eyes on me, but she didn't push. She let me process it all in my own time, knowing that whatever was bubbling inside me needed space to breathe.

The silence between us wasn't uncomfortable. It was heavy, yes, but there was an understanding in it, a shared grief that we both carried. Her heart had broken with mine – shattered, just like I had written. And now, we were both sitting in the pieces, trying to figure out how to put it all back together.

"I don't remember writing the note," I whispered finally, my voice barely above a breath. The confession was difficult, like admitting to something I didn't even want to believe was true.

My mum's hand found mine again, her fingers curling around my palm with a gentle, reassuring squeeze. "That's okay," she said softly, her voice steady but fragile. "It's okay if you don't remember. What matters is that you're here now, Lily. We have time to heal."

Time. The word hung in the air between us, both comforting and terrifying. Time was the only thing that could help, but it also meant facing everything – the choices I had made, the pain I had caused. I wasn't sure I was ready.

"I'm scared, Mum," I admitted, my voice cracking under the weight of the words. It felt like I had been holding onto that fear for so long, pretending it wasn't there, pretending I could handle it. But now… now it was all spilling out.

She nodded, tears glistening in her eyes once more, but this time she didn't try to hide them. "I know, sweetheart. I'm scared too."

Her voice wavered, but there was strength beneath it – a strength I hadn't realized she still had. "But we'll get through this. Together."

I closed my eyes, letting her words sink in, trying to believe them. Together. For the first time in what felt like forever, I wasn't trying to shoulder everything alone. The fear, the guilt, the shame – it was all still there, but it didn't feel as crushing when she was beside me.

"I'm sorry…" I whispered again, the apology spilling from my lips before I could stop it.

"You don't need to apologize," she said, her thumb stroking the back of my hand. "What happened… it wasn't your fault. You were hurting, and I didn't see it. But I see you now, Lily. I'm here, and I'm not going anywhere."

Her words cut through the fog that still clouded my mind, reaching a part of me that had been locked away for too long. I had been lost in the darkness, and she had pulled me back, just like she always had when I was little – when I was scared of thunderstorms or bad dreams. Only this storm had been so much bigger, and I had almost lost myself in it.

"I'm so tired," I admitted, my voice barely more than a breath.

"I know," she said gently. "You've been carrying too much for too long."

I nodded, unable to say anything more, the exhaustion settling deep into my bones. My mum's hand never left mine, her touch grounding me as the silence stretched between us again. But this time, it felt different – softer, safer.

I wasn't sure what tomorrow would bring, or the day after that. I wasn't sure how I was going to move forward, how I was going to face the world after everything that had happened. But for now, I had my mum. I had this moment. And maybe that was enough.

As the room grew quieter, I felt my eyes growing heavy, the weight of the day pulling me into a state of drowsiness. My mum's hand was still in mine, her presence anchoring me as I let the tiredness take over. Slowly, the fear and pain started to blur at the edges, and for the first time in weeks, I let myself believe that maybe – just maybe – I could heal.

Chapter 16
You For Me

The sterile hum of the hospital was unnerving, like the universe was holding its breath. The air felt heavy, thick, as if even the walls were weighed down by the silence, and the ceiling stared back at me like an unforgiving judge. This room, with its pale blue walls and its cold, artificial lighting, felt like a waiting room between life and death – neither place offered solace.

I shouldn't be here. I wasn't supposed to be here.

The ache in my chest wasn't just from the lingering effects of whatever drugs they had used to keep me under. It was something deeper, something that felt like it had carved out a hollow space inside me, filling it with confusion and bitterness. I could feel the echo of my pulse in my ears, each beat a painful reminder that I had failed.

Alive. I was still alive. Why?

The weight of that thought pressed down on me, suffocating. I had made a decision, a deliberate choice, and yet here I was, my heart still beating, my lungs still drawing breath. Each inhale felt like a betrayal.

The bed beneath me felt too small, like it could barely contain the storm swirling inside. I shifted, the scratchy hospital blanket grazing my skin like sandpaper, and turned my head toward the window. But the blinds were drawn, the world outside hidden from view, leaving me trapped in this artificial, timeless place. It could have been any hour, any day, and I wouldn't have known the difference.

There was no time here. Only stillness. Only waiting.

I tried to remember what had happened, but the memories slipped through my mind like sand through fingers, fragmented and hazy. I remembered the pills. The note. But the rest was a blur, like a movie I had only half-watched. Somewhere in the haze, I saw my mum's face, her tear-streaked cheeks, her voice breaking as she called my name.

I glanced at the empty chair by the bed. Her jacket was draped across it, a silent witness to the hours she must have spent here. She had been waiting, watching over me, even when I couldn't see her. Guilt crept up my spine, twisting in my stomach like a knife.

I failed her, too. I failed everyone.

My eyes moved to the table beside me, where a small, leather-bound notebook sat – my journal. Its pages were crisp and untouched, like a blank slate waiting for me to fill it with the mess of my thoughts. Writing had always been my only escape, my only way to make sense of the chaos inside my mind. But today, even the pen felt too heavy to hold.

I looked down at my hands, pale and trembling. They didn't feel like mine. They felt like someone else's, someone who was still stuck between two worlds – one she had tried to leave, and one she was too broken to rejoin.

I thought of Ava, and the wound deepened. The memory of her smile flashed in my mind, but it was jagged, splintered, like a photograph torn in half. She had always been my light, my compass. But now? Now she felt like a ghost haunting the edges of my vision, always out of reach. I missed her with an intensity that scared me, but there was something darker beneath that longing, something bitter and twisted. How could I want someone so badly, and yet resent her so much for not being here?

But she didn't know. How could she? Maybe it was better this way.

And then, there was Leo.

His name slipped through my mind like a whisper, soft but undeniable. He had been my rock, my constant, the one person who had never let me fall. But even he hadn't been able to save me from myself. I could almost hear his voice, steady and warm, telling me I was stronger than this. Telling me that I mattered. But those words felt hollow now, like they belonged to someone else, someone stronger, someone who wasn't lying in a hospital bed, trapped between the world of the living and the abyss she had so desperately tried to fall into.

I wondered if he even knew. If he had been sitting by my bed like my mum had, his heart breaking just as hers had. But the truth was, I didn't want to know. The thought of his face twisted in pain was too much to bear. He had been everything I needed, and yet, even that hadn't been enough.

I let out a shuddering breath, the silence pressing in on me from all sides. The hospital room felt too small, like the walls were closing in, suffocating me with their sterile brightness. I wanted to scream, to claw my way out of this place, out of my own skin, but I couldn't. I was trapped in this body, in this life, and I didn't know how to live in it anymore.

I reached for the notebook, my fingers trembling as they brushed against the leather cover. The coolness of it grounded me for a moment, pulling me back from the brink. I flipped it open, the blank pages staring up at me like a challenge. This was where I always found my way – through words. But today, even that felt impossible.

Still, I picked up the pen, my hand trembling slightly as I pressed it to the page. The words came slowly, trickling out at first, but then they began to flow, spilling from me like blood from a wound. Each word was a piece of me, a sliver of my soul that I didn't know if I would ever get back.

I wrote about Ava. About Leo. About the loneliness that had swallowed me whole. I wrote about the weight of waking up in a world I no longer understood, about the way my mum's heart had shattered alongside mine. I wrote about the fear – the fear of living, the fear of dying, the fear of everything in between.

As the words spilled onto the page, something inside me shifted, like a floodgate opening. I couldn't stop, even if I wanted to. The pen moved as though it had a mind of its own, pulling out every secret, every thought, every piece of hurt I had buried deep. I wrote about how I missed her – Ava. How her absence felt like a hollow echo that reverberated through my entire being. I wrote about the sharp, bitter edge of betrayal, cutting deeper every time I remembered her walking away.

I thought about the way her eyes had shone when we were happy, like I was the only person in the world. But that light had dimmed, hadn't it? I saw it – how her gaze would shift, how her laughter had turned hollow. Maybe I had been too blind, too wrapped up in my own pain to see the cracks forming between us, like tiny fissures in a fragile piece of glass.

Ava had always been the sun, and I had revolved around her, drawn to her warmth. But that sun had set, and I was left in the cold, wondering if I'd ever feel its warmth again. And Leo... Leo had always been there, steady, like the moon, reflecting the light I'd lost. But he wasn't the sun. He wasn't her.

Still, the thought of him tugged at something inside me. A different kind of warmth. One that was softer, quieter. One that didn't burn the way Ava had. But that only made the guilt fester deeper. Leo deserved more than my fractured heart. More than my shattered pieces. How could I let him carry the weight of something that even I didn't understand?

I paused, the pen hovering above the paper, the weight of my own words hanging in the air around me. I wasn't sure where to go from here, or if I even had the strength to keep writing. My body ached, my mind ached, and the sharp edge of reality cut into me with each passing second.

Why was I still here?

I wasn't ready for answers, and maybe I wasn't ready to ask the right questions either. But I couldn't deny the pull of the past – the longing for what had been and the fear of what was to come.

The sound of footsteps outside the door pulled me out of my thoughts. I tensed, my heartbeat quickening as I waited for someone to come in, to disrupt this fragile bubble of solitude. But the footsteps faded, and the door remained closed. I let out a shaky breath, my body sinking deeper into the bed.

I glanced out the window, at the small sliver of sky visible through the gap in the blinds. The sun had begun to set, painting the sky in shades of orange and pink. It reminded me of the sunsets Ava and I used to watch together, sitting by the water, the silence between us comfortable, filled with unspoken promises. We had believed that we had all the time in the world. But time was cruel, wasn't it? It slipped through your fingers when you weren't looking, and suddenly, you were left with nothing but memories and regrets.

I turned my gaze back to the notebook, the words blurring as fresh tears pricked at my eyes. I missed her so much that it hurt. But missing her didn't change the fact that she had walked away. It didn't change the fact that she had chosen someone else – chosen Sophia.

Sophia. Her name made my stomach twist, a bitter taste rising in my throat. I hadn't wanted to think about it. About them. About what had happened after that night at the party. The images haunted me, unbidden, a relentless assault on my mind. I imagined them together – laughing, kissing, touching. It made me want to scream. I hated that I couldn't stop thinking about her, about them. Hated that I still wanted her, despite everything.

I took a deep breath, forcing the thoughts away, trying to regain some semblance of control. But control felt so far out of reach these days, like a distant star I couldn't grasp no matter how hard I tried.

IN DARKNESS

A part of me wanted to shut the notebook, to push it all away and bury it like I always had. But another part of me – the part that had survived this long – knew I couldn't do that anymore. I had to face it. Even if it hurt. Even if it broke me all over again.

I picked up the pen and began to write, my hand steadier this time, the words coming easier:

June 6, 2018

Today and tomorrow and for the rest of my life,
I will forever regret how I let you slide by;
You ran far away before I could blink my eye,
But for today and forever there are some things I cannot deny.

Perhaps I should have told you what I wanted and needed,
Or perhaps I should have shown you what you meant to me;
For now there is nothing but a faint hint of hope,
For deep down inside I still believe that we are meant to be.

Life can drag us farther and farther apart,
Life can introduce us to others in this world;
But life will never allow me to have a love quite like ours,
For life will constantly remind me of what the stars had observed.

When our paths cross together and our eyes meet again,
I promise that I will show you how things were meant to be;
I promise I will confess to you what I should I said I wanted,
For what I wanted and for what I want is you for me.

I put the pen down, my hand trembling from the release. I stared at the words for a long time, reading them over and over until they blurred together. They felt like an admission, a confession I wasn't sure I was ready to make. Not to Ava. Not even to myself.

The door creaked open, and I flinched, quickly closing the notebook and setting it aside. My mum stepped into the room, holding a small bag in one hand, her eyes searching my face for any sign of change.

"I brought you something to eat," she said softly, her voice like a lifeline pulling me back from the edge. But I wasn't hungry. The weight in my stomach was too heavy, the ache in my chest too overwhelming.

"I'm not hungry," I mumbled, my voice barely audible.

She set the bag down on the table, her eyes lingering on me for a moment longer. "You don't have to eat right now," she said, "but maybe later." There was an unspoken sadness in her voice, a sadness I didn't have the strength to acknowledge.

She turned away for a moment, busying herself with something on the other side of the room, giving me space. But I could feel her concern like a shadow hanging over us, always there, always watching.

I lay back against the pillow, closing my eyes for a brief moment, wishing the heaviness would lift, even just for a little while. But it didn't. It stayed with me, settling deeper into my bones. And despite the warmth of the room, I felt cold, so cold.

Chapter 17
The Gloomy Meadow

The door clicked softly behind my mum as she stepped out to take a call, leaving the room in a strange, almost suffocating stillness. I knew she wasn't going far – just down the hall to check in with her boss – but the moment she was gone, the air seemed to thicken, and a quiet dread crept in, seeping through the sterile walls of the hospital room. The white-tiled floors gleamed under the fluorescent lights, and the scent of antiseptic hung heavy in the air, sharp and intrusive, like a constant reminder of where I was. I hated it.

The loneliness felt different now. It wasn't just the physical absence of my mum; it was the crushing weight of everything – everything I had been through, everything I would have to face, alone. My body felt heavy, rooted to the bed, as if the thin blanket draped over me was made of lead. Breathing seemed harder, the rise and fall of my chest almost too much effort. Each inhale felt shallow, strained, like the air in the room was too thick to fill my lungs properly.

I glanced toward the muted television, where a documentary about meadowlands played softly. The narration, distant and almost robotic, described the fragile balance of nature. But the words didn't matter. They floated over me like a thin mist, irrelevant. All I could focus on was the image of a crow on the screen, its sleek black feathers rippling as it took flight over the meadow, wings outstretched as it cut through the sky.

I stared at it, mesmerized, the steady rhythm of its wings lulling me into a haze. It looked so free – gliding effortlessly, unbound by anything. That crow didn't have to deal with this hospital room, the constant check-ins, the medication, the endless talks about recovery. It didn't have to think about the shattered pieces of its life, about the people it had hurt or the battles it was still too weak to fight.

It was free.

I envied it. I envied the way it could just... leave. It could soar, disappear into the vastness of the sky, and no one would stop it. No one would ask it to stay behind and mend the cracks in its wings, no one would demand it to be whole again before it could take off. I was the opposite of that bird – trapped. Trapped in this hospital bed, in this sterile, lifeless room, in my own body that still felt foreign to me.

The world outside moved on. Cars hummed in the distance, people walked the halls just beyond my door, but here, in this room, time seemed to stand still. The walls, the bed, the machines, they all felt like a cage, one I didn't know how to break free from.

For a moment, I closed my eyes, imagining what it would feel like to be that crow – to spread my wings and fly far away, to rise above everything. To leave behind the heaviness, the guilt, the pain. To feel weightless.

But when I opened my eyes, I was still here. Still tethered to this place, to my reality. I couldn't escape. The crow on the screen was long gone, but I was still stuck, unable to move forward, unable to fly.

The door creaked open, pulling me out of my thoughts. I turned my head, expecting to see my mum, but instead, it was Dr. Byrne. My mum followed closely behind him, her mobile now tucked away in her pocket. She walked back to the chair beside my bed, the tension in her face barely concealed as she took her seat, eyes never leaving Dr. Byrne.

"Good afternoon, Lily," Dr. Byrne said, his voice soft but professional, as he entered the room with his clipboard in hand.

I nodded, my throat too tight to offer much more than that. My mum moved closer to the edge of the bed, her eyes glued to Dr. Byrne, waiting for him to speak. The tension in the room was palpable, like we were all bracing ourselves for something.

"I wanted to check in with you both," he began, sitting down on the edge of my bed, "and talk about the next steps for your recovery."

I could feel my mum tense up beside me. She reached for my hand, squeezing it gently as if preparing us both for whatever was about to come.

"You've made significant progress, Lily," he continued, "and we're pleased with how you're doing physically. However, before we can discuss discharge, there are a few things that still need to happen."

I swallowed hard. Discharge. It felt like a word I wasn't ready for – like it belonged to someone else, some other version of me.

Dr. Byrne glanced between the two of us. "You'll need to be cleared both medically and psychologically before you can leave. Physically, you're healing, but we need to make sure you're stable mentally as well. We've arranged for you to meet with Dr. Maeve Donnelly, one of our top psychologists. She specializes in adolescent trauma and will be guiding you through the next phase of your treatment."

My mum's grip on my hand tightened. I could feel her breathing shift as she tried to steady herself. She was always the one asking questions, making sure every detail was covered. This time was no different.

"How long will this take?" she asked, her voice shaking slightly. "I mean... how long before she can come home?"

Dr. Byrne exhaled softly. "It varies. It really depends on how Lily responds to treatment. The psychiatric evaluation and therapy sessions are key. Dr. Donnelly will need to ensure that Lily is emotionally and mentally stable before we can consider discharge. I know this isn't easy to hear, but it's critical for her recovery."

I felt my mum's eyes on me, filled with concern and fear. I wanted to meet her gaze, to say something that would reassure her, but I couldn't. The words just wouldn't come. All I could do was sit there, feeling the weight of this new reality press down on me.

"I understand," my mum said quietly, her voice strained but resolute. "We'll do whatever it takes. We just want her to be okay."

Dr. Byrne offered a sympathetic smile. "We're here to help, and Lily, we're going to support you through this process. But it's important to take things one step at a time. Dr. Donnelly will be in contact soon, and we'll start developing a plan together."

The room fell silent after he spoke, and I could feel my mum's heartbreak simmering beneath the surface, as if each word shattered her hope just a little bit more. She had been strong for me, but I could tell this news hit her hard. I didn't want to look at her, but I knew she was fighting tears, holding it together for me.

Dr. Byrne stood up, placing a hand on my shoulder. "You've been through a lot, Lily. I know it's overwhelming, but you're not alone in this."

I nodded again, still too lost in my own thoughts to fully respond. As he left the room, I felt the tightness in my chest grow.

My mum leaned in, her voice soft but trembling. "We'll get through this, Lily. I promise. We'll take it one day at a time."

I nodded, but I wasn't sure if I believed her. The meadow on the screen was still there, and I found myself lost in it again – the crow flying away, while I remained trapped in this bed, in this hospital, in my own mind.

Dr. Byrne rose from his seat, his expression still warm and encouraging. "I'll be checking in on you regularly, but Dr. Donnelly will take the lead on your psychiatric care. We'll be with you every step of the way, Lily."

He gave me one last look, then turned to my mum, offering her a reassuring nod before heading toward the door. As the door clicked shut behind him, the room felt smaller, like the walls were closing in.

I turned to my mum then, finally meeting her gaze. Her eyes were red-rimmed, the tears barely held at bay. She looked at me with a kind of fierce love, but beneath it, I could see the cracks – the same cracks that had broken me were now breaking her. I was watching her heart shatter in real-time, and it was my fault.

She moved from her chair and perched on the edge of my bed, pulling me into her arms. I didn't fight it. I just let her hold me, let her wrap me in her warmth and love, even though I didn't feel like I deserved it.

Her voice was soft, barely above a whisper. "I was so scared, Lily... I thought I lost you. I can't lose you."

Tears welled up in my eyes as I buried my face in her shoulder, her words hitting me like a punch to the gut. The guilt, the shame, it all came flooding back, drowning me in it.

"I'm sorry," I whispered, my voice cracking. "I'm so sorry, Mum."

She held me tighter, her tears mixing with mine. "We'll get through this," she whispered back, her voice breaking. "We'll get through this together."

For the first time since I woke up, I let the tears come. I let them fall, hot and unrelenting, as I clung to my mum, the only anchor I had in this storm.

After what felt like hours in my mum's arms, she finally pulled away, wiping the tears from both of our faces with a soft smile that didn't quite reach her eyes. She pressed a kiss to my forehead and gave my hand one last squeeze before excusing herself, saying she needed to check in with her boss.

"I won't be far, love," she assured me. "Just down the hall. I'll be back before you know it."

The silence of the room pressed in on me after my mum left, a hollow feeling settling in the pit of my stomach. The documentary still played on the TV, the steady voice of the narrator a distant murmur. I tried to tune it out, but the images on the screen kept pulling me back.

Meadows.

At first glance, they seemed alive – so full of color, movement, life. But beneath the surface, there was decay. I could see it now. The slow, inevitable dying that happened just out of sight, hidden in the shadows of tall grasses and bright wildflowers.

I felt that. I knew that feeling too well.

The crow swooped into the frame, its black wings cutting through the golden dusk. It looked so free, so unburdened by the weight of the world beneath it. I envied it – how it could escape. How it could fly away from the mess of life below. But I wasn't like the crow. I was trapped, tethered to the earth, to this hospital bed, to this broken body.

The meadow was its home, but it was also a graveyard. Things died there. And part of me had died too.

I stared at the screen, feeling a heaviness in my chest that I couldn't shake. The documentary continued, but I barely heard the words. My mind was lost in the darkness of that meadow, in the decay that quietly spread beneath the surface. Was that me now? Was I just waiting to wither away, unnoticed and forgotten?

My thoughts spiraled, chasing the crow in my mind. What would it be like to fly away? To leave all of this behind – the hospital, the pain, the endless expectations of getting better? What if I didn't have to fight anymore?

But then again, wasn't that what got me here in the first place?

I blinked, the sting of unshed tears in my eyes. The meadow faded into twilight on the screen, and I turned my head away, staring at the blank wall instead. The weight of it all felt crushing, like I was drowning in this in-between place. I couldn't move forward, but I couldn't go back either.

The crow had flown away, but I was still stuck here, grounded.

I glanced at the new journal beside me. Its blank pages seemed to mock me, waiting for words that I wasn't sure I had anymore. But maybe writing them down would help – maybe it would make sense of the chaos swirling in my head.

I reached for the pen, my fingers trembling slightly as they wrapped around it. The ink felt heavy as it touched the page, but once I started, the words flowed out, almost as if they'd been waiting all along:

June 7, 2018

The meadows of darkness that keep you awake,
The meadows of darkness that do not take a break.

Gasping for air when you succumb to their darkness,
Searching and scanning through the bristles of sharpness.

The dark and gloomy meadow is not obsolete,
The dark and gloomy meadow is not a retreat.

Crows swarm so sweetly in the wake of the night,
Making their nests before taking quick flight.

Get stuck in this mess of thick goo and gunk,
Get stuck with a mind that is all in a funk.

This sanctum makes home for new thoughts and new missions,
This sanctum makes way for a new wave of traditions.

Be cautious and careful as you navigate through the stream,
For in the gloomy meadow no one will be able to hear you scream.

Chapter 18
Midnight Thoughts

The hospital was never truly dark. Even in the dead of night, there were always glowing lights in the hallways, faint murmurs of nurses' conversations, the distant hum of machines. But tonight, it felt like the world was quieter, like everything had settled into a stillness that left me alone with my thoughts.

The clock on the wall blinked midnight. The hours had slipped away, unnoticed, and now I was stuck in that liminal space between one day and the next. It wasn't just time that felt suspended – it was everything. I was suspended, waiting for something, though I didn't know what.

The weight of the day had settled on me like a blanket, suffocating and heavy. My thoughts were all over the place, ricocheting off memories and worries, bouncing from one unresolved feeling to another. I couldn't sleep. My body was exhausted, but my mind wouldn't shut off. It spun in circles, replaying every conversation, every decision that had led me here, to this sterile room in the middle of the night.

I glanced at my mobile, resting on the table beside me. Leo. I hadn't heard from him in days, but I didn't know if that was because of me or him. Maybe it didn't matter. Maybe he was just trying to give me space. But I needed something – some kind of lifeline to hold onto in this endless night.

Before I could talk myself out of it, I picked up the mobile and sent him a quick message: *"Aye... are you up? I'm having a hard time sleeping."*

It felt strange, reaching out. But I didn't know what else to do. The silence was pressing in, and the thoughts were too loud.

I stared at the screen, watching the message send, and then set the mobile back down. I leaned back against the pillows, closing my eyes, but the thoughts kept creeping in, like shadows dancing just out of reach.

I tried to breathe deeply, hoping it would calm me, but everything just kept swirling. It was like I was trapped inside my own head, with no escape. Maybe writing would help. It usually did.

I grabbed my journal, my fingers shaking slightly as I opened it to a fresh page. The pen felt heavy in my hand, but I pressed it to the paper anyway, letting the words flow:

June 8, 2018

The clock chimes midnight as the night shines through that window crack,
And the thoughts come crashing through the glass like a fastball through the
                                                                                                        sky.
The shattered glass lies on the floor as it glistens a canvas abstract,
In this moment in time you ponder the thought of what would come after you
                                                       have reached the
                      high.

As the clock chimes midnight and you fade away —
Your thoughts find you as their prey.

I set the pen down, staring at the words for a moment. It didn't make the thoughts go away, but it helped. A little. The weight of everything didn't feel quite so suffocating.

The mobile buzzed beside me, pulling me out of my head. I glanced at the screen – Leo.

"Yeah, I'm awake. You okay?"

I hesitated, my fingers hovering over the screen. Was I okay? No. Not really. But how did I say that?

"Not really," I typed back. *"Can we talk?"*

Seconds passed, and then the mobile rang.

I answered quickly, pressing it to my ear. "Aye."

"Aye," Leo's voice was soft, gentle, the same way it always had been. "What's going on?"

I let out a long breath, sinking back into the pillows. "I don't know. I just... can't sleep. My mind won't stop. Everything feels so... loud."

He was quiet for a moment, his voice calm when he finally spoke. "Yeah. I get that. I've been thinking about you a lot."

A warmth spread through my chest, unexpected but not unwelcome. I didn't know how to respond to that, so I just stayed quiet.

"I was going to come see you tomorrow," he continued. "I didn't want to push, but... I miss you."

My throat tightened, and I had to swallow hard against the tears that threatened to fall. "I miss you too."

We sat in the silence for a while, but it wasn't uncomfortable. It was almost soothing, just knowing that someone was there, someone who cared.

"Leo?" I whispered.

"Yeah?"

"I don't know how to... do this," I admitted, my voice cracking. "I don't know how to... be okay."

"You don't have to be okay right now," he said softly. "You just have to keep going. One step at a time. We'll figure it out together."

Tears welled up in my eyes, but for the first time in a long time, they weren't from despair. It felt like some of the weight had lifted. Not all of it. But enough.

"Thank you," I whispered.

"Anytime, Lily. I'm always here."

We talked for a while longer, about nothing in particular. It was comforting, just having someone to talk to. Eventually, I started to feel the exhaustion creeping in.

"I'll come see you tomorrow," Leo promised again, his voice soft and reassuring. "We'll get through this."

I nodded, even though he couldn't see me. "I'd like that."

As I settled back against the pillows, I felt a little lighter. It wasn't fixed – none of this was – but maybe it didn't have to be. Not right now. Tomorrow, Leo would be here, and that was enough for now.

"Leo?" I murmured, my eyelids growing heavy.

"Yeah?"

"I love you."

There was a pause on the other end of the line, but then he spoke, his voice warm and full of something I couldn't quite place. "I love you too, Lily."

A small smile tugged at my lips, and for the first time in what felt like forever, I felt at peace.

Chapter 19

In Darkness

The morning light filtered through the thin curtains of my hospital room, but it didn't bring any of the warmth or comfort it usually did. Instead, it felt cold, distant, like it had no place here. The weight of the world seemed to press down on me, and everything felt muffled, as if I were underwater, trapped beneath the surface.

Leo's visit had been a brief reprieve, a break in the constant heaviness that had settled on my chest since I woke up. But now, as I lay in bed, staring at the blank ceiling, it was hard to hold onto any of that light. I felt like I was sinking again, slowly slipping back into the shadows that had been haunting me for so long.

I was lost in my thoughts when a soft knock at the door pulled me back to the present. My doctor, Dr. Byrne, stepped inside, his expression neutral but kind. Behind him was someone new, a woman with kind eyes and a soft smile. I knew immediately who she was.

"Lily, this is Dr. Donnelly," Dr. Byrne said, gesturing toward the woman beside him. "She'll be working with you over the next few weeks to help with your recovery, both physically and mentally."

I nodded, my mouth dry. I wasn't sure I was ready for this. I wasn't sure I was ready to face everything I had been trying so hard to push away.

Dr. Donnelly smiled, stepping forward. "It's a pleasure to meet you, Lily. We'll take things at your pace, okay? There's no rush. We'll work through things together."

Her voice was soothing, but I could feel the anxiety bubbling up inside me. I wasn't used to talking about my feelings, about the things that were buried so deep inside me. And yet, there was something about her presence that made me feel like maybe, just maybe, this wasn't impossible.

"Would you like to talk now?" Dr. Donnelly asked gently. "We can meet in the office if that's more comfortable."

I hesitated, glancing over at Dr. Byrne and then back at her. The idea of leaving this room, of stepping out into the world beyond these four walls, felt overwhelming. But staying here, in this space that had become both my sanctuary and my prison, wasn't much better.

"Here is fine," I said quietly, my voice barely above a whisper.

Dr. Byrne gave me a reassuring nod before excusing himself, leaving me alone with Dr. Donnelly. She took a seat in the chair beside my bed, her movements calm and unhurried. It was like she had all the time in the world, and somehow, that put me at ease.

For a few minutes, we just sat in silence. It wasn't uncomfortable, but it gave me space to think, to breathe. I wasn't sure where to start, but Dr. Donnelly didn't push. She just waited, giving me the time I needed to gather my thoughts.

"I don't... I don't know where to begin," I admitted, my voice barely audible.

"That's okay," she said softly. "There's no right place to start. You can begin wherever you feel comfortable."

I took a deep breath, staring down at my hands in my lap. "I don't feel... anything. Or maybe I feel too much. I don't know."

Her gaze remained soft, understanding. "That's completely normal, Lily. You've been through something incredibly difficult. It's okay to feel overwhelmed."

I nodded, but it didn't make it any easier. The words were there, somewhere deep inside me, but they were tangled, trapped in the darkness I'd been carrying for so long.

"I don't know how to talk about it," I said finally. "Everything feels... wrong."

Dr. Donnelly leaned forward slightly, her expression gentle. "Would it help to write it down?"

I looked up at her, surprised. "Write?"

"Yes," she said. "Sometimes writing can help when the words are too difficult to say out loud. If you'd like, we can try that."

The thought of journaling again – of putting my feelings into words on paper – felt both daunting and oddly comforting. Writing had always been my way of processing things, but lately, even that had felt too hard. Still, something about the suggestion felt right.

"I can try," I whispered, reaching for the journal beside my bed. My hands shook slightly as I opened to a fresh page, the weight of the pen feeling heavier than usual. But as I pressed it to the paper, the words began to flow, tentative at first, but then faster, like a dam breaking:

June 10, 2018

The light fades away as the autumn breeze takes wind,
The leaves falling from the trees delicately and swift;
The dwelling thoughts of nature's most frivolous actions,
Has the whole wide world left blind.

There is a bitter tranquility regarding the ominous night,
That has overtaken the way of the land;
Suddenly a world full of laughter and joy,
Has been left in darkness on whose demand?

Perhaps this is a trick of time that will work to make amends,
Or perhaps this is an intentional play from above that means to change a life;
Regardless of who has cast this forbidden spell of dark,
The world shivers as we feel its mark.

Not a light beams high through the southern sky,
Not even a star seems to shine tonight;
The lights and the lampposts seem to be out of commission,
As the darkness takes control of all that remains in sight.

Who knows how long this midnight horror show will last,
It feels as if it has become a lifetime;
Could there be an unspoken message of hope,
Lying idle in the darkness of the past?

The candles seem dim and the moon loses its luster,
As the world expends all the strength that it can muster;
The stars realign in a harmonious cluster,
While through the darkness that light is a buster.

I closed the journal, my chest tight with emotion. The words didn't fix anything. They didn't make the darkness disappear. But they were there, on paper, outside of me. And for now, that was enough.

Dr. Donnelly waited patiently as I gathered myself. "Would you like to share what you wrote?" she asked gently.

I nodded, even though the thought of reading it aloud made my throat tighten. But something inside me wanted to try, wanted to give this a chance.

So I read the words aloud, my voice shaking slightly, but growing stronger as I went. When I finished, there was silence between us, the kind that felt like understanding.

Dr. Donnelly gave me a small, encouraging smile. "Thank you for sharing that with me, Lily. I know this isn't easy, but this is a great start."

A start. That's all it was. But for the first time in a long time, it didn't feel like I was drowning. Maybe, just maybe, I was starting to swim.

As I set the journal aside, Dr. Donnelly reached into her bag and pulled out a small notebook, flipping through a few pages before looking up at me.

"I think it would be helpful for us to meet once a week for now," she said. "We can adjust the frequency as we go, depending on how things progress. But for now, I'd like to focus on building a routine, something consistent."

I nodded, the idea of structure feeling both reassuring and daunting at the same time.

"And," she continued, "I encourage you to keep journaling. It seems like it's a powerful way for you to express what's going on inside. You don't have to share everything you write, but bringing your thoughts to our sessions, whether they're written down or spoken, can help us work through them together."

Journaling before our sessions. It felt like a tangible step, something I could actually do. Even when the words were hard to say, they seemed to flow more easily onto the page.

"That sounds... good," I said quietly.

Dr. Donnelly smiled again, her warmth unwavering. "Take your time with it, Lily. This is your journey, and I'm here to walk through it with you, at your own pace."

For the first time in what felt like forever, I didn't feel completely alone in this. Maybe, with time, this darkness wouldn't feel so suffocating. Maybe I could find my way through it.

Chapter 20
Demons

The week had felt like an eternity, every day dragging on as if time itself had slowed to a crawl. I spent most of my hours lost in thought, replaying memories I wasn't ready to face and emotions I didn't know how to process. There were moments when I'd catch myself staring out the window, watching the world outside move on as if everything was fine, while I felt frozen in place.

I had tried to write a few times over the past days, to capture what was happening in my mind, but the words just wouldn't come. The page stayed blank, mocking me with its emptiness. And so I let the days slip by, avoiding my thoughts, avoiding the journal, avoiding everything.

But now, as the next appointment loomed, I couldn't avoid it any longer. Dr. Donnelly had asked me to bring my thoughts to our sessions, to use the journal as a way to communicate when words felt too hard to say. I needed to write something, even if it was just a starting point.

I sat at the desk in my room, staring down at the open journal. The pen felt heavy in my hand, like it was weighed down by the demons that had been following me all week. I wasn't sure where to begin.

Demons.

The word lingered in my mind, hovering just at the edge of my consciousness. I didn't know why it felt so significant, but it did. Maybe it was because everything I was going through – the pain, the fear, the confusion – felt like some kind of dark presence, something I couldn't shake no matter how hard I tried.

I pressed the pen to the page, the words coming slowly at first, then gaining momentum as I let myself go:

June 17, 2018

They come and conquer your wildest dreams,
And leave you questioning all that seems.
Concentrate and focus on who you are,
And these demons will not follow you all that far.

They are fueled by your anguish and feed on your cries,
And they seek to reckon those crystal-clear blue skies.
Follow your journey and trust your path,
And show all these demons your unmatched wrath.

They choose to come and go as they see fit,
And continue to lurk for as long as you submit.
Regain your strength and your will to survive,
And take away the pain these demons need to thrive.

They can bring about change that you would never see coming,
And these changes can be made out to be mind-numbing.
Remember you are right where you are meant to be,
And these demons will surely soon set you free.

They cannot hang on when you have regained control,
And they cannot hang on to the purest of soul.
Write your own journey and love who you are,
And these demons will not follow you all that far.

As I set the pen down, I felt a strange mixture of emotions. The words were raw, and they didn't fix anything. They didn't make the demons go away, but they were there now – on paper. It felt like an acknowledgment, like I had taken a small step toward facing them instead of letting them control me.

I leaned back in my chair, staring at the journal. There was still so much I didn't understand, so much I wasn't ready to confront. But writing, even when it was difficult, helped in a way I couldn't quite explain. It made the chaos in my mind feel a little more organized, a little less suffocating.

As I flipped back through the pages, I could see the thread of my journey – scattered, broken, but there. I wasn't sure where it was leading, but I could feel the pull of something just beyond my reach. Hope, maybe. Or at least the possibility of it.

I sighed, closing the journal and setting it aside. I still had a long way to go, and the weight of the coming therapy session settled on my shoulders. Dr. Donnelly had been patient, but I knew she was expecting more from me – more openness, more vulnerability. And I wasn't sure if I was ready to give her that.

Even deciding where to meet had been a challenge. But after spending days isolated in my hospital room, I had opted to have today's session in Dr. Donnelly's office. I needed a change of scenery, to feel like I wasn't completely stuck in place.

As the nurse wheeled me down the long corridor, I couldn't shake the feeling of how dependent I had become – on everyone and everything around me. The wheelchair, though necessary, felt like a cage. It wasn't just my legs that were confined; it was my thoughts, my voice, my very self. I wasn't sure which was harder to admit – my physical weakness or my emotional one.

Dr. Donnelly's office was a quiet sanctuary amidst the chaos of the hospital. Soft, muted colors covered the walls, and a painting of an open road, winding through hills and disappearing into the horizon, hung just behind her. I couldn't take my eyes off it. It seemed so simple, yet the more I stared, the more I realized that road was me – uncertain, never knowing what was beyond the next curve.

"How are you feeling today, Lily?" she asked gently, folding her hands in her lap.

I hesitated. "I don't know. I wrote… I wrote something. It helped, I think."

"Would you like to share it?" she offered, her tone open and non-pressuring.

I wasn't sure if I did. But I nodded anyway, pulling the journal from my bag and flipping to the page with the poem. My hands shook slightly as I began to read aloud, the words feeling different now, like they held more weight coming from my own voice.

When I finished, Dr. Donnelly took a deep breath, her eyes thoughtful. "That was incredibly insightful, Lily. You're acknowledging these demons, and that's a huge step. Writing can be a powerful way to give shape to those feelings. How did it feel to put those thoughts on paper?"

I shrugged, unsure. "It helped a little, I guess. It made them real, but it didn't make them go away."

"That's okay," she said gently. "They don't have to go away all at once. What matters is that you're giving them space, allowing yourself to recognize them. That's part of the healing process."

I nodded, feeling a small flicker of understanding. The demons weren't gone, but they didn't feel quite as overwhelming now. Maybe Dr. Donnelly was right – maybe it wasn't about banishing them completely. Maybe it was about learning how to live with them, without letting them control me.

Dr. Donnelly's voice was soft, but her question was sharp: "What do you think is the hardest part of facing these demons?"

The room seemed to narrow around me. For a moment, I wasn't sitting in Dr. Donnelly's office anymore. I was with Ava, on that last night before everything fell apart. She had looked at me with eyes so full of love, yet so full of something else – something darker. I remembered the feeling of her hand slipping from mine, the weight of what I couldn't say, and what she wouldn't say.

"Do you trust yourself, Lily?" Dr. Donnelly's question hung in the air, heavy with meaning.

I looked at her, unsure of what to say. Trust myself? I hadn't even thought about it. My entire life felt like one mistake after another, each one pulling me further away from who I used to be.

"I don't know," I admitted, my voice barely a whisper. "How can I trust myself when everything I've done feels wrong?"

Dr. Donnelly's eyes softened, and she leaned forward slightly. "Trusting yourself doesn't mean being perfect. It means believing that you can make it through, even when things feel impossible. It's about finding that small voice inside that tells you to keep going."

We spent the rest of the session talking through the week, unpacking the emotions that had been swirling in my mind. It wasn't easy, but by the time the session ended, I felt like I had taken another step forward. It was small, but it was something.

There were moments when Dr. Donnelly would sit in silence, her eyes calm, waiting for me to say something. But the words got stuck somewhere between my heart and my throat, as if they were afraid of being heard. I wanted to speak, I really did. But then a part of me wondered if putting everything out in the open would only make the pain more real, more concrete, something I couldn't ever take back.

As I was wheeled down the hallway, I glanced out the narrow window and saw the sun breaking through the clouds, casting a soft ray of light onto the garden below. A small bird flitted by, struggling against the wind, but still flying. The sight was fleeting, just a brief moment in the blur of everything, but it caught me. It was a reminder that even when the sky is heavy, light can still break through. And maybe, just maybe, that was enough to remind me that tomorrow didn't have to feel so impossible after all.

Chapter 21

Nightmare

The night before had been restless. Sleep didn't come easy anymore, and when it did, it brought with it a barrage of dreams that left me shaken. This one was no different. The nightmare had clung to me like a second skin, its details vivid even now as I sat in bed, staring blankly at the hospital room ceiling.

In the dream, I was trapped in a house – dark, cold, the walls too close, suffocating. There were voices in the distance, voices I knew but couldn't reach. No matter how fast I ran or how loudly I screamed, the house twisted around me, bending time and space until I was lost. I woke up gasping, my heart pounding in my chest, soaked in sweat.

It wasn't the first time I'd had dreams like this, but something about this one felt different – more intense, more real. Like it wasn't just a nightmare, but a reflection of the cage I felt trapped in, the suffocating weight of my own life pressing down on me. I could still feel the panic in my chest, lingering long after I'd opened my eyes.

I sat up in bed, my thoughts swirling around the nightmare and how much it mirrored the way I felt. How trapped I was in my own head. I couldn't shake the feeling that it meant something, that the dream was trying to tell me something about where I was headed – about what I needed to face.

Today, I had another appointment with Dr. Donnelly. I thought about what I would say, about how much I wanted to open up, but there was still this part of me that wasn't ready to be fully vulnerable. Dr. Donnelly had been patient with me, always letting me take the lead, but this time… this time I had to face it.

I didn't want the nightmare to own me, and I knew I couldn't run from it. I wanted to tell her about it, but how could I explain that it wasn't just a dream – it was the embodiment of everything I feared? The trauma, the depression, the deep-seated pain that had built up over the years. I had never really let anyone in on how suffocating it all felt.

I reached for my journal, knowing it was time to process everything before I walked into her office. The journal had become my way of sorting through the chaos in my mind, and I knew that writing it down was the first step toward confronting it in the session:

June 24, 2018

It is like a dream that you can't quite shake,
With moments that force your brain to ache.

You spring up from slumber with a panicked mentality,
As you are faced with the notion that this was not a dream but a reality.

Those scenarios that play through your mind last saw,
What may end up being deemed as your tragic flaw.

Do not let the nightmare gain full control of your motions,
And work to maintain control of those conflicting emotions.

Do this and you will undoubtedly soar to new limits,
Even as you attempt to count down to your last minutes.

Maybe you think it would be easier in the end,
Or perhaps maybe you should just try to pretend.

Regardless of the choice you know one thing true,
You will no longer be the same person you once knew.

These nightmares have their way of intrusion,
These nightmares have their way of confusion.

It is like a dream that you can't quite shake,
With moments that force your brain to ache.

Once I finished, I closed my journal and sighed. The words on the page felt heavy, but there was some relief in seeing them there. I knew it was time to face it head-on, to stop letting the nightmares consume me. I was ready to talk about it, no matter how hard it would be.

The past week had been a slow crawl through a dark tunnel. I'd spent most of my days lying in bed, too exhausted to do much of anything. There were moments where I'd force myself to sit up, pretend I was getting better, but the weight of everything still bore down on me, dragging me back into the darkness.

Leo had visited a couple of times, his presence a strange mix of comfort and awkwardness. He was trying so hard to make me laugh, to distract me from my thoughts, but nothing seemed to break through the wall I'd built around myself. I appreciated his efforts, but I couldn't shake the sense of loneliness that gnawed at me, even when he was there.

Then there was the physical therapy. The doctors were encouraging me to move more, to regain my strength, but even the act of walking left me feeling drained. My legs were shaky, my body uncooperative, and every step felt like a battle I wasn't sure I had the energy to fight.

And the nightmares – they'd been relentless. Every time I closed my eyes, they were waiting for me, dragging me back into that cold, dark place where nothing made sense. I'd wake up gasping for air, heart pounding, the panic lingering long after the dream had ended. I hadn't talked to anyone about them yet. Not even Leo. I wasn't sure how to.

But today, as I prepared for my session with Dr. Donnelly, I knew it was time. I couldn't keep running from it. The nightmares were part of the reason I was here in the first place. They were a manifestation of everything I was feeling, everything I was afraid to confront. And if I was going to move forward, I had to start facing it.

That afternoon, as I was wheeled to Dr. Donnelly's office, the nightmare was still lingering in my mind like smoke that refused to clear. But as I sat in her office, I knew it wasn't just about the dream anymore. The unease I had been feeling, the restlessness, was deeper than the nightmare itself. It was the manifestation of everything – my past, my present, and the fear of what was still ahead.

Dr. Donnelly leaned forward, her eyes filled with that same understanding patience she always carried. She didn't push me to speak, but the silence stretched on, urging me to start. I felt the journal heavy in my hands, my words sitting on the page like a confession waiting to be read.

"How are you today, Lily?" she asked, breaking the stillness with her calm, soothing voice.

"I don't know," I replied truthfully, barely above a whisper. "I… I had this nightmare. And it's not going away." My voice wavered, the vulnerability creeping in like a flood I wasn't prepared to hold back.

"Tell me about it," she prompted, and for the first time, I didn't feel the usual hesitation to answer.

I handed her my journal and let her read the entry. The room was silent except for the faint ticking of the clock on her desk. As her eyes moved over my words, I felt that familiar tug of fear – the fear of being too exposed. But at the same time, there was a strange comfort in it. Like maybe, just maybe, I didn't have to carry all this alone.

"The dream was vivid," I started, my voice gaining a little strength. "It felt like I was trapped. I was stuck in a house, and no matter how hard I tried, I couldn't escape. It was dark and cold… and there were these voices, voices I recognized, but I couldn't reach them. No matter what I did, the house kept closing in on me."

I paused, my heart racing as the memory of the dream resurfaced. "It was suffocating. And it felt… it felt like it wasn't just a dream. Like it was real, and that house was a reflection of everything I've been feeling."

Dr. Donnelly didn't look away from me as she placed the journal down gently on the table between us. "It sounds like the dream is mirroring your current emotional state," she said softly. "You feel trapped – by your thoughts, your past, and maybe even by the things you haven't confronted yet."

Her words hit a nerve, and I felt my chest tighten. She was right. I had been avoiding the deeper parts of my pain for so long that they had started to seep into every corner of my life.

"I think it's more than just the nightmare," I admitted, my voice shaking slightly. "It's everything. My dad... Logan... Ava... even Leo." Saying his name felt like a betrayal, but I couldn't deny the confusion that had been building around him.

Dr. Donnelly raised an eyebrow but remained silent, allowing me to continue.

"I don't know how to explain it," I continued, feeling the weight of all those names. "I've lost so much. And it's like every time I think I'm healing, something pulls me back. I can't let go of any of it. I think about my dad and Logan, and all the things that went unsaid... and then Ava. I thought she was my future, and now she's just... gone. But with Leo..." I trailed off, unsure how to finish.

Dr. Donnelly tilted her head slightly, her eyes narrowing in thought. "Tell me about Leo," she said, her voice gentle yet probing. "What's different about him?"

I took a deep breath, trying to sort through the tangled mess of emotions that had been building for weeks. "He's... he's always been there. He's my best friend, and he's been through everything with me. But lately, it feels... different. Like there's something more. And I don't know if it's real or if it's just because I'm desperate to hold onto someone."

The words tumbled out faster than I'd expected, and the weight of them hit me hard. I had never said that out loud, not even to myself. But here, in this quiet room, it felt like the truth.

Dr. Donnelly leaned forward, her face thoughtful. "It sounds like Leo has been your anchor, especially during this difficult time," she said. "But it also sounds like you're afraid of what that could mean. Are you worried about losing him too?"

The question sent a jolt of panic through me. Was that it? Was I clinging to Leo because I was terrified of losing another person I loved?

"I don't know," I whispered, my voice barely audible. "I don't want to lose him. But I don't want to ruin what we have either. And I don't even know if what I'm feeling is real or if it's just... grief."

"Grief can blur the lines between emotions," Dr. Donnelly said, her voice steady. "It's possible that the feelings you have for Leo are tangled up in everything else you've been going through. But it's also possible that what you're feeling is real. The important thing is that you allow yourself to explore those feelings without judgment."

I nodded, unsure of how to process everything she was saying. The truth was, I didn't know what I felt. Leo had been my rock for so long, but now... now it was like the ground beneath us was shifting, and I didn't know where we would land.

Dr. Donnelly smiled gently. "We don't have to solve everything today," she said. "But I think it's important that we keep exploring these feelings, especially the ones that make you uncomfortable. You've been through a lot, and it's okay to feel conflicted. What's important is that you give yourself the space to process it all."

I swallowed hard, feeling the familiar weight of uncertainty pressing down on me. "It just feels like too much sometimes," I admitted. "Like I'm carrying all of this... and I don't know how much longer I can hold on."

Dr. Donnelly's expression softened, and she leaned forward slightly. "You're not carrying it alone, Lily," she said. "I'm here with you. And so is Leo. You have people who care about you, who want to help you through this."

I blinked back tears, the weight of her words settling over me like a warm blanket. I wasn't alone. I had people who cared about me, who wanted to see me heal. But still, the fear lingered. The fear of losing more, of letting people down, of failing myself.

As the session continued, we delved deeper into the traumas I had been avoiding – my father's death, Logan, the unresolved guilt and grief. We scratched the surface of those old wounds, but Dr. Donnelly was careful not to push too hard. She knew, as I did, that healing would take time. There were no quick fixes, no easy answers.

"I think we've made a lot of progress today," she said as the session came to a close. "But I want to wait a couple more sessions before we start putting any labels on what's happening. For now, I want you to continue journaling and focusing on the things that are coming up for you. And don't be afraid to reach out to Leo. It sounds like he's been a real source of comfort for you."

I nodded, feeling both relieved and anxious. There was so much still left unsaid, so many pieces of the puzzle still missing. But for now, I had done enough. I had scratched the surface, and that was a start.

As I left her office, the sun had started to set, casting long shadows across the hospital grounds. The nightmare still lingered at the edges of my mind, but it felt less suffocating now. I had taken the first step toward facing it, and for the first time in a long time, I felt like maybe I was strong enough to keep going.

Chapter 22
Major Depression

The sunlight filtered through the small window in the hospital room, casting long beams of light across the bed where I sat, my fingers tracing absent patterns on the blanket. Outside, I could see a few birds gliding through the air, their wings outstretched, riding the invisible currents of the wind. They looked so free, so effortless. But here I was, grounded – chained, really – by the weight of what lay ahead. Dr. Donnelly had asked me to think about how I felt, what I wanted from our session today. But the truth was, I didn't have the energy to write anything for her this time. I wasn't going to bring my journal, no planned thoughts, no neatly packaged revelations. I was going in with an open mind, prepared to let the conversation flow wherever it needed to.

Last week had been… strange. A blur of ups and downs. There had been moments where I thought I was starting to feel something again, a flicker of hope perhaps, but they were fleeting, swallowed up by the waves of numbness that followed. There had been the quiet mobile call with Leo, our conversation filled with his reassurances, but the silence afterward was louder than anything he had said. Then there was the night I stared out at the moon for what felt like hours, wondering if anyone out there was feeling the same way I was, lost in their own darkness. But even in those moments, I couldn't seem to capture the emotions enough to write them down.

And then there was the overwhelming exhaustion – the kind that made it hard to move, to breathe, let alone process my feelings. I was tired of trying to put them into words, tired of pretending I could make sense of the mess in my head. So today, for the first time, I wasn't going to journal before my session. I was just going to talk. Or try to, at least.

There was an odd tension between the bright, clear day and the storm swirling inside of me. It felt like the universe was mocking me. The world was full of light, yet here I was, trapped in my own darkness. My stomach twisted with nerves, not for the first time. The therapy sessions always brought something heavy with them, some truth I wasn't ready to face. I rubbed my hands over my arms, suddenly cold despite the warmth outside.

What had I even achieved this week? I couldn't tell. Some days, just getting out of bed felt like a victory. But the constant buzzing in my head, the lingering thoughts of Ava, of Logan, of everything I had lost – those stayed with me. And through all of it, Leo remained my steady anchor, though lately, I'd been thinking more about what that really meant, about the way his presence seemed to ground me in a way no one else did. But I couldn't let myself go there. Not yet. Not with everything else still hanging over me.

Later that afternoon, I was wheeled down the sterile, sunlit hallway toward Dr. Donnelly's office. My progress, if you could even call it that, felt agonizingly slow. Every turn of the wheels beneath me was a reminder of how trapped I felt – trapped in this body that wasn't moving the way it should, trapped in a mind that kept spinning in circles. I hated it. The dependence on others to get me from place to place, the way I still couldn't walk on my own, the way the world kept moving while I felt stuck in this endless limbo.

As we passed by the hospital windows, I caught glimpses of the outside world – the trees swaying in the breeze, people walking without a second thought, the sun hanging low in the sky. It seemed like such a small, ordinary thing – to be able to walk outside, to feel the grass under your feet. But for me, that felt like a lifetime away.

When we finally reached Dr. Donnelly's office, the familiar scent of lavender greeted me as it always did, soft and calming. Normally, that smell helped to settle some of the tension inside of me, but not today. Today, my frustration was too sharp, too jagged to be smoothed over by a bit of lavender oil.

She was already sitting in her chair, her face lit with that calm, patient expression she always wore, waiting for me to speak. But the words weren't coming. I was too tired to dig them up, too drained from fighting the same battle day in and day out. What could I possibly say that she didn't already know?

Dr. Donnelly waited for a moment, allowing the silence to stretch between us before she spoke. "I know it's been a tough week," she said softly. "You're dealing with a lot, both physically and emotionally. That's not something that changes overnight."

Physically. Emotionally. It felt like she was naming the two sides of me that were at constant war. "I'm trying," I mumbled, though it felt like a hollow admission. Was I really? Or was I just going through the motions, pretending that I could somehow push through it all without really believing I could?

"I can see that," she said, her voice warm. "But I also want you to know that it's okay to feel frustrated. Healing – physically, mentally – it's not a straight line. There are ups and downs, and it's natural to feel like progress is slow, even when you're moving forward."

I nodded weakly, though it didn't feel like I was moving forward. Not really. "I just... I don't know. It's like every time I take one step, I fall back ten more."

"That's a normal feeling," Dr. Donnelly reassured me. "But I think part of what's making this journey so difficult for you is that you've been carrying a lot for a very long time, even before the recent events." She paused, studying my expression. "We've touched on this before, but I think it's important to talk about the things that happened in your past. They're still shaping your present."

Her words hit a nerve, and I felt my chest tighten. I knew she was right, but the idea of opening those wounds again felt unbearable. I stared at the floor, the weight of her words pressing down on me.

"Lily, I want to help you carry some of that weight," Dr. Donnelly said gently. "We don't have to dive in all at once, but we need to address it. Because these things – they don't just go away on their own."

My throat felt dry, and I swallowed hard. "Where do I even start?" I whispered, my voice cracking under the strain.

"We can start wherever feels right," she said. "But I think you know where some of the pain comes from."

I nodded slowly, the memories flashing through my mind like ghosts. My father. Logan. Ava. The things I'd tried so hard to bury were rising to the surface, one by one.

"It's my family," I began, my voice shaking slightly. "I thought I had dealt with it, but it never really goes away, does it?"

"No, it doesn't," Dr. Donnelly said softly. "Losing your father and Logan – it's a grief that doesn't just disappear. It stays with you, even when you think you've moved past it."

The mention of their names brought a sharp pang of emotion, and for a moment, I struggled to keep it together. I could still remember the day Logan died so clearly. It was like watching a slow-motion train wreck, and I was helpless to stop it. The guilt still gnawed at me, no matter how much time had passed.

"I don't think I ever really got over losing them," I admitted, my voice barely audible. "It feels like... like a part of me was buried with them."

"I can't imagine the pain of losing them," Dr. Donnelly said softly. "It's a loss no one should have to face, especially at such a young age. But Lily, carrying that pain alone is too much for anyone. It's okay to talk about it. It's okay to feel it."

The tears I'd been holding back slipped free, trailing down my cheeks. "I just... I didn't know how to deal with it," I said, my voice cracking. "I still don't. It's like it's always there, lurking in the background, but I try to ignore it."

"That's understandable," Dr. Donnelly said gently. "But ignoring it doesn't make it go away. It's part of why you feel stuck now. There's so much unresolved grief, and it's manifesting in other ways."

I nodded, wiping at my tears with the back of my hand. "And then there's... other stuff," I added hesitantly, my voice faltering. "Things I don't even like thinking about, let alone talking about."

Dr. Donnelly gave me a soft, encouraging look, waiting patiently for me to continue. I took a deep breath, knowing that this was the part I had avoided for so long.

"There was... someone," I whispered, the words barely escaping my lips. "Someone who... who hurt me."

Her expression remained calm, though I could see the concern in her eyes. "Are you ready to talk about it?" she asked gently.

I shook my head, the emotions too raw, too tangled. "Not yet," I admitted. "But I know it's... it's a part of why I am the way I am. Why I can't... trust people the way I should."

Dr. Donnelly nodded, understanding. "That's okay, Lily. We can take this step by step. What's important is that you're acknowledging it. Healing doesn't happen all at once – it's a process, and it's on your terms."

The weight of her words settled over me, but this time, it didn't feel crushing. It felt like an invitation to begin, to start peeling back the layers, even if it hurt.

"And Ava?" Dr. Donnelly asked softly, her voice laced with compassion. "She's been a big part of your life, and I know that losing her has been a source of deep pain."

At the mention of Ava, my chest tightened again. "It's... complicated," I whispered. "She was... everything to me. But I couldn't hold onto her. And now, it's like... I'm not sure who I am without her."

"That's understandable," Dr. Donnelly said. "It sounds like Ava represented a lot for you – comfort, connection, love. And losing her has left a void. But it's also okay to grieve that loss. It's okay to feel the pain of it."

I stared down at my hands, clenching and unclenching them. The weight of everything I had been holding onto felt unbearable, but for the first time, I wasn't running from it. I was acknowledging it, facing it head-on.

"I just feel... broken," I whispered. "Like there's nothing left of me that's worth saving."

Dr. Donnelly shook her head gently. "You're not broken, Lily. You're hurting. There's a difference. And you don't have to do this alone. You're here now, and that's a huge step. It means you want to get better, even if it doesn't feel like it yet."

Her words were kind, but the fear and doubt still lingered. "What if I can't?" I asked, my voice barely audible.

"You can," Dr. Donnelly said firmly. "It's going to take time, and it's going to take work. But I believe in you, Lily. We're going to take this one step at a time. Together."

For a moment, I sat there, letting her words wash over me. It wasn't a solution, and it didn't make everything better. But it was a start – a tiny flicker of hope that maybe, just maybe, I could find my way through the darkness.

Dr. Donnelly smiled, though it was filled with a sadness that suggested she understood more than I wanted her to. "Let's take things one step at a time today," she said gently. "There's something I want to discuss with you – something we've touched on, but I think it's time to explore more deeply."

I glanced at her, my heart suddenly heavy with the weight of whatever was coming. I had a feeling I knew what she was going to say.

"You've shown a lot of resilience, Lily," she began. "But based on everything we've discussed, and the symptoms you've described, it's clear that you're showing signs of Major Depression. I'd like to explore this diagnosis with you, talk about what it means and how we can address it together."

Major Depression. There it was, out in the open. I felt the words settle in my chest like lead, heavy and cold. I wasn't sure why hearing it said out loud made it feel so final, so real. I had known, deep down, that something was wrong. That this wasn't just grief or sadness – it was deeper, darker. But now, with the label attached to it, I wasn't sure what to do with that truth.

Dr. Donnelly waited, letting the silence sit between us before she continued. "It's not your fault, Lily. This is something we can work through together. I know that hearing it can feel overwhelming, but a diagnosis like this doesn't define you. It's just a part of what's happening inside your brain, a part we can address with the right approach."

I swallowed hard, trying to keep my emotions in check. But the floodgates were dangerously close to opening. "So what does that mean?" I asked, my voice barely a whisper. "What... happens now?"

Dr. Donnelly leaned forward slightly, her tone gentle but firm. "Major Depression, or Major Depressive Disorder, is a condition that affects not only your emotional state but also how your body functions and how you think. It's more than just sadness or feeling down – it's a persistent feeling of emptiness, hopelessness, and often a disconnection from the things that once brought you joy. It changes the way your brain processes information, the way you feel physically, and even how you relate to those around you."

I looked away, feeling the weight of her words. *It changes everything*, I thought.

She continued, "It's like your brain is stuck in a cycle of negative thoughts and emotions that are hard to break free from. The neurotransmitters in your brain, which help regulate mood – like serotonin, norepinephrine, and dopamine – become imbalanced. That imbalance affects your ability to experience pleasure, to sleep well, and even to think clearly. That's why, at times, it feels like a fog is hanging over everything."

I nodded slowly, absorbing each word.

"Major Depression can also lead to physical symptoms – fatigue, changes in appetite, aches, and even a weakened immune system. It's as much a physical condition as it is a mental one. The heaviness you feel, the exhaustion, the difficulty in doing even the simplest tasks – those aren't just in your head. They're very real effects of the disorder."

I could feel the familiar weight of exhaustion settling on my shoulders again, but this time, there was a sense of validation in it. The heaviness wasn't just me failing or being weak – it was a symptom of something bigger.

Dr. Donnelly's voice softened as she continued, "Depression can affect everyone differently. Some people may feel numb, disconnected from everything. Others may feel an overwhelming sense of guilt or worthlessness, like they're a burden to those around them. It can even distort your thinking, making you believe things that aren't true – like that you're alone, or that things will never get better. But these are all symptoms of the condition, not reflections of reality."

A flicker of something – maybe hope – passed through me as I listened. It had always felt like something was wrong with me, something broken inside, but now it was starting to make sense.

"And like any other medical condition," she added, "Major Depression is treatable. It doesn't mean you're stuck feeling this way forever. It means we can develop a plan to help you regain control, to stabilize your mood, and to get back to a place where life feels manageable again."

I stared at her blankly, my mind overwhelmed by everything she is sharing with me.

"Think of it this way," she continued. "Depression can be caused by a combination of factors. There's a biological component – an imbalance in the chemicals that regulate mood in your brain, like serotonin, norepinephrine, and dopamine. These chemicals help to control your mood, sleep, and even how you respond to stress. When they're out of balance, it can lead to feelings of sadness, hopelessness, and exhaustion, sometimes to the point where you can't even do the things you used to enjoy."

She paused for a moment, giving me time to continue to absorb her words.

"It also has psychological factors," she added, her eyes searching mine for any sign of understanding. "Past trauma, unresolved grief, and the relationships we build – or lose – can contribute to depression. The loss of your father and Logan, your relationship with Ava, the other things we touched on today... all of that shapes how you see yourself and the world around you. Those experiences can sometimes leave emotional scars that make it harder for you to process new challenges."

I nodded, my chest tightening with the weight of her words, realizing that without any acknowledgement she would continue to reveal the same diagnosis – trapping me in a cycle like a bird in a cage. I had never thought of my brain as something that was chemically broken, something that could betray me. I always thought I was just... weak.

"That's why Major Depression can feel so consuming," Dr. Donnelly said softly, reading the thoughts on my face. "It's not just emotional pain. It's physical. Your body reacts to it. Fatigue, difficulty sleeping, changes in appetite, and physical aches are all symptoms of depression. Your mind and body are intertwined in ways that can sometimes feel overwhelming."

She leaned forward slightly, her expression serious but kind. "But here's the thing, Lily. Major Depression is treatable. It's something we can work through together. The treatment is multifaceted, meaning it's not just about one approach, but several that come together to help you regain control."

I swallowed hard, the word *treatable* standing out like a beacon in the fog of everything else.

"What are the options?" I asked quietly, my voice shaky. I had a feeling I wasn't going to like some of them, but I needed to know.

"Well, there are several options for treatment," she began carefully. "We'll continue with therapy, of course. That's going to be a key component in helping you manage and process your emotions. Cognitive Behavioral Therapy, or CBT, is a common approach we'll use. It focuses on identifying negative thought patterns and learning how to challenge and change them. Depression often tricks your brain into believing things about yourself that aren't true – that you're worthless, or that nothing will ever get better. CBT helps you break that cycle."

I stared at my hands, trying to wrap my mind around all of this.

"And then," she continued, "there are medications that can help manage the chemical imbalances in your brain. Antidepressants – such as SSRIs, which are selective serotonin reuptake inhibitors – are commonly prescribed for Major Depression. They work by increasing the levels of serotonin in the brain, which can help improve mood and emotional stability."

I tensed at the mention of medication. The thought of pills made my stomach twist. It reminded me too much of the prescription drugs I had once abused – drugs that made me numb and distant from the world. Dr. Donnelly must have sensed my discomfort because she quickly added, "I know your history with prescription drugs, Lily. And I understand that this is something we need to be cautious about."

I let out a small, shaky breath. "I don't want to go down that road again."

"I understand," she said softly. "And I would never push medication on you without considering your past experiences. We're not going to take any steps that make you feel uncomfortable. But I want you to know that, when used correctly and under careful supervision, antidepressants can be a useful tool for some people. It's not the only tool in the toolbox, but it's something we could explore together if and when you're ready."

I nodded, still wary but less resistant.

"We can also explore lifestyle changes," she added. "Things like diet, exercise, and sleep routines can have a significant impact on your mental health. Exercise, for example, has been shown to increase endorphins, which are natural mood lifters. We'll work to create a balanced routine that supports your mental well-being."

She paused again, letting her words sink in. "Ultimately, Lily, treatment for depression is about finding what works best for you. There's no one-size-fits-all solution. Some people benefit from therapy alone, some from medication, and others from a combination of both. The important thing is that we work together to figure out what's going to help you feel better."

I exhaled slowly, trying to absorb everything she had said. Therapy, medication, lifestyle changes... It sounded like so much, like more than I could handle. But Dr. Donnelly wasn't rushing me. She wasn't pushing anything on me. She was giving me options, guiding me, and for the first time in a long time, I didn't feel completely lost.

"What happens next?" I asked, my voice barely above a whisper.

"We take it one step at a time," she said gently. "We'll start with regular therapy sessions, and if you ever feel ready to explore medication, we'll do it carefully and thoughtfully. You're in control here, Lily. My job is to help guide you and give you the tools to navigate this. But you're the one steering the ship."

For a brief moment, the weight on my shoulders felt a little lighter. It wasn't all fixed, not by a long shot. But it was a start. Maybe, just maybe, I could find my way through this.

The session had drained me. As I was wheeled back to my room, the hallway felt longer than usual, like it was stretching out endlessly before me. Each rotation of the wheelchair's wheels sounded louder, echoing in the narrow corridor. The sterile smell of the hospital seemed thicker, suffocating. I kept my eyes on the floor, the tile pattern beneath me blurring together, but my mind was somewhere else, replaying Dr. Donnelly's words, *Major Depression.*

It clung to me, the diagnosis. Not just a label but a weight, pressing down on me, demanding to be understood. I hadn't wanted this – this explanation for why I felt so broken. But there it was, following me like a shadow.

A nurse pushed open the door to my room, and I wheeled myself inside. It was quiet, too quiet. The small television hummed in the corner, muted, and the window at the far end of the room framed the fading light of the late afternoon. Everything felt suspended in time, as if the world outside was still moving, but my life had hit pause.

I sat there for a moment, letting the silence wrap around me, before slowly making my way to the bed. My journal sat on the small table beside it, waiting patiently, just like it always had. I stared at the cover for what felt like an eternity before finally reaching for it. My fingers brushed against the worn edges of the pages, familiar, comforting, but today it felt different.

I positioned myself on the edge of the bed and placed the journal on my lap. The room was bathed in the golden light of the setting sun, which cast long shadows on the walls. The warmth of it clashed with the coldness inside me. I opened the journal to a blank page, the starkness of it mirroring the empty feeling in my chest. My hand hovered over the page, unsure, hesitant, but the pen felt like it belonged there, as if it had been waiting for me to pour everything out.

Major Depression.

The words echoed in my mind, their weight pressing down on me. I scrawled them onto the page in shaky handwriting, barely legible. Writing them down made them real. I tried to capture the enormity of it, the way it had reshaped everything I thought I knew about myself. But how could I? How could I put into words the depth of this pain, the confusion, the anger? I wasn't just dealing with a diagnosis – I was dealing with the realization that everything I had been feeling for so long now had a name. But it also meant I was sick, and that part scared me.

I let the ink flow, each word bringing a small sense of release, like I was letting pieces of the burden spill onto the paper instead of carrying it all inside. My hand moved faster as the emotions poured out: *fear, isolation, anger, sadness.* The confusion of it all, the unfairness. It wasn't just depression – it was everything else that came with it. Losing Logan and Dad, feeling like I was constantly drowning in grief and now, adding this to the pile.

I paused for a moment, my pen hovering just above the page. The light from outside had softened, casting golden hues on the walls. The sky beyond the window was a deepening blue, the last traces of daylight slipping away. I glanced at my reflection in the mirror across the room. I hadn't really looked at myself since waking up here, not fully, and now that I did, it startled me. The girl staring back seemed different – more fragile, more burdened. Her eyes, my eyes, were tired, but behind them, there was a quiet resilience. I was still here. I hadn't given up.

The journal lay open in front of me, the pen still in my hand. I sighed deeply and, with a few last words, finished my entry. The sun was nearly gone now, just a thin line of orange on the horizon. I closed the journal softly, as if sealing away everything I had just written. The weight of the words still lingered, but at least they weren't trapped inside me anymore.

As I sat there, the shadows lengthening around me, I thought about tomorrow. About the fact that I had made it through today, and that was something. Maybe it wasn't a victory, but it was survival, and right now, that was enough.

I glanced at the journal again, the familiar weight of it grounding me. Tomorrow, the fight would continue. But for tonight, I allowed myself to breathe. Just a little. Just enough.

With smooth, bold strokes, I collected my thoughts and finished the write:

July 1, 2018

A feeling of intense sadness and sorrow,
Masking the possibility for laughter and joy;
A feeling that nearly half of the world may know,
Creating a new world of no more tomorrow.

A sensation laced with crippling fears and dreams,
Following humankind like a hitman on a mission;
A sensation easily described as endless misconception,
Manipulating the mind to meet an unrealistic condition.

All hope may be lost one day more than any other,
That is one thing that comes within the realm of this state of mind;
And often urges its' subjects to make that unworldly confession,
Tell me what it is like to live with major depression.

Chapter 23
Chaos

The physical therapy room buzzed with the steady hum of machines and the soft murmurs of other patients trying to regain pieces of themselves they'd lost along the way. I was just another body in the lineup, yet I felt entirely disconnected from the world around me. The sterile scent of antiseptic clung to the air, sharp and cold, much like the harsh reality of my present.

The straps holding my legs in place dug into my skin as the therapist tightened them, his hands steady, confident. "Ready, Lily?" His voice was calm, reassuring, but I could only nod. I was too far inside my head, trying to convince myself that this time would be different. But the nagging doubt was loud, overwhelming, like a drumbeat that wouldn't quiet.

"Focus on one step at a time," he reminded me, the repetition of his words more frustrating than helpful. Every time he said it, I felt a surge of guilt – like I should've been able to do this by now, like I was failing just by needing the reminder.

The first attempt of the day was pitiful. My legs felt like concrete, refusing to obey the commands my brain sent them. The therapist's encouraging words barely registered as I struggled to lift my left foot. I felt the chaos bubbling up inside me – thoughts of failure, shame, frustration – and it clouded everything else.

I shut my eyes for a moment, gripping the handrails tighter until my knuckles turned white. The tension in my muscles mirrored the battle in my head, and with every ounce of effort, I tried again.

Lift. Move. Step.

But it wasn't enough. My leg buckled beneath me, and I collapsed into the chair behind me. The ache in my muscles was nothing compared to the weight in my chest. I wanted to scream, to cry, to just give up entirely.

"You're doing great," the therapist said, and I hated him for it. For his optimism, his patience, his insistence that I could still achieve something when everything inside me felt like chaos. I swallowed the anger. He was just doing his job.

Each failed attempt was like a kick to my pride, and as I sat there, waiting for the next round, I could feel the tears burning behind my eyes. Not here. Not now. I tried to swallow them down, but the chaos in my mind wouldn't relent. It swirled, reminding me of every loss, every misstep, every moment of weakness that had led me to this chair.

Minutes passed, and I tried again, but with no progress. The chaos in the room – the soft clatter of equipment, the voices, the distant sound of wheels on linoleum – it all felt too loud, too overwhelming. My body wasn't mine anymore. It was just a vessel that refused to obey, like the chaos had spilled into my muscles, hijacking even my physical form.

And then, something inside me snapped. I wasn't going to leave this session without a win. I couldn't. I had to reclaim some part of myself.

"One more try," I said, my voice barely above a whisper. My therapist's gaze met mine, and he nodded, moving into position to support me again. But this time, I didn't rely on his words or his encouragement. I tuned everything out – the noise, the failures, the chaos – and I focused on the task at hand.

Lift. Move. Step.

My foot moved. Not much, but enough to feel a flicker of hope.

"Good, keep going," he said, but I blocked him out. This was my moment, not his.

I gritted my teeth, pushing through the burn in my legs, the exhaustion that weighed me down like lead. I shifted my weight forward, moving my other foot in front of the first. A second step. This time, it didn't feel like defeat. It felt like survival.

But just as quickly as it had come, the strength in my legs gave way, and I stumbled back into the chair. I wasn't standing anymore, but I had taken two steps. Two steps that I hadn't taken the day before. My breath came in shallow gasps, but a faint, tired smile tugged at the corners of my lips.

It wasn't much. It wasn't enough. But it was something.

"That's progress, Lily. You should be proud," the therapist said, patting my shoulder gently. I nodded, but I barely heard him. My mind was already elsewhere – already back in that chaotic space, replaying the events that had led me here, reminding me how much farther I had to go.

Still, for the first time in weeks, I had won something. A small victory, buried beneath the chaos.

As the session ended, I let them wheel me back toward my room. The wheels squeaked on the linoleum floor, cutting through the silence of the hallway. I stared ahead, lost in thought, but something outside the narrow window caught my attention. The sun had started to set, casting an orange glow over the hospital garden below. The sky was still light, but there were clouds in the distance, threatening to overtake the bright evening.

I felt like those clouds – hovering on the edge, waiting to be swallowed by the dark.

When we reached my room, the therapist left me in the doorway. I was alone again, alone with the noise in my head. I wanted to celebrate those two steps, to feel pride in what I had accomplished, but all I could think about was how long the journey still was, how much more chaos I had to endure.

My journal lay on the bedside table, untouched since the last entry. With a deep breath, I reached for it. The pen felt heavy in my hand, but as I opened the book, the words started to come:

July 4, 2018

The world erupting around me,
My thoughts collapsing my rhythmic breath...
I think about who I need to be,
As I am facing certain death...
I only wish that I could see,
The chaos that controls my life in depth...

I finished my journal entry with a sigh, my fingers tracing the edges of the paper. The weight of the words I had just written still hung heavy in the room, pressing against me. It was as though I had spilled every bit of pain onto the page, yet it didn't feel lighter. If anything, it felt thicker in the air – dense and overwhelming. I closed the journal quietly, setting it aside on the small table next to me. I could still feel my emotions clawing at the surface, begging for release.

The room seemed too quiet now. The walls too sterile, the air too heavy. I tried to focus on the small victory from earlier – the way I had pushed myself, taking those few steps during physical therapy. I had felt a surge of pride, but now, it felt like a distant memory, something I had lost as quickly as it came. My legs still ached, the burning reminder of how fragile my body felt.

I ran my hands over them, trying to ground myself, but the hollowness lingered, unshakable. I was drowning in it again, sinking into the familiar darkness.

Then, a soft knock pulled me from my spiraling thoughts. I looked toward the door, my heart skipping a beat. For a moment, I froze, not sure if I wanted company or solitude. But the door creaked open, and my breath caught in my throat.

Leo.

He stood there in the doorway, his eyes soft, and for a brief second, it felt like everything around me stopped. The room didn't seem so cold, so sterile anymore. It was like his presence filled the space, warming it in a way I hadn't felt in a long time.

"Lil," he said, his voice low and familiar, his lips curving into a small, reassuring smile. He stepped inside, closing the door behind him, his gaze locking onto mine with that look I'd come to know so well – kind, gentle, grounding.

"Leo…" I barely managed to whisper his name, afraid that if I said it too loudly, this moment might dissolve into nothing, that he might vanish.

But he didn't. He crossed the room quickly, his footsteps barely making a sound, and before I could say anything more, he wrapped me in his arms. The warmth of him, the familiar scent of his cologne – it flooded my senses, pulling me out of the darkness I had been sinking into. For the first time in what felt like hours, I let myself relax, sinking into his embrace. I let my head rest against his chest, breathing in deeply.

He was solid, real. And I needed that.

"I heard you've had a rough day," he whispered, his voice close to my ear, his breath soft against my hair. He pulled back slightly, just enough to look at me, his eyes searching mine, trying to understand without me having to say anything.

I nodded, unable to find the words. My throat felt tight, my chest heavy. I didn't even know where to start, how to explain the storm that had been raging inside me.

"Figured I could keep you company for a bit," he said softly, sitting down in the chair next to my bed. His hand lingered on mine for a moment, that comforting touch grounding me in ways I hadn't realized I needed. "If you don't mind."

"I don't mind," I whispered, my voice breaking slightly. "I'm glad you're here."

For the next few hours, we talked. About everything and nothing. Leo asked me about physical therapy, about how I was holding up. He cracked a few jokes, the kind that made me smile despite myself. And for a while, I let myself forget the weight of the day, the heaviness that still clung to my bones. I let myself sink into the familiar comfort of his presence, feeling the storm inside me calm, if only for a little while.

For a moment, with him sitting there, talking about trivial things and making me laugh, the world didn't feel quite so heavy.

Chapter 24

Amnesia

The week had passed slowly, each day blending into the next in a haze of half-formed thoughts and blurry memories. It was as if time had lost its grip on me, slipping through my fingers like sand, while I sat there, frozen, unable to make sense of the fragments that remained. I found myself trapped in a fog, both mentally and physically, as I navigated the hospital halls, confined to my wheelchair. The weight of the world pressed down on me, but what haunted me most was the feeling that I had been removed from my own life, like a spectator watching from afar.

I couldn't grasp the events that led me here. It was like the days and hours before my attempt were hidden behind a thick curtain, just out of reach. I knew something had happened – I had done something – but the details eluded me, like shadows slipping through cracks in the walls. I kept trying to remember, forcing my mind to pull together the pieces, but the harder I pushed, the more the memories seemed to unravel.

It felt like someone had taken a paintbrush to my memories, smearing them with broad strokes, leaving behind only vague impressions. Moments blurred into one another – Ava's face, the way the light filtered through my bedroom window that night, the sound of my mum's voice calling out to me, and then... nothing. A hollow, yawning gap in the timeline of my life.

I couldn't shake the feeling that something important was missing, that I had buried it deep within myself, but I didn't know if I had the strength to dig it back up. The idea of uncovering those lost memories terrified me. What if they were worse than I could imagine? What if I couldn't handle the truth?

I felt like I was living between two worlds. In one, I was conscious, aware of the present, the sterile hospital room, the constant hum of machines, and the soft whispers of nurses in the hallway. In the other, I was lost in the black hole of my own mind, a place where time had no meaning, where I floated in the void, disconnected from everything and everyone.

I searched my mind for any thread that could lead me back, any clue that could help me remember how I had fallen so far. But it was like reaching into darkness – my hands found nothing solid to grasp. The harder I tried to make sense of it, the more distant the memories became.

There were flashes of moments – brief and unsteady – like scenes from a movie I'd seen once but couldn't fully recall. I remembered the suffocating weight of hopelessness, the overwhelming sense of being swallowed whole by grief. I remembered staring at the pills, counting them, my hand shaking as I tried to rationalize the decision that would come next. But after that... my mind shut down. It had locked the door and thrown away the key.

I wasn't sure if I was ready to open that door, to face the flood of emotions and memories that lay behind it. What if I couldn't handle what I found there? What if it was too much to bear?

Each time I tried to reach back, it felt like I was running in circles, trapped in a labyrinth of my own mind. The confusion gnawed at me, tearing at the edges of my sanity. And then there was the fear. Fear of the unknown, of what I might find if I kept searching. Fear that whatever had driven me to that dark place still lingered, waiting to pull me under again.

My heart raced as the realization hit me – I didn't trust myself. I couldn't trust my own mind to give me the answers I needed. It had betrayed me once, led me to the edge of the abyss, and now, in the aftermath, I wasn't sure if I could climb my way back out.

Back in my room, I reached for my journal, my fingers trembling as I flipped it open to a fresh page. The emptiness of the paper stared back at me, reflecting the blank spaces in my memory. Maybe writing would help. Maybe if I put the fragments down, one by one, I could begin to stitch them together, make sense of the chaos swirling inside my head.

But as I stared at the page, the words felt heavy, weighed down by the fog that had settled over my mind. I didn't know where to begin. It felt like my life had been fractured into a thousand pieces, and I was too scared to pick them up, afraid that I would cut myself in the process.

The pain was real, but it was elusive, shifting just out of reach whenever I tried to confront it. I didn't know how to move forward, but I couldn't go back. I was stuck here, in this liminal space, trapped between what had been and what was yet to come.

I took a deep breath, gripping the pen tighter. Maybe writing would help me make sense of it all. Or maybe it would just be another reminder of how lost I truly was.

July 8, 2018

It is hard to tell the difference between night and day,
And at times my mind feels like it has gone astray.
My memories are clouded by the pain of the past,
And the amnesia begins to settle fast.

I cannot control what happens to my mind when it fails,
But deep down I know that it is me who I hope prevails.
The monsters come and change the way I feel,
And the amnesia quickly comes and starts to steal.

My life has vanished right before my eyes,
I cannot seem to move past my perilous cries.
I wish I could recall the moments of haze,
But something continues to set my mind ablaze.

I am left with only what remains of me,
When suddenly I become set free.
By now it's far too late to see,
What amnesia does not guarantee.

I will hope and pray that one day it will be a new story,
But until then allow me to continue to restore my glory.
I am sorry that the monsters maintain control,
And give and take bits of my soul.

I wish you all the best indeed,
And hope to one day see you succeed.
But a part of me will always be,
Regretful that you chose to flee.

Amnesia here has been a curse,
But I do not want to allow it to get worse.
To gain control is all that I ask,
And finally I am ready for the task.

I set the pen down, staring at the words that filled the page. I wasn't sure if they made sense, or if they were even true. But there they were. I hoped that maybe they could offer me something to hold onto when everything else felt so far away.

Later that afternoon, as I was wheeled to Dr. Donnelly's office, the weight of the journal entry still lingered in my mind. The therapy sessions had been challenging, but this felt different. There was something raw, something I wasn't quite ready to face, yet it was already spilling onto the page.

When I arrived in Dr. Donnelly's office, the air felt heavier than usual. The sterile scent of the hospital lingered in the room, mixing with the quiet hum of the overhead lights. Dr. Donnelly sat across from me, her eyes soft but sharp, always watching, always ready to listen. I handed her my journal, my fingers trembling slightly as I passed it to her. She took it without a word, flipping open to the latest entry I had written.

The silence stretched between us as she read, her eyes scanning the lines. I sat there, trying not to squirm in my wheelchair, feeling exposed in a way I hadn't anticipated. The weight of my words was hanging in the air between us, and I wasn't sure if I was ready to confront them again – let alone through her gaze.

Finally, she looked up, setting the journal on the table between us. "This is a powerful entry, Lily," she said softly. "You're acknowledging not just the gaps in your memory, but the fear that surrounds them. The struggle of not knowing – of having pieces missing from your past – it's weighing on you."

I swallowed hard, feeling the tightness in my throat. "I just… I don't know how to fit all the pieces together. I can't remember the days leading up to everything. It's like I'm missing something important, but I can't even tell what it is."

Dr. Donnelly nodded, her expression understanding but serious. "That's common in trauma. Your mind is protecting itself by blocking those memories, and that's okay for now. It's a form of survival. But those memories, Lily – they haven't disappeared. They're still a part of you. They're what we call *rememory*."

"Rememory?" I echoed, the unfamiliar term hanging in the air.

"Yes," she continued, leaning forward slightly. "Rememory is the idea that memories, especially traumatic ones, don't simply vanish. They exist, but sometimes they're hidden away, not fully accessible until your mind is ready to process them. It's not about forcing them to come back; it's about understanding that, in time, they might surface naturally, and when they do, we'll work through them together."

I stared at my hands, the weight of her words settling over me. "I don't know if I *want* them to come back. What if remembering makes everything worse?"

Her voice was calm but unwavering. "That's a valid fear, Lily. But healing isn't about rushing to uncover everything all at once. It's about learning to live with the uncertainty, with the gaps, and knowing that you're not defined by those missing pieces. You're more than what you remember."

I felt a tear escape and trail down my cheek, and I wiped it away quickly. "I just… I don't want to feel like I'm broken. Like there's this part of me that's missing, and I'll never be whole again."

"You're not broken," Dr. Donnelly said, her voice strong. "You're healing. And healing doesn't mean returning to who you were before the trauma. It means growing around it. Learning to carry it with you in a way that makes you stronger, not weaker."

The words hung in the air, but they felt distant. I wasn't sure if I believed them yet. The amnesia – the holes in my memory – they weren't just blank spaces; they were walls I couldn't see past, and the idea of unlocking them terrified me.

Dr. Donnelly continued, "You've gone through so much – your father's and brother's deaths, the loss of relationships, and now the aftermath of this attempt. Your mind has compartmentalized those traumas, shielding you from the full weight of them. That's not weakness, it's survival. But as we keep working together, those memories may start to emerge."

I looked at her, feeling small under the weight of all the things I hadn't allowed myself to process. "And if they do? If they start coming back?"

"We'll face them together," she said. "One step at a time. You don't have to carry them alone."

I nodded slowly, my gaze falling to the journal between us. The entry I had written felt like a lifeline – something solid in the midst of all this uncertainty. "I don't even know what's real sometimes. It's like the past is this dark cloud that I can't see through. It's blurry, and the more I try to focus on it, the more it slips away."

"That's part of the process," Dr. Donnelly said. "Your mind is trying to protect you from things that are too painful to remember all at once. But in time, Lily, you'll be able to revisit those memories. And you'll find that you're stronger than you think."

I nodded, trying to take in her words, though the idea of facing my past still terrified me. But somewhere deep inside, there was a glimmer of hope. Maybe I didn't have to be defined by the things I couldn't remember. Maybe I could find a way to move forward, even if the past remained blurry for now.

Dr. Donnelly looked at me across the table, her hands resting gently on her lap. "I know this is overwhelming, Lily," she said softly, leaning forward a little, "but I think you're beginning to open the door to a part of yourself you've kept closed off for a long time. These memories – what we call rememory – they don't just go away because we want them to. They linger, reshape themselves, and sometimes even hide. The work we're doing is going to help you bring them to the surface, to face them, and ultimately, to heal."

The word "rememory" echoed in my mind. It felt foreign, yet so painfully familiar. Dr. Donnelly had explained before those memories – especially traumatic ones – could warp over time, hiding behind emotions or even other memories, making them difficult to process. But the idea of rememory, that these pieces of my past had always been there, buried deep within me, waiting to resurface, felt suffocating.

She continued, her voice steady and calm. "Sometimes, the mind protects us by locking away the things it thinks we can't handle. But the problem with that is, they're still there. They affect us, they shape us, whether we remember them clearly or not. And when these memories start to resurface – when we begin the process of rememory – it can feel like you're walking through a fog, unsure of what's real and what isn't."

I nodded slowly, trying to make sense of everything. Dr. Donnelly always had a way of explaining things so clearly, yet it still felt like I was drowning in confusion. The idea that my mind had been working against me this whole time, hiding away the truth of what happened, made me feel powerless.

"That fog you're feeling?" she said, her eyes never leaving mine. "That's what we're going to work through. We'll take it slowly, piece by piece, and when you're ready, those memories will become clearer. But it won't happen overnight. This is a process. You'll get there, Lily. I promise."

There was a heaviness in her words, but there was also hope. I could feel it, faint but present. For the first time, the idea of facing these memories didn't seem like an insurmountable task. It felt possible.

"Tell me about your thoughts leading up to that day," Dr. Donnelly gently prompted, bringing me back to the moment. "What do you remember feeling?"

I thought back to those hazy days before everything went dark. The memories were disjointed, like pieces of a puzzle that didn't quite fit together.

"I remember feeling... numb," I said slowly, my voice barely above a whisper. "I was just so tired. Of everything. Of feeling too much and then not feeling anything at all. It was like I was walking through life, but nothing really mattered anymore. And I didn't know how to make it stop."

Dr. Donnelly nodded, encouraging me to continue.

"I don't remember every detail. It's all so blurry," I admitted, my fingers gripping the armrests of the wheelchair as if trying to hold onto something tangible. "But I do remember the emptiness. That hollow feeling inside of me, like I was sinking and couldn't find a way out. It felt like everything was spinning out of control."

Dr. Donnelly sat quietly, giving me space to find my words.

"And then... then there was nothing. I don't remember making the decision. I don't remember what I was thinking when I did it. I just... I wasn't there."

She let a few moments of silence pass before speaking again. "Lily, it's common for the mind to blur out those moments, to shield you from the intensity of the pain you were feeling. But as we move forward, we'll work together to help you reclaim those memories – not to relive them, but to understand them, so they can lose their hold over you."

Her words felt like a lifeline. The idea of reclaiming the memories, of taking back control, gave me a sense of purpose I hadn't felt in a long time.

Dr. Donnelly paused, glancing at my journal before meeting my gaze again. "Lily, I want you to keep writing, especially after our sessions. Use the journal to explore the thoughts and feelings that come up. Sometimes, you'll find the words come easier when you're not saying them aloud. And if you ever feel overwhelmed, we can work through what you've written together."

I nodded, feeling a small flicker of determination ignite within me. Writing had always been my refuge, and maybe – just maybe – it could help guide me through this storm.

As Dr. Donnelly stood up and walked toward the door, she gave me a reassuring smile. "This is going to take time, but we'll face it together. I'm proud of you for opening up today."

I watched her leave, the door softly clicking shut behind her. The room felt quiet again, but this time, the silence didn't feel so heavy.

I glanced down at my journal, my fingers tracing the edges of the pages. There was so much more to unpack, so much more to uncover. But for now, I would take it one step at a time. One memory at a time.

I stared out of the window, watching the clouds drift lazily across the sky. The sun was beginning to set, casting a golden hue over the horizon. It wasn't much, but in this small moment, it was enough.

The light from the setting sun filtered through the window, casting long shadows across the room. I could hear the faint hum of the hospital outside, but for now, it felt like the world had slowed down, giving me space to breathe. I rolled the wheels of my chair back a bit, gazing out at the orange and pink hues blending into the sky.

There was still so much I didn't understand – so much that remained tangled in the fog of my mind. But Dr. Donnelly's words replayed in my head, offering a small sliver of clarity: *rememory*. The notion that all the pieces were there, waiting to resurface. It was a frightening thought, knowing that everything I had tried to bury would eventually come back. But somehow, today had felt like a start.

The wheelchair creaked as I shifted, glancing down at the journal still resting in my lap. My fingers moved to open it, but I hesitated. For the first time since I had started writing again, I wasn't sure what to say. The words were stuck, swirling inside me, but not ready to come out just yet.

And maybe that was okay.

I wasn't going to solve everything today. I wasn't going to unlock every memory, heal every wound. But I had made it through another session, another day of confronting the parts of myself I'd tried so hard to hide. That felt like progress, even if it was small.

Chapter 25

Intoxication Blues

The morning began like most mornings had since I arrived at the hospital: gray, quiet, with the sound of muffled voices and beeping machines echoing down the sterile corridors. But inside my mind, there was no such calm.

I glanced toward the window, watching raindrops roll down the glass. Each droplet seemed to race the other, a small competition in an otherwise monotonous world. I wondered if they felt the same pull that I did, the inevitable drag downward.

Today felt heavier than usual. My thoughts had been spiraling since the session with Dr. Donnelly, where we'd begun to scratch the surface of my past. But there was one part of my life I hadn't mentioned. Something I'd been avoiding for years – my mum and the bottle she used to keep under the kitchen sink.

As I lay in bed, my mind drifted back to those days when the house had been filled with grief. After Logan and my father died, our home turned into a battleground, not just between my mum and me, but between her and her addiction. It felt like the walls had absorbed the sadness, the lingering smell of alcohol mixing with the scent of her old perfume. There was a time when I couldn't walk into the kitchen without finding her sitting at the table with a half-empty bottle of Jack, her eyes bloodshot and distant.

I never asked her why she drank, never needed to. I knew why. I knew how grief could destroy a person, how it could seep into your bones and make you want to forget the world. But what I didn't know was how to live with the fallout.

In those days, I learned to hate the sound of ice clinking in a glass. It became the soundtrack of my life, a constant reminder that my mum wasn't really there. She was drowning in her own sorrow, and I was left to figure out how to survive in the wreckage.

With a sigh, I threw off the covers and sat up in bed, the cold floor stinging my feet as they hit the ground. My mind still felt tangled in the past, and I knew that today's therapy session would be harder than the ones before. I would have to confront things I'd buried, things I hadn't wanted to admit to anyone, least of all myself.

A nurse arrived shortly after breakfast to wheel me down to Dr. Donnelly's office. I still hadn't regained full strength, so the wheelchair was a necessity, another frustrating reminder that I was far from the person I used to be.

As I was pushed down the hallway, the fluorescent lights above flickering with a dull hum, I felt the familiar knot of anxiety tighten in my chest. What was I even going to say today? How could I begin to explain what it was like to watch the strongest person in my life fall apart, only to turn into someone I didn't recognize?

The therapy room was quiet when I entered, with Dr. Donnelly sitting in her usual spot, her calm eyes studying me as I wheeled in. I had already decided that I wouldn't write anything before today's session. It felt too forced, too manufactured. I needed to speak from the rawness inside me, even if I wasn't sure where to start.

"Good morning, Lily," Dr. Donnelly greeted me as I was settled into my usual spot. "How are you feeling about today?"

I shrugged, unsure how to answer. "I don't really know."

"That's okay," she said gently, folding her hands in her lap. "We don't need to know everything right away. Why don't we just start by talking? How's your week been?"

I thought about my week – the way my mind had been drifting between memories and the present, how hard it had been to stay grounded. "It was... a lot," I admitted. "I've been thinking about my mum. And how things used to be after my dad and Logan died."

Dr. Donnelly's eyes softened, but she didn't push. She just nodded, letting me continue at my own pace.

"She drank a lot back then," I said, my voice barely above a whisper. "It was like... she wasn't my mum anymore. She was someone else. Someone I didn't know how to reach."

Dr. Donnelly leaned forward slightly. "That must have been really difficult for you, especially when you were dealing with your own grief."

I nodded. "It was. But I also get it, you know? I understand why she did it. She was trying to escape."

"And how did that affect you?" she asked, her tone gentle, encouraging.

I swallowed, feeling the weight of the question. "I... I hated her for it. But I also loved her. And I didn't know how to handle both of those feelings at the same time. I was angry that she wasn't there for me when I needed her. But I also knew she was hurting too."

We sat in silence for a moment, the weight of my words hanging in the air between us.

"I think..." I began, my voice faltering, "I think I'm afraid of becoming like her. I'm afraid that I'm going to end up the same way."

Dr. Donnelly nodded slowly. "It's understandable to feel that way, especially with everything you've been through. But it's important to remember that you are not your mum. Your journey is your own."

I stared down at my hands, my fingers picking at the edge of the blanket on my lap. "She stopped drinking after a while. But the damage was already done. And I still don't know how to... deal with that."

"It sounds like there's a lot of unresolved pain there," Dr. Donnelly said softly. "Have you ever spoken to her about it?"

I shook my head. "No. I don't think I could."

Dr. Donnelly was quiet for a moment, then she spoke again. "Lily, you've carried so much for so long. And it's okay to feel conflicted. It's okay to love someone and be angry with them at the same time."

I nodded, but the knot in my chest didn't loosen.

We spent the rest of the session delving deeper into the tangled web of my emotions, those conflicting threads of guilt, resentment, and love that had been knotted together for years. It wasn't easy, and every word I spoke felt like it was dragging out something I'd buried so deep I wasn't sure I even wanted to find it again.

"I feel guilty," I admitted, my voice barely above a whisper. "For being angry at her when she was grieving, too. But at the same time, I was angry because... because I needed her to be strong for me. And she wasn't."

Dr. Donnelly's eyes were steady and compassionate, giving me the space to speak, to feel. "It's okay to feel both of those things at once, Lily. You were also grieving, and it's natural to want support from someone who wasn't in a place to give it."

I hesitated. "But... shouldn't I have been more understanding? I mean, I was young, but I knew she was hurting. Shouldn't I have done something?"

She shook her head gently. "You were a child, trying to survive your own pain. It wasn't your responsibility to take on hers."

I stared at my hands, feeling the weight of the truth settle over me. It wasn't just that I had felt abandoned by her during those years – it was that I had tried so hard to pick up the pieces for both of us. And I had failed. I couldn't be what she needed any more than she could be what I needed.

Dr. Donnelly spoke again, softly. "What do you remember feeling the most during those times?"

"Alone," I replied immediately, the word escaping before I had a chance to process it. "I felt so alone. I mean, Logan was gone, my dad was gone, and then it felt like she was gone, too. I didn't know what to do with all of that."

She nodded. "That's a lot for anyone to carry, especially at such a young age. Do you think you've been carrying those feelings ever since?"

I nodded slowly, the realization sinking in like a stone. "Yeah… I think I have."

The room fell quiet for a moment, the only sound the distant hum of the hospital machinery outside. Dr. Donnelly gave me a moment to process, but I could feel the next question brewing before she even asked it.

"And what about now?" she asked gently. "Do you still feel that way? Alone?"

I hesitated, feeling the familiar sting behind my eyes as tears threatened to break free. "I don't know," I whispered. "Sometimes, I guess. I mean, I have Leo, and I know my mum loves me, but… it's hard to let people in. I'm always waiting for them to leave."

"And why do you think that is?" Dr. Donnelly pressed, her voice never losing its calm, never pushing too hard, but always urging me to dig just a little deeper.

"Because they always do," I said, the words slipping out before I could stop them. "Everyone leaves. And I can't… I can't go through that again."

Dr. Donnelly didn't say anything right away. She just let the silence settle between us, letting me sit with the weight of my own admission. When she finally spoke, it was in that same steady, understanding tone.

"Lily, you've been through more loss than most people experience in a lifetime. It makes sense that you would be afraid of it happening again. But the fear of being abandoned can sometimes make us close ourselves off, even from the people who want to be there for us. Do you think that's what's been happening with Leo?"

I blinked, the mention of his name stirring something inside me. "I don't know. Maybe. I mean, he's been my best friend for as long as I can remember, but lately… I don't know what's happening between us. It's like things are changing, and I don't know if that's good or bad."

"Change can be uncomfortable," Dr. Donnelly said, leaning forward slightly. "But it doesn't always mean something bad. Sometimes, it's just part of growing."

I nodded, though the knot in my chest hadn't loosened. There was so much swirling in my head, so many emotions I didn't know how to name. "I just… I don't want to lose him," I admitted quietly. "He's the only one who's never left."

Dr. Donnelly's eyes softened. "Have you told him that?"

"No," I admitted, my voice catching. "I don't know how to."

"You don't have to have all the answers right now," she reassured me. "But maybe that's something you can explore when you're ready."

The conversation shifted after that, touching on other wounds that had been left open for far too long… Logan's death, my father, and even the relationship trauma I had carried from Ava. Each memory was like peeling back another layer, exposing things I hadn't realized were still raw.

By the end of the session, I felt like I had been torn open and stitched back together all at once. There was no neat resolution, no sudden sense of peace. But there was something else. Something like hope.

As I wheeled back toward my room, I felt the weight of everything we had uncovered in the session, a mix of exhaustion and relief pulling at my chest. The hallway felt longer than usual, the distant hum of the hospital buzzing around me, but inside, I was quieter, more reflective.

Back in my room, I sat by the window, watching the world outside. The day had grown darker, the sun swallowed up by the heavy clouds that loomed overhead. The rain was still falling, soft and steady, but it felt less oppressive now. More like a quiet reminder that even in the storm, there was a chance to breathe.

I reached for my journal, knowing I needed to capture the whirlwind inside before it slipped away into the background noise of my mind.

With the journal in my hands, I took a deep breath, feeling the familiar weight of it grounding me. There was still so much left to figure out, so much I didn't know how to solve. But I knew one thing for sure: I needed to get these thoughts out of my head, to put them somewhere where they could stop swirling and start making sense. Somehow, writing it all down always made the chaos feel a little less overwhelming.

I opened the journal, the blank page staring back at me, waiting. And for the first time today, I let the words flow freely.

July 14, 2018

The whirlwind above eats at the thoughts below,
All around there are some frightening whispers;
You turn the corner to see a beam of light,
That half empty bottle that has begun to glow.

Each sip contains an elixir of hope and fear,
A way for you to forget about life's current slate;
But this trance only lasts a few hours longer,
Suddenly you must address your mental state.

You look at the bottle that lies on the floor,
And look in the mirror with a tear in your eye;
In that moment you remember what you sought to forget,
That hope that someday you escape from this debt.

Above the cabinet in the corner where that picture hangs,
Stands a bottle of jack nesting in bed;
You reach for the bottle and pour yourself a shot,
As you lose yourself to the intoxication blues.

Chapter 26
It's You

The soft morning light filtered into the room, stretching across the white hospital linens like an invitation to wake up and face the day. But as I lay there, staring at the slow-moving clouds outside my window, I couldn't shake the weight pressing down on my chest. Each day felt like a quiet battle, one I wasn't sure I had the energy to fight anymore.

I'd been going through the motions – sessions with Dr. Donnelly, attempts to open up, to heal – but the progress felt invisible, like trying to see your reflection in a fogged-up mirror. The more I tried to clear it, the more smudged and distorted everything seemed.

My thoughts drifted to Ava, as they often did. No matter how hard I tried to pull away, she was still there, hovering in the back of my mind like a storm cloud I couldn't outrun. I hated that she still had this kind of power over me. Even after everything, I couldn't shake the memory of her; the way her eyes used to light up when she laughed, the sound of her voice when she whispered my name. It was ridiculous, really. Ava had hurt me, shattered me, and yet here I was, still tethered to her in ways that made no sense.

Unfortunately for me, it was her. Unfortunately for me, it always had been.

The emotional pull I felt toward her was irrational, I knew that. And yet, every time I tried to sever the connection, I found myself tangled back in it. The longing, the memories, the what-ifs – they were all part of a past I couldn't seem to let go of.

I closed my eyes and tried to breathe through it, the ache in my chest dull but constant. As the seconds stretched into minutes, my thoughts began to shift. They drifted away from Ava and toward someone else – someone who, over the past few weeks, had been a steady presence, even when I didn't deserve it. Leo.

Leo had been there from the beginning, quietly supporting me through everything. He wasn't the chaos that Ava had been; he was something else – something calm and grounding. When I thought about him, it wasn't with the same kind of fire that Ava ignited, but with a warmth that made me feel like maybe, just maybe, everything could be okay again.

I wasn't ready to think too deeply about what that meant, not yet. But the idea that my feelings for Leo could be something more than just friendship lingered in the back of my mind, like a whisper I wasn't quite ready to hear.

I sighed and glanced at the clock, realizing it was almost time for my therapy session with Dr. Donnelly. Today, I wasn't going to write anything in my journal ahead of time. I wanted to go into the session with an open mind, to talk about whatever came up, without the pressure of having pre-planned my thoughts. Maybe that would help me sort through this mess.

Dr. Donnelly's office felt suffocating today, the usual calmness replaced by the weight of everything unsaid. The ticking of the wall clock seemed louder, more persistent, like each second was reminding me of how much time had passed since Ava had been a part of my life. How long had it been now? Weeks? Months? Yet, she was still with me in every unguarded thought.

"Tell me what's been on your mind this week," Dr. Donnelly said, her eyes meeting mine with that soft, unrelenting patience she always had.

I didn't answer immediately. Instead, I stared out the window behind her, watching the trees sway in the late afternoon breeze, feeling the pressure of unspoken words build inside me. Finally, I let them out.

"Ava," I whispered, my voice barely audible.

Dr. Donnelly nodded, not surprised. "It's been a recurring theme for you."

"It's like she's everywhere," I admitted, my voice gaining a little more strength. "In every song, every memory, every… everything. I don't know how to let go. I want to, but I can't stop thinking about her. It's like I'm stuck in this loop."

Her expression softened. "Grief isn't just about losing someone to death, Lily. It's about the end of relationships, too – the end of love. What you're feeling is natural, but what I want you to understand is that moving on doesn't mean erasing her from your life. It doesn't mean pretending the relationship didn't happen."

"I know," I murmured. "I know it shouldn't be that simple. But I don't know where to start. It still feels like… like she's a part of me. Like letting go of her means losing part of myself."

Dr. Donnelly leaned forward slightly, her hands resting calmly on her knees. "You shared a deep connection with her, and it's understandable to feel like part of you is tied to that. But what if letting go isn't about losing part of yourself? What if it's about reclaiming the parts of yourself that have been overshadowed by that relationship?"

'Reclaiming myself?'

I hadn't thought of it that way. I had been so focused on what I had lost, so obsessed with the pain of not having Ava, that I had forgotten who I was outside of her. I had forgotten what it felt like to live for myself, to breathe without the weight of her name pressing against my chest.

"What do you think moving on looks like?" Dr. Donnelly asked, her voice bringing me back to the room.

I shrugged, feeling a strange hollowness in my chest. "I don't even know what that means. How do you just let someone go when they've been your whole world?"

"You don't let go all at once," she replied gently. "It's a process, and it's a slow one. But maybe it starts with accepting that Ava isn't your whole world anymore. She was part of your story, but she doesn't have to be the defining chapter. Moving on is about making space for yourself again, for new experiences, new relationships. It's not about forgetting her. It's about finding balance."

Her words echoed in my mind, a slow reverberation that felt like a wave crashing against a wall I had built so high around myself. Balance. I hadn't felt balanced in so long. Everything in my life had been consumed by the shadows of Ava, by the pieces of her that still lingered in every corner of my mind.

"But how do I start?" I asked, my voice cracking slightly as the vulnerability crept in. "How do I even begin to move on when it still hurts this much?"

Dr. Donnelly's eyes softened, and she leaned back, as if giving me space to breathe. "Start with small steps. Acknowledge that the pain is still there. Let yourself feel it. But also give yourself permission to focus on the future – your future. What does Lily's life look like without Ava? What does it mean to live fully for yourself again?"

Her question lingered in the air, almost suffocating in its simplicity. What did my life look like without Ava? I hadn't even dared to ask myself that. The thought scared me – terrified me, really. It felt like a leap into a void I wasn't ready to face. But maybe that was the point. Maybe that leap was the only way to find out what was waiting for me on the other side.

"I don't know," I whispered, swallowing hard as the weight of that uncertainty pressed down on me. "But I think… I think I want to try."

Dr. Donnelly smiled a warm, reassuring smile that made me feel like maybe – just maybe – I could survive this. "You don't have to have all the answers right now, Lily. But this is a start. You've already taken the first step just by being here, by talking about it. We'll work through it together."

There was a moment of silence, the kind that stretched on just long enough to make me realize how far I had come in this session. I had started with so much pain, so much confusion, and now… there was still pain, but there was also a glimmer of something else. Hope. A small, fragile hope that maybe I could get through this. Maybe I could let go of Ava without letting go of myself.

"I want to move on," I finally said, more to myself than to Dr. Donnelly. "I don't want to keep hurting like this."

She nodded, her voice soft. "Then we'll work on that together. And remember, it's okay to still care about Ava. It's okay to feel everything you're feeling. But let's focus on finding a way forward, one step at a time."

I closed my eyes for a moment, taking in her words, letting them settle deep within me. There was so much work ahead – so much pain to process, so many memories to untangle. But maybe, just maybe, I could start to reclaim the pieces of myself that had been lost along the way.

As I was wheeled back to my room, I glanced out the small window in the hallway. A single ray of sunlight broke through the clouds, casting a patch of warmth over the hospital garden below. There was something oddly comforting about it – a reminder that even in the midst of all this chaos, there was still light to be found. Maybe that was all I needed to hold on to for now.

Back in my room, I pulled out my journal, my thoughts swirling as I tried to make sense of everything. The words came slowly at first, then faster, until they poured out onto the page.

July 16, 2018

Unfortunately for me,
It's you.
Unfortunately for me,
It will always be you.

Just as I closed the journal, the door creaked open, and there he was – Leo, standing in the doorway with a wide grin on his face and a bag full of snacks in his hand.

"I brought reinforcements," he said, his voice warm and teasing.

I blinked in surprise, feeling my heart do a strange little flip in my chest. "Leo," I whispered, the sound of his name soft on my lips.

He walked in like he owned the place, dropping the bag onto the bed and flopping into the chair beside me. "You looked like you could use some cheering up," he said, already rummaging through the snacks. He pulled out a candy bar and waved it in front of my face. "Come on, you know you want it."

I couldn't help but laugh, the tension easing from my body. Leo always had a way of making everything seem lighter, even when I felt like I was carrying the weight of the world. His presence was like a balm to my soul, and for the first time all day, I felt like maybe things would be okay.

"You always know how to show up at the right time," I said, smiling softly at him.

He grinned. "It's a gift."

We spent the next hour talking about nothing and everything, the conversation flowing easily between us. Leo had that way about him: he could turn even the darkest moments into something bearable. For the first time in weeks, I found myself laughing. And it wasn't forced. It was real.

At one point, he said something so ridiculous that I burst out laughing, a deep, genuine laugh that made my stomach hurt. And in that moment, I realized how much I had missed this – missed him.

But then, as the laughter faded, I felt something else settle over me. It was warm, and it wasn't just from the laughter. It was from Leo. The way he looked at me, the way his presence filled the room with light.

And that scared me.

I caught his gaze, and for a brief second, something passed between us. Something unspoken, something more than just friendship. My heart sped up, confusion swirling in my mind. Was this just the comfort of a friend, or was there more? And did I even want to know the answer?

Leo smiled at me, oblivious to the storm brewing in my chest. "You okay?" he asked, his voice soft.

I nodded, though I wasn't sure I believed it. "Yeah. I'm okay."

But even as I said the words, I knew that things were shifting. I wasn't ready to face it yet, but it was there, simmering beneath the surface, waiting to come to light.

As Leo started packing up the snacks, he caught my eye again, and this time, I couldn't look away. There was something there, something real and raw and terrifying.

I wasn't ready for this. Not yet. But maybe someday, I would be.

Chapter 27

Second Love

The air in the therapy room felt thick today, dense with anticipation that clung to me as I sat on the bench. Sunlight filtered through the high windows, casting pale squares on the smooth linoleum floor. It was the kind of light that didn't quite warm you, but reminded you of life beyond these walls, of moments waiting to be touched. Today, that quiet room with its muted tones and sturdy equipment felt different, somehow more intimate – like it held its breath along with me.

My hands rested on my lap, trembling just slightly, as I absorbed every detail around me: the worn handles on the equipment, the encouraging posters tacked on the walls, the faint scent of antiseptic mixing with sweat. Today, each step toward the parallel bars felt like more than a physical movement; it was like reaching for a new beginning. My physical therapist, a young woman with warm, steady eyes, hovered close but gave me space, her smile holding the promise that today could be different.

Taking a deep breath, I placed my hands on the cold metal bar, steadying myself. The air held a quiet tension, and every muscle in my legs felt taut, like a coiled spring just waiting to be released. For a moment, a flood of memories washed over me – of days when walking was second nature, and when the effort of a single step wasn't enough to set my heart racing. I felt the weight of each step that had brought me here, the pain, the falls, the recovery. It was all part of this one, simple goal.

My fingers gripped the bar tighter, and I could feel the cool metal bite into my skin, grounding me, keeping me from floating away under the weight of my own anticipation. How many times had I sat here, staring at these bars, afraid to take that first step? Today, though, was different. Today, there was no excuse left, no reason to hide behind caution. I could feel the fragility of my strength and the weight of my own expectations colliding, swirling within me in a tense balance.

As I inhaled slowly, a strange blend of emotions filled my chest – determination laced with fear, excitement woven with doubt. A thousand memories flickered through my mind: the feel of grass under my bare feet as a child, the solid ground I'd once taken for granted, the carefree days when movement was effortless. But those moments felt distant, like they belonged to someone else entirely, someone who had not known loss or struggle. I had once walked through life without a second thought, taking each step without hesitation. Now, each movement felt precious, deliberate, almost sacred.

I wanted this. I wanted to reclaim that part of myself that I'd lost somewhere between grief and survival. But beneath that desire lurked a familiar fear – what if I couldn't do it? What if I faltered, right here on the cusp of something I had yearned for so desperately? Or worse, what if I succeeded and nothing changed? I could feel the walls of self-doubt pressing in, questioning whether I was truly ready, whether I was worthy of this next step forward.

I squeezed my eyes shut, pushing away the noise. The fear, the doubt, the memories – they would have to wait. Right now, there was only this moment, only the feel of my body, my muscles quivering in anticipation. A part of me wondered if this was how it felt to come alive again, to shed the weight of all the "what ifs" and simply exist in the now.

I opened my eyes and looked ahead, focusing on a spot across the room. My destination. A place that, on any other day, might have seemed unremarkable, but today, it held everything I'd been fighting for. Taking a deep breath, I released my grip on the bar slightly, loosening my hold, preparing myself to let go.

With a final breath, I let my hands hover above the bar, fingers twitching, bracing for what came next. My muscles felt tense, alive, each one on edge, and I could feel the small, nervous tremor in my legs. I glanced down, watching as my right foot inched forward, as if it, too, was unsure of the path ahead. The sole of my foot met the ground with a hesitant pressure, testing its steadiness, as if the earth beneath me might slip away.

My weight shifted, tentative, and I felt my left leg begin to respond. This small movement, this almost forgotten instinct to move, to reach forward, was something I once did without thinking, and yet now, I was conscious of every sensation – muscle, balance, and determination, each one holding me upright, steadying me. I gritted my teeth and whispered a quiet encouragement to myself, barely audible over the pounding of my heartbeat.

As I took another step, a slight quiver ran through my legs, but I refused to let that stop me. The ground felt solid, more solid than it had in a long time, and in that brief, miraculous moment, I was moving forward – not out of necessity or pressure, but simply because I could. It was a step, my step, forward.

The room was silent, save for my own labored breaths, and as I lifted my gaze, I saw Dr. Byrne standing nearby, his eyes watching me closely, a subtle, encouraging nod echoing his belief in me. For the first time, I dared to believe I could do this. I was walking.

One step turned into two, the second followed by a third, each one feeling like a defiance against everything that had tried to hold me back. But as I reached the end of my strength, my legs began to tremble under me, and I felt my balance waver. Before I could catch myself, I crumpled, sinking back down, but not with defeat… with a breathless, aching pride.

Lifting my head, I found Dr. Byrne's gaze stuck upon me, and I couldn't help the small, weary smile that crept onto my face. I had taken those steps. They were mine.

As I sat back after those first few steps, my mind drifted into a memory of Ava, one that felt too vivid to ignore. I could almost feel her hand in mine, steadying me, her laugh breaking the silence. She'd always had that way of making me feel invincible – like I didn't need to walk alone because she'd always be there, right beside me.

In this memory, we were walking through the gardens behind her house on a late spring afternoon, flowers blooming on either side of the path. I remember how the sun caught in her hair, lighting up those moments where she'd look back at me and smile. It was a time I thought I'd never have to let go of, where everything felt whole, like I could take on anything with her there.

But now, as the memory faded, I was left feeling that same bittersweet ache, a realization settling into my heart like a weight. Back then, I had relied on her to steady me emotionally, the way I now relied on physical therapy to help me stand again. And yet, I was moving on from that dependence with every step, leaving pieces of that old life behind. Maybe that was okay – maybe it was what I needed. But the thought of it, of leaving her behind, was harder than I wanted to admit.

As I made my way down the hall to Dr. Donnelly's office, each step brought a jolt of ache to my muscles – a reminder of how far I'd come, and how much further I still had to go. I settled into the chair across from her, feeling the weight of all that I carried, and for a brief moment, I wondered if she could see it too.

She welcomed me with her usual warmth, but there was an unspoken curiosity in her eyes.

"I heard about your progress in PT," she began with a gentle nod of approval. "That's a huge step, literally and figuratively."

A hesitant smile surfaced, and I shifted my gaze down, tracing patterns on my hands. "Yeah, I guess it is."

"What's going on in that head of yours?" she asked, leaning in slightly, her tone inviting me to spill the mess that had knotted itself in my thoughts.

I hesitated, the words swirling but refusing to form. Finally, I managed, "It just... didn't feel the way I thought it would. I thought taking those steps would feel like conquering something, like freedom. But instead, it feels... lonely. Like every step forward takes me further away from what I knew – from the people and moments that kept me grounded. Especially Ava."

Dr. Donnelly's eyes softened, a quiet understanding reflecting back at me. "That feeling of distance is so real, Lily. Moving forward often brings up a mix of emotions we may not expect. Every step away from the past can feel like a loss."

"Yeah." My voice barely rose above a whisper. "It's like... letting go of her feels like letting go of myself. I feel guilty for even thinking of it."

She leaned forward, her gaze never wavering. "Grief often binds us to the ones we lose, but sometimes it binds us in a way that makes forward motion seem like betrayal. What you're feeling isn't just about Ava; it's about the you that existed when she was by your side. You're learning who you are without her presence, and that change can feel uncomfortable, even painful."

My breath hitched as I absorbed her words, each one landing heavily. The pain had become familiar, a constant companion in the chaos. The thought of letting go – of allowing even the smallest sliver of peace – felt like abandoning her.

"I'm scared I'll lose the part of me that loved her," I admitted, surprising myself with the rawness. "That felt... alive with her. If I let go, I'm afraid I'll forget her."

Dr. Donnelly nodded slowly, her expression unwavering. "That's a very human fear, Lily. Sometimes, we think moving on means erasing the past, but it doesn't. Moving on can be about carrying the parts of those we've loved with us, even if they evolve into something new."

Her words resonated deeply, peeling back a layer of the fog I had been living in. "How do I carry her forward without letting her control where I go?"

"It's a balance that takes time and reflection," she replied. "Maybe start by acknowledging that she's part of who you are – one chapter in your life that helped shape you. But chapters end, and that doesn't mean their impact does. Honoring her memory doesn't mean staying stagnant in it."

I nodded, feeling the knot inside me loosen just a bit. Perhaps Ava's memory could live with me in a way that felt more like presence than pain, like a gentle reminder of the love I once knew, rather than the constant ache I carried.

"And, Lily," she continued, "as you learn to carry her memory in a healthy way, you'll start to realize that there's room for more love, more connections, more moments. It's not about replacing her, but allowing your heart to open, even if that love feels different."

"Different…" I echoed, glancing down at my hands as I twisted my fingers together. "It's hard to imagine that right now. I feel like I'll always carry this weight."

"That's okay, too," she said gently. "Healing isn't about losing the weight entirely but learning how to carry it. You've already shown such resilience, Lily, and that strength will only grow."

For the first time, her words felt like a balm, soothing places that had been raw for so long. I could move forward, not by forgetting Ava, but by learning to carry her in a way that allowed me to keep living.

With Dr. Donnelly's words still echoing in my mind, I returned to my room. The hallway felt quieter than usual, a stillness settling around me that softened the edges of everything. The weight on my heart had eased, even if only a little, replaced by a glimmer of something I hadn't felt in a long time: hope.

Once back in the quiet of my room, I took a moment to sit by the window, watching as the sun dipped lower, casting long shadows across the hospital courtyard. Memories of today's session flickered through my thoughts, each one anchoring me to something steadier, something I wanted to believe I could hold on to. The soft glow of the fading day felt like a gentle reminder that there were more moments ahead, more chances to reshape everything that had once weighed me down.

With a deep breath, I reached for my journal, letting the familiar weight of it settle into my hands. As I opened it, I felt the pull of my own words waiting to be released, the urge to capture the quiet revelations that had surfaced today. I let the ink bleed onto the page, writing not only for today but for the days when grief would strike again, when I'd need these words as a reminder.

July 21, 2018

This love comes with quite the burden,
With twists and turns that are quite uncertain.
You want to believe this love is better than the last,
But it simply leaves you hurt and fast.

This love can show up in different ways,
And may even fluctuate by the day.
It is laced with pain and guilt and sorrow,
But you will continue holding on until tomorrow.

This love teaches you lessons to use forever,
And pushes you into your future endeavor.
The manipulation of this love will hurt,
But will help you remain on high alert.

This love is a love you wish would work,
And often times leaves you without that smirk.
It tends to be laced with toxicity and insecurity,
But this often comes with immaturity.

This love is a special love you cannot deny,
Even after you both say goodbye.
This love it leads you to your third true love,
One that is symbolized by the pure white dove.

I closed the journal, feeling a mixture of exhaustion and calm as the weight of my own words began to settle within me. Somehow, seeing everything in ink made it real and, strangely, manageable. I traced the edges of the journal cover with my fingertips, feeling the textured surface that had become so familiar – a reminder of the countless nights spent wrestling with thoughts that no one else could see.

A gentle knock on the door pulled me from my thoughts. A nurse peeked in, smiling softly as she brought in my evening tea. I took the warm mug in my hands, grateful for the comforting heat. The room felt peaceful now, as if the act of writing had purged it of shadows.

I sipped the tea slowly, allowing myself a moment of quiet contentment. There was still so much to face, so much to heal, but for tonight, I was okay with that. Tomorrow would come soon enough, and with it, another chance to rebuild.

Chapter 28
Falling

The courtyard felt almost peaceful as I sat on the bench, trying to let the fresh air fill the spaces inside me that had been empty for so long. Around me, the early spring blossoms were just beginning to open, tiny buds against the branches, each one a reminder that something fragile could still survive the cold. I'd missed that feeling – simple, almost easy – like the world hadn't completely changed.

I heard Leo's voice before I saw him, the familiar lilt bringing me a sense of calm even as my pulse quickened. He was grinning, holding a small paper bag in the air like a trophy. "I brought provisions," he announced, settling beside me. "Because, well, obviously, hospital food isn't cutting it." He handed me a packet of crackers, his hand brushing mine just slightly, the touch warm, familiar... and somehow different. It was such a small thing, but I felt it linger, spreading like warmth in the pit of my stomach, leaving me caught somewhere between comfort and a strange, restless feeling.

He tore open his own bag, crunching down on a cracker as we sat there in easy silence, looking out at the garden. But he didn't just look at the garden; he looked at me, studying my face as if trying to memorize every line and curve. I met his eyes, just briefly, but when he saw me looking back, he glanced away, his cheeks coloring ever so slightly. I'd never seen him blush like that. I felt my heart skip, as if it was waking up after a long, cold sleep, as if this – whatever this was – had been there all along, waiting for the right moment to be felt.

I shook off the thought, focusing on the snack wrapper in my hand, trying to act casual, unaffected. We both tried to fill the silence with more pointless chatter, but each time he looked over at me, something in his eyes pulled at me, breaking down walls I hadn't even realized I'd built.

After a while, he grew quiet, holding a cracker between his fingers and staring off at something in the distance. His expression shifted, softened. "You know, it was strange without you around," he began, his voice lower now, almost a whisper. "Like… like something was missing. I kept thinking about all the things I never said. About what I wish I'd told you sooner."

I swallowed, feeling my throat tighten. His words hung there, almost like a confession, and I couldn't bring myself to respond. The meaning beneath his words was there, waiting for me to acknowledge it, but I was frozen, caught between the familiarity of his presence and the sudden, dizzying realization that I might feel more for him than I'd ever dared admit to myself.

He glanced down, a hesitant smile playing on his lips, and for a moment, neither of us moved. His hand rested on the bench between us, close enough to touch if I reached out. Slowly, almost without thinking, I let my fingers drift toward his, grazing his hand. It was a small, almost imperceptible motion, but he noticed. His fingers curled around mine, his thumb brushing the back of my hand, warm and gentle, like he was afraid I might pull away. But I didn't.

We sat there like that, his hand in mine, the connection a silent promise that felt more real than any words we'd shared. When he looked up, I saw something new in his eyes – a softness, an openness I hadn't seen before. His gaze flickered to my lips for the briefest moment, and my heart jolted in response, a spark that felt fragile yet undeniable.

Just as I was about to say something, the moment was broken by the voice of a nurse. "Leo, visiting hours are nearly over." She sounded apologetic, as though she could sense she'd interrupted something important.

Leo's fingers slipped from mine reluctantly, his gaze lingering on me, leaving an ache I hadn't felt in so long. "I'll be back," he said quietly, his voice holding a gentle certainty. "You know where to find me."

I nodded, watching him walk away, trying to steady the swirling emotions that had come rushing to the surface. His touch had left me with a warmth I hadn't expected, a feeling I wanted to hold onto, even as it left me with questions I wasn't ready to face.

I stayed on the bench for a while after he left, my hand resting where his had been, as if the warmth of his touch could linger long enough to fill me up. The air around me felt both lighter and heavier, weighed down by this feeling I didn't know how to navigate, a feeling that had planted itself and was now spreading through me, unfurling in ways I couldn't yet understand.

Eventually, I made my way back inside, the familiar sterile scents and stark walls of the hospital greeting me like an unwelcome reminder. Each step felt like it should have been steady, confident, but instead, I was lost in my thoughts, the memory of Leo's hand in mine looping in my mind like a song I couldn't shake. By the time I reached my room, I felt like I'd been wading through fog.

Settling down on the bed, I pulled out my journal, needing a place to set these emotions down, to somehow organize them into words I could understand. I held my pen poised over the page, waiting for the right words to come, for some kind of clarity. But nothing seemed right; everything I could think of felt like it only scratched the surface. And as much as I wanted to write it all out, I was afraid of what those words might reveal, of what admitting these feelings might mean.

Instead, I wrote the simplest thing I could manage, something true, even if it didn't capture all of it:

I didn't expect him to mean this much to me, but here we are.

The words felt small, barely able to hold the weight of what I felt, but it was something. I closed the journal gently, running my fingers over its worn cover, a quiet reminder of how much this space had come to mean to me. Each entry had been like another step in a long climb, where the path was jagged and rough, but each word somehow found its way. And now, sitting here in the quiet stillness of the hospital room, I let myself fully feel the impact of everything. Leo. His hand in mine. That look he'd given me – the one that had lingered just a second too long, too full of something I hadn't expected to see.

I didn't want to admit it, but that look had left me breathless in a way that felt new, like a spark lit beneath layers of ash. But was I ready for that kind of flame? Or even for the possibility of it? I'd barely managed to hold onto myself, to navigate each day without the world feeling like it was crumbling beneath my feet. And yet… and yet, I couldn't help but wonder. Wonder if it was safe to let someone in, to let someone like Leo, who had been there from the start, who had seen me in my most shattered states, close enough to touch those broken pieces.

With a sigh, I let my head fall back against the pillow, staring up at the ceiling. Shadows moved across the room as the evening light filtered through the blinds. There was something comforting about the quiet, the way the hospital had its own heartbeat, its own rhythm of life moving around me while I was still. I closed my eyes, letting the softness of the silence settle over me, sinking into the comfort of knowing that maybe – just maybe – someone was out there who understood, who wanted to share this journey with me.

But the words I hadn't yet written gnawed at me, pulling me back toward the journal. Reaching for it again, I opened it to a blank page, letting the pen rest against the paper as I gathered the fragments of my thoughts, the feelings too big to keep inside any longer:

July 23, 2018

F
 A
  L
   L
    I
     N
      G

For you today and tomorrow;
From this moment until the end of time —
And I will simply drown myself in sorrow,
As I struggling to even make this rhyme.

F
 A
  L
   L
    I
     N
      G

For you more and more each day;
As I stare from a distance while you drive away —
I think about what you would always say,
Praying that all of this will end up being okay.

F
 A
  L
   L
    I
     N
      G

For you with each living breath;
Longing for laughter and your gentle touch —
Next to you I evaded death,
But without you I'm within his clutch.

Chapter 29
Full Moon

The night was quiet and still, save for the occasional rustle of leaves in the breeze. I wrapped my arms around myself, the chill biting at my skin, grounding me in the moment. The hospital courtyard stretched out in front of me, but it was the sky that drew me in. A full moon hung like a beacon overhead, illuminating the world in soft, silvery light. Everything appeared sharper under its glow, but it was a light that held shadows close by – just like the pieces of myself that lingered in the dark, refusing to fully reveal themselves.

I hadn't stood under a sky like this in what felt like years, though I knew it was only weeks. The moonlight was intoxicating, bathing the world in a beauty so stark it almost hurt. There was something ominous yet oddly comforting in its glow, like it understood the pain I carried and didn't judge it. The silver seemed to reach out, wrapping around the silent trees, turning the world into a mystical landscape that demanded reflection.

It reminded me of how time seemed to stretch and fold here in the hospital. Each day bled into the next, defined only by small, quiet moments – much like tonight. The moon pulled at me, urging me to consider where I was and how far I still had to go. The stars above blinked down like old friends I hadn't seen in a while, bringing with them memories of a life that felt worlds away.

Standing here, I let myself think of the path I'd taken to get to this moment. The highs, the lows, the countless nights staring at the ceiling, wondering if things would ever feel whole again. And yet, here I was, still searching for answers under the same sky that had watched over every sleepless night, every journal entry, every desperate thought.

The cold began to seep in deeper, but I didn't move. The moon seemed to hold something for me tonight – hope, maybe, or just the clarity of knowing I was still here. The reflection of my own scars seemed painted across the night sky, woven into every shadow and every star.

Beneath the full moon, I felt something shift inside me. It was subtle, but undeniable, like the whisper of a memory from a time when I hadn't been burdened by so many fractured pieces. The air was crisp, filling my lungs with a sharp clarity that contrasted with the muddiness of my thoughts. It was strange – how something so vast and distant could stir something so deep within me. The moonlight spilled across the courtyard, illuminating patches of frost that clung to the grass like glistening fragments, mirroring the shards of myself that felt so scattered.

I walked slowly across the courtyard, my footsteps echoing faintly in the stillness. Each step seemed to carry weight, grounding me but also reminding me of how fragile everything still felt. I glanced up at the branches of an ancient tree standing tall in the corner, its limbs stretched out like fingers reaching for the sky. In the darkness, it seemed both alive and somber, its roots buried deep, yet its branches free to sway with the wind. I wondered if I'd ever feel that balanced; rooted, yet able to sway with life's changes without breaking.

As I looked around, I noticed the shadows cast by the bushes and trees, stretching long and thin under the bright glow. There was something poetic in how they shifted and danced, unwilling to be fully captured by the light. Shadows like these had always existed within me, hidden just beneath the surface, holding pieces of myself

I was too afraid to face. But under the moonlight, everything seemed sharper, more honest. And tonight, for the first time, I didn't want to turn away from them.

A cool breeze swept past me, and I closed my eyes, letting it carry away the tension that clung to my chest. My thoughts wandered to all the people I missed, the places I hadn't seen in so long, and the girl I used to be before all of this. That girl who used to look at the sky with wonder, who once believed in a future that wasn't painted in shades of pain and loss. I wondered if she was still here somewhere, buried under layers of scars and heartbreak.

And then there was the loneliness, lurking in the corners of my mind like an old friend. It was heavy, almost comforting in its familiarity, yet I felt the urge to release it… to let it dissipate into the cold night air like fog lifting with the dawn. There had been too many nights spent in darkness, wrapped in silence that echoed louder than any words could. But now, standing here under this ancient moon, I felt the faintest glimmer of something different, something that wasn't despair. It was the whisper of a new beginning, the fragile promise of a dawn I hadn't believed in until now.

My gaze drifted back to the moon, as if it held the answers to all the questions I was too afraid to ask. Its silvery glow bathed the world in an ethereal light, casting everything in shades of hope and uncertainty. Perhaps it was silly to look for meaning in a celestial body, but in that moment, it felt like the moon understood. It had seen countless cycles, endless endings and new beginnings. It was constant, even when it disappeared from view, it was always there, just waiting for its time to shine again.

Maybe, just maybe, I was like that too.

The moon hung overhead as if watching, and the air grew still. I took a deep breath and opened my journal, letting the pen slide effortlessly across the page as if the moon itself had inspired the words:

July 26, 2018

Shining bright in the sky during an ominous night,
A full moon overshadows the pain that you are trying hard to fight.

Laying on the ground with shivers sent through your spine,
Staring up towards the sky awaiting for a new sign.

You cannot quite place the feeling in the pit of your heart,
You cannot quite place the fact that you no longer fit your part.

So write a new story and begin a new chapter,
For that moonlight will help guide you to see that new life factor.

The new moon shines bright beyond the stars in the sky,
There are many more moving pieces than what meets the eye.

This next phase of your journey that you have yet to see,
Lies in the beyond of that eerie willow tree.

Prepare your spirits and align your vision,
For you are about to be faced with the toughest decision.

To stay or to go is the name of the game,
Look up to the sky at what that full moon became.

Allow it to guide you while you feel drained and weak,
For it is in these moments that give you the strength to speak.

As one final notion from those stars up above,
One day you will experience this journey with love.

Chapter 30

The Weeping Willow

The air was soft and cool as I made my way to the willow in the far corner of the hospital garden, the familiar sway of its branches greeting me with a quiet strength. Once, this place had felt like a wound left open – a reminder of moments I'd shared with Ava, moments I could barely look at without feeling shattered. But now, each leaf seemed to tell a different story, one of survival, not sorrow.

The sun had begun its descent, casting a warm glow across the garden. I felt its fading light pass through the willow's branches, dappling the ground beneath in shadows and patches of golden light. The breeze caught, rustling the leaves in a soft whisper, as if it was trying to speak to me.

I lowered myself onto the ground, feeling the familiar pull of this place, though it no longer stung with that raw ache. There was something different now. I wasn't here to mourn or feel haunted; I was here to reflect. To heal.

The memories weren't absent, but they felt distant, softened. I thought of Ava's laugh echoing through a spot that mirrored this one, her hand intertwined with mine. I'd once felt that her absence took this place from me. Yet, sitting here now, I felt a quiet resilience building up, as if the willow itself was lending me a part of its strength – its ability to bend without breaking, to weather storms and stand steady as seasons passed.

In the calm of this moment, beneath the sheltering canopy of leaves, I felt like I was finally untangling from the past, allowing myself to see this place, and my own reflection, with clarity. This willow had once held my grief, my longing, but now, it held my hope, my resolve. It was no longer just a tree tied to memories of someone else; it was a part of my journey back to myself.

The willow stood above me, its branches stretched out like open arms, reaching toward the earth in a graceful arc. Each leaf, fluttering softly in the wind, felt like a quiet witness to everything I had been through. This tree had seen it all, from the days when sitting here felt like sinking to a place I'd never escape, to now, where it felt like a lifeline back to myself. Its roots, twisted and strong, were buried deep in the ground, so much like the memories that had become part of me, interwoven with who I was.

I let my fingers trail along the earth, feeling the cool, damp texture under my skin. It was grounding, each handful of soil a reminder of the life that existed even in the hardest of times. The willow's roots, both hidden and exposed, seemed to mirror my own scars, some buried deep within, others etched into my daily life. Sitting here now, I felt like I was connecting to something ancient, something that understood the cycles of growth, decay, and rebirth far better than I did.

This tree, once shadowed by memories of Ava, held a power over me that was different now. I used to see her here, feel the pain of what we had been, and the emptiness left behind. But now, instead of sorrow, there was something gentler, an understanding that the tree could hold it all – the pain, the love, the letting go. Its branches swayed with a kind of acceptance, as if to say, "Yes, you have suffered, but you have also survived."

And in that survival, there was something new growing, fragile but real. I felt it in the way my heart wasn't racing like it used to, the way I could look at the branches and not be pulled back into the depths of grief. It was as though the tree had taken my pain and held it, cradled it in its ancient arms, and now returned it to me transformed, softened. Ava's memory was still here, but it was quieter now, a distant echo rather than a raw wound. I didn't need to fear this place, or that part of my past, anymore.

Leaning my head back against the trunk, I let my eyes drift closed. My breath settled into the rhythm of the wind moving through the branches. I felt a sense of peace that was unfamiliar, like a balm over a long-healed scar. The world around me, the distant chatter of people, the occasional bark of a dog, all faded until it was just me and the tree, rooted and still.

It struck me, then, how much I had in common with this willow. We had both bent under the weight of life, swaying and giving, but never breaking. I could feel a quiet strength growing within me, a determination to keep going, to keep bending without letting go of myself. The willow had become more than just a place tied to memories of Ava; it was now a symbol of resilience, of transformation, of surviving even when the world tried to pull you under.

When I finally opened my eyes, it was with a new clarity. I wasn't entirely free from the past, but maybe I didn't have to be. Maybe, like the willow, I could carry it with grace, letting it shape me without defining me. There was a beauty in that, in the way life left its marks on us, scars and all. I smiled, a small, private smile that felt like a promise to myself.

As I stood up, brushing the soil from my hands, I looked back at the willow one last time. It stood tall, the branches swaying as if in a silent farewell. And as I walked away, I felt lighter, as though I was leaving behind a part of myself that I no longer needed. The past, the memories, Ava – they would always be a part of me, but they were no longer a weight to carry. They were just another layer, another root in the soil beneath my feet, grounding me as I moved forward into whatever came next.

Leaving the willow, I felt an unanticipated sense of calm settle over me. I moved with ease I hadn't felt in months, maybe years. It wasn't a release from everything weighing me down, but it was enough for this moment, a step forward. I crossed the winding path, breathing in the crisp air that hinted of lingering winter but promised spring. Each step felt deliberate, intentional, a reminder that I was still here and still moving.

As I approached the exit of the garden, the sun dipped lower, casting a golden glow over the landscape. Shadows stretched long, but they felt less ominous, softer somehow, as if the light was reminding me that even the darkest parts of us have a beauty when we look at them differently. A group of friends laughed as they took photos beneath a tree, their voices carrying a warmth that reached me, making me realize how much I missed that simple joy of being in the world without the heavy cloud of grief hanging over me.

There was still so much to face, of course. But somehow, the weight felt a little easier to bear, the path a little clearer. I didn't need every answer today; all I needed was the courage to keep going, one small step at a time. And maybe, if I allowed myself to lean on those around me, I could navigate the twists and turns that lay ahead.

As the last rays of sunlight faded, I walked back inside, each step echoing with a newfound resilience. The willow, my anchor for so long, was now a part of me, a quiet reminder of what I had endured and the strength I had found. The journey would continue, with shadows and light alike, but for now, I was ready to face it.

Returning to my hospital room felt strange, almost surreal after the calm I'd found beneath the willow. The still air and quiet hum of the machines reminded me of where I was – here, in the present, but carrying with me the peace from that tree. The willow had changed somehow from a symbol of old hurts with Ava into something... therapeutic. Almost like it had absorbed all the sadness I'd once tied to it, giving me the space to breathe in a different meaning.

I moved toward the window, watching the pale light stretch across the room, touching everything with a quiet softness. A bird landed on the ledge, peering in, head tilted in that curious way birds do. A faint smile tugged at my lips. Here, in this hospital room, where it was hard to feel much besides the steady pulse of loss, that little scene was an unexpected reminder: life still moved outside these walls. Maybe I could too.

I walked to my bedside chair, easing myself down, and picked up my journal. The weight of it felt different in my hands today, like the pages knew they were about to carry something more than my usual thoughts. My fingers lingered on the cover before I opened it. Under the willow, I'd felt things I hadn't let myself feel in so long – the idea of letting go, of moving past what I'd held onto so tightly. Somehow, that tree had helped me to start gathering myself back together.

I started writing, pouring the day's reflections into the lines, trying to hold onto that steady feeling I'd found under the branches. With each word, I felt like I was taking a small, hopeful step forward, my voice soft but steady, like I was finding a way to stand on my own again.

July 30, 2018

Towering above the field of green,
Casting shade on what lies between.
Hear the screams of the crows and fiends,
And stretch the mind beyond its means.
You can and will be who you are,
So sit down beside that star.
Beyond the body of that darkened billow,
Stands the grounded Weeping Willow.

Chapter 31
Gravity

As I stepped into the hospital garden that morning, the air was cool and gentle against my skin, carrying the faintest hint of autumn as if nature itself was starting to change with me. The willow tree stood tall and familiar at the far end of the path, its branches swaying lazily in the breeze, casting shifting shadows on the ground beneath it. This tree, once the painful keeper of memories with Ava, had somehow softened in my eyes. It had weathered seasons just like I had, and now it seemed less a reminder of what I'd lost and more a quiet guardian of what I could become.

I walked slowly, feeling each step in my core as if they were marking something significant. When I reached the tree, I leaned back against its trunk and let my eyes close. Memories drifted in, but they felt less like knives and more like softened edges – reminders of things I was beginning to leave behind. There had been laughter here, whispers and shared secrets beneath this tree, but there had also been heartache and promises that fell away with the leaves. Now, those memories seemed to belong to someone else, a younger version of me. It felt as if the tree had seen me grow, from that girl lost in love and pain to someone who, just maybe, was starting to find herself again.

Opening my eyes, I looked up at the way the sunlight filtered through the branches, painting the ground in dappled patches. And then, like an unbidden thought, Leo's face floated into my mind. A surge of warmth hit my chest, confusing and unexpected. I found myself wondering how I could even entertain feelings for someone new. But there was something undeniable in the way Leo had been there, a steady hand when I felt like I was slipping. And yet, the uncertainty lingered; I couldn't tell if this was comfort I needed or something deeper. I wrapped my arms around myself, trying to hold onto the faint feeling that maybe, just maybe, I could still open up again, even if it was terrifying.

Later that afternoon, I walked myself to Dr. Donnelly's office, catching her pleased smile as she noticed. Her approval didn't need words. Each step, each movement felt like a small victory – a way of reclaiming what had been lost. She gestured for me to sit as I settled, her calm eyes watching.

"It's so good to see you getting more comfortable moving around," she began, warmth in her voice. "You're getting stronger, Lily. I can see it."

I nodded, though a part of me wasn't sure if I believed it fully. "Some days… it doesn't feel like enough," I admitted. "Like I'm still so… lost, so unsure."

She nodded gently, understanding. "Progress isn't always about certainty, Lily. It's about moving, even when things feel unstable. And that's exactly what you're doing."

The conversation then shifted to my relationships, and, as if reading my mind, Dr. Donnelly brought up Leo. Her question lingered in the air, inviting me to explore what I felt – what I wanted. I took a breath, feeling vulnerable.

"With Leo," I started hesitantly, "I feel… safe. Like he understands what I need without even asking." My voice softened, trying to pin down the unfamiliar sensation that followed. "But I don't know if it's real or just… because I'm lonely. I've never wanted to hurt someone, and I feel like… I don't even know how to want him or anyone right now."

Dr. Donnelly's face softened. "It's okay to feel conflicted, Lily. The heart doesn't always rush into new feelings with a clean slate. Sometimes, it carries its scars, and those take time to heal." She paused, her gaze encouraging. "Take things at your own pace. Let it be gentle with yourself and with him."

As we delved into what life after the hospital might look like, Dr. Donnelly leaned forward, her voice steady but warm. "Lily, the transition home will feel overwhelming at first. That's normal. One way to soften that feeling is to establish a few consistent, meaningful routines," she explained, her eyes holding mine to make sure I understood. "We're talking about small actions – anchors, if you will – that can ground you, keep you connected to yourself."

I let her words settle, but the idea of "life anchors" felt foreign, distant. "What does that... actually mean?" I asked, the words coming out hesitantly. "I mean... I've never thought of myself as someone with routines. Not good ones, at least."

Dr. Donnelly nodded, her voice reassuring. "Think of it as building a foundation, something reliable and steady that you can turn to each day. It doesn't have to be complex – simple, meaningful practices that make you feel in control, even on difficult days."

She suggested a few possibilities, like setting aside a specific time each morning to step outside, even if it was just to stand in the doorway and breathe. Or maybe making a habit of stretching before bed, something to mark the end of one day and the start of another. "These routines help reinforce a sense of purpose," she continued. "And purpose, Lily, is powerful. Even if it starts small, it grows."

I felt something shift within me as I listened, the idea beginning to take shape. I wanted something meaningful, not just a placeholder for the day.

"What about journaling?" I offered, glancing down at my hands. "Writing... it's helped me more than I expected. Maybe it could be something I do every day, even just a few lines?"

Dr. Donnelly's face softened, and she nodded thoughtfully. "Journaling would be a beautiful way to stay in touch with yourself.

It's a place where you can be completely honest, where there are no judgments. And it can serve as a reminder of how far you've come."

For the first time in a long time, I felt a small flicker of anticipation. The thought of capturing my days, of giving myself space to unravel and understand – maybe even grow – felt like something worth holding on to.

"You know," Dr. Donnelly continued, "life plans don't have to be grand visions. Sometimes, they're simply small commitments that remind us of who we are and who we want to be. Yours can be just that."

She paused, and then with a kindness that felt oddly intimate, added, "And Lily, if ever your path feels too daunting, remember you can reach back to these small practices. They'll be here to ground you, like that willow tree you mentioned."

It was a new feeling, this glimmer of trust in myself and in the process. And as I looked at her, I felt like, maybe, I could be strong enough to build this life, one small step at a time.

I left her office with a strange blend of emotions, somewhere between relief and anticipation. As I passed the small window overlooking the hospital garden, my gaze instinctively found the willow tree. The sunlight fell in a delicate arc around it, highlighting its branches as if in a silent benediction. The memory of this tree and the day's reflection echoed in me, a soft reminder that I could withstand more than I'd ever believed.

Sitting alone in the quiet of my room, I reached for my journal. The day had left a mark on me, stirring feelings I wasn't yet ready to face fully. The pull of memories was as strong as ever, like gravity keeping me tethered to places and people I was trying to move beyond. Yet, the journal was the only place I could let those feelings settle. As the ink met the page, I let the words come naturally, my own quiet testament to everything still unresolved.

August 6, 2018

It has a push so strong it can hold you together,
And a pull so strong it can control the weather.

There is something about the feelings that I have for you,
Since gravity keeps on revealing to me what is true.

The stars align under the midnight sky,
And I still find reasons to keep wondering why.

I wish that this was a different story to tell,
Because I still wear the effects of your ancient love spell.

My love for you will never cease to grow with age,
And I'll continue to proclaim it here on center stage.

With a push and a pull that can change your way,
Gravity keeps its hold on what you seek to convey.

If I could rewrite our story it would end with love,
Instead of my staring at you from high above.

There is a force that has a strong grip on my heart,
As gravity continues to pull us farther apart.

I remain full of hope that our stars will realign,
As I begin this journey of my minds redesign.

Keep shining bright and chase your wildest dreams,
And do not ever forget the rays of sunshine that your smile beams.

Our paths will not be easy as we sail away,
But here is to letting gravity take hold and lead the way.

The silence settled around me after I closed the journal, heavy yet oddly comforting, as though it, too, was something I could hold onto. I traced the journal's worn edges with my fingers, feeling the weight of each word that now lived within its pages. In that silence, a strange calm took root, weaving itself through the air like a delicate thread binding me to something greater than myself, something timeless.

Outside, a faint glow was visible through the small window, the last light of evening as it merged with the coming night. Shadows danced along the walls, shapes moving in rhythm with my thoughts. They were fragments of memories, each one holding a different version of myself – ones I'd let go of and others I still held close. I breathed deeply, letting the coolness of the night slip into the room as if it could soothe the restless ache in my chest.

I looked at the world beyond the glass, where the sky stretched vast and endless, holding secrets and stories I might never understand. The stars had begun to emerge, each one a tiny light surrounded by darkness. And yet, there they were, defiantly shining in the face of it all. I envied them – their consistency, their resilience. They didn't question their place in the universe; they simply existed, burning and flickering, never demanding more than what they were given.

And maybe, just maybe, I could learn to do the same. To exist, to let go, to trust that gravity, that quiet, unseen force, would guide me forward.

The thought gave me a sense of calm, fragile and fleeting, but there all the same. I sank back against the pillows, letting myself feel the depth of that silence, the weight of everything left unsaid, as it washed over me. I allowed my eyes to drift shut, knowing that the stars, that silent audience to all of life's moments, would watch over me until morning.

Tonight, I could be still.

Chapter 32
The Darkest Hour

The rain drummed against the window, each drop sliding down the glass like a silent tear. The world outside looked blurred and washed away, muted under the heavy clouds that hung low in the sky. I couldn't help but feel that the storm outside had seeped into my bones. The dull, leaden feeling had settled into my chest, the same weight that seemed to greet me every morning since I could remember. But today, it was stronger, as if the grayness outside fed the shadows inside me. I wasn't just tired; I was exhausted down to my very core.

I'd watched other patients passing by earlier, their laughter and muffled chatter just audible from my half-open door. It seemed like they were somehow exempt from this heaviness, like life still held some warmth for them. I envied their ease, the lightness in their steps, and the way they seemed to take the sun for granted when it chose to peek through the clouds. For me, it felt like the light only served to remind me of the shadows.

I turned my gaze to the window, watching droplets racing down the glass, splitting and rejoining in a silent, aimless flow. It reminded me of how I felt, as if all my thoughts and memories were dripping, seeping away, without purpose. I closed my eyes and let my mind wander, almost afraid of where it would go, yet unable to resist the pull of old memories.

In flashes, I saw pieces of my past, fragments of what once was. Logan's laughter came first – clear and vibrant, that infectious laugh he'd release when we'd chase each other through the greenhouse after school. I could almost see him there, darting around the rows of flowers, his grin wide, and his eyes bright with mischief. The smell of soil and blooming lilies filled the air, wrapping around me, grounding me. His laughter felt so real I nearly believed he was there beside me, reaching out, just out of touch.

Then came my father – his quiet strength. The memory shifted to those moments he'd kneel beside me in the garden, his hands rough and worn from the work he loved, guiding mine as he taught me how to plant the seeds. He'd place a comforting hand on my shoulder whenever I doubted myself, his touch warm and steady, like he was passing on a piece of his own resilience to me. I could feel the warmth, that same calming weight, the way he'd look at me with such pride. It was as if he was reminding me that I was strong, even when I felt lost, even when the world felt far too big to bear.

Then, there was Ava. The world seemed to soften around her memory, blurring into those golden afternoons when it was just us, her hand resting in mine, a quiet warmth passing between us, grounding us in our own little world. I could see her face... the slight curve of her smile as she'd tilt her head, her eyes catching mine in that way that made everything else disappear. We would lie beneath the willow tree, sunlight filtering through the branches, creating a mosaic of light across her skin. Her laughter, softer than Logan's but just as warm, would fill the air, and I'd feel the world slow down, as if time had granted us this moment alone. The way her hand fit perfectly in mine, her thumb grazing my skin as if it were second nature, felt like home. Her voice, saying my name softly, lingering like a melody, whispered through the memory.

Each memory left a lingering ache, a bittersweet reminder of something beautiful, something real, something I could never retrieve. They felt alive within me, yet distant – like watching an old film, each scene flickering and fading. The laughter, the warmth, the love – they were all echoes now, fragments of a life that felt like it belonged to someone else. But they were mine, part of me, part of the emptiness I carried. And, in this quiet, the ache became the weight I had to bear.

It seemed almost impossible that I had lived those moments. They felt like scenes from someone else's life, faded, blurry, yet carrying a pain that was uniquely my own. I wanted to reach out, to grasp those fleeting images, but they always slipped through my fingers. Today, they felt like ghosts haunting me, echoes of a life that no longer existed.

I opened my eyes, pulling myself back to the present, the weight of it pressing down on me like the heaviest anchor. I could feel myself sliding, the familiar pull of the darkness beckoning me, inviting me to sink deeper. The edges of my vision seemed to close in, narrowing to that one window and the rain that wouldn't stop falling. I wondered if it would ever stop, if this storm, both outside and within, would ever pass.

Without thinking, I reached for my journal, fingers cold as I turned to the next blank page. My hand trembled as I held the pen, my mind swirling with the weight of everything I couldn't say out loud. I took a breath, forcing myself to begin, the words bleeding onto the page as if they had been trapped inside me, desperate to escape:

August 9, 2018

There is time before the brightest day where things seem out of place,
A time where chaos meets the world and drives your soul away;
Before you lose all hope and give up your future,
Just for a moment try to seize the day.

In that moment in time will you either conquer or fold,
As the weight of the world becomes yours to carry;
And you will not be weak if it is too much to burden,
Or if in the darkest hour you remain uncertain.

When the words fail to speak your mind,
Just listen closely to what has met the eye;
The light may not shine consistently or bright,
But it is in these things where you yourself will find.

There is time before the brightest day where things seem out place,
A time where chaos meets the world and drives your soul off base;
Moments left to set your memories displace,
In your darkest hour you will learn how to embrace.

The words stopped, and silence filled the room like a weight I hadn't noticed until it lifted. My hand lingered on the cover of my journal, my fingers tracing the faint indentations left by my pen as if feeling for the shape of my thoughts. There was something grounding about the texture beneath my fingertips, a reminder that the words were real, the pain was real, and somehow, by writing it all down, I had anchored it outside of myself. The hollow ache was still there, but now it felt bearable, like an echo I could listen to instead of running from.

I glanced out the window, noticing the rain had softened, its relentless drumming now a gentle, rhythmic patter against the glass. It was a lullaby of sorts, and I closed my eyes, letting the sound seep into me, weaving through the cracks. With each breath, I felt myself sinking deeper into the moment, the quiet merging with my own heartbeat; a rare sense of calm wrapping itself around me, fragile yet solid enough to hold.

In the stillness, memories lingered but no longer clawed at me, settling like the fading light on the horizon. The idea of tomorrow felt strange and daunting, but not as impossible as before. The darkness was there, but tonight, I could look at it from a distance, no longer drowning in its depths. I couldn't say what the future held or how long this calm would last, but for now, this small pocket of peace was enough. I let myself breathe in the quiet, hoping – perhaps foolishly, but hoping nonetheless – that one day, there might be more moments like this. Days where I wouldn't have to fight so hard to keep myself afloat.

I didn't know if tomorrow would be brighter or easier, but as I sat there, feeling the steady rhythm of my breath, I realized that tonight, I'd survived. And in this moment, that was all I needed.

Chapter 33
Sadness

I sat up slowly, eyes barely open as I squinted at the soft morning light slipping through the blinds. Everything felt blurred, hazy – like my mind was still in the thick fog of a dream I couldn't shake. Reaching for my journal, I flipped to a blank page, staring at it. The words didn't come, no matter how long I waited, the emptiness of the page mirroring the hollow feeling inside me.

After a few minutes, I closed the journal, frustrated. My thoughts, like the sky outside, were heavy and scattered, clouded with a sadness that never seemed to let up. Standing by the window, I pressed my forehead to the cool glass, letting my eyes trace the clusters of gray clouds hanging low across the sky. They drifted and shifted aimlessly, almost taunting me with their weightlessness, their freedom. And yet, they still looked like they carried a storm. I couldn't tell where the clouds ended and my own thoughts began.

The walk to Dr. Donnelly's office felt both strange and freeing. It was the first time I'd walked this path on my own, but every step felt heavy, as if I were dragging a weight behind me. I moved carefully, steadying myself with each footfall, allowing the simple rhythm of walking to ground me in the moment. Yet even as I walked, the familiar ache of sadness pulsed inside me: a dull, relentless reminder of everything I'd been through, everything I was still facing.

I entered her office and settled into the armchair across from her. Dr. Donnelly's welcoming nod was like a signal, a cue to let down the walls. She sat with her notebook resting on her knee, her gaze gentle yet probing.

"So, Lily," she began, her voice calm but curious. "Tell me what's been sitting with you lately. What's been at the forefront of your mind?"

I shifted, finding myself staring at the pattern in the rug beneath my feet. "Sadness," I admitted, the word feeling both small and enormous. "I can't seem to shake it. It's… always there, no matter what I try to do."

She nodded. "Sadness can be persistent, especially when it's tied to so much loss and change," she replied. "But sometimes, it helps to explore what that sadness is connected to. Has anything specific been coming up in your mind recently?"

My throat felt tight as I thought about her question. "A lot," I whispered, glancing away. "I guess it's… it's everything. Losing Dad and Logan… and now with Ava, it feels like… I don't know, like I'm losing myself too."

Dr. Donnelly's expression softened. "Grief often brings an echo of all our losses," she said. "It's not unusual to feel overwhelmed when past and present pain start blending together. Do you feel that it's the loss of these relationships, or perhaps the feeling of being left alone that hits the hardest?"

I swallowed, considering her words. "Both, I think. There's this… emptiness. And it feels like no matter what I do, it just keeps growing."

She leaned forward slightly. "Loss often leaves spaces in our lives that we don't know how to fill, spaces where people once were. And sometimes, these spaces can trick us into feeling that they'll remain empty forever. But Lily, healing doesn't mean filling these spaces with anything or anyone else. It's about learning to live around them, finding ways to honor what you had without letting it define what's still to come."

The sadness felt sharp in my chest, yet her words carried a kind of truth I hadn't allowed myself to consider. "It just feels like it's all tangled up inside me," I admitted. "And every time I think I'm okay, something happens, and... and I just go right back to that place."

Dr. Donnelly nodded again, her gaze steady and compassionate. "It sounds like you're carrying a lot on your own. But healing doesn't have to happen in a straight line, nor does it have to be something you do alone. And, as we've discussed before, even when things feel overwhelming, there are tools and ways to help bring you a bit more balance and support."

She paused, carefully choosing her next words. "Lily, how do you feel about revisiting the idea of medication? It's simply another tool, not a solution, but something that could create a bit more stability as we work through these deeper feelings. I know we've discussed your concerns, especially with your past experiences with your mum. But it's something we could start very gradually, and with close monitoring."

I bit my lip, the memory of my mum's distant gaze lingering. But this wasn't about her... it was about me. And maybe, just maybe, this could be a chance to approach things differently.

"I'm... I'm open to trying," I said quietly, meeting her gaze. "As long as... as long as I don't lose myself in it."

Dr. Donnelly offered a reassuring smile. "You won't lose yourself, Lily. This is all about helping you reconnect with yourself in a safe way."

As the session continued, Dr. Donnelly guided me back through memories I'd barely allowed myself to revisit – each a doorway into the parts of my heart still aching, still raw. We spoke about Dad, his deep laughter that used to echo through our home, and the way he'd lift me onto his shoulders, making me feel like I could reach the stars. Now, the echo of that laughter was like a ghost, lingering in the corners of my mind but fading whenever I tried to hold onto it.

"I don't remember the exact moment I realized he was gone," I confessed, my voice quiet. "It was like... one day, he just wasn't there. And no matter how hard I tried to make sense of it, to fill that space with memories, it never... it never worked. It just left this void."

Dr. Donnelly nodded, her gaze steady and compassionate. "Grief often leaves us with unfinished spaces, ones we try to fill but somehow never can. Sometimes, we have to accept that those spaces are part of us now."

Then there was Logan, my twin, my other half – the absence of him was different. It was more like losing a piece of myself. I remembered how he'd tease me about the smallest things, how he knew just what to say to make me laugh when I didn't think I could.

"It feels like there's this... emptiness," I told her, my voice trembling. "Like I'm reaching out, but there's nothing to grab onto anymore. Sometimes, I imagine he's just somewhere out of reach, like I might see him again if I turn the corner fast enough. But he's not. And that... that hurts in a way I can't describe."

Her words wrapped around me gently, helping me face the memories I'd been holding at arm's length. "Those pieces of you," she said softly, "they're precious. And even though they're gone physically, they're woven into you. Honoring them doesn't mean they fade away; it means they can be part of you as you keep going forward."

And then there was Ava. That wound was fresher, more jagged, and raw in a way the others weren't. Loving her had brought me so much joy but losing her had cut just as deeply. I tried to explain to Dr. Donnelly the way I'd felt after she left, the sense of freefall, the feeling that I wasn't enough to make her stay.

"With Ava, it's different," I murmured, almost afraid to say the words. "It's like... I keep replaying every moment, every fight, trying to see what I could've done. As if finding the answer might make the pain go away. But it doesn't. It just keeps circling, bringing me right back to where I started."

Dr. Donnelly looked at me with understanding. "Sometimes, with love, we try to make sense of things by finding reasons. But maybe it's not about what you could've done differently, Lily. Sometimes, relationships end not because of one person's actions but because they've served their place in our lives. And while the love you shared with Ava was real, maybe its purpose wasn't to stay forever but to help you grow."

I sat with her words, letting the truth of them sink in. Each of these people I'd lost had shaped me, filled parts of me that now felt hollow. But maybe, as Dr. Donnelly had said, I didn't have to fix or fill those spaces. Perhaps I could simply learn to carry them with me, to honor them without letting them consume me.

By the time we finished, I felt as if something heavy had lifted, a weight I hadn't realized I was carrying. There was a lightness now, fragile but real, like a small flicker breaking through the thick darkness. It wasn't much, but it was enough to remind me that maybe, just maybe, there was still a path forward.

Back in my room, I sat by the window, letting the afternoon light fill the space around me. My journal lay open on my lap, the blank page waiting. Dr. Donnelly's words echoed in my mind: sadness, grief, healing. I took a deep breath, feeling the weight of everything settle within me.

Then, slowly, I began to write:

August 13, 2018

When the dark masks the light in the morning dew,
And the moon shines bright in the crisp autumn air —
Your mind and your heart are both laced in blue.

The days are restless while the nights are sleepless,
And the thoughts in your mind just keep rearranging —
That feeling of sadness keeps you quite speechless.

Allow your mind to heal and your soul to breathe,
And the world to become a place where you can be —
That feeling will finish with a sense to seethe.

Remember who you are and where you have been,
And the experiences that have come to cleanse those thoughts —
For your life's greatest journey is soon to begin.

Do not succumb to that dark cloud that lays high above,
And do not allow your heart to betray your mind —
For one day soon that sadness will turn into love.

On that day that will likely be filled with madness,
You will think back to a time when you did feel such darkness —
And suddenly you will then forget about that sadness.

Chapter 34

Dandelion

I stepped into the garden, greeted by the earthy scent of freshly turned soil, mingling with the soft sweetness of honeysuckle and lavender. The morning sun cast a golden glow across everything, gentle and warm, wrapping the small plot of nature in a kind of softness that felt rare and precious. Each step felt different here, cushioned by the grass beneath my feet instead of the sterile linoleum floors inside. Here, the harshness of hospital life faded away, leaving a sense of peace and vibrancy that only nature could bring.

This garden was a hidden gem, tucked into the far corner of the hospital grounds, as if it offered itself only to those willing to seek it out. There were winding paths bordered by a mosaic of wildflowers – purple asters, deep red dahlias, and sunflowers that stretched up tall, their faces turned reverently toward the light. Around me, bees flitted from bloom to bloom, humming softly, a rhythm of life that felt as steady as a heartbeat. It was strange, how just a few steps outside the walls could feel like stepping into a different world.

As I walked along the narrow stone pathway, I let my fingers trail over the tops of the flowers, grazing their delicate petals. There was something grounding in that simple touch, as if each bloom held a small piece of clarity that it was willing to share. The garden seemed to reach out to me, urging me to look closer, to breathe deeper. The vibrant life around me felt somehow contagious, as if its energy could seep into my bones and pull me back to life.

Turning a corner, I came to a patch of dandelions. They were scattered through the grass, their sunny heads turning to the sky, their soft, feathery seed balls shimmering in the light. One of the seeds broke free, drifting up on a whisper of breeze, spiraling lazily in the air. It caught the sun just right, casting a tiny sparkle as it floated, free and unburdened, spinning through the space between here and somewhere far beyond.

I watched it, mesmerized by how effortlessly it moved, how it seemed content to just… be. I felt an impulse I couldn't quite explain, and I reached out instinctively, hand open, hoping to catch it. My fingers brushed against it, just for a second, before it twisted away, slipping through the air like a whisper of something half-remembered. I watched it drift higher, out of reach, lost to the light. My hand fell back to my side, an ache settling in my chest, soft but insistent.

The memory came, then – unbidden but undeniable – of love, as fleeting as those dandelion seeds, impossible to hold onto even if I tried. I thought of Ava, of the way her laughter used to fill the silence, of how we'd once floated through life together, side by side. And just like that seed, our love had drifted away, a beautiful thing that wasn't meant to stay. I stood there a while longer, letting the memories settle, each one flaring up briefly before fading again, like sparks flying up and disappearing into the sky.

Feeling the weight of it all, I sank down onto a nearby bench, pulling my journal from my bag. The cover was worn from countless days of flipping through its pages, of capturing moments I couldn't bear to let go. I opened it slowly, and my pen hovered over the page as the words formed on the edges of my mind. This was a moment I knew I had to capture, the memory of those seeds slipping through my fingers, the acceptance that some things, like love, couldn't be held onto forever.

August 15, 2018

And just as quickly as it fell into my hand,
Our love floated away through the air —
Like the seeds from a dandelion,
Freshly picked and blown through land.

But as those seeds fall to the earth below,
Watch them as they allow a new flower to grow.

I closed my journal slowly, pressing the cover as if to hold the words in place, feeling the weight of them settle deep within me. For so long, I had thought love was something you kept, something you fought to hold on to, but maybe... maybe I had been wrong. Perhaps love was meant to be like those dandelion seeds – beautiful, yes, but free, moving on to find new places to bloom. My fingers traced the spine of the journal, each stroke a silent acknowledgment of what I had carried and what I was learning to release.

I watched as the breeze picked up again, stirring the patch of dandelions beside me. More seeds lifted from their stems, twisting in graceful spirals as they drifted away. Each tiny seed, so fragile yet so full of possibility, carried with it the memory of a flower that once was. And I realized that maybe that was what love could be: a gentle thing, something to be admired, cherished, and let go of when the time was right. Love, like those seeds, left behind its trace, its impact, a reminder of something that had grown and flourished, even if it was no longer in my grasp.

The ache in my chest softened, giving way to something else, something quieter and strangely comforting. It was as if, by watching those seeds float away, I was letting go of the version of love I had clung to for so long. For once, I didn't feel the urge to chase after it, to pull it back to me and keep it for myself. Instead, I let it drift, knowing that it would find a place to land. And maybe, in some way, I would too.

I stayed there on the bench, captivated by the gentle dance of the seeds in the sunlight. One by one, they floated higher, catching glimmers of light, becoming tiny, fleeting stars against the clear blue sky. Each one carried a piece of my past, my love, my longing. And as they drifted farther, I felt a strange sense of peace washing over me, filling spaces that had long been empty. It was a feeling of release, a breath I hadn't realized I'd been holding. It felt like forgiveness... forgiveness of myself, of the choices I'd made, of the things I'd held onto too tightly.

Eventually, the garden around me seemed to change, as if seeing it anew. The sun seemed to cast everything in a softer glow, turning the edges of the flowers to gold, illuminating every petal, every leaf, with a warmth that felt personal. The colors were more vivid, each hue brighter, each bloom a testament to life's ability to renew itself. Even the grass beneath my feet seemed to pulse with energy, as if the earth was breathing, inviting me to do the same.

As I finally rose from the bench, I felt lighter. The memories, the pain, the hope – all of it seemed to settle in a way that felt right. I took one last look at the dandelions, now sparse, their seeds having journeyed out into the world, seeking new ground to grow. I couldn't help but feel that I, too, was on my own journey, moving forward, reaching for a life that had been waiting for me beyond all this sorrow.

As I walked back toward the hospital, the weight of the past seemed to lift, replaced by a quiet resilience. For so long, I had feared returning to those walls, fearing they would pull me back into the darkness I had known there. But this time, the doors felt welcoming, like the hospital was less a place of confinement and more a place of healing. And I felt ready to let it be that.

Inside, the familiar hallways seemed brighter, the sterile lights somehow softer, casting a gentler glow on everything. I felt a small smile tug at my lips, the kind that comes not from joy but from a deep, settled acceptance. I knew the heaviness would return in waves, that grief and love and loss would continue to find me, but I also knew that I could face it.

For today, for this small, fragile moment, I had found a precious piece of peace… and today… today that was enough.

Chapter 35
The Quill

The week leading up to my next therapy session felt different. Each day wasn't necessarily easier, but there was a subtle lightness, an almost imperceptible shift that I couldn't quite name. The routine had been the same – meals, medication, short walks in the garden, journaling – but I found myself able to hold onto moments of calm, even when the shadows crept in. With each journal entry, I sensed a deepening connection, not only to the memories and feelings I poured out but to the act of writing itself.

One afternoon, Leo visited. He arrived with that familiar energy of his, a mix of laughter and warmth, as if he carried the sunlight in with him. He asked about my sessions with Dr. Donnelly, and his encouragement lingered in the air, giving weight to each piece of advice he shared. When he left, there was a part of me that felt undeniably anchored, as if his presence left a mark that would hold me through the coming days.

During another morning, I felt the same pulse of life through a simple walk in the garden. I had been aimlessly observing the flowers when a breeze swept through, scattering petals from the dandelions. I watched them drift on the wind, disappearing into the sunlight as if each petal carried a part of my own longing. It reminded me of how life continues, regardless of the weight we carry, and I wondered if my words could do the same – float out into the world, becoming lighter with each page I wrote.

In these moments, I felt the faintest hint of clarity, as if each day and each memory allowed me to shed something heavy and old, making space for something new. It was subtle, fragile, but I clung to it, knowing that even these small moments of peace were victories. And it was this shifting awareness, a quiet yet persistent hope, that I carried with me into my next session.

As I opened the door to Dr. Donnelly's office, the room seemed to welcome me with a quiet warmth. Sunlight filtered through the window blinds, casting delicate beams across the walls. I took a slow breath, allowing the light to settle in me, as if each ray were a bridge reaching into the parts of myself that still felt raw, untouched.

Dr. Donnelly gestured for me to sit, her smile as reassuring as ever. The journal rested on my lap, heavier somehow – maybe from the hundreds of thoughts that it now contained, each word like a breadcrumb of the journey I'd been traveling.

She noticed it, of course. "I see you've brought your journal, but something feels different about today. How are you feeling?"

I paused, fingers tracing the edge of the journal's worn cover, noticing its softened edges. "I think I'm realizing that these pages aren't just a way to release pain or document memories. They're… well, they're like pieces of me that I'm putting together."

Her nod was slow, absorbing every word. "So, it's more than a record – it's an expression of who you are and where you're going."

"It feels like my voice," I said, a faint tremor in my tone, "and for the longest time, I didn't think I had one. When I write, I'm not just reacting. I'm creating something. It's like holding a quill… like I'm sketching out the life I want, even if it's different from what I've been through."

Dr. Donnelly leaned forward, her eyes reflecting the warmth of the sunlight that spilled across the floor. "I want you to imagine that quill, Lily, really feel its weight in your hand. Writing isn't just a form of expression; it's a tool to shape your life. With it, you can draft, rewrite, even erase parts of the story that feel incomplete."

I closed my eyes briefly, picturing it: a quill made of something ancient and enduring, a feather stained with ink that had survived countless pages. In my hand, it felt heavy, imbued with the power of all the words I'd ever written and those yet to come.

"It's strange," I whispered, opening my eyes to meet her gaze. "When I think of writing that way – as a tool – I start to see my words differently. They're not just my fears or memories; they're a way forward, a way to reclaim… everything."

"Yes," Dr. Donnelly murmured, her voice like a soft exhale in the quiet room. "That's the essence of it, Lily. Your words are an extension of you. When you write, you're not just recording – you're becoming. You're creating, not only who you are but also the person you hope to be."

The imagery of the quill deepened with each word she spoke, and for the first time, I felt its weight settle firmly in my grip. I thought of every story I'd ever told myself, every painful moment I'd scribbled away, and suddenly I could see them, not as scars on a page, but as brushstrokes in a larger canvas. Each entry was a part of me, a mosaic of experiences I could choose to expand or release, one careful stroke at a time.

"Writing is powerful," she continued, "because it connects us to parts of ourselves that may be too hard to face otherwise. It's a way of holding memories in a safe space while also creating new meaning."

I looked down at the journal. "It's strange… I've always thought of my words as fragile, but maybe they're strong too. Maybe they're what's been holding me together, even when everything else has fallen apart."

Dr. Donnelly's eyes glistened, a quiet understanding passing between us. "You've been using your quill to survive, Lily. Now, it's time to use it to thrive. When you write, let it be not only a reflection of what's behind you but also a map of where you wish to go."

The words struck me, lingering in the air like a promise. My journal, once a vessel for my pain, had become my compass. I wasn't merely recording; I was crafting a life, one page at a time. And with each stroke of the quill, I was reminded that there was power in choosing what I wanted to remember and what I wanted to create anew.

As the session continued, Dr. Donnelly and I spoke about the weight of that responsibility – how holding the quill meant facing the past while still daring to imagine a future. I admitted my fear, that some memories felt too heavy, some stories too raw, but her voice reassured me, steady and warm.

"It's not about writing it all at once," she said, her hand resting lightly on her notebook. "Healing is a process, Lily. Each page you write is a step. There's no rush to finish, only the courage to keep going."

By the end of the session, I felt different… lighter, maybe, as if I'd glimpsed a new part of myself in the ink-stained pages of my journal. It was as though each word I'd ever written had gathered here, guiding me gently forward. I could feel the weight of it all, the stories that had once been my burden, shifting now, morphing from shadows into something warmer, something that felt almost like hope.

This quill I held was no longer a simple instrument; it was a gift, one that held within it the power to transform my darkest hours into something beautiful, something enduring. It was a bridge between who I had been and who I wanted to become. Each word I placed on the page was like a seed, each stroke of the pen a tiny declaration of faith, of resilience. It made me feel both grounded and expansive, tethered to my past yet free to grow beyond it.

As I rose from the chair, the journal felt solid in my hands, its pages a tangible reminder of the journey I was on, the miles yet to come. Clutching it close to my chest, I walked slowly out of Dr. Donnelly's office, the sunlight warming my skin as if blessing each step. I knew this journey wasn't over; it was only beginning. The path was unwritten, a blank canvas where each page held endless possibilities, and for the first time, I felt ready – ready to let my words lead me toward a life I could finally claim as my own.

Leaving Dr. Donnelly's office, I moved down the hall at a pace that felt almost reverent, each step pressing into the floor with a new sense of grounding. The air was clearer, lighter, and each breath felt like the start of something I hadn't yet fully realized. A warmth pulsed in my chest, a gentle flame that I wanted to carry carefully, without rushing or overburdening it. For once, I felt like I wasn't just trying to survive the day – I was beginning to embrace it.

The sunlight spilled through the tall windows lining the hall, casting golden patches across the tile. It seemed to touch everything differently, even the worn linoleum, illuminating details I'd never noticed before. Shadows and light interplayed softly, reminding me of brushstrokes on a canvas. As I passed a small, potted fern beside the nursing station, I slowed, reaching out to let my fingertips brush against its soft leaves, grounding myself in the texture of the world. It was as if the hospital was letting me see its gentler side – a promise hidden among the antiseptic and routine.

With each step, pieces of my conversation with Dr. Donnelly unraveled and reassembled in my mind, like loose threads weaving into something whole. I could feel the shift inside me, the realization that writing was more than a pastime or an escape; it was a lifeline, a bridge that could lead me back to myself. It held a part of me that no diagnosis, no sadness, could touch. And in some quiet corner of my mind, Leo's voice echoed, his words like soft beacons. He had seen this in me all along, even when I had forgotten. His belief, his encouragement, had been a light, and now, piece by piece, I was beginning to see myself through his eyes – a person worthy of hope, worthy of joy.

When I reached my room, I paused, letting the door swing open slowly, savoring the quiet that awaited me. Inside, the air was still, touched by the gentle hum of a nearby fan, and sunlight poured in through the window. The chair by the window was angled just out of its reach, so I took my time, moving it gently, positioning it to catch the full warmth of the sun. It was a small act, but somehow it felt important, like arranging the pieces of a space that would welcome new beginnings.

I eased into the chair, my journal cradled in my lap, its pages a blank canvas open to all the possibilities of this day. The sunlight spilled across me, warm and grounding, like a touch from something greater than myself. Outside, a few wisps of clouds floated lazily against the vast blue, their movements slow and unhurried. I sat there for a moment, breathing in the stillness, letting the quiet settle deep within me.

When I finally opened my journal, I felt the words come, each one a gentle revelation. I wasn't just writing to survive anymore; I was writing to live, to connect with parts of myself I had once thought were lost forever. The pen moved over the page with a sense of purpose, as if it had been waiting for this moment as much as I had. Each line was a declaration, a vow to keep moving forward, even when the path felt uncertain.

The quill in my hand held secrets that felt sacred, truths I could barely acknowledge until now. But, for the first time in my life, I was fully prepared to accept my past, focus on my present and dream of the future. With these thoughts, and bold strokes, I wrote:

August 20, 2018

The quill knows the secrets of its holder,
Far before the holder knows the truth;
The bond that is shared may never waver,
And the truths that be told may be bolder.

The quill is trusted to execute a story,
Far before the eyes can read;
These stories based off happenstances,
And the hope for what lies ahead.

The quill may come with quite the cost,
As it writes your name into history;
For if you do not create a sense of security,
It will send your mind into obscurity.

The quill has magic both good and evil,
The way it leans is up to the holder;
Build a trust that is based on truth and hope,
That evil will be unable to control the slope —
Build a trust that is based on deception and lies,
And you will see the light magic reach its demise.

The quill knows the secrets of its holder,
Far before the holder knows the truth;
Keep that quill close to your chest,
And you will need not worry about feeling colder.

Chapter 36
Lost Love

The day began quietly, as if the world itself were holding its breath. Outside my window, a blanket of low-hanging clouds softened the landscape, casting everything in a muted shade of gray. Raindrops gathered on the glass, slipping down in soft streaks, painting delicate patterns that blurred the view beyond. I sat alone, cocooned in the stillness of the room, watching those droplets merge and dissolve, letting myself take in the peace they brought.

In that moment, a subtle sense of anticipation stirred within me, a sensation so rare I almost didn't recognize it: a lightness, a feeling that I might be standing on the edge of something new. The thought felt fragile, like that dandelion seed I was too afraid to catch, yet unable to ignore. As I let my mind drift, memories from the past week surfaced, blending together like the clouds moving outside my window.

Ava's face flickered at the forefront, as if she were watching me from within those memories. I could see her smiling, her hands entwined with mine, and that familiar laugh of hers that used to make the world feel right. The memory washed over me, gentle yet sharp, carrying that deep ache I knew all too well – an ache that once felt impossible to let go. But now, though still present, it was quieter, softened by time.

Yet, amid the bittersweet reminders of Ava, other memories appeared, ones that I hadn't expected. I thought of Leo, his infectious laugh, the way his jokes had caught me off guard and made me laugh so freely, almost as if the heaviness I carried had lifted, if only for a moment. I remembered lying in bed, getting lost in the pages of a book for the first time in ages, feeling a simple joy in something so ordinary. These small moments, ones that would have meant nothing to me a few months ago, had found a way to anchor me, reminding me that even the smallest things could bring solace.

Maybe, I thought, for the first time, I could let Ava go. The love I'd held onto so tightly, the memories I'd cherished and mourned – it was time to place them gently in the past. I breathed in deeply, the air cool and cleansing. The ache that had defined me was loosening its grip, leaving space for something new, something that felt lighter.

Dr. Donnelly greeted me with a warm smile as I settled into the chair across from her. Her gaze was steady, reassuring, a silent promise that this space was safe, that whatever I brought forward would be met without judgment. "It seems like you've made tremendous strides since we last spoke," she began, her voice warm and patient. "How are you feeling?"

I hesitated, glancing down as if the words I was searching for might be written there on the floor. I hadn't realized how loaded such a simple question could feel. Eventually, I met her eyes and spoke softly, "I feel... like I'm finally ready to let go of something that's been a part of me for too long."

She nodded with that familiar kindness, leaning forward just enough that her presence felt closer, as if offering her support in more than just words. "You've been carrying this love for a long time, Lily," she said gently. "Love, especially when it's deeply rooted, can leave marks on us, etching itself into our identity. But you've been brave to even consider placing it gently in the past. Letting go doesn't mean it was any less important; it simply means you're allowing yourself to grow beyond it."

Her words washed over me, each one like a balm, nudging memories to the surface – memories of Ava's laugh echoing through quiet afternoons, the way she used to take my hand without a word, the countless dreams we whispered late into the night. For a moment, the emotions swelled, sharp and vivid, but there was an unexpected softness to them too, like something precious I could admire without needing to grasp so tightly.

"I never thought I'd get here," I admitted, my voice wavering. "For so long, the idea of moving on felt like losing a part of myself. But now... now, I think I can start to place that love somewhere safe, somewhere it can rest without pulling me back."

Dr. Donnelly's expression softened, and a gentle smile curved on her lips. "This love, as profound as it was, doesn't have to define you entirely, Lily. It shaped you, and it will always be a cherished part of you. But it's also okay to create space for new experiences, for love that feels steady, without the shadows of guilt or fear."

Her words settled over me like a comforting weight, grounding me, and I felt a clarity I hadn't realized I was missing. The love I'd held onto with Ava had been real, beautiful even, but it was also something I could choose to step back from, to let drift like the dandelion seeds I'd watched just days before.

I looked up, gathering my thoughts, trying to capture the relief blooming within me. "When I think about love in the future," I murmured, feeling a gentle conviction I hadn't known I possessed, "I want it to be... less painful. I want it to come without the burden of my past or the fear of losing myself in it."

Her smile widened, and I felt her understanding wash over me. "That's a beautiful revelation, Lily. You're discovering what healthy love looks like, what it feels like, and that's a remarkable step forward. And now, maybe it's time to start imagining what your own future could look like – one filled with love that nurtures you."

In that room, with her encouraging gaze meeting mine, I felt the permission I'd been searching for – permission to love without loss, to grow without guilt, to create a new future in which I could hold onto the best parts of my past without letting them weigh me down.

As Dr. Donnelly continued, her expression shifted to something slightly more serious, but still warm. "Lily, we've talked a lot about your progress, and I can't emphasize enough how far you've come. But I want to talk about what's next. Have you given any thought to maintaining this stability once you're discharged?"

The question hung in the air between us, and I found myself instinctively tensing up. I nodded slowly, swallowing the instinct to retreat. "I know I want to keep feeling... steady, like I've finally started to stand on solid ground again," I admitted, though there was a flicker of fear behind my words. "But I'm scared of... slipping."

Dr. Donnelly nodded, leaning forward, her gaze sincere and unwavering. "That's entirely understandable. It's natural to have reservations, especially after everything you've been through. And sometimes, a little help can make a big difference. We're considering a mood stabilizer as part of your release plan. Something that could support you without taking away who you are."

The mention of medication triggered a surge of memories – the foggy, numbing haze from years past when I had leaned too hard into prescriptions. My throat tightened, the taste of resistance familiar. "I don't know, Dr. Donnelly," I murmured, glancing down at my hands. "Last time, it... it wasn't good. I lost pieces of myself. I felt numb."

She paused, absorbing my hesitation with her usual calm. "I know, Lily. I'm not here to take away your spirit, your emotions, or your voice. We would do this gradually, checking in often. You'd have agency every step of the way, adjusting as needed. This isn't about numbing anything; it's about giving you the tools to feel secure in the stability you've fought so hard to achieve."

I took a deep breath, her words creating a strange warmth inside me. "So... it wouldn't be like before? I wouldn't feel like a shell of myself?"

Her expression softened, and she reached across the table, her hand resting near mine without intruding. "No, Lily. That's not the goal here. We'll work together to find a balance that lets you experience life fully – where you still feel like you. The medication is just a piece of the puzzle, not the whole picture. You have more control over this journey than you think."

I nodded slowly, her words beginning to lift the fog of past experiences. "I guess I thought... taking meds would be like admitting I'm broken or something."

She smiled gently. "Not at all. It's actually a testament to your strength and commitment to yourself. Choosing to try something new to protect the progress you've made – that takes courage."

In that moment, I felt a shift, a tiny flicker of trust reemerging, like a spark rekindling within me. "Maybe... maybe I can try it. I can't lose what I've fought so hard to regain."

"Exactly," Dr. Donnelly said softly. "We're not here to take anything from you, Lily. We're here to help you build on what you already have. You're in control, every step of the way."

She handed me my journal, as if it were a silent invitation. I took it, feeling that familiar urge to capture what I was feeling in words. With the pen in my hand, I wrote, letting my heart pour onto the page, letting go in the only way I knew how:

August 27, 2018

You wake up one morning with a note left beside you,
The love that you once had made the decision to leave;
You are unexpectedly forced to question your own self-worth,
But perhaps in this very moment you are meant to grieve.

Grieve over the love that you have lost,
Grieve over the pain that you have been caused —
Grieve over the memories that you had hoped would last forever,
Grieve for a moment and then realize the unfathomable cost.

You begin to navigate your new day in the life,
And question just what love means when it is gone;
But that is the magical thing about it —
It may not be here or there or near;
Though it will always be the piece of your heart that makes a perfect fit.

Love is a delicacy that is hard to comprehend,
With one small misdirection it can be hard to defend;
Treat it with kindness and passion and care,
For the love that is lost was a love that was quite rare.

But instead of sulking in the sorrow of yesterday,
Remember that love that ignited your passion;
For while that love may be lost there is one thing that remains —
All those memories that you shared will continue to fuel all your veins.

One final thing before you lose hope for love,
There is a light that will shine from above;
Pointing you onward through your journey of —
When you least expect it you will find your true dove.

As I finished writing, I looked up, catching Dr. Donnelly's gaze. Her eyes held something gentle and unspoken, a quiet understanding that didn't need words. In that moment, I felt the fullness of all I had just expressed, each word from my journal lingering like an echo in the room. Holding my journal close, I nodded, murmuring a soft, "thank you." I took a final glance at her, noting the faint smile that seemed to hold a world of encouragement before I turned toward the door.

The walk back to my room felt deliberate, almost ceremonious. Every step seemed to lighten as if I were shedding layers of the weight I'd carried for so long. The corridor stretched out in front of me, but it no longer felt daunting – it was an invitation, leading me toward something new. I caught my reflection in the glass panel lining the hallway, pausing as I noticed a faint, yet familiar, expression staring back at me. It was my own face, but softened, less burdened by shadows.

For a moment, memories flickered gently in my mind. Ava's laugh, the warmth of our shared moments, drifted in like a soft breeze. I could see her smile, but for the first time, it didn't bring a sting or a pang of longing. It felt like a whisper of the past, something that once was but had settled quietly in the background. I let the memory breathe for a moment before allowing it to drift away, like a feather carried off in a gentle wind.

Arriving at my room, I hesitated just outside the door, my hand resting on the handle. The silence around me felt rich, full of possibility rather than isolation. I took a deep breath, the air filling my lungs like I was breathing in a new beginning. As I stepped inside, the room felt different, warmer, as if it too was ready to hold this new version of me. I closed the door gently, listening to the faint click as it settled back into place, grounding me in this quiet moment.

I lingered there, holding onto that silence, knowing that as this door closed behind me, somewhere, unseen but waiting, another door was ready to open.

Chapter 37
Distance

Sitting by the window, I let my eyes drift to the horizon. There was something about the way the sky stretched into infinity that made me think of distance – not just the physical gaps between people but the kind that settled in, quietly, between hearts. That unseen force that could take the place of old laughter and familiar embraces. It was strange, really, how a single step backward, a few inches even, could make people feel worlds apart. And yet, I couldn't deny the bittersweet truth: that same distance was the reason I was here today, feeling more grounded than I had in months.

I thought about Leo. He had been right there, so close yet so far, like a faint whisper in my life, echoing just enough to remind me he was still there, waiting, supporting me from a place I couldn't see. We'd both changed in ways we might never have understood if it hadn't been for that distance, but now, each step I took in recovery, each breath I took in a new kind of air, felt like one small step back toward him, toward everyone.

As I sat there, tracing the invisible line between the sky and the earth, I felt a strange kind of pride. The distance between where I was and where I'd once been felt vast, like looking back across an ocean I'd barely managed to swim. There was a time I didn't think I'd make it to this shore, where the ground beneath me felt more solid, less like the quicksand of my own thoughts. Yet here I was, breathing, feeling, thinking... stronger with every passing day.

In the stillness, I felt the echoes of the past few weeks ripple through me, like the calm after a storm when the sea finally settles, reflecting the world above in the quiet glass of its surface. It was an odd comfort, knowing I'd been reshaped by each moment, that the distance I'd traveled within myself had built new bridges where walls had once stood.

And as I thought of those bridges, my mind inevitably wandered to Leo. He'd always been there, steady and patient, but with a certain quiet restraint, like he was waiting on a distant shore of his own, one he wasn't sure I'd ever reach. Leo was like gravity in my life; something I didn't always see or fully understand but always felt, pulling me closer to the ground when I thought I might float away. There had been days when even the thought of him was painful, when our shared memories were like thorns, reminders of everything I thought I'd lost. But now, with each step forward, it felt less like an ache and more like a soft pull, a gentle reminder that maybe, just maybe, something beautiful still connected us across that distance.

In that moment, I understood something that Dr. Donnelly had been hinting at all along: distance doesn't have to be emptiness. It could be growth, a space where two people can become more of themselves before they finally come back together. It was in that gap, in that stretch of silence between us, that I had found the strength to become someone whole, someone worthy of a life beyond the shadows.

I took a deep breath, fingers hovering over my mobile screen. There were so many things I could say, so many words that felt trapped somewhere in my chest, but somehow, I didn't need them all right now. Sometimes, closing the distance wasn't about saying everything; it was about finding the one thing true enough to span the gap, something that could speak for itself.

I miss you.

It was simple. But as I hit "send," it felt like I'd dropped a pebble into a still lake, watching the ripples spread, connecting me to someone who had seen me at my worst and stayed.

For a moment, I sat in the quiet, feeling the weight of the words settle over me. The reply came quickly, his response lighting up the screen almost before I'd had a chance to exhale.

"I miss you too, Lily. I always have."

A warm pulse spread through my chest, softening the edges of everything I'd held so close. And just as I started typing to ask if he could come visit, another message appeared.

"Look behind you."

I glanced up, my heart pounding, and there he was, standing just inside the doorway with a tentative smile, his hand raised in a quiet wave. There was something so natural, so easy about him standing there that for a split second, it felt like nothing had ever changed.

"Leo..." My voice caught, and I swallowed hard, feeling the wave of relief and joy mingle in my chest as I got to my feet.

He stepped inside, closing the door softly behind him. Without another word, we met in an embrace that felt like coming home. His warmth, his familiar scent, all of it wrapped around me, grounding me in a way I hadn't felt in months.

Finally, I pulled back, looking up at him, feeling a softness in my smile that felt as new as it was old.

"You're here," I whispered, my voice barely breaking the quiet. He nodded, his own smile gentle.

"As long as you need me, Lil. Always."

As the light outside turned soft with evening, I let myself lean into the comfort of that moment, knowing that maybe, just maybe, I could keep moving forward with him beside me. And with the door swinging closed behind us, it felt as though a new one was opening somewhere in the distance, waiting just up ahead

With the warmth of Leo's embrace still lingering, we found ourselves lost in an honest, quiet exchange. The room softened, and

I felt a vulnerability come to the surface, one that hadn't had a voice until now. Sitting side by side on the edge of my bed, I finally broke the silence.

"It's strange… this relief and fear all at once," I admitted, casting my gaze to the window. "I'm finally starting to feel like myself, but there's this… space between me and everyone else. As if I've been standing outside my life, watching it all happen from a distance."

Leo's eyes met mine with a kind of steady compassion. "I've felt that too," he confessed, his tone thick with unspoken weight. "The distance wasn't just physical, you know. When you… when you were gone, it was like I was drifting too. It's been hard, Lily." His voice softened, and he looked down, almost embarrassed by the admission. "But I'm here, now. No distance, just… here."

A quiet stillness filled the room, his words settling between us with a truth I wasn't ready to face. But as his hand grazed mine, an unspoken question lingered in his touch, his fingers brushing lightly over my own. It was such a small gesture, yet in it, I felt the weight of a feeling we'd both been too afraid to name.

I looked up, catching his gaze, and for a moment, I let myself consider what could be. There was warmth in his eyes, a gentleness that held so much understanding and promise, and I felt myself drawn to it. But as the moment lingered, I pulled back, uncertainty rearing its head. I wasn't ready for this, not yet. The wound of my past was still fresh, and even the idea of moving forward felt both a relief and a risk I wasn't ready to take.

Leo seemed to sense my hesitation, his hand slipping back without pressure, his gaze softening into acceptance. "We don't have to rush anything," he murmured, his smile a quiet assurance. "I'm just… happy to be here with you."

The tension lifted, and after a shared glance, we decided to step out for a walk around the hospital's garden. The air was crisp, the late afternoon sunlight casting a soft glow over the carefully tended paths. As we strolled side by side, conversations meandering from shared memories to unspoken dreams, it felt like a continuation of something we'd started long ago.

When we reached a shaded spot beneath an old tree, we stopped, resting against its trunk, and Leo turned to me with a gentle reminder. "Distance doesn't always mean losing something," he said, his voice low. "Sometimes it just strengthens what's already there, even if it doesn't look like it at first. This…" he gestured between us, "this is proof of that."

His words settled in my mind, echoing long after he spoke. I reached for my journal, feeling an unexpected wave of comfort at the thought of writing with him nearby. With a soft nod, I opened it, letting my thoughts spill onto the page while Leo remained silently by my side. In the quiet of that moment, we shared an unspoken understanding, a bond deepened by distance, healed by proximity.

August 29, 2018

They say that with distance comes progress and growth,
They say that it is spoken like some sort of oath.

But distance can sometimes be a challenge you see,
For between this point and that point you will change who you'll be.

But growth in this status is meant to bring you no harm,
Growth in this status can be quite the good luck charm.

Buckle up and smile for this ride will be intense,
Buckle up and smile for your life is about to commence.

And always remember to ask for assistance,

You will have support no matter the distance.

With my words laid bare on the page, I closed the journal and took a deep, grounding breath. An unexpected lightness filled me, as though the simple act of writing had released a weight I hadn't realized I was carrying. Leo's gentle squeeze on my shoulder reminded me he was still there, a steady anchor beside me, holding me in a place of quiet strength and peace.

As we walked back to my room, the air felt different, lighter somehow, and each step was guided by the comforting presence beside me. When we reached the door, I stopped, glancing back to catch Leo's eyes, which shone warmly, softened by the day's fading light.

Inside, the quiet wrapped around us. The room was dim, and the familiar hum of the hospital grew softer, as though the world was allowing us this fragile, precious moment. I could feel my heartbeat steady, the vulnerability lingering from the day settling into something gentler.

I looked at him, feeling an urge I could barely explain. "Leo…" I hesitated, my voice barely a whisper, "would you… would you stay? Just tonight?"

For a heartbeat, his eyes searched mine, his own expression softening. He didn't speak right away; instead, he gently moved a chair next to the bed and sat beside me. "Of course," he murmured, his hand reaching for mine, a comforting weight and warmth that settled the lingering edges of fear I hadn't realized were still there.

As he took my hand, I felt the smallest, softest smile curl at my lips. His presence was like a lullaby in the quiet night, a reminder that despite everything, here was a piece of safety, a shield against the darker thoughts.

We sat together in the stillness, not needing to fill the space with words. The soft hum of the night around us was enough, the shared warmth of our hands a quiet promise of safety. With Leo close, I felt my breathing slow, the day's weight gently dissolving, and I let my eyes close, knowing that, for once, I didn't have to face the darkness alone.

Chapter 38
In Some Life

The soft, filtered light from the hospital window spread across my room, casting a gentle glow that softened the sterile lines of the walls. Mum had brought a few things from home: a thermos of tea, a pastry from the bakery down the road. The scent of cinnamon and sugar mingled with antiseptic, and somehow, it was comforting. She sat across from me, sipping her tea quietly. Just her presence made the room feel more grounded.

I glanced over at her, my heart caught in the tangle of words I didn't know how to say. Talking about Leo and how things had shifted between us felt surreal, almost fragile. But the steady warmth in her eyes, the quiet way she just waited, it felt safe.

I finally broke the silence. "Mum... I've been feeling... different. About Leo."

Mum set her tea down carefully, her gaze sharpening in that way only mums can. "Different how, honey? What's going on between you two?"

A shaky breath escaped me, and I looked down at my hands, fidgeting with the edge of the pastry wrapper. "I don't know. It's just... when he's around, everything feels... less heavy. Like I can breathe a little easier. I can't explain it, Mum. I didn't see it coming. He's always just been... Leo, you know?"

She nodded slowly, a small, knowing smile tugging at her lips. "You'd be surprised how often the most important people in our lives are the ones we don't expect."

I bit my lip, wrestling with the unfamiliar emotions. "I think he... cares about me more than I realized. And I think... maybe I care about him too. But, Mum," my voice cracked, betraying the fear I'd kept bottled up, "What if I'm only feeling this way because I feel so empty? Or because he's the closest person to me? I don't want to confuse comfort with something else, you know?"

Mum reached across the table, her hand warm over mine. "Sweetheart, love doesn't always fit neatly into boxes. Sometimes, it just... grows. And yes, sometimes it grows out of need, but that doesn't make it any less real. It's okay to be unsure. You've been through so much, and it's normal to be scared." She squeezed my hand gently, letting her words settle over me. "It's okay to take your time."

I let out a shaky laugh. "I guess I'm worried that I'm just looking for someone to fill the empty spaces left by everything that's happened. What if I ruin things with Leo because I'm... trying to find meaning in all the wrong places?"

Mum's eyes softened, her hand still holding mine. "What if he's not there to fill the spaces but to help you walk through them? What if he's the person you lean on while you figure this all out?"

I looked away, blinking back the prickling in my eyes. "I feel like... like I have these broken pieces, and he somehow makes them feel okay. Like I'm not... just a mess."

"You're not just a mess, Lily," she said, her voice gentle but firm. "You're healing, and sometimes, we find people who help us find our strength. Leo's been a constant for you, hasn't he?"

I nodded, a flood of memories filling the silence. "Yeah... I keep thinking of the way he looks at me lately. It's like he sees the real me, and it doesn't scare him. I mean, it scares me half the time." I gave a soft laugh. "He sees past all of this." I gestured to the room, to the hospital gown, to the ache that was still very much part of me.

Mum's smile deepened, her eyes glistening slightly. "Sweetheart, sometimes we find love in places we'd never expect. He's been by your side for so long, through the darkest parts, hasn't he?"

I nodded, her words settling into my chest. "Yeah. He has."

"Maybe that's the kind of person you can build something beautiful with," she continued, her words soft but certain. "Sometimes, real love shows up when we're at our lowest. He's not filling an emptiness, Lily. He's been holding space for you to find yourself."

The knot in my chest unraveled slightly, her words wrapping around the hidden hope I hadn't been able to admit. I thought back to the gentle ways Leo supported me – the way he listened, the way he didn't flinch when I told him about the hardest parts of this journey.

"Do you think... maybe... he could be more than just a friend?"

Mum's face softened even further. "I think he already is, sweetheart. The real question is, do you want him to be?"

I swallowed, the weight of that question settling into my bones. The images of our moments together, the way his voice had become a kind of anchor, all flooded back. "I don't know... I think so." I looked down, my heart beating a little faster. "I guess I'm just... not sure. It feels like opening a door that I'm not ready for. Like I might lose the one person who's... kept me steady."

Mum's hand rested on mine, a gentle comfort. "That's the risk, isn't it? Real love means risking what we're afraid to lose. But love also gives us courage, Lily. And if you're not ready, that's okay. Leo will still be there, whenever you are."

Her words wrapped around me like a promise, filling me with a cautious hope. The journey with Ava had been filled with so many sharp edges, but with Leo, things felt... softer, somehow.

I looked up at her, feeling a bit more grounded. "Thanks, Mum. I... I think I just need time to let this settle. I don't want to rush into something, but maybe I don't need to be as afraid as I thought."

Her warm gaze held mine, a quiet encouragement. "Take your time, honey. Love is patient, and Leo... he's shown that he can be too."

I leaned back in my chair, a strange sense of calm settling over me.

As the conversation with Mum wound down, we sat in companionable silence, sipping our tea and letting the weight of her words settle around us. The room was quiet, filled with the soft hum of the air conditioning and the occasional muffled sounds from the hallway. It was peaceful – something I hadn't felt in a long while.

Eventually, Mum rose, gathering up our empty mugs and giving my hand a final squeeze. "I'm going to check in with your doctor, but I'll be back soon." She smiled softly, touching my shoulder. "Take your time, okay?"

I nodded, watching her leave, and as the door closed, I felt a wave of reflection surge over me. I wasn't alone in this. Not really. Leo had been my steady presence, and now, with this gentle encouragement from Mum, something fragile but hopeful took root. Maybe Leo and I were meant to be a different kind of close. I wasn't sure how or when I'd be ready, but I could feel that he wasn't just a friend. He was something more... a light that had always been there, growing brighter when I needed it most.

I let my eyes wander around the room, resting on the framed photo Mum had brought in of our family. Dad and Logan's faces beamed back at me from a sunny day in some happier, far-off time. The dappled light streaming through the blinds cast patterns over their faces, as if they were somehow close by, a reminder of the love I'd lost and the love I still had.

I couldn't let myself sink back into sadness, though the familiar pull was there, tempting me. Instead, I reached for my journal, opening to a fresh page. My fingers hovered over the pen, feeling the words just waiting to escape.

September 1, 2018

I choose to believe that in some life,
Whether this one of the next —
You and I will be side by side,
Moving together through this ride.

Chapter 39
Moving On

The first glimmers of dawn crept over the horizon, casting soft, amber light across the room. I blinked, surprised to feel a strange but welcome calmness. It was as if, for the first time, I could simply be – a feeling so unfamiliar it almost startled me. I rose from bed, slipping on a jumper over my thin hospital shirt, and decided to take a quiet walk through the hospital gardens before the day began in earnest.

Outside, the air was cool and damp, and I savored each breath as I wandered through the small, winding paths lined with flowers and shrubs. There was a simplicity here – a natural beauty and peace that, though I'd seen it before, seemed new in the light of everything I'd been through. It reminded me of all the things I had clung to, all the pieces of myself and my past I'd held so tightly that I'd become almost afraid to let go. Each flower and leaf seemed to represent a memory I'd carried… memories both joyful and painful that had woven themselves so deeply into my identity.

As I rounded a corner, I caught sight of Dr. Donnelly standing near one of the benches, sipping her coffee as she glanced over some notes. She looked up, surprised, and offered me a warm smile.

"Lily! Up early, aren't we?" she said, her voice gentle but filled with that familiar steadiness that had guided me through so many difficult days.

I gave a small nod, a little hesitant. "Yeah... something felt different this morning. Like I just needed to breathe, to walk."

She gestured for me to sit on the bench beside her, and I joined her, tucking my hands into my sleeves.

"You've come a long way, you know," she remarked, her gaze thoughtful. "I can see it in how you carry yourself. There's a lightness now that wasn't there before, a willingness to look forward rather than back."

I looked down, kicking a stray pebble with my shoe. "It's strange, because part of me wants to keep holding on. There's a safety in the familiar – even in the painful memories. Letting go feels... terrifying."

Dr. Donnelly nodded, her expression softening. "It's natural to feel that way, but letting go isn't about forgetting. It's about giving yourself permission to live without the weight. Moving on doesn't mean you leave behind the love or the lessons; it just means you create space for new experiences to find you."

Her words settled into my mind, echoing in a way that felt like truth. Moving on didn't have to erase what I'd been through; it could just mean embracing the possibility of something more. I felt a flicker of hope and found myself nodding in agreement.

"Thank you," I murmured, the words feeling small but true.

Dr. Donnelly gave my shoulder a gentle squeeze before she stood, leaving me alone with my thoughts and the quiet beauty of the garden.

As I left the garden, a gentle breeze tugged at my hair, as if whispering that it was time to return inside. I walked through the quiet, dimly lit hallway, each step echoing softly against the tile. There was something about these walls, usually confining, that now felt protective, as if they held the weight of everything I'd faced here. It was strange to think that in just a short while, I'd be leaving this place behind. But somehow, in this moment, the thought didn't feel daunting; it felt right.

I paused just outside my door, taking in a breath before stepping inside. The familiarity of my room greeted me – a space that had witnessed my darkest moments, my breakthroughs, and everything in between. As I crossed the threshold, a calmness settled over me, a lingering warmth from my conversation with Dr. Donnelly, wrapping around me like an invisible shield.

I glanced around, and my eyes fell on the small collection of mementos from my past with Ava brought – my mum brought remnants from home that she felt would be important to my recovery journey. These were scattered across the table and shelf, little remnants of a love I had cherished deeply and fiercely. I walked over to the table and picked up a photograph of us together, one where she was laughing, her head tilted back, eyes closed, completely unguarded. I remembered that day so well – the feeling of her hand in mine, the soft glow of the setting sun casting a warm light on her face, illuminating every freckle, every smile line.

But as I held it now, the photo felt different. It wasn't a wound, raw and painful; it was a memory, a moment that I'd carried with love but no longer needed to hold so tightly. It was time to let go, not to forget but to release. Each piece I held seemed to represent a moment, a feeling, a part of who I'd been with Ava. I gathered them, one by one, the faded letters, the small trinkets we'd collected together, and placed them into a small box I'd found in the closet.

I lingered over each item for a moment, allowing myself to feel its weight, its history, before gently laying it to rest. The last item was a ticket stub from a concert we'd gone to together – our first date, her hand in mine as the music washed over us, her voice singing softly along to the chorus. I ran my finger over the faded ink, then set it in the box, and closed the lid with a quiet exhale.

This wasn't an erasure, I reminded myself. It was an honoring of the love I'd felt, a love that had helped shape me but no longer defined the person I was becoming. With the box tucked away on a high shelf, I returned to the window and sat down, the morning light pouring in, casting a warm, golden glow around me.

After placing the box on the high shelf, I took one last glance around the room. Everything felt lighter somehow, as if those remnants of the past had held a weight that I hadn't realized until now. I took a breath and turned toward the window, noticing the soft golden light casting warmth across the floor.

I walked over and lowered myself into the chair, pulling it close to the window's edge to watch the world outside. My fingers brushed the pages of my journal on my lap, and a familiar energy surged through me as I held my pen, yet this time it felt different… grounded, steady, ready to tell the truth without hesitation or doubt.

In the quiet of that moment, I let my thoughts flow freely, each line of the poem feeling like a gentle release, a letting go:

September 3, 2018

Stuck in one place without the ability to move,
Is no way to live a life;
Stuck in one place fixating on you,
Has left me feeling quite blue.

To find peace and happiness in this game of life,
There must be a way to move on;
Put one foot forward and pick yourself up,
Live like your mind will morph you into a swan.

Let go of the pain and the sorrow and guilt,
Let go of the choices that made you into who you are;
Pay no attention to the looks that dwell upon,
Become comfortable with the thought of moving on.

As I set the pen down, a sense of calm settled over me, like a quiet wave washing the shore. I closed the journal gently, feeling the weight of each word as if they had etched themselves not only onto the paper but deep within me.

I leaned back in the chair, letting my gaze drift out the window once more. The sun was dipping lower now, casting a soft glow across the horizon, painting the sky in shades of lavender and amber. The world outside felt like it was on the brink of something new, a transition from one day to the next.

For the first time, that mirrored my own sense of readiness. I felt it in my bones – in the way I was breathing, slower and steadier, in the way my shoulders had finally relaxed.

I stood, walked across the room, and reached for the door, hesitating just for a heartbeat. As I turned the handle, I felt the weight of the past loosen, and as the door closed softly behind me, it was as though another one had quietly opened somewhere ahead, leading me into whatever was waiting next.

Chapter 40
Let Go

I took a steadying breath as I left my room, knowing that this was it: my final therapy session. The weight of it settled in my chest, a combination of excitement, uncertainty, and a strange sadness I hadn't expected. My hand clutched my journal as I made my way down the hall, the walls I'd seen so many times somehow looking different today. I noticed the warmth in the faces of the hospital staff, the gentle hum of voices, the small details that I'd overlooked on previous walks. With each step, it felt like a piece of me was finally stepping into the life I'd worked so hard to reclaim.

Dr. Donnelly's office came into view, and I straightened up, pushing back the hint of nerves that surfaced. She was already waiting, her smile warm and encouraging as always.

"Ready?" she asked gently.

"As ready as I'll ever be," I replied, taking my seat across from her one last time.

The session started with my weekly recap, though today, the words didn't come as reluctantly as they once did. There was a strange lightness to them, a calm that seemed to echo the quieter spaces I'd found in myself lately. As I talked, I could sense that this peace wasn't fleeting – it felt earned, rooted in the shifts I'd begun to trust. I shared with Dr. Donnelly how my days had felt a little fuller, less marked by the hollow ache that used to greet me each morning.

Even the simple acts of sitting by the window or listening to a song seemed to carry a renewed meaning.

I spoke about the moments with my mum, how our conversations had taken on a depth that felt healing. We'd talked more about my dad and Logan, opening up parts of our shared grief that we'd kept hidden away. Somehow, it didn't hurt in the same way it used to. Instead, it felt like we were stitching together the pieces, filling in the spaces left by their absence with memories that no longer cut as deeply.

"And then there's Leo," I murmured, feeling a faint blush rise as I glanced away, unsure of how to capture the intensity of what I'd been feeling. "It's like... something's changed. And, at first, I didn't want to see it. But he makes me feel safe, in a way I can't ignore."

Dr. Donnelly's eyes softened, and she nodded encouragingly, as if giving me the silent permission to explore it further. "These are meaningful changes, Lily. It's important to recognize them. They're proof of all the work you've put in."

Her words sank in, grounding me. I realized, in a quiet way, that these shifts – the laughter, the warmth, even the lightness in my thoughts – they weren't just coincidences. They were proof of my journey, little markers that, in some way, I was finally moving forward.

"I can see it in you, Lily," she said, her tone quiet but sure. "You're really stepping into a new chapter of your life."

A small smile played on my lips as I nodded. "I feel it, too. There's been... a peace, I guess. Something I haven't felt in so long."

"That peace you're feeling," she said, "is the result of letting go. You've been through so much – loss, self-blame, regret. But you're releasing it now, and it's allowing space for something new."

Her words struck a chord, and for a moment, I sat in silence, letting them sink in. I'd spent so long carrying pieces of my past, like weights I thought I'd never be free from. But here I was, lighter, even as my chest swelled with the emotions of it all.

I opened my journal, the familiar comfort of the pages grounding me. The words began to flow, as if they'd been waiting for this final moment of release:

September 8, 2018

When things begin to feel weighted or even out of place,
Let go of the painful feeling that this is not meant to be your path;
Everything happens for a reason and that we know for sure,
Let go of the painful feeling that makes it difficult to embrace.

Life is full of challenges and obstacles to face,
But you are capable of being the one you need to be;
Let go of the memories of yesterday that keep you from moving on,
Let go of the memories of yesterday and a smile is a guarantee.

It may not be what you had in mind for the life you chose to live,
Although the choices you make define the person you are —
There is a no need to disrupt and change the flow,
When you can simply just let it go.

Dr. Donnelly gave me space as I wrote, her quiet presence there, steady and patient. After I finished, I looked up, and she reached out, placing a gentle hand on mine.

"You've done the hard work, Lily. And it's allowed you to come this far. I want you to keep this journal as a reminder of that. And as you go forward, keep writing. It will be your anchor, and it will remind you of the strength you've carried through every step of this journey."

Her words hit a deeper note, settling like a balm over all the fears I hadn't even realized I was still holding onto. "Thank you, Dr. Donnelly," I murmured, my voice thick with gratitude. "I don't think I can fully express how much this means."

She gave me a warm smile. "It's been an honor to be part of your journey, Lily. You're ready for what comes next. And Dr. Boyle will be visiting you this evening to go over your next steps and finalize everything."

The weight of it hit me fully… this was real, the end of one chapter and the start of another.

As I walked back to my room, everything seemed sharper, clearer. The faint sounds of the hospital filled the air, grounding me as I let each step carry me forward. Inside my room, the evening light was beginning to cast warm, golden hues through the window. I set my journal on the table and gazed out at the quiet sky, a final moment of reflection settling over me.

A few hours later, Dr. Boyle walked in, clipboard in hand but with a softer expression than usual. He pulled up a chair beside me, his calm presence putting me at ease.

"Lily," he began, his tone warm but direct, "I wanted to go over what the next few steps look like for you." He paused, searching my face as if to gauge if I was truly ready. "You've done incredibly well here, and it's time to transition back home. But there are things we'll continue to monitor – ways to help make sure that support is in place as you go forward."

I nodded, feeling a mixture of gratitude and trepidation at his words. "I understand. I just… it feels like stepping into a whole new world."

"And in many ways, it is," he agreed, leaning in slightly. "But it's your world, and you're ready to be a part of it in ways you couldn't before." He glanced at his clipboard. "I'll be prescribing a mood stabilizer – something that'll be monitored carefully. We'll schedule follow-ups with both me and Dr. Donnelly. You'll have check-ins, adjustments if needed. You're not alone in this, Lily."

The mention of medication didn't land lightly. I bit my lip, the weight of the word "prescription" settling in my mind. "Dr. Boyle… I'm nervous about relying on something else. I've had… struggles with that in the past."

He nodded, understanding. "I know. And we'll approach this carefully. This isn't about losing control; it's about supporting the strength you already have. We'll keep an eye on everything, and you'll have Dr. Donnelly and me working closely with you."

"Thank you," I said, feeling the nerves begin to settle. "I trust you both."

We discussed more of the discharge details: the follow-up schedule, the support system they'd arranged, and even a few grounding techniques he suggested I carry into my daily life. I listened, feeling the weight of each word, absorbing it all with a quiet resolve. When he finally stood to leave, there was a moment of shared understanding, a recognition that this was no longer just a hospital room but a place where I'd begun to rebuild myself.

"Remember, Lily, this is a process," he said gently. "One step at a time. And if there's anything you need, reach out."

I stood by the window as he left, letting the last light of day wash over me. Outside, the sun dipped below the horizon, the colors deepening into a calm twilight. The darkness wasn't something to fear but felt like a quiet invitation to embrace this new beginning. And as the door to my room clicked shut, another door seemed to open somewhere ahead, the path forward clearer than it had ever been.

Chapter 41
Healing of the Broken Heart

The morning light streamed softly through the hospital room window, casting a warm glow over everything it touched. It seemed to bring a quiet reverence to each corner, like it too understood the weight of this day. I sat up slowly, feeling the familiar heaviness in my chest begin to ease, as if the light was gently reaching into the cracks I'd spent these weeks trying to mend. The knowledge that I'd be discharged soon filled me with a strange mixture of hope and hesitation – a thrill as if I were standing on the edge of a cliff, ready to leap but unsure where I'd land. These walls had become both my sanctuary and my battleground. And now, I'd have to let them go.

Around me, the room was filled with the objects of my recovery – books with pages dog-eared, letters and notes from friends, the gifts brought to me on quiet afternoons, and my journal, its edges worn from the countless times I'd opened it. Each item held a piece of these last few months, like small anchors reminding me of how far I'd come. They were mementos from the days I thought I wouldn't make it, through the nights that felt endless, through the quiet dawns when I'd finally find some peace. The idea of leaving them felt both daunting and liberating. But I knew I couldn't stay in this place forever. I had to let it go, to move forward, even if each step felt as uncertain as the last.

I picked up a small photo frame with Logan's picture. It was a candid shot from when we were kids, our arms slung around each other, grins stretched wide across our faces, his laugh so vivid in my mind that I could almost hear it. Running my fingers along the edge of the frame, I grounded myself in that memory of him – the way he made me feel safe and invincible. This journey of healing wasn't just for me; it was for him, too. Keeping him close meant learning to move forward. I could still carry him with me without holding myself back. Letting go didn't mean losing him. In fact, it felt like the best way to honor him.

My journal lay open on the bed beside me, its pages filled with fragments of my heart – pain and hope woven into each entry. It held my lowest lows and small victories, a testament to everything I'd fought through. As I read back over some of my words, a quiet pride stirred within me. The ache in my heart wasn't as sharp as it had been. It had softened, and now that ache seemed to hold a quiet resilience. This discharge wasn't an end; it was the beginning of a life I was learning to want again.

A soft knock at the door pulled me from my thoughts. Dr. Donnelly stepped in, her presence a steady, familiar comfort. Her smile was gentle, her gaze kind and understanding, as though she knew that today was more than just another session. She went over the final steps of my discharge, reminding me that I'd face new challenges and that this wasn't a finish line – it was just a turning point.

"Your discharge is coming up," she said, her voice gentle, anchoring me in the present. "You've worked so hard, and I want you to remember that healing isn't a straight line. There will be good days and challenging ones, but the tools you've gained here are part of your strength now. You have what it takes."

I felt a mixture of anticipation and uncertainty stirring within me. She must have sensed it because she leaned in, her tone steady but full of encouragement.

"Lily, you've come so far. You have the strength to handle whatever comes next."

I realized I'd been clutching my journal, holding it tightly against me like it was part of me. Dr. Donnelly glanced at it, her smile deepening with understanding. "Keep writing," she added softly. "There's power in those words. They'll ground you just like they have all along."

With that, she left, leaving a soft warmth in the room as I opened my journal. In its pages, I let my thoughts flow freely, capturing the fear, the hope, and the strength that had carried me to this moment:

September 10, 2018

Do you ever find yourself wondering why,
There is an emptiness left behind that wild goodbye?
As if the push and pull of all the prior laughter,
Was enough to keep you happy after.

There is nothing worse than that empty feeling,
Except for what comes next with healing.

There is no pain worse than an empty broken heart,
As that pain is enough to tear your entire world apart.

Hold on to the memories of your favorite days,
For those moments can help you clear the haze.

That empty feeling will be what remains,
As those bursts of emotions run through your veins;
But what is important to know is that one morning,
You will wake up no longer in mourning.

Everything happens for a reason even if it's hard to see,
And everything in your life will end up the way it's meant to be.

Roads are meant to be traveled slow,
For that is how these lessons will grow.

The only way to succeed in self-healing,
Is to fully embrace what inside you are feeling.

Today is one day but tomorrow is another,
Do not let that empty feeling inside you smother.

Regain control over yourself and your mind,
And follow your journey that is being redesigned.

That empty feeling inside of you will grow,
Unless you have the strength and power to know:
From these feelings you will continue to glow,
For you are the most important star of your show.

As I finished, the pen lingering over the last word, a quiet calm settled over me – a kind of peace that felt rare, like it had been waiting patiently for this very moment. I closed the journal slowly, running my fingers over the worn cover, feeling the weight of everything these pages held. They had been my constant companions, silent witnesses to my battles and my breakthroughs. Setting it aside felt like setting down a piece of my soul, but it also felt freeing, as if I were leaving behind the darkest parts of myself and embracing the light that lay ahead.

I stood up, stretching as if shedding a skin that had clung to me for too long. The room was still, bathed in the soft afternoon light that streamed through the window, and in that silence, I took in every detail: the chipped paint, the small cracks in the ceiling, the clock ticking gently. This space had been both sanctuary and confinement, a place where I had faced my deepest fears and begun to heal. Now, it felt as though I were standing in a cocoon, just moments before breaking free.

With a steady breath, I walked to the window one last time, looking out at the world beyond these walls. The gardens lay sprawled below, with the sunlight dappling the paths and trees, casting a golden hue over everything. There, a single dandelion drifted lazily through the air, its tiny seeds catching the breeze and scattering into the open sky. I watched it, feeling that same sense of possibility and vulnerability, like I, too, was ready to let go and scatter myself into the unknown.

Turning back, I gathered my few belongings with a newfound resolve, as if each item were a small piece of the journey I'd walked. I ran my fingers along the side of my bed, feeling the cool metal that had once seemed confining, now softened by the understanding I'd gained here. I glanced around one last time, taking in the echoes of all the conversations, the tears, and the moments of clarity that had filled this space.

Then, I opened the door slowly, stepping into the hallway and glancing back over my shoulder. The door closed behind me with a soft click, the final seal on this chapter of my life. And though part of me felt a quiet sadness, a greater part of me felt ready. Ready to step through into the unknown, ready to face what lay ahead, knowing that somewhere, just beyond the bend, a new door was waiting, ready to open.

Chapter 42

The Light

The morning sunlight seeped softly through the window, casting a warm, golden glow over the room. I lay still, feeling its gentle warmth dance across the walls, illuminating the edges of the room that had held me through the darkest days. In that moment, I realized this room, with its sterile hum of machinery, faint antiseptic scent, and soft, sterile light, had somehow grown familiar, almost comforting. It was no longer just the place where I had been confined; it had become a silent witness, a confidant in the backdrop, holding the weight of all the unspoken moments that had defined my time here.

I remembered the days when despair felt so overwhelming that even moving felt impossible. The nights when the loneliness was thick, the weight of my thoughts pressing down on me, making me question if I'd ever find my way back to myself. And yet, it had been here, in this small, quiet room, that I had started piecing myself back together. This room had seen me cry, laugh, collapse, and stand tall again. Today, as I prepared to leave it, I knew it would always be a part of me, as if fragments of its four walls and all the memories within them would travel with me wherever I went.

Sitting up slowly, I let the silence settle over me, letting myself breathe it in like an old friend. The last few months played through my mind like scenes from a distant memory – the first time I took a step without help, the hours spent in therapy sessions that felt both painful and healing, and the moments of isolation that, over time, transformed into a peaceful solitude. Each memory felt like a piece of a puzzle, coming together to form a clearer image of who I was now – someone who had been broken, mended, and who had found a new purpose along the way.

Today wasn't just about leaving a hospital. It was about stepping into something entirely new.

A soft knock on the door gently pulled me out of my reverie. I looked up as Dr. Donnelly entered, her familiar warm smile a comfort I'd come to count on, followed closely by Dr. Boyle, who gave me a reassuring nod. They both took seats across from me, their expressions a mix of pride and sincerity, a subtle sense of ceremony present. These two people had walked beside me through the storm, and now they were here to witness the clearing skies.

Dr. Boyle's voice was steady and gentle as he began. "Lily, today is a milestone. You've made remarkable physical progress, and I have every confidence that you'll continue building strength and resilience beyond these walls. Your journey doesn't end here, of course, but you should know just how far you've come. Listen to your body; self-care will always be vital, just as important as any therapy or treatment. And we'll still see each other for check-ins. For now, though, I want you to savor the freedom you've worked so hard to reclaim."

I nodded, his words settling over me like an anchor, grounding me. In that moment, it was as if his words formed a foundation beneath my feet, something solid I could stand on as I looked toward what lay ahead.

Dr. Donnelly leaned forward, her voice as warm as her gaze. "Lily, you've shown strength that's truly inspiring. You've confronted so much here – grief, self-worth, trauma. But you're emerging stronger than before. Healing doesn't stop here; it goes on, but you're carrying with you the tools, support, and most importantly, the inner resilience you need to face whatever comes next."

I felt a tightness in my throat, a well of gratitude and emotion bubbling up, and I swallowed back tears, feeling their support as something tangible, almost like a physical presence. "Thank you," I managed, my voice thick with sincerity. "Thank you both. When I came here, I didn't see any way forward. But now, I do. And it's because of everything you've given me."

Dr. Donnelly placed a gentle hand on my shoulder, her touch warm. "Remember, Lily," she said softly, "you did this. We just gave you the tools, but it was your strength that brought you here. Don't ever forget that."

With one last warm hug from Dr. Donnelly and a firm handshake from Dr. Boyle, they stood, offering me gentle, encouraging smiles as they quietly stepped out of the room, leaving me with these last moments to absorb the stillness and say my silent goodbyes.

With care, I packed my things, each item carrying a fragment of this journey. A soft comforter, worn and familiar, that had cocooned me on the coldest nights; my stack of journals, filled with thoughts once too heavy to bear alone; and the flowers Leo had brought that transformed the room into a sanctuary on days when the outside world felt impossibly distant. I lingered by the window, gazing at the hospital garden one last time, feeling the weight of the past few months settle over me like a comforting blanket, grounding me.

The knock at the door drew me back, and I turned to see my mum standing there, her eyes brimming with a mixture of pride and tenderness. She stepped into the room, folding me into a hug that carried the warmth and weight of so much that words couldn't express. As she held me, I felt the strength of her heartbeat steady against mine, a silent reassurance that whatever came next, we'd be okay.

"I can't believe it's finally time," she murmured, pulling back slightly to look into my eyes. "You've come so far, Lily. You have no idea how proud I am of you." Her voice was soft, almost reverent, and I could see in her gaze the journey we'd both been on, in different ways, and how we'd both emerged from it changed.

We took a slow walk down the corridor, side by side, the fluorescent lights casting our shadows on the sterile floor. I let my gaze drift over each familiar doorway, each corner of the hall that had been a part of my world for so long. I could feel my heart tugging between the fear of leaving and the excitement of moving forward.

The elevator doors opened, and as we descended to the lobby, my mum squeezed my hand, a gesture of strength and quiet encouragement. I held on, grounding myself in her presence, drawing from the love that had carried us both through this.

When we stepped outside, the world felt almost too bright, the air too crisp. Everything was sharper, louder, as if the world itself had shifted to greet me. Together, we walked to the car, the gravel crunching beneath our feet a reminder of the earthiness, the realness of this new chapter. I felt lighter with each step, like I was shedding pieces of the pain that had kept me bound.

Once we were settled in the car, my mum gave me a soft smile and a nod, as if signaling the transition from this place back to the world waiting for us. As she started the engine, I opened my journal, knowing this would be my last entry within these pages. I felt the hum of the road beneath us, steady and grounding, as I let the words pour out, each line lifting the remnants of the weight I'd carried within these walls:

September 13, 2018

The flick of the light that shines bright in the sky,
Propels you up to the top beyond the eye.

It was gone for a while when life got in the way,
It became hard to survive the day.

In the darkness of yesterday was that drop of life,
That left you face to face with all your strife.

Lend a hand to the face behind the gaze,
Fight through that crippling cloudy haze.

When tomorrow comes you feel the grip of hope,
Creating a new way to live through this scope.

Reality shifts forward and through that dainty looking glass,
When in the mirror you see what is coming to pass.

So smile and nod and shine bright like the stars,
Let us co-create the life that is ours.

The flick of the light that shines bright in the sky,
Propels you high up above the eye.

As I closed the journal, a wave of calm washed over me, flowing through me like a quiet tide after a long storm. The hum of the car, steady and sure, felt like a heartbeat, anchoring me to this new beginning as we moved down streets that felt both familiar and foreign. Every tree, every building, even the soft gray of the overcast sky felt like it was layered with meaning, as if the world was welcoming me back, ready to show me that things could be different this time. I glanced out the window, watching the landscape drift by, each passing scene grounding me, a reminder of the life waiting beyond those hospital walls.

My mum's hand reached over and gently covered mine, her warmth seeping into my skin like a silent reassurance. I looked over at her, catching the soft smile on her lips, and felt an ache, tender and deep, that spoke of the journey we had both endured. Her gaze held something unspoken – a promise, perhaps, that whatever came next, we'd face it together. In that moment, I felt an unbreakable bond, a connection stronger than words, one that had been built through every tear, every quiet moment, every small step forward.

The car continued its gentle rhythm, each turn bringing us closer to home. I leaned back, letting my shoulders drop, feeling the weight that had clung to me for so long start to lift. The scenery outside became a blur, a wash of color that seemed to echo the hues of hope I felt unfurling inside me, gentle yet steady, like a sunrise breaking through the darkest night.

My fingers brushed over the cover of my journal, feeling the familiar texture beneath my fingertips, the last entry still fresh inside. I let my eyes close, savoring the quiet peace that had settled over me, a sensation that felt almost surreal. In the silence, I knew that something had shifted, a final thread released, freeing me from the grip of my past.

With every mile, I felt a little stronger, a little lighter, as if the road itself was carrying me forward, guiding me toward a place I had only glimpsed in fleeting moments of hope. The past few months had been a journey through darkness, but sitting here, with my mum's hand in mine and the open road ahead, I felt something I hadn't known I could – peace. As the familiar turns brought us closer to home, I knew that this chapter, filled with so much pain yet laced with resilience, had come to its natural end.

I wasn't sure what lay beyond, but I felt ready to step into it, one foot in front of the other. And as the car pulled into the driveway, I took a deep breath, feeling the calm settle into every part of me. This was the beginning of something new, a door opening, inviting me forward. And as we stepped into the warm light of home, I knew I was finally, beautifully, moving on.

Chapter 43
Saving Grace

The evening air was cool, carrying a soft bite as it curled around me, lifting strands of my hair like whispers. Tonight had a different feel to it, a newness that tugged at my heart as I waited for Leo. I felt strange – excited but almost nervous, an anticipation that buzzed quietly in my chest. This was my first time meeting him outside the hospital since discharge, and yet it felt like more than that. It felt like stepping into a new world, one where each moment felt uncertain yet filled with the promise of something I couldn't quite define.

A car door clicked shut in the distance, and I saw him walking toward me, hands in his pockets, shoulders relaxed, as if he'd always belonged to this moment. A faint smile lifted his lips as his gaze found mine, and in that instant, something inside me softened. He looked at me with a warmth that reached right through the layers of silence and unease that had shadowed the last year. My heart fluttered as he finally reached me, wrapping me in his arms in a quiet, grounding embrace. It was as if all the missing pieces of my world had found a place here, in his steady presence.

"You look good, Lil," he murmured, his voice wrapped in sincerity, his arms still gently holding me.

"Thanks." I barely recognized my own voice, a whisper almost lost in the lingering warmth of his touch. "I missed this," I admitted, allowing myself to lean into the strength of his arms a moment longer.

He looked down at me, something tender in his expression that made me feel seen in a way I hadn't in a long time. We lingered there, silently acknowledging what words couldn't capture, then decided on a simple walk to a scenic overlook, letting the city lights below be our backdrop. We strolled in silence at first, the rhythm of our steps matching the calmness of the descending twilight. The sky above stretched in soft hues of lavender and deep blue, the last golden traces of the sun slipping behind the hills. It felt symbolic somehow; a quiet blessing marking the end of one chapter and the uncertain, exciting beginning of another.

Our conversation began light, a weave of our familiar banter and shared memories. He made me laugh as he recounted our reckless adventures from years past, like the night we snuck out to watch the stars only to end up shivering, half-frozen, by dawn. There was an ease, a comforting rhythm in our talk, and it allowed the weight on my shoulders to slip away, inch by inch, as if Leo could absorb my worries with every word and laugh.

After a lull in our laughter, a sudden impulse to share rose within me. "Leo…" I started, hesitant, glancing at his profile as the twilight cast gentle shadows across his face. "I don't think I've ever told you just how much you've done for me… I don't even know if I can." My throat tightened as I tried to find the words. "You were there through everything, even when I wasn't sure I'd make it. And I don't know if I ever said it, but… you've been my anchor. In every way."

He stopped walking and turned toward me, his hand reaching for mine, his thumb gently grazing over my knuckles in a comforting rhythm. "Lily, you don't have to say it." His voice was soft, resonant, each word steady and strong. "I'd have been there a thousand times over if you needed me. But if I'm honest… there were times I didn't think I could hold on any longer. Times I thought I'd lose you." His words wavered, a tremor of vulnerability breaking through. "It hurt, Lil, to watch you struggle like that and feel helpless… and all I could do was hope you'd find your way back."

The rawness of his words, their unfiltered honesty, made my heart tighten with a feeling I couldn't fully grasp. In that moment, I felt his unwavering presence settle even deeper within me, as if his support, his care, had become a part of who I was. We reached a quiet bench by the overlook and sat, his hand still holding mine. His touch was a silent promise, grounding me in the calm assurance I'd come to associate with him. For a while, we just sat there, the night stretching out in a sacred silence around us, his presence a quiet comfort that seemed to reach into every aching part of me.

A thought flickered within me, a small and tentative spark, something that stirred the memories of what we once had and ignited something unfamiliar yet comforting. I found myself reaching for his hand, a gentle, instinctive gesture, and as our fingers intertwined, a warmth flooded through me. It was as if all my unspoken words, my guarded emotions, could finally breathe in his quiet understanding.

After a while, Leo rose, saying he'd get us something warm to drink from a nearby stand. I watched as he disappeared into the shadows, his figure fading into the night, and a sense of emptiness stirred beside me. I didn't know how or when, but somehow his presence had become essential to the part of me that was rebuilding itself, steady and unshakable. I reached into my bag, pulling out my journal, feeling the familiar weight of it – a place where I could pour out my heart without fear, where the words could be as raw as the emotions behind them.

Under the dim glow of the city lights, I penned my thoughts, each word pouring out from somewhere deep within me:

September 15, 2018

I remember where my mind was when we first met,
Full of chaos and heaviness and left in disarray;
But when our eyes crossed paths and we spoke hello,
Much of that rooted fear seemed to melt away.

You do not know how grateful I am for you,
And you may not know the impact you had;
But let me share one thing about that meeting,
To shed some light on what I wish I knew.

Life works strange in moments of darkness,
And at times may leave you feeling different emotions;
But if you trust your path and carry forward;
Something will find you when you least expect it.

My life shared with me something I could not see coming,
For in that moment I was not yet seeking;
The feelings that I felt with you,
And now I can't seem to stop myself from running:

To you, my love, my saving grace.

When he returned, he handed me a cup, his familiar gentle smile easing the tension that lingered within me. His presence was like a balm, a warmth that seeped past every guard I'd ever put up. As we sipped our drinks in comfortable silence, I watched him from the corner of my eye, savoring this feeling – this rare, inexplicable peace that he brought me. The lights of the city stretched out before us, shimmering like distant stars, painting the world in a soft glow that matched the feeling within me.

Each sip seemed to ease a different ache, a quiet reprieve from the memories I often found myself lost in. With Leo beside me, I didn't feel the weight of everything that had happened, the heaviness of my past mistakes. For a moment, I simply existed, free from the clutches of regret, tasting a sliver of joy, something I'd thought had slipped from my reach long ago.

He shifted, drawing my attention back to him, and our eyes met: a spark, unspoken, a silent acknowledgment of all we'd been through. I wanted to tell him everything, to lay my heart bare and thank him for every time he had shown up, every time he had stayed when I'd thought I was unlovable, unreachable. But words felt too small, too fragile. So I let them settle unspoken, feeling a quiet resolve that they would come in time.

And then, he reached for my hand, his fingers intertwining with mine in an unhurried, grounding gesture. The pulse of his touch echoed through me, a gentle rhythm that felt as steady as my own heartbeat, as if reminding me that no matter how far I had fallen, I was not alone. He was here, beside me, and the thought was so simple, yet so powerful.

We walked back, the world seeming to slow around us as each step matched the steady cadence of my newfound hope. The air was cool and comforting, whispering promises of a future that felt possible for the first time in forever. As we approached my door, I felt the weight of the day settle softly within me, not heavy or daunting, but warm and reassuring.

I squeezed his hand, a silent thank you, a quiet promise that whatever lay ahead, I was ready for it. His hand tightened in response, and as I stepped inside, I looked back at him one last time, his silhouette framed by the city's glow.

And in that final, shared glance, I knew that while the journey was mine to walk, he would be there every step of the way – my saving grace.

Chapter 44
Out of the Darkness

The park lay hushed as I entered, enveloped by shadows that stretched across the path, elongating like the past I had once carried so heavily. The air held a faint, earthy smell of leaves, their edges just beginning to curl with autumn's approach, blending with the lingering warmth of the day. There was a change in this place tonight, a subtle shift that mirrored something within me, as if the air itself acknowledged that I was no longer the person who used to haunt this path with such burdened steps.

I walked slowly, each step purposeful, as if I were savoring the weight of the ground beneath me, feeling the strength in each stride. The familiar ache, once so present in every movement, seemed distant, softened somehow. There was a lightness in my chest, a fragile feeling that I didn't dare question, only allowing it to fill me as I approached the willow tree.

The willow loomed ahead, its long branches swaying gently in the evening breeze, whispering as they brushed against one another. I lifted a hand to touch the bark, my fingers grazing the rough texture, feeling each ridge and groove, the tree's resilience rooted deep in the earth. It was strong, unyielding, as though it had faced countless storms and still stood, quiet and certain. Once, this tree had felt like a symbol of every heartbreak I'd endured, every loss, every shadow I couldn't shake. But tonight, it held a different energy, a kind of solemn acceptance that felt... safe.

I leaned into that feeling, closing my eyes, letting the willow's silent strength wash over me. Memories drifted in, soft as the wind, images that had once cut sharply now easing through me like gentle streams. They were no longer wounds but distant echoes, and as I stood there, I could feel each one loosening its hold, fading into the soft hum of the evening. The tree, this silent witness to my pain, seemed to absorb those memories, as if gathering them, carrying them away with each breeze that rustled its leaves.

When I opened my eyes, the first stars had emerged, pinpricks of light against the twilight. They were steady, unwavering, like tiny markers of resilience set against the vastness. I breathed in deeply, feeling the remnants of past weight drift away, leaving only a raw sense of lightness in its place. Here, beneath the canopy, I felt the past releasing me, a parting gift, as if the tree itself were acknowledging that I was ready to move forward.

I lowered myself to the ground, settling against the willow's roots, and reached for my journal. The blank page waited, patient and unassuming, as if it had known all along that this moment would come. With a deep breath, I placed the pen against the page, letting my words flow, each line a testament to everything I had faced and everything I was letting go.

September 16, 2018

Stop
And for a moment take in the scene,
For the monster inside of you soon it would seem —
Will vanish right here in the in between.

Wait
And for a moment know it will be okay,
For the monsters all around you are not here to stay —
The pain is only temporary and will someday go away.

Think
And for a moment look ahead at what may come,
For the monsters are what set you on this path that you are on —
These monsters are what compose the past that you are from.

Go
And for a moment live only in the present,
For the monsters cannot catch you when you are focused on what may save you —
And maybe the life you are living could perhaps be quite pleasant.

Stay
And for a moment know everything happens for a reason,
Notice what is missing from your mind and your heart racing?
It appears you have gained control over your darkest season.

Dream
And know that what will come is well worth it,
This pain and sadness in your heart is only temporary —
Buckle up for an adventure that you will not want to omit.

I closed my journal softly, feeling the cool leather beneath my fingertips as I traced slow, deliberate circles along the cover, letting its familiar feel settle into my palm. It was as if the words I had written on the page were more than just letters or phrases, more than thoughts and reflections – they were promises. They were the pieces of myself I had gathered and fused together, my commitment to move beyond the shadows and embrace whatever lay ahead. Each line felt like a small vow, a pact with myself, delicate yet resilient, something I would hold close from here on.

As I sat, absorbing the weight of what I had just let go, I felt an ache – the kind that lives quietly beneath the surface but deepens once acknowledged. Rising slowly, I steadied myself, placing one hand against the willow, feeling its bark, rough yet comforting, pressing against my palm. The touch was grounding, as though I were absorbing its ancient wisdom, its silent strength, drawn from years of weathering storms and watching the world turn.

I closed my eyes and let out a slow, steady breath, feeling the remnants of my old burdens sink into the earth beneath my feet. The willow seemed to hold it all, as though it were receiving and understanding everything I had poured out, every sorrow, every moment of pain, and every whisper of hope. For a fleeting moment, I imagined it breathing with me, its leaves rustling softly in time with my own release. It felt as though I were leaving parts of myself there, parts that no longer served me, absorbed into the roots of something larger, something that could bear the weight without judgment or strain.

Turning to leave, I glanced back at the tree, feeling a wave of gratitude rise in my chest. I whispered a silent thank you, as if acknowledging the role it had played in this journey – my confidant, my witness, my grounding anchor. It had been there through it all, standing tall even as I felt lost, offering its quiet strength each time I found myself at its roots, struggling to hold myself together.

The sky had darkened around me, but as I stepped away from the willow, the night seemed to soften, its edges blurred by a gentle glow from the stars above. They appeared brighter than before, casting a faint shimmer over the path that stretched out before me, each star like a small beacon lighting the way forward. I felt the cool night air brush against my skin, as if the universe were welcoming me back, letting me know I had stepped into something new, something lighter.

With each step I took, I felt the past loosen its hold, falling away like the dried leaves at my feet. There was no hesitation in my stride, no lingering shadows clinging to my heels. There would be more moments of light and darkness ahead; I knew this. But for the first time, I felt sure-footed, certain that I could move forward. This path was no longer one of fear or doubt. It was a new beginning, grounded in acceptance and a sense of purpose.

As I walked, I held my journal close, my fingers tracing its familiar edges as if touching a part of myself. It was a reminder of where I had been, and as I felt the pulse of my heartbeat steady in my chest, I knew it was also a reminder of where I was going. This was my journey, my story, and with each step, the path behind me faded as the one before me opened wide. There was only the road ahead, waiting – one step, one breath, at a time.

Chapter 45

Happiness

The morning light filters through my curtains, casting a warm, gentle glow across the room, softer than usual, as if the world itself is encouraging me to linger in its embrace. The sun's rays stretch like delicate fingers, caressing the worn fabric of my quilt and dappling the wooden floor in scattered golden patches. There's a tender quietness in the air, a stillness that feels almost sacred, as if this moment belongs to me alone – a fragile, perfect pause before the day truly begins. I pull the quilt a little closer, savoring the simplicity of a morning untouched by worry, cocooned in the softness that seems to mirror my own growing ease.

In my lap lies my journal, its familiar cover worn smooth under my fingers. I open it slowly, brushing my fingertips across the pages, feeling the faint indentations left by past entries. Each groove, each line holds pieces of me – pain, resilience, fleeting moments of joy, quiet despair. I'm here, between these pages, stitched together in ink and memory. Yet today, my hand feels steady, grounded, my heart oddly quiet, as if it, too, has found a new rhythm. There's no heaviness pressing down, no reluctant words fighting their way out. Instead, my thoughts flow with an ease that surprises me, like a gentle stream over well-worn stones, calm and clear.

The pen glides effortlessly, each stroke carrying a weight that is, for once, gentle, almost buoyant. The words that spill onto the page are a testament to where I've been, but today, they're lighter, free from the shadows of yesterday. There's a hint of something new, something tender beneath the surface of each line – a small, steady pulse of hope. It's as though the ink itself carries a quiet promise, whispering that maybe, just maybe, I've reached a turning point. I breathe in deeply, letting the air fill my lungs, feeling a calm settle within me. In this moment, I'm whole, grounded, and I realize that perhaps, the worst is finally behind me.

September 17, 2018

In the darkest of moments that you may soon regret,
Look towards the light reflecting the moon;
Allow that glow to push you forward,
And regain the happiness that you sought to forget.

For the time you have spent looking down unto yourself,
Should have been time that you spent rebuilding your life;
It is not too late to begin the journey of healing,
You just need to let go of that internal strife.

Your happiness is one that you can control,
So chase what you want and never let go;
For in your weakest moments please remember me this,
There is nothing more filling than a life full of bliss.

It may seem impossible at this moment in time,
But trust in the process of this journey you're on;
It was never said to be an easy journey to happiness,
One thing is for certain and it is not always right there.

Patience is key as your mind fills with ease,
All those dark lonely feelings will begin to freeze;
In your darkest of moments that you may soon regret,
Remember that there is a happiness waiting for you that you have not yet
met.

I close my journal, a soft smile lingering on my lips, feeling a quiet anticipation stirring beneath the calm. Today feels different. There's a subtle spark, a whisper of possibility hanging in the air, like the world around me is holding its breath, waiting for something more. I can feel it – a gentle tugging sensation, somewhere deep in my chest, hinting at an unknown yet enticing possibility.

Tonight, there's no looming shadow, no weight of expectation. It's as if the universe has decided to align, weaving together the pieces of my world, whispering promises of the unexpected. For the first time in a long while, I'm not only willing but eager to lean into the unknown, to let the night unfold as it wishes.

And perhaps, just perhaps, it could be a night to remember – a moment where everything shifts, where two hearts could finally connect without hesitation, without fear.

When Leo arrives that evening, he's holding a warm bag of food, the smell of spices and roasted garlic filling the air as he steps in. Just seeing him, feeling his presence in my space, lifts something inside me. It's as if a weight melts away, replaced with something warmer, softer.

We decide to stay in, spreading out the food on the coffee table, and soon the room fills with our laughter. Every shared glance, every small brush of his hand as we reach for plates, carries a meaning that feels like it's been there all along, waiting to be felt.

"You know," he says, his voice dropping slightly, "I was scared for you, Lil. I was so afraid I'd never see you sitting here like this again."

I meet his gaze, finding myself caught in the warmth of his eyes. "I was scared too," I admit, feeling a vulnerability I've held back for so long. "But you… you kept me going, Leo. Even when I couldn't see it. You've been… my anchor."

He reaches over, tucking a loose strand of hair behind my ear, his fingers brushing my cheek with a gentleness that sends warmth flooding through me. I lean into his touch instinctively, my pulse quickening at the contact. Silence settles between us, our eyes locked, words unnecessary.

As Leo's fingers linger at my cheek, a warmth unfurls inside me, one that reaches deeper than comfort. There's a spark, an undeniable energy that thrums between us. His hand stays there, holding me in a moment that feels as fragile as it is charged. It's as if we're teetering on the edge of something vast and unknown, but neither of us dares to look away. His thumb brushes against my cheek in slow, gentle circles, and I close my eyes for a brief second, savoring the warmth radiating from his touch.

We sit there, letting the silence fill the air around us, yet every inch between us feels alive, humming with possibility. Slowly, my hand reaches for his, instinctively closing over his fingers. Our eyes meet, and I feel him lean in, his breath warming my skin. His gaze moves over my face, as if memorizing every detail, and I find myself doing the same, taking in the way his eyes soften, the way his lips curve in the gentlest of smiles.

As our lips meet, it feels like every barrier, every unspoken feeling, dissolves into this kiss. His hand slides into my hair, pulling me closer, and his other arm wraps around my waist, bringing me against him. My heart races, but in his arms, I feel a calm I hadn't known I was missing. We move as if we've done this a thousand times, like this was always meant to be, every touch growing bolder, every kiss leaving me breathless.

He pulls me down beside him on the couch, our laughter mingling and fading into something deeper, something I've only ever dreamed about. His hands trace gentle patterns along my spine, and I find myself sinking into him, trusting him in a way that feels both exhilarating and terrifying. His fingers brush my collarbone, and I shiver, feeling as if every touch leaves a spark, like we're creating something fragile and beautiful in the spaces between us.

Our breaths quicken, each inhale and exhale mingling, fueling the rising heat between us. His lips travel down my neck, grazing over my skin with a delicate intensity that sends shivers rippling through me. I feel his fingertips tracing paths down my spine, each touch lighting up nerves that had laid dormant, igniting sensations I hadn't realized were waiting there. It's a slow discovery, a delicate unwrapping as we inch closer, savoring every second as our bodies press together, skin against skin, warmth meeting warmth.

My hands slip under his shirt, gliding over the smooth planes of his back, feeling the strength beneath his skin. His muscles tense under my touch, and he lets out a low groan, his own hands moving to explore the lines of my body, pressing and holding as though he can't quite believe this is real. Our eyes meet, and in that moment, an unspoken promise fills the space between us, words that don't need saying as he lifts my face, capturing my lips in a kiss that's slow, savoring, yet laced with an undeniable urgency.

Piece by piece, our clothes are shed, falling carelessly to the floor as our bare skin meets, igniting a fresh wave of desire. His hands find my hips, pulling me closer, our bodies aligning as though we were made to fit this way. I run my fingers along his chest, feeling the steady beat of his heart beneath my palm, matching the thudding rhythm of my own. He presses me back against the bed, his weight settling over me, warm and steady, grounding me even as he stirs something wild inside.

Every touch, every glance, every kiss feels like it holds a universe of meaning, his lips trailing down my collarbone, his hands mapping the curves of my waist, my legs, pulling me under with him. I'm aware of every inch of him, every slow, careful movement, the way he pauses to look at me, to take me in, like he's memorizing this moment. There's a gentleness in his touch, a care in the way he brushes his fingers through my hair, before the urgency rises again, more intense, more consuming.

We move together, a natural rhythm taking over, instinct guiding us as our bodies find a perfect sync. There's something raw, something deeply vulnerable about it, and I let myself go, let myself feel everything, let myself be fully here with him. His lips find mine again, deepening the kiss, and I'm lost, pulled into the tidal wave of emotions, of passion, of love and trust that feels both new and timeless.

The world outside disappears, leaving only this – our shared breaths, our bodies intertwined, our heartbeats echoing one another. His name slips from my lips in a soft whisper, and he responds in kind, his voice filled with a mix of tenderness and passion that sends a thrill through me. We move as one, building higher and higher, until the sensation reaches a fever pitch, crashing over us like a wave, leaving us breathless, weightless, wrapped in each other's arms.

Hours drift by, but in this space, time feels suspended, like we're the only two people in the world. The world outside doesn't exist, and right now, neither of us needs it to. I'm entirely absorbed in the rhythm of his heartbeat, its steady cadence echoing beneath my fingertips as I trace circles on his chest. The warmth of his body against mine is grounding, a steady anchor that I find myself clutching onto, afraid to let go, yet completely unafraid within his hold.

His laughter, low and soft, vibrates against me, filling the quiet spaces between whispered words and gentle touches. It's a sound I could lose myself in, and as I close my eyes, I feel him smile against my hair, his lips brushing the top of my head, sending a shiver down my spine. Every word spoken is intentional, quiet, and so deeply connected to something I hadn't allowed myself to feel in what seems like forever. The lines between us blur, the boundaries that once felt impenetrable are now gone, leaving only trust and warmth.

As the night deepens, the outside world fades further away, until it's just us. He presses a tender kiss to my forehead, his fingers weaving through my hair, calming and stirring me all at once. We shift, adjusting to find comfort in the way we fit together – like we were always meant to meet here, in this moment. His arm wraps around my waist, drawing me closer, his embrace firm yet gentle, like he's holding on to something fragile, something precious.

I lay my head on his chest, feeling his breath rise and fall, a rhythm I let myself sync to as he holds me close. The weight of his arm draped over me feels safe, a warmth that soaks through to my bones, melting away the cold spaces I had long carried within me. I listen to the sound of his heartbeat, a quiet melody that fills the night, and I feel something in me relax, something I'd been bracing against for too long.

When we finally settle, tangled together in a closeness I've craved more than I ever knew, I realize with a gentle ache that something has shifted. The spaces between us, once cautious and filled with questions, now feel complete, intertwined in a way that makes me feel whole. His touch speaks a thousand words, telling me without language that he's here, that he's staying, that he'll be there even when I'm afraid to look forward.

He pulls me even closer, his arm resting protectively over me, his thumb tracing gentle patterns along my shoulder as though he's memorizing every inch of me. And as I lie there, held tightly in his embrace, the world feels right for the first time in a long time. The weight I've carried for so long fades, replaced by a peace I hadn't dared to hope for, a happiness I'd once thought was out of reach.

In his arms, I finally find the courage to close my eyes, surrendering to the calm that settles over me. Here, in the dark warmth of night, with him beside me, I feel whole.